I0572297

Lia Karra Tembo
L.N. O'Rourke

Perth, Western Australia
**Picardie Press**

# Copyrights




National Library of Australia Cataloguing-in-Publication Data, catalogue record for this book is available on request from the National Library of Australia.

ISBN Number: 978-0-6457138-1-7

# Acknowledgement

Thank you to Damien Mander, who, through his Sixty Minutes Australia interview and his creation of the International Anti-Poaching Foundation, inspired me for the theme of this story.

A special note to SAVE African Rhino Foundation in Perth, Western Australia, who was also instrumental in some of the content of this story and supplied the opportunity to meet with Damien Mander at Perth Zoo in 2017.

# Preface

When everything you thought you knew turns out not to be as important as you thought, it puts life into perspective.

Some of the content in the story is based on actual events, some on personal experience and yet other parts came about through exhaustive old-fashioned research and owed their adaptation to too many sources to mention.

Although this book is targeted primarily for the entertainment of anyone who enjoys action, adventure, drama and a touch of romance, I would hope that the message is not lost in the fictional aspect of the story because the subject of what the story is really about should be important to everyone who loves animals and the triumph of good over evil.

# Chapter 1

Intermittent flashes of light played on the tarmac under the halo of the slowing rotors belonging to a Jet Ranger helicopter.

Continued buzz filled the cabin, my passengers thanking me over and over for the great time they had whilst they hung up their headsets and gathered their belongings.

Helping them step from the helicopter, I accompanied the two couple's while still air-side. Eagerly tittering about the highlights of the adventure they had on one of our Great Barrier Reef Tours.

With them barely drawing breath, I couldn't help but grin to myself as they followed me towards the small reception area in our building that served as the terminal for Station to Coast Heli Services, Mackay Airport in Queensland.

Some said I had a dream job, and it was moments like this that I would have to agree.

After the final thank yous, the last of my tourists bid goodbye and I was left to make my way to the office to complete the flight paperwork.

"This came for you Annie," said Chris, the chief pilot, who was sitting at his desk, holding up a pretty silver envelope.

I hated being called Annie and he bloody well knew that, but at least it wasn't 'Orphan Annie' anymore.

I still bristled.

I frowned in confusion. I never got mail, unless it was a bill of course.

"Where's it from?" I asked quietly.

Chris shrugged waving the letter in the air impatiently. He was always indifferent with me and it all started when he thought he had a chance with me and I knocked him back the first, the second and the third time he asked me out.

It wasn't professional and it was too soon. It was still too soon.

His bruised ego sometimes shared the limelight with his jealousy thanks to my familial ties with the company I worked for.

I was after all the boss's honorary kid sister.

Not that I expected any favours, I worked as hard, and probably harder than the others, which earned me the reputation as one of the most respected young mustering pilots in the industry.

Coached by the best.

Biting my bottom lip, I thought back to the first time I'd set eyes on Jayme.

*-He shut down his tiny Robinson 22 and changed his headset and peaked cap for an Akubra, he was dressed in fitted jeans and a navy long sleeved shirt with Station to Coast Heli Services embroidered on the chest pocket. I was fifteen at the time and there he was all tall and dark and handsome... and so much older.*

*Uncle Kyle had finally been able to pin down "The Robbo Cowboy" and I for one couldn't have been happier. That Easter my life changed irrevocably...-*

Without a thought, I reached down and laid my hand over the large silver belt buckle, the feel of the intricate image of a wedge tailed eagle with its wings spread in full flight, ironically earthing me to his memory.

"Oi!" Chris interrupted my reverie. "I'm not your personal letter holder Stedman!" He could be such a douche bag. Even so, I had to admit that he was a great Chief Pilot and ran a tight ship.

Narrowing my eyes at him, I grabbed the fancy mid-sized envelope and turned it over, squinting through the dark lenses of my Aviators at the calligraphy printed elegantly across the elaborate stationery that looked suspiciously like a formal invitation. Noting the return address, I let a girly giggle escape.

Girly giggles weren't something that I did and as a result, I could feel Chris' questioning eye on me when it caught his attention, so I blocked him out by turning my back to him and walking away. I heard him huff before I pulled my shades off and plopped into a chair at the only other empty desk in the room. I couldn't believe the mail was from my best friend Carley. A wave of guilt engulfed me and not for the first time, I certainly hadn't earned the title as her Best Friend for far too long now. Opening the envelope, careful not to rip the pretty paper, I pulled out the matching invitation. A smile grew on my lips, Carley was getting married and not only was she inviting me to her and Blair's wedding, but to be her bridesmaid too!

We hadn't spoken to each other since... the smile fell off my face and I shook my head, pushing the memories to the back of my mind.

It had been three years.

We had emailed though. It was easier to control the conversation that way and I could think about what I wanted to say, thereby avoiding any unpleasant subjects that would make things so awkward in a normal conversation.

Still, I felt like such a lousy friend, neglecting the companionship for as long as I had. It was high time to change that, time to make up for it. I owed Carley big time and therefore, the decision to agree to support her on her wedding day was a no brainier.

Another chopper beating its path back to base interrupted my thoughts, that meant that Pete was on his way home. I grinned again and packed the invite away before finishing my paperwork and heading outside with the plan to put both of the company's Bell 206's to bed.

"Hey Chicky." Pete waved as he approached me with his passengers.

"Hey Pete, I'll put your bird down for the night if you want."

"Thanks Anna." He said with a wink, striding over, then slowing his pace and pulling up just before he passed by me. "Hang on a minute, what do you want?" He asked taking off his Aviators and arching a suspicious brow at me.

Apparently, it wasn't often that anyone around here offered anything for no reason so near knock off time. Busted.

"Mint?" I smiled, offering him small plastic case of tiny white lollies to distract him. He grinned, shaking his head at me in mock disappointment.

Pete was the boss, the owner of STC, he was a very talented guy at the best of times and could fly the pants off just about anything, but he also had a really finely tuned BS radar.

I understood his confusion though, because I'd never once exercised that muscle in the time that I'd worked at STC.

"I'll catch up with you in a bit." I smiled. He nodded, still looking a little suss before continuing to usher his passengers across the tarmac.

I tidied both choppers, covered the windscreens, air intakes and pitot's while I worked out how much leave I'd need. With Carley and I being at opposite ends of the country, I couldn't really help her the way I probably should. Her wedding was in October, so the boys and I would still be busy mustering the dregs for the season. As it was, I'd been taken off mustering for a week because one of the guys called in sick. It was already crazy, with it being the middle of tourist season, my schedule was chockablock and I wouldn't be able to get back to chasing cows till after the weekend. I shook my head at myself, it was still a few months away and surely Pete would be able to cover me, right?

Thankfully, I was in luck. When I got back to the office, Chris had already left for the day and Pete had no problem letting me book leave for the almost two weeks leading up to Carley's wedding date and a few days thereafter.

"It's about time you nicked off, you've been working non-stop since you started," he said with a grin after signing off on the schedule.

"I can feel the love," I replied, placing my hand over my heart "Oh and the HF's still got a dicky dial on Echo. I've made a note in the Log," I added, with regard to the radio in the helicopter I flew today.

"Okay I'll get Baz to look at it first thing. Now go on," Pete nodded to the door, "go home before I change my mind."

I was out of that door in a flash.

## Chapter 2

The mustering season was full on and the months flew by, October was here before I knew it and I was walking into the Perth domestic terminal eight hours after my departure from Mackay. I swear half of that was spent waiting for my connecting flight in Brisbane.

When Carley picked me up from the airport, she hugged me fiercely. "It's so good to see you again," she said, her voice thick with emotion as she struggled to keep herself from crying.

"It's been too long, I'm so sorry..."

"No!" She scolded, holding a finger up, "you're here now and it's a happy occasion, so get happy Stedman."

I smiled and I would try to get happy for her.

I stayed at her place leading up to the wedding. Blair was in his last year at Uni, finishing his engineering degree so he didn't have much time for organising anything, not that Carley would have let him anyway, she was more than content to take charge of proceedings and he was more than happy to let her. They hadn't really seen much of each other as a consequence and during my stay, I only briefly saw him on the odd occasion, but I was sure they'd more than make up for it on their honeymoon.

They were spending three weeks touring the world.

"So, the first week we're staying here," Carley said, slapping a brochure in front of me on the long bench of her big open plan kitchen, "it's a game reserve just bordering Kruger National Park." She beamed, bouncing in her chair with excitement.

"Wow! I'm so insanely jealous!" I said leafing through the glossy pages, "You guys'll get to see the big five and I'll be stuck here chasing dust." I said, in a whiny tone.

I loved large animals and had dealt with big stock at Uncle Kyle's Hidden Valley Station in Western Australia's remote Kimberley. That's where I originally adopted my horse Blue who, incidentally I was already missing like crazy.

*-Blue came to me when Travis Sanosi from the neighbouring station, Mahria Downs needed to remove a large herd of old style station horses. These animals popped up from time to time and had bloodlines that go back as far as settlement or something.*

*Travis was going to shoot them because they were competing with his cattle but said we could give them a chance because they seemed like fairly decent stock. Our station had a reputation for producing some of the best stock horses in Australia and I don't mean the pretty registered show ponies you got in the big smoke. I mean hardy, tough horses that could work all day carrying a hundred kilos and stay sound.*

*When Bill, our head stockman and I finally tracked them down, they were definitely far too nice to cull, so we herded them into a cattle truck -poor buggers- and took them the two hundred clicks home to Hidden Valley to be vetted and broken in. Those that didn't make the cut were culled out, but the majority were of excellent type, well put together and had good feet.*

*We picked out the 'Eyes' for Hidden Valley and the rest were sold off to other stations. Anything that had balls was cut except one black colt with white stockings, a baldy face and one icy blue eye.*

*I smiled at the thought, he was my soul horse in every way, my Blue, the other love of my life, a bit of Thoroughbred, a dash of Arab and a heap of heavy horse. He was about sixteen two and built like a brick outhouse with fluffy feet and a great big beard in winter, but boy could that horse work!*

*He was smart as a whip too and I'd taught him to sit and bow and pick up my hat if it fell off. He'd do anything for mints.*

*Apart from horses, I'd also broken in Hidden Valley's stud bull, Sherman, - after the tank- he weighed twelve hundred kilos and was one heck of an animal but the biggest pussycat you'd ever come across. I actually used him whenever the cattle were in the holding yards. The cattle stressed less with Sherman than with horses and that bull would quietly work the herd anywhere you'd want them with minimal fuss.*

*And then there were the camels, I broke a few of those as well, but they just took up too much of my time, so a guy from Broome would come up every so often to take a bunch off our hands in the same way we'd taken the horses from Mahria and use them for his camel rides on the Beach. Any good ones he didn't need, would be exported to the Middle East. He said that Australia had the best camels in the world. The rest were good on the BBQ, though I preferred beef myself.*

*That was station life.-*

I looked down at the glossy brochure, at a picture of a herd of elephants out in the open savannah. Standing as high as their mother's elbows, cuter than cute, the young calves caused my heart to skip a beat and a smile to dance on my lips.

I wondered what it'd be like to ride an elephant.

"Anna?" Carley interrupted.

I looked at her, feeling a little embarrassed, "Sorry what did you say?"

"I said, I'll take heaps of pictures!" She said brightly before sliding another brochure in front of me. "And the other two weeks are gonna be spent travelling Europe."

"That's awesome Carley!" I tried to sound enthusiastic, but my thoughts were still on the elephants. After quickly scanning the other locations she was intending to visit, I looked up at her. "I think you're going to need a holiday to get over your holiday."

"I know, right?"

We stared at each other, the grin on her face so huge, she looked like she was about to burst.

"Oh my god!" Her voice broke into a higher pitch, "I'm getting married to the love of my life, how lucky is that!" She said, throwing herself at me and hugging me fiercely.

I smiled, nodding as I swallowed thickly, glad she couldn't see my face.

Her and Blair had been high school sweethearts, Carley was my only friend at boarding school here in Perth, I'd been home schooled until I was high school age and Blair was a year above us at the all boy's college up the road.

Carley and I were roomies, and she took me under her wing when a clique of those 'mean girls' took great joy in teasing me, pointing out what a freak I was and how no one could ever look at me and take me seriously appearing the way I did.

Carley was socially savvy and shut them up by threatening to tell the headmaster what they were really doing in their free study period.

While it stopped them in their tracks, it didn't do anything for my self-esteem and I forever carried with me, a blemish that couldn't be unseen, but Carley came through for me there too.

She found a brilliant idea that would hide my ugly defect and with the elephant no longer in the room, it proved that mean girls were fickle creatures with very short attention spans and pretty soon I was yesterday's news!

Much to my relief.

Blair and Carley had been inseparable when they weren't "in school" and always attempted to include me and not have me feel like a third wheel.

That consideration worked both ways and I often made it easier for them to rendezvous when they shouldn't have been. It was only fair, but there were some things that a third wheel just shouldn't have to witness.

That was harder said than done sometimes, because those two just melted even at the mention of each other.

Just like I used to melt when I thought about Jayme.

Now I just feel the emptiness in his absence, the pain in my lip served to keep the tears at bay as I bit down.

*-He had looked just as gorgeous as he did the year before, even more so, my memories didn't do him justice at all.*

*I melted the moment he gave me his lopsided smile when I picked him up from the airstrip in my new/old farm ute, complete with daggy "P" plates.*

*And I melted as Jayme looked at me over my cake while singing happy birthday with the rest of the Station crew at the barbeque bash that was put on in my honour that fateful evening.*

*My birthday wasn't the only celebration that year. In the week leading up to his arrival at the station, Jayme had also won his first National Champion Bull Rider buckle at the National Rodeo Finals in Queensland. It was a prestigious award and the highlight of the Australian National Circuit. I thought cowboys were nuts trying to stay alive on the back of a giant bull while it rearranged the human anatomy for eight seconds.*

*Unless that bull was Sherman of course.*

*It didn't stop me from melting though, when he caught me on the way back to the homestead after the party and he handed me a pretty blue box with silver ribbon that laid heavy in my palm.*

*"Happy birthday sweet sixteen," he said with a beautiful smile that made his eyes twinkle even in the low glow of the veranda lights.*

*That belt buckle was the first he'd ever won, he was eighteen at the time and he gave it to me for inspiration, he said it had served its purpose and it was time for him to pay it forward. He told me I should have dreams and to never let anyone get in the way of them.*

*I was so overwhelmed, that all I could do was squeak a thank you and be grateful that the light sucked, because I could feel the heat rise from my chest all the way to the top of my head.*

*Thing was, cowboys never gave away their belt buckles to girls.*

*Never.*

*If they did, and that's a big if, it meant they were together. And I mean together-together, so that night I wondered what he really meant by the precious gift. I wondered if I read too much into it, but the way he looked at me, it was different, wasn't it?*

*I flipped between thoughts and doubt crept in, of course he didn't think the same way I thought of him, he was at least ten years older than me, a man, I was a teenager, a little girl by comparison.*

*What could he possibly see in me? Regardless, Jayme's belt buckle was the best Birthday present ever.-*

# Chapter 3

The rest of the wedding preparations were for the most part uneventful. I'd been thinking of Jayme a lot lately, which made me feel melancholy, but for Carley I put on a smile and went to the hair and make-up trials, the cake tastings and the dress fittings. The gowns were floor length and elegant with halter necks and low backs, all were blue but in different shades, mine being the lightest, almost teal, that Carley assured was 'my colour'. Thankfully they could be worn at other functions besides weddings, not that I ever went anywhere fancy enough to be able to wear a dress like that ever again.

Three days before the big day was Carley's hen's night, which meant it was also Blair's bucks night. The whole mob drove down to Margaret River in two separate Coaster buses.

The girls begged me to have a drink, but drinking was something I never really did, certainly not in public, so I opted to be skipper since I had the bus licence thanks to Pete needing a few people to be able to do hotel transfers with the STC courtesy bus, so we were set.

We toured around the Southwest town and its stunning surrounds, twenty partying women on a pub crawl of the wine region, and you know how it is, it's all fun and games until someone gets hurt.

One of the girls tripped up the steps of the bus and chipped a tooth. So instead of risking any more injuries, they opted to continue the festivities back at the chalets... after the purchase of a box of assorted wines.

There, the afternoon turned into night and the girls went nuts when the mandatory group of very lovely looking strippers turned up.

Of course, I was embarrassed beyond mortification thanks to my lack of inebriation and 'life' experience when I had to sit down and endure a lap dance. Luckily the stripper in question had no such lack of life experience and was in his words 'gentle with me.'

The party started winding down when the boys left and a few of the girls decided to continue into the wee hours. I left them to it and went to bed.

I was woken by yelling. Very, very loud and distraught yelling, coming through my open window over the sounds of the waves crashing on the beach.

It came from Carley. "I can't fucking believe it!" She screamed.

"I'm sorry babe, I was drunk, I didn't know what I was doing." I heard Blair's voice plead.

"What? You mean you tripped over her and your pecker accidentally slipped into that... that trash...?"

"Babe... it was a joke... the guys... they..." Blair stuttered and pleaded hopelessly.

"Don't you dare 'babe' me. C'mon Blair, it doesn't take a genius to work out what happened. God! I hope the skanky hoe was worth it, cause you're sure as hell never coming near me again!"

Uh oh. By the time Carley had finished her rant, she was sobbing, and I had managed to pick my way through the mass of fallen bodies to where the couple were in dispute. Carley was hunched over, and Blair, wearing only his boxers, was looking exceedingly guilty and at a loss as to what to do.

"We're still getting married, aren't we?" Blair asked hopefully, triggering a brand-new wave of uncontrollable sobs from my friend.

"Seriously?" I asked him incredulously.

Blair scowled at me. Evidently, he didn't appreciate me calling out his flippancy. "Stay out of it, Anna!"

"Little late for that now don't you think?" I asked, gesturing around me at the gathering crowd before I moved to throw an arm over the still distraught Carley. "C'mon hun, let's get out of here."

Carley complied and we turned to leave. At that moment, I felt his hand grab my shoulder.

"Hey!" Blair said, raising his voice, "I said..."

An instinctive reaction kicked in, that feeling you get where everything happens in slow motion yet a blur all at the same time.

Pulling my arm back, I made a fist, turned abruptly, and let fly in a smooth motion. The accuracy and momentum surprisingly hitting home... hard.

I registered a sickening crack before recoiling and shaking out my hand, the noise not coming from me.

"You broke my nose!" Blare's voice pitching in a tone of pitiful disbelief.

I stayed silent in my own shock, but that only lasted a moment before I returned to Carley's side. She was still an incoherent mess.

Then Blair started to advance.

"Don't!" I warned, rounding on him again with a pointed finger.

He flinched reflexively.

With her arms wrapped around her middle like she was trying to hold herself together, Carley continued to quietly sob. The scene made all the more heartbreaking with eager expressions of fascination coming from the silent onlookers, some with their phones at the ready to record the moment.

"You've got to be kidding," I said loudly, "some friends you are!" I added before the said friends seemed to think better of it and had the decency to lower their devices.

"C'mon Carls, I'll take you home," I said softy.

The crowd parted like the red sea as I walked her back to the chalet. I asked one of the girls who'd come down by car if she wouldn't mind giving us a lift back to Perth. She was great and ended up giving me the keys, saying she'd go back on the bus. I nodded hoping that there was someone among the group who could actually drive the damn thing, but at that moment I didn't quite care enough to find out.

Hitting the road, it was just as well that I wasn't a drinker, because everybody else would have still been well over the limit. It didn't take long for us to add the miles, driving in relative silence at least until we got to Busselton.

"Thanks for that by the way," she said, after explaining some of the finer details that led up to the connection between my fist and Blair's face.

"Anytime," I said, opening and closing my fist, the knuckles starting to become stiff and swollen.

"We should have taken some ice for that," she said, her grief for her situation changing to concern for me, "It looks ouchy."

"Meh, it'll buff right out," I said.

Carley managed a chuckle. "Who thought you had it in you, Stedman?"

"I know right?" I said, agreeing with her.

After Carley finished ranting, crying some more, asking why her, and extricating all manner of other emotional outbursts, we laughed hysterically. Apparently no one had told Blair that he was on a beach that banned dogs, evidenced by the fact that he'd been found tied to a signpost that stipulated the rule according to the local council.

The girl involved in the tryst and located not too far from him, was also found all tied up. To a rubbish bin no less! Of course we couldn't help but to laugh out loud at the irony.

We weren't sure who'd had the foresight to tie their naked arses to their prospective structures, but it was genius and they deserved a medal.

"It all makes sense now, the extra credit card expenses that I thought were because of the wedding, 'no time' due to study," she said making air quotes, "all acceptable huh?" She asked with a shake of her head. "God, I was so stupid."

"Shit Carley, he's the stupid one," I assured her.

"What am I going to do?" She asked, running her hands through her loose shoulder length auburn hair. "The guests, the reception, we've got Buckley's getting even half the money back that we've paid out."

"We'll sort it when we get back, I'm sure you'll get some of it back hon," I said, rubbing her arm.

The next two days proved hectic because I had to help support Carley by fronting first of all, the close relatives on her side of the family, then mediating between her and Blair to sort the financial stuff out. After the last round of angry tears from Carley, he gave up fighting and basically threw his hands in the air and said everything was hers.

How nice of him.

I may have been mildly euphoric that he had a brace on his nose and that he was sporting two swollen black eyes.

We made quick work of cancelling everything and collecting about ten thousand dollars after the non-refundable deposits and cancellation fees were processed. Sending all the guests the news that the wedding was off all became too much for Carley, so I took it upon myself to spend a whole day trying to get in touch with as many guests as I could.

It was finally the day before I was due to leave and we had an awkwardly silent dinner at her home. We had brought Chinese on the way back from picking up all the table decorations from her parent's place that were now obsolete. She would try to sell them on one of those internet trading sites.

I finished the last bite of my stir-fry when I gasped. "What about the honeymoon?"

"Shit! I completely forgot!" Carley closed her half-eaten container and tapped the lid as she thought it over. Slowly, a wicked smile spread over her face, which was kind of odd considering the last few days she had pretty much been a basket case, "That bastard might have ruined my life for now but he's not ruining the trip."

"Huh? You're still going?" I asked in confusion.

"Hell yeah!" She answered with a nod.

"What are you, a masochist? I can't imagine you'd want to spend any more time with him" I said, taking a sip of water.

"You got that right," she said, grinning mischievously. "There's no way he's going."

"Well, you know, you shouldn't really go alone, ..."

"Oh, I won't be," she said, her grin was becoming more wicked by the second and I wasn't sure if that was actually a good thing.

"Okay then, I'll bite Ms Smug Secret Keeper. Who are you taking, your mum? She deserves a holiday especially after this, or your sister, she'll make it a wild ride."

Carley was still staring at me intently, her grin was positively evil now.

"Ooook, who then?" I asked, feeling a nervous flutter in my chest.

"You silly! Oh Anna, we'd have so much fun, a girl's holiday, I've booked tours and everything, what do you say?" She asked, bouncing in her seat.

"Me? I-I don't know Carley," I said rubbing the back of my neck.

"Oh come on! You could use the time away, it's exactly what you need," she said pointedly, "and besides, you almost broke your knuckles on that oxygen thief's face, and did you see the smile on dad's when we told him? That alone makes you the obvious choice, and the fact that you're my besty and that we haven't seen each other in like, forever. Please?" She begged.

Weighing up the pros and cons, I was sure she could hear the cogs grinding in my head.

"Don't over think it. Just jump in! What's the worst that could happen?" She asked, sitting on the edge of her seat, every inch of her vibrating with her new-found excitement. How could I possibly refuse her pout and her puppy dog eyes and that quivering chin?

"Okay then, I'll come with you. Bu..."

She squealed, clapped her hands, then jumped up out of her chair and tackled me, forcing an "Ooof" from my lungs and almost throwing me off my seat.

Would I ever get used to her explosive enthusiasm?

Awkwardly patting her back, I waited for her to loosen her hold. Taking her by the shoulders, I waited until she gave me her full attention. "But. We'll first have to see if we can transfer the tickets and stuff 'kay? And if I can take more time off..."

"Oh, stop being so practical and let me bask in my joy will ya?"

"Okay then." I giggled when she hugged me again briefly, before letting go.

"This is gonna be so much fun, you'll see," she paused, before the smile dropped from her face. "You do have passport don't you?" She asked, the worry clearly evident in her tone.

"Yeah I do," I said as I remembered the last time that I almost used it. "I'll have to go back home and pack before we go though," I said thinking of my little flat in Mackay. "And tie up all the loose ends while I'm there," I added thoughtfully.

"You do that, and I'll sort out the name transfers. Isn't this the best idea ever?" She said with such excitement, that she couldn't sit still.

I was amazed and worried at the same time with my friend's sudden carefree attitude. After the disaster that unfolded only so many days ago, was that even normal? I was still having problems getting over Jayme and that was three years ago and I knew that was definitely not normal, but I couldn't help it. Maybe Carley was right, maybe this time away was exactly what I needed.

Exactly what I needed to get away from the memories even if it was for just a little while. My mind transported me again to another time, my teeth automatically finding their mark.

*-The day after I received the best birthday present ever, one of the Jackeroos had too much to drink and needed to stay back a day or so and get hydrated before the outback killed him. Bill cleared a seat for me in the cab and loaded Rowdy's motorbike onto the back of one of the farm utes to run us out to where the boys were mustering. There was no way I was allowed to head out that far on my own.*

*To my joy, Jayme flew me back to the homestead the following day after dropping Rowdy off. "You want to take the stick?" He asked referring to what I later learned was called the Cyclic.*

*I was so nervous I could barely move let alone take the controls of the chopper, but with gentle coaxing, I was keeping the helicopter straight and level before the airstrip came into view. The flight left me feeling as free as I felt when I rode Blue out by myself, just me and the open space around me.*

*We had flown over the red dirt, the ironstone hills, the light green tufts of Spinifex and the lush pastures tall with green Buffel grass during the wet season, now browned and dry, our life blood as the main forage for our cattle. Then there were mostly bare tracts with the occasional stand of Acacia trees and a smattering of low bushes and Boab trees. Closer to the river, the open country gave way to multi coloured sandstone gorges, lined with greenery, the waters teaming with Barramundi and freshwater crocs. There was a powerful contrast in the harsh Kimberley country.*

*From the air, the uncapped bores looked different from when I camped at their water's edge with Blue. Hot water spewed from deep within the earth onto the parched landscape. The man-made wetlands created an oasis in the tinder dry surrounds.*

*It was interesting that all that water often brought shore birds in from the coast, we even got pelicans in from time to time.*

*The flight was over too soon, and I missed Jayme the moment his helicopter flew out of earshot. Uncle Kyle was at the airstrip to pick me up and take me back to the homestead. I'd be going back to school in two days and that evening, my adoptive parents handed me an official looking envelope from some Lawyer. Now that I was sixteen I had been handed part of a trust fund.*

*"You know sweetheart you can do with it what you want, although we'd prefer it if you put it in the bank." Aunt Rose said a little nervously.*

*Uncle Kyle looked agitated but held his tongue, I smiled though and thanked them, because I knew exactly what I wanted to do with it.-*

## Chapter 4

Once back in Mackay, I began to feel the excitement bubble at the prospect of going overseas for the first time! It was nice to have something to look forward to again. I packed my bags, found my unused passport, thinking about the last time I intended to use it with Jayme. I didn't feel as sad as I thought I would when I flicked though it's blank pages. It was long overdue for me to get away from here for a while and perhaps the timing couldn't have been more perfect.

Pete had been on about me traveling at some point, but I just wasn't ready. Certainly not if I was to do it only for my own benefit, but going with Carley filled me with a thrill that I hadn't felt in a while. That and the fact that Carley also wanted so badly for me to go with her was an added bonus.

Over the next few days I got the call from her to say all the name transfers had been made so it was confirmed. Pete needed to juggle everyone around, and all the guys seemed pleased that I'd finally made the decision to piss off as they put it.

"Way to make a girl feel appreciated," I mumbled.

"Anna, you need a change of scenery hon, go enjoy yourself, seriously." Pete said, always one to encourage me.

"Yeah but I feel like a shit leaving you at such short notice," I said frowning a little.

"Psht, don't be daft, it's winding down now, we'll be right, you've been working like a dog for three years, I owe ya," he said jovially, nudging my shoulder playfully. "I'm guessing you haven't told Kyle yet?"

I shook my head.

"And I suppose it'd be too much to drop a line?" He looked at me sceptically.

"Yep." I clenched my jaw.

"Alright then," he said with a shrug and wave of the hand. It was clear that he didn't agree with me, but he knew that I couldn't be swayed.

He sighed, changing the subject. "So, you'll be careful, won't you?"

"Yes dad," I said rolling my eyes.

He stood and came around his desk to give me a hug. "No, I'm your big bro, don't you forget it, now scoot, and get some sleep, jet lag's a bitch."

"I'll see you when I get back." I said, smiling as I turned to go.

"Who knows Anna, you might get the travel bug and never come back," he said half-jokingly with a grin on his face.

"Not bloody likely," I said with a chuckle. Because that was about as unthinkable as me flying a fixed wing aircraft.

Time flew and before I knew it the Taxi beeped its horn and my two suitcases and myself were on our way to the airport. That night, I would fly to Brisbane and then to Perth with Qantas first thing in the morning. There was a connecting flight with South African Airways later that day to Johannesburg, a total of forty hours on the go or something ridiculous. I'd be waiting (sleeping) in the airport terminal overnight and I'd catch some Z's at Carley's place in Perth before we would check in for South Africa nine hours later.

It was great to see Carley again so soon. Never again would I let so much time pass by. I'd been an idiot for being off her radar for so long, but like they say about true friends, now that we were together it's like we'd never been apart.

That night we watched a movie and had a healthy meal of pizza and coke since Carley had completely emptied her fridge. I nodded off not even halfway through the flick when I was nudged awake, "C'mon, let's get some proper shut-eye, we've got a holiday to go on!"

As soon as I'd slipped under the cool sheets, sleep claimed me, it only felt like minutes before Carley woke me with a steaming hot cup of tea and cold pizza. After we checked and double-checked that we hadn't missed anything, we took a Taxi to the Airport. A couple of hours later, we had boarded on a giant Airbus A340, bound for my first overseas trip.

Carley and I were super excited since we left her place and that didn't stop until the excitement wore off an hour into the flight at thirty-six thousand feet. The first hour of many passed and instead of sitting back to an in-flight movie, I thought I'd try and catch up on resting.

I wouldn't say I really slept but I did doze on and off until I heard and smelled the early breakfast being prepared in the galley, which was only a few seats down from where we sat. Out of Carley's window seat, the sun was just starting to illuminate the dark morning sky with a thin bright line cresting the curve of the earth.

"You missed the movie," she said pulling the foil from her cooked breakfast.

"Did I?" I buttered my mini croissant, "What was on?" I asked licking my fingers before looking at her.

She was grinning. "Oh some movie about an elephant in a Circus."

"Ha, funny considering we're on our way to a game reserve, you think they do that stuff on purpose? You know, tug at the heartstrings to save the wildlife and all that?" I never really watched animal movies, it always irritated me that the animals were often depicted inaccurately.

"Probably, you know I booked an Elephant Back Safari for us?"

"I think you mentioned it once or twice." I said, looking sideways at her.

"See, you're saving the fluffy animals already, that's so cool," I said shoving half the buttery goodness into my mouth.

"Yeah, thought it would be better than just a four-wheel drive tour, you know really be part of the experience." She looked off dreamily.

"Gees, you've been reading too many brochures," I teased.

"You have no idea," she said while playing with some plastic looking scrambled eggs on her plate.

After walking around the cabin to ward off the DVT and taking a bathroom break, I watched the next in-flight movie. I didn't really get into it because it was about Rugby or something, but it did have Matt Damon in it which was quite nice. The movie was set in South Africa and I was sure that the movie themes were no coincidence at all.

How Patriotic.

We touched down in Johannesburg and endured the long customs process before boarding a puddle jumper to Pretoria where a shuttle bus drove us for another hour to the Resort.

We were both barely able to sit upright we were that jet lagged. I took my time to gaze out the windows and watch the landscape pass by. It wasn't all that different to the scrub county from the station, red dirt, low shrubbery, and spindly water wise trees. Mile after mile rolled past us. With a break in the trees every so often there was a glimpse of a mountain range to the Far East, white puffy clouds looking peculiarly like wet season build up dotted the sky on the far side of the peaks.

The minibus slowed and turned into a fancy driveway, lined on each side by a huge log fence that stood about four metres high. It morphed into an equally high multi stranded electric fence, some of the wires would have been thick enough to tow a boat with.

"Is that to keep the tourists in or the game out?" Carley asked the driver.

The driver chuckled. "That would be to keep the game out ma'am," he said politely, "Welcome to Saanastia Game Reserve," he said as the heavy iron gates moved automatically.

The Driveway was long and wound itself through the native vegetation before opening out onto a large lawned area revealing those ecofriendly safari glamping tents, motor homes and a few caravans parked to the left. There were also more permanent buildings that looked like the ablutions for the visiting guests.

The whole area married elegantly with the resort ahead, which was almost hidden by the tall lush timber that surrounded it.

Stepping off the bus, the humid air hit us.

"Should have booked in the dry," Carley said with a huff, blowing her hair from her forehead.

"We'd probably freeze, it's not that bad Carley. Be thankful it's not hitting 45 degrees, this is nice." I said as the group followed the bus driver to the luggage trailer. "I reckon you've gone soft living in Perth," I teased shaking my head at her being so darn precious.

Carley grumbled at my comment. "Shut up, not all of us enjoy living in a sweat box, Stedman." She frowned causing me to chuckle and I found my lethargy easing with the banter.

Once we were handed our bags, we thanked the dark-skinned gentleman who flashed us a bright white toothy smile and we made our way to the resort lobby.

The building was impressive and looked like a massive hunting lodge. It was all huge wooden logs, stone walls and windows that towered floor to ceiling.

The gardens were meticulously maintained and somewhat tropical in appearance. Huge boulders were strewn throughout the grounds, which tied in with the building and stylishly set off the acres and acres that surrounded the resort.

We hung back, while the rest of the guests made a mad rush for the entrance, eager to get out of the heat.

Walking across the decking to the lobby, the doorman bowed slightly and politely pulling open the large glass entry. I was just about to thank him and because I was looking at the doorman instead of where I was going, I didn't see the battering ram who shoved me aside.

Careening back into Carley, the tall man rushed past without any regard. "Hey!" I yelled out, but the only acknowledgement I received was his retreating back stalking away like it didn't even happen.

He was on a two way.

"I'll call Jerry, the helo's on its way..." Was all I caught before his voice trailed off out of earshot.

"What's his problem?" I asked no one in particular.

"I am sorry ma'am," the doorman said in a heavy accent. "It looks like Mr. Staadman has got some bad news."

"No need to apologise for him Sir," I said, righting myself and continuing on inside.

"What a dick," I said to Carley, my skin prickling deliciously as the cool air-conditioning surrounded us upon entering the lobby.

"You get all the luck," Carley said, pretending to pout.

"Now I know you're tired, open your eyes girl, I was just about assaulted out there."

"I know, but oh to be assaulted by someone that looks as hot as that," she said, giving me a sideways glance and an impish look.

Clearing my throat, I may have retorted a little too quickly. "I didn't notice, I was too busy trying to stop myself from hitting the deck."

I may or may not also have noticed the tall frame, broad shoulders, and the hand gripping his messy Dark blonde coloured hair or the peaked cap stuffed in the back pocket of his stereotypical cammo' kaki's and his American accent.

Helo? Really? Who even uses that term?

I shook my head.

Nope, didn't notice anything.

In my mind, I rolled my eyes, knowing I was lying to myself.

I looked around the lobby, the place was cavernous. The timber and stone walls were so masculine, that I half expected there to be antelope heads hanging off the walls and zebra hides covering the floors, but there was none of that. Instead there was a huge array of artwork and large carvings that appeared to be native, not that I had any idea. The polished wooden floors were swathed in finely woven grass matting that you'd pay a bloody fortune for back home. The furniture was tasteful, heavily carved and covered in beautiful handwoven fabric.

"Welcome to Saanastia, my name is Martha, how can I help you," a friendly voice cut through my perusal as an older woman greeted us at reception.

"Just checking in thanks," Carley said wearily, she looked just about as wrecked as I felt.

We gave our names and were handed the keys. A man called Mathus took our bags and promised he wouldn't be too long to deliver them for us while Martha pointed to the large double doors that led all the rooms.

The resort was only two stories high and once at the top of the stairs, we entered the full length corridor that only had doors to one side. The opposing wall was made entirely of glass, almost completely unobstructed, and reached from the ground floor all the way to the eaves. It was the perfect viewing platform that had several pieces of furniture to sit on while enjoying the vista in the comfort of the cool air conditioning.

Unable to look away from the beautiful landscape, I took in the view to the east. The large green paddock ended at an almost invisible distant fence which appeared similar to the high cable fence I saw earlier. Past that fence, the landscape changed to the open range and in the far distance, the mountains rose to frame the picture. It was simply breathtaking.

For the moment, there was nothing happening outside and after tearing my gaze from the panorama, all I really wanted to do was wash off the aircraft grime and get some decent lunch into me.

As promised, Mathus arrived with our bags and we could finally get cleaned up. The room was nicely decorated with deep dark wooden furniture, freshened by ivory coloured drapes, cushions and bedding. The theme was similar to the lobby with grass matting and attractive artwork on the walls. The large sliding glass doors led out to a balcony facing west to take advantage of the sunsets that would undoubtedly be as nice as the ones we got at the station.

The bathroom was huge with a spa bath, double shower and vanity and there was also a separate toilet.

I stripped off and luxuriated under the warm spray before washing my hair and willing all the tension away via the plughole.

I dressed in a clean version of what I was wearing earlier and used the in-house hair dryer out in the room while Carley took her turn to freshen up.

Once ready to eat we started making our way down the stairs when the familiar beat of helicopter rotors sounded in my ears. Looking through the expanse of glass facing the sea of green, the flash of a red Bell Jet Ranger, minus its doors, flew towards the north east and disappeared into the distance.

Carley nudged my side and grinned, "Come on, I thought you were hungry."

I smiled not even realising that I had stopped to watch the chopper leave. "Yeah, I am," I said as I joined her.

We made it downstairs past the reception and asked Martha for directions. While she was pointing to the set of doors to our left that led to the restaurant, she also handed over two flyers that invited us to the annual Handle This Trunk With Care Gala Ball, explaining that it was a charity event to help fund the fight against rhinoceros and elephant poaching. It would be held in the dining room of the hotel in three days and was free entry to guests already staying at the Resort.

Carley had a knowing look on her face that she tried to hide, without success. I knew the girl was up to something.

## Chapter 5

We climbed the stairs to the second story of the main building and entered the very impressive entrance to the dining hall. While waiting to be seated, I perused the large space, it appeared grand and characteristic of the resort. In keeping with the other part of the building, a glass wall of windows had also been installed and overlooked an animal enclosure.

At closer inspection, the glass walls were actually sets of large accordion style doors, each section could be opened to the expansive alfresco area on the deck outside. Tables were scattered almost to the edge but were barricaded by a railing and also a series of stainless steel braided wires running the entire length of the deck.

"Oh wow," I said in realisation, "you could just about touch the animals from out there, you could get so close."

The maitre'd introduced herself as Michelle, dragging my thoughts back into the room and my eyes from the view outside.

"Please come this way." She turned away to pull a couple of menus from under the podium before leading us to the middle of the room.

There were about a dozen guests already scattered around the restaurant, casually chatting away, the subtle clink of crockery and cutlery filling the space with a relaxed ambiance. We were ushered to a table just inside the tall glass doors so we could see all the movements happening outside.

"You are right of course," she placed the menus on the table for two as we pulled our seats out and settled down, "the deck is built for interaction with the elephants and sometimes the giraffes."

"Oh that's just so cool," Carley said, her face brimming with excitement, "when do they usually come in, so we can see them?"

"Usually at evening dining," Michelle answered, "but you're not always guaranteed to touch them, they're sometimes too interested in their hay to bother coming by. They've seen it all before, but occasionally we get lucky, and usually it's Pragtig who is the instigator."

"Who's Prag- Prag?" Carley tried to get her tongue around the grating sound of the 'gs'.

"Hark up the 'g', Carley," I joked.

Carley looked at me a little grossed out, but when Michelle suggested, "Pronounce it like Prak-teck and you won't spit everywhere." She giggled. "And we'll still know who you mean." She winked.

"An elephant named Prak-teck, does that mean anything?" Carley asked, cocking her head.

At the same time as the word Beautiful suddenly came to mind, Michelle said, "Yes it does, it means beauty, magnificent or gorgeous and she is, she's the matriarch of our elephant herd. The leader." She smiled warmly and was clearly proud of the unique facility that allowed the animal/human interaction.

"Is there anything I can get you ladies to drink while you check our menu?"

We asked for a bottle of water to share and ordered our meal shortly after, two club sandwiches on rye and found they were just about the best we'd ever tasted, maybe it was the typically shitty airline food that made them taste top shelf or maybe they were really that good, but it didn't matter, they were just delicious.

"So what was that look you gave about this Gala thing earlier?" I asked before taking an obscenely large bite from my sandwich.

Carley smiled as she chewed, giving herself away.

I narrowed my eyes at her suspiciously as I wondered what she was up to.

She swallowed and wiped the crumbs from her mouth before dusting off her hands "Oh I may have already known about it," she said taking a sip of water and smiled broadly.

"So you're going?"

"Yup, and you're going too," she said with a sly smirk, before picking at some bacon from her plate and popping it in her mouth.

"Ugh Carley...I don't think..." I said curling my lip and shaking my head. I never was one for dances or dressy events, "I didn't bring anything to wear, it would be a formal evening and I only brought jeans and shorts and stuff."

"Oh, dear sweet Anna, I expected as much," she shook her head at me in mock sympathy, "which is why I brought your bridesmaid dress, just for the occasion." She bubbled with excitement, lightly bouncing in her chair.

I gaped at her. "I knew you were up to something." I narrowed my eyes at her, before taking another sip of water.

I shouldn't have been surprised.

"You planned this?" I asked.

"Uh huh, it's all part of the original itinerary, I liked the idea of the wildlife conservation thing, and how often do young bushies like us get to go to a black tie event huh? I mean, I've been to a B&S Ball, but it doesn't really count when you wear cowboy boots under a mini dress," she said, giggling at the memory. "And you babe, haven't done anything bigger than a barbeque." She tapped her nose knowingly.

I shook my head, "I don't know," I said hesitantly, grimacing at the thought.

"Oh come on Anna, you're on holiday, you might even enjoy yourself."

"You're not letting this go, are you?" I asked, scowling at her.

"Nope," she said popping the 'p' and shaking her head in the way that you knew she wasn't going to budge.

I slumped back in my chair and groaned.

"I suppose you have the shoes too?" Hoping that she didn't, but unfortunately, I also knew that was wishful thinking.

She fixed her eyes on me and dead panned. "Of course, as if I'd forget those."

We finished our lunch and I popped a mint, offering one to Carley, which she readily took. We were determined to fill our afternoon with something, the name of the game was to stay awake and get a full night's sleep, so we'd shed the jet lag as soon as possible. We met with Martha again because she looked like she was clearly in the know. She didn't disappoint and said that there was baby elephant playtime every afternoon in the enclosure, open to the public. This was right up our alley and it would start in ten minutes.

We decided to book the slot and wait around for one of the staff to take us through to view what promised to rate highly on the cuteness factor. I'd only ever seen baby elephants in pictures and on T.V. and I couldn't imagine what it would be like to see them playing while I was there with them. I could barely contain myself and my normally excitable best friend was calming me down for once.

Other guests started to gather and by the time one of the keepers came to collect us, - dressed again in the stereotype khaki camouflage clothing - the group had expanded to about twenty.

"Popular event," I whispered to Carley.

She agreed and we were ushered outside to the enclosure via a restricted electronic door.

The heat hit us but it wasn't oppressive, the distinct smell of outdoors and farmyard filled my nostrils and that wasn't oppressive either, the place was kept meticulously clean and only added to the feel that we were visiting an animal sanctuary.

The keeper explained that we weren't to purposely reach out for our interactions, we were to wait for the calves to come to us. For those that were nervous of the animals, there was a heavy post and rail viewing area, where both animals and humans could still reach through, but both could retreat without feeling pressured.

"Who's watching who?" I asked, chuckling at the corralled men and woman behind the fence, because naturally Carley and I were both confident enough to brave the baby elephant walk.

The keeper went on to explain that the interactions weren't just for the benefit of the tourists but that the elephants needed to be exposed to lots of people. They were all traumatised orphans and had probably watched their mother's get shot.

To get their trust back took years because it wasn't a myth that elephants had fabulous memories and they needed five to ten years of education to be a good member of elephant society. It amazed me that they sometimes took that long to wean depending on their mother's pregnancy status. They did however have equally fabulous forgiving natures and it was game reserves like Saanastia that helped to rehabilitate the pachyderms to being able to sustain themselves.

As if on cue, a distinct soft-footed rush of mini elephant feet ambled towards the enclosure, the area looked to be a few acres and was fenced. The bouncing, shuffling flapping calves ran in with about six men running alongside. The whole group was chasing of all things a giant soccer ball!

"Oh for goodness sake, isn't that the cutest thing you've ever seen?" Carley said, gushing over the scene unfolding before us.

I couldn't deny it and gasped for want of words that I couldn't speak while my heart tugged in my chest. My hands flew to my mouth as the herd of grey came towards us cavorting and pushing each other in attempt to get to the ball. The ball had stopped rolling when one of the handlers blocked its movement and the red cloud of dust that had risen behind the incoming herd, caught up to the guest area, engulfing the group and setting off one lady's allergies in a sneezing attack.

"I so want to take one home and love it, how utterly adorable," another lady cooed from behind the rails.

"And you won't need to pack a thing, they even have their own trunk!" One of the male guests joked sending a smatter of laughter into the air.

"As delightful as we know this appears," the keeper said with a chuckle, "this is a serious lesson for our babies. The trainers, called Mahouts are with them all the time, teaching them how to be elephants."

"I love their wriggly little trunks, aren't they just darling?" Asked another woman in a classic upper-class American accent.

"Yes they are," the keeper agreed. "That is why we need to be with them at all times, there are over fifteen thousand muscles in their trunks, and the babies have to learn how to use them, it takes years," he said, as the mixed group of hip to head high babies shuffled closer.

"Just stay still and let them come to you," the keeper encouraged.

Within minutes the world around me became unimportant as a little floppy trunk softly slapped the side of my head.

"Hello there." I said, feeling the little ones trunk. It was like soft, wrinkly thick leather, but still surprisingly pliable and with the bristly sparse hair that also covered the rest of its body.

Again the little trunk was in my face and I steadied it with my hand, blowing into the end gently.

"She likes you, you have experience with large young animals," the mahout said knowingly. He was older but had smooth dark skin and large brown eyes, he was tall and thin, every bit a proud African man.

"Yes," I said as the little one pressed her trunk to my face again, "Poddy calves and foals. They have a similar curiosity."

Then a second trunk felt its way up my body, I giggled because I was ticklish and in a moment, I had two little trunks busily checking me out.

I was completely engrossed by these little (well not really that little) souls. Their big flappy ears folded back to their bodies, streamlining them, their tuskless little faces and rather boggley eyes showing their whites at this young age. Their clumsy yet soft movements, innocent though full of mischief had me completely enamoured.

They messed my hair up and put their trunks in places they probably shouldn't have, completely unaware of social human etiquette and then one of them found what was in my pocket.

"Hey cheeky, you found my mints, hey?" I said with a giggle as I gently took the packet from the little fella before it could be absconded with. I looked up, and most of the guests were gone now; I hadn't realised that I'd been out there for so long; I was left with probing trunks and the keepers looking on quietly with contented looks on their faces.

Carley was sitting on the top rail of the fence to the viewing area, her feet resting on the second rail from the top. She was leaning with her chin on her hands and her elbows on her knees, looking bored.

"Finally, you grace us with your presence," she joked, her face looked relieved and I had no idea why.

"Huh?" I managed to utter as my brain attempted to make a connection with my mouth and failed miserably.

"You've been 'playing'," she said with air quotes before checking her watch, "for the past hour."

"Rea...lly?" I asked as another trunk smooshed me in the mouth. I eyed my surroundings, the staff members were smiling widely, their white teeth looking brighter in contrast to their dark skins.

"Oh crap, I'm sorry to have taken up so much of your time," I said trying to extricate myself from the throng of grey that had me pinned to the spot.

The elephants were dispersed just enough for me to be able to weave my way through them to the relative safety of the corral.

"What are you, the pied piper now?" Carley teased with a smirk on her face.

"I don't know Carley, that was..." I breathed deeply in contentment "Wow, just...Wow." I shook my head. I had no other words.

"Would you like me to ask if it is okay for you to come back to bottle feed later?" The oldest man in the group asked.

"Seriously, is that like, even allowed?" My eyes grew wide in disbelief.

"Well let's just say it's not part of our normal guest experience, but I will ask, we are a few people short this evening, we could use the help, and you look capable enough."

My heart seemed to grow in my chest, I felt truly privileged that these experienced people would allow these precious babies to be handled by me.

"Really? That would be amazing, thank you so much, I'd be honoured." I couldn't contain the huge smile that I was sure started from my toes. "What time do you start?"

"We'll be in the stables at four so anytime from there would be fine, I will let Martha know if I get the okay and she can also call one of us to escort you."

"Thank you, thank you," I shook his hand, and tried to contain myself somewhat, I didn't want to startle the calves by jumping around like some clueless girly girl.

"You are welcome... Miss?" He said, enquiring about my name.

"Anna." I said quietly.

"Miss Anna. Wonderful," he said joyfully. "I am Caseous, but you can call me Cass," he said turning towards the door to the resort.

"Well Cass, I'll see you in a couple of hours," I said as Carley and I followed him, "can Carley come too?" I asked.

Carley spoke before Cass could answer, "Na that's okay, the animals are more your thing, these little guys are cute, but I need to find me some other entertainment." Even though she grew up on a sheep station, Carley never really embraced the lifestyle completely, she was more of a city slicker.

She used to ride horses once upon a time, but that's as far as it went, it would have been a surprise had she jumped at the chance to bottle feed a baby elephant, god forbid she get formula on her three hundred dollar Ariat hiking boots.

Once we said good-bye to Cass, we made our way back through the lobby, passing Martha at reception. She was on a two way and caught our attention, by waving Carley and I over with a big smile.

Signing off, she turned her focus on us. "Ladies," she said brightly. "That was Cass, he tells me that you'll be helping make up the numbers at the barn this evening?"

"That was quick!" I said with excitement. Letting out a very uncharacteristic squeal, I nudged Carley. "How good's that Carls? How lucky am I?"

"You are Anna, you're the first guest in a long time to bed down with the babies, with three of the boys gone this afternoon the others could do with the help, Lloyd will be pleased that everything's still running to schedule here, lord knows that boy's got enough on his plate," she said with a strained look on her face.

I raised my eyebrows without thinking, which automatically prompted the motherly figure to continue.

Her brow furrowed with worry, moving closer, she said softly, "we have a new rhino baby being airlifted back here today."

This immediately piqued my interest, "Oh, what's wrong with it?" I asked.

"It was shot." Martha said, wringing her hands.

Carley gasped and her hand rose to her mouth in alarm.

"Oh no! Who would shoot a baby rhino?" She whispered, her voice breaking with the horror of what she'd been told.

I stepped closer to the desk and leaned in slightly. "It's mother?" I asked quietly.

Martha shook her head, her neat tight bun not moving an inch, "Butchered," her mouth set into a tight line as she appeared to fight of a quivering chin, "it's the third baby we've brought in recently."

"That's so sad," Carley said, her eyes glassy with tears. She may not have been naturally passionate about animals, but she had about as much compassion for them as anyone I'd ever met and she'd almost run herself off the road, rather than accidentally hit a bird with her car.

Then a thought struck me as hard as that guy had earlier in the day out the front of the lobby. The man that clocked me, was more than likely this Lloyd character, and while there was no excuse for not even acknowledging my presence, I mean let's face it, I was a guest at the facility that payed his wages, I could understand the irate mood he was in.

"Yes dear it's a travesty, the poor little mite will be here in an hour or so, if she makes it. Jerry, our vet," she smiled warmly at the mention of his name, "flew out with Lloyd earlier, the lad was in such a state but," she sighed, "if there's any chance at all, it'll be with those two."

"Cruel bastards," I whispered under my breath. It really was a wonder how there were people in the world who thought nothing of these sorts of actions.

"Yes dear, they are and they are the sole reason for Lloyds existence, his dream is to keep the Rhinos from becoming wiped out, the only consolation to this young calf is that she'll be a valuable addition to add to the numbers. If she survives." Martha shook her head as her voice drifted off, she looked like a worried mother hen until she suddenly snapped out of it. "Now enough of that, so..." she brightened somewhat but her eyes gave her away, for the smile didn't reach them, "are you two beautiful ladies coming to the Gala?"

I nodded absently. The images of men with big guns. Then of them cutting the horns off a mother Rhinoceros while her baby was caught in a catch twenty two, scared out of its mind and remaining in grave danger whether it stayed or left the place where its mother fell filled my mind. I could have wept but I clenched my jaw hard in an attempt to ward off the tears.

"... auction to dance with the town's most eligible bachelors, I'm sure you girls would like to contribute, Anna?" Martha smiled at me interrupting my reverie.

"I'm sorry, what?" I looked at her.

"Martha was just saying we might get to dance with some hotties at the Gala if we pay enough." She laughed, "I think I might need to blow some of that wedding money chick, can you imagine what that no good cheating ex of mine would think if he found out I spent some of his 'hard earned' cash paying for a stranger to dance with me?"

I chuckled despite the lingering darkness of my thoughts, figuring that Carley was going through a revenge faze at the moment, I had a feeling it was going to be a big night for Carley, that girl was going to do some serious partying.

"Mothers lock up your sons," I said, sending out a warning to the universe and only half joking, because I'd seen Carley's Girl's Gone Wild side in the past.

"I sure hope there are lots of sons at the Gala!" Carley said, rubbing her hands together with glee.

Martha followed suit saying, "That's the spirit," in an uplifting tone and I couldn't help but laugh at their antics.

She gave us a handful of glossy brochures, one that explained the main conservation goals at Saanastia, one about the Gala, and yet another which Carley was perusing, that listed additional activities at the resort.

There was the usual. We could go upstairs to the resort bar to shoot some pool or play darts. Outside we could explore the grounds - within the safety fence of the human zoo of course - play tennis or we could go swimming at the pool while sipping on some drink that held a mini umbrella.

But Carley and I weren't really up to anything too vigorous and instead, were happy to find something that would serve to simply keep us awake.

After some discussion, we opted to stay in the air-conditioned comfort of the library instead.

Carley was an avid bookworm and found something to read almost right away, but I just couldn't tear my mind away from this whole poaching thing and continued to study the brochures that Martha had gaven us.

All I could think was wow. I assumed Saanastia was just a hotel game reserve that managed wild animals in their equally wild habitat. A popular draw card for the tourism and the economic dollar. There was nothing inherently wrong with that in my opinion because the animals benefited no matter how the funds were raised. It was worth it to keep the environment they lived in as safe as possible.

That view was rapidly amended this afternoon, with the time we spent alongside the babies and there was also the nursery for young elephants and rhinos that I was invited to visit. But what struck me most was what happened after they'd survived to adulthood. The elephants were educated to carry tourists on the elephant safaris that Carley was talking about the other day and the rhinos were entered into a breeding program they were DNA tested, and selectively bred so the bloodlines weren't too close. Any doubling up would result in a swap with zoos and reserves from a pool thereby keeping numbers as diverse as possible.

Saanastia reared both Black and White Rhino, sadly they were all offspring derived from poached mothers. The awareness campaign to the plight of these animals was also a priority and education seemed to play an integral part of Saanastia's goals, the Gala Ball just one of the drives to raise money for the cause. It was all very impressive.

This gave me a new-found respect for the place, and I couldn't wait to get a glimpse behind the scenes later this evening.

When the time did come to go and feed the elephants, I barely interrupted an engrossed Carley who clearly wasn't going to miss me for a couple of hours and no doubt would still be in the library when I was done. She was completely oblivious to her surroundings as she disappeared into a fictional world of her own.

Martha seemed to have left for the day and a young red headed guy was now at the helm. Within minutes, I was whisked out the door into the wildlife enclosure and through the wide gate and rustically fenced off gardens hiding the large sheds from immediate view of the resort. Once the path ended, there was another equally wide gate that opened out to a massive barn like complex.

George, the guy who had taken me through the complex was another smooth, dark skinned, whiter than white toothy, grinning, lanky member of the elephant nanny community. He showed me to a large sterile looking room that was clad in stainless steel and concrete. It was a vetting room and to the right of the entry was a large stainless sink that was the size of a trough. In it, were a dozen or so five litre plastic containers that looked more like spare fuel tanks that you keep in the shed for your mower. The only difference was that these didn't have a nozzle screwed onto the end of them, they had a teat instead.

"These have been sterilised, we fill them with a custom mixture for each elephant or rhino depending on age and health. The charts," he pointed to the line of clipboards hanging off the front of a row of large stainless steel storage containers, "constantly change as the babies get older, milk strengths change, additions of vitamins and minerals, sometimes charcoal sometimes antibiotics, anyway it's all in the charts and we must follow it meticulously," he said as he took the first bottle labelled Boabo. He matched the bottle up with the corresponding chart and then set about adding the correct measures of various ingredients, marking them off as he went.

"How much do those little fellas drink George?" I asked as he handed me a large two litre measuring jug and guided me to a stainless elevated vat with a tap at the bottom of it.

"Can you pour three litres into Boabo's bottle?"

I nodded and he smiled before he picked up the next bottle.

"With a newborn it starts at about ten litres a day, divided into three hourly feeds around the clock. The quantity increases from there but the feeds are reduced. Generally they need between one to two percent of their bodyweight a day to grow properly," he informed giving me the next bottle, "four litres please," he said, collecting the first bottle and double checking the clear measuring strip on the side. He then gave the bottle a vigorous shake, placed it on a trolley and lastly, he ticked it off on the chart.

Half an hour later all the bottles had been filled and the other keepers started to file into the vet room to pick up a couple each. I then followed George, who led the way pushing the still laden trolley into the barn. "This is Makimba, she's the little one that was stuck to you earlier." George smiled as he unlatched the steel railed gate to one of ten or so massive elephant stables that lined one side of the huge barn.

Makimba knew it was feed time and you could hear her begging for her bottle. She was wearing a blanket to keep her warm. It was strapped around her girth with a rope and looked very snugly.

For an elephant that is.

"Just hold it up she knows the rest."

I followed his directions with ease, everything was familiar to me, those Brahman calves were the same.

"Ah, I am reminded of your expert skills Anna." He grinned at me and I couldn't keep the smile from my face.

Makimba tipped her head up, curling her trunk out of the way and started suckling.

"Touch her as much as she'll allow, they need as much interaction with different people so as not to get too bonded to any one person," he explained as a few more keepers made their way into the breeze way to collect bottles from the trolley. "I'll be in the next stall with Nambi if there's a problem but then I need to get the operating room ready."

"Because of the rhino?" I asked over the strong sucking sounds.

"Yes, we have to remove the bullet."

I frowned.

"Now don't be sad Anna," he said, perceptively. "Makimba will know and be sad too."

I nodded and concentrated on avoiding the froth spilling from the corners of Makimba's mouth which instantly pepped me up.

I fell into the zone again and I didn't even notice when George left while Makimba drank her milk.

There was a towel hanging over the hole at the gate latch and I wiped at the corners of her mouth, drying off my hands too. The cheeky little thing grabbed onto the towel and started waving it around.

"You like that little one, huh?"

I started rubbing her all over just like I would when I desensitised a horse, being methodical and rhythmical.

Hearing the helicopter arrive, there was a brief commotion of voices until the chopper landed and wound down. After that, there were only muffled voices and a little bit of banging and clanging followed by the barn sounds.

"Guess you might have a new friend to play with, hey?" I said soothingly, thinking of the rhino that was currently in the operating room with its life in the balance.

To think that those callous poachers would leave a young animal in that state was appalling. I shook my head, who was I kidding? Those same poachers had no qualms shooting the mothers of these babies so why would they care if the bullet didn't finish the little guy off first up, it would die eventually anyway right?

Pretty soon Makimba plopped down in a heap, tired from her day's exploits. So I decided to sit next to her in the straw, rubbing her and chatting to her. I yawned after only a few minutes and heaped a bit of straw up to lean into. I popped a mint into my mouth and instantly Mikambo's little trunk was exploring my face, sniffing at my mouth. I blew gently and after a few minutes I was able to hold the end of her trunk in my hand as it rested on my thigh.

Before long that little elephant had drifted off and my eyes also grew heavy at the sight of the sleepy little critter...

"Ms. Stedman wake up please," the smooth voice stage whispered near my ear.

Warmth spread through my shoulder before it was shaken gently. Coming to, I took a deep breath and the warmth was withdrawn. I opened my eyes, only to be met with the icy blue ones that belonged to the voice I had just heard. I scanned my strange surrounds and was reminded that I was asleep with a baby elephant whose trunk I was still holding.

When I looked back at the man, the eyes were gone. Their owner rising with the graceful ease of a big cat, which was fitting since we were in big cat country.

"Ms. Stedman you may leave now, George will be here in a moment to escort you back to the Resort," he said in an American accent that I finally placed as my human bulldozer.

"Oh," I said in a sleepy voice before I rubbed my eyes with the bottom of my shirt, Ow! Bad move, I still had the contacts in.

"Um how's the rhino baby?" I asked.

"As well as can be expected," he said bluntly holding out his hand and wriggling his long fingers as he urged me to get a hurry on.

I instinctively met the man's hand half way and he helped me up off the straw with no apparent effort at all. My heart fluttered without my permission. Thankfully, he was wearing his baseball cap and diverted his gaze by looking at the ground, because right then there wouldn't have been any other way to hide the embarrassing blush that the interaction caused.

After an awkward silence, I found my voice "You're Lloyd right?" I asked, regretting it instantly when he simply grunted at me before turning away with his hands on his hips.

Ok then, I get when I'm not wanted.

I was saved from any further embarrassment when George finally returned, Mikambo was stirring and I knelt down to touch her before she woke up fully, soothing her till she stilled again. Without a sound, Lloyd took my place and settled himself on the bed of straw.

"You did a wonderful job, Anna," George whispered. "Your assistance was invaluable this evening, thank you." He flashed that big white toothy smile at me. "It was just what we needed, right boss?" He prodded.

Lloyd grunted again, reclining onto the straw pillow I'd made and pulling the peak of his hat lower over his eyes.

What was his problem?

I decided to let it go, I'd had the most beautiful experience this evening and I wasn't going to let my holiday be ruined but some grumpy bastard with PMS - no matter how attractive he was.

I could have kicked myself for my involuntary thoughts.

There was nothing remotely attractive about a guy who practically knocks over a woman without so much as an acknowledgement, nor one who can only answer in caveman when asked perfectly reasonable questions. Besides, I hadn't even seen him properly, the way he hid under that cap, he was probably really unattractive to look at too.

At least that's what I'd keep telling myself.

I left the stable, accompanied by George and we walked back to the resort, it was barely light and I still needed to shower and change before tracking down some dinner.

"Uh, thanks George, Mikambo is just gorgeous." I said at the door to the resort.

"You're welcome my dear," his musical South African accent rolled off his tongue gently, "and don't you worry about Mr. Lloyd, he is a little bit intense, he gets more so when he's trying to save a rhino, they are endangered and there have been too many in such a short time."

I smiled at him and nodded, not quite sure why everyone was so quick to defend 'Mr. Lloyd' to me.

"That's okay George no harm done."

"Okay my dear I will let you be," he said with a slight bow and his trademark toothpaste commercial grin before he disarmed the door and opened it for me to walk through.

Hearing the door click shut behind me, I was only two steps into the lobby when I was startled by a voice.

"Ah Anna, there you are!"

Martha sounded jovial.

"Oh, hi Martha, I thought you'd gone home for the day." I said, giving her a wide smile.

I couldn't help but be affected by her demeanour, she was such a sweet lady.

"Oh no dear, this is my home," she said proudly, gesturing to the space around her.

I looked at her with surprise. "You live here?"

"Why yes, I do, have for years and so does Lloyd, we live in the guest quarters at the homestead," she said, her own smile not leaving her face.

"Oh okay" I was a little taken back. "All the staff live here then?"

"No Anna, just the management and sometimes the keepers if it's really busy, Saanastia never really sleeps." Picking up on my confusion, she continued. "Oh sorry dear, I should explain I'm the Resort Manager. I was filling in at the front desk today because Natalie had to go to hospital this morning. She broke her finger in the car door before she even left home poor thing." She said, shaking her head with worry.

Martha quite obviously was a bit of a mother figure for all the staff here.

A yawn escaped me without warning.

"Oh, goodness I'm holding you up, of course you'd be weary after today, you've not even had a proper rest since your flight I'm sure, I should let you have your dinner and then you need to get yourself a good night sleep."

She was motherly to her guests too, so it seemed. It was a nice feeling that she cared so much. I smiled, a little embarrassed at yawning in her face and waved off her concern with my hand "I'm fine, I shared some straw with Makimba for a few hours."

She nodded with that knowing look she seemed to own. "Yes dear, but I would think that a full stomach and comfortable bed will be far better for you."

I sighed.

"You're right of course," I said, because she was.

Then, a thought for the man who was giving up his bed after a hard day crossed my mind.

Martha smiled with a look of victory on her face, she told me the restaurant would be open till ten, so there would be enough time to freshen up beforehand.

I took that to mean I probably stunk like an elephant stable, so I went upstairs and greeted Carley who was reclining on her bed reading.

She looked up briefly. "Well, seems that the four legged company around here has you hooked, I was just about to eat without you. How was it?" She asked, finally setting the book aside and sitting up to pay attention.

"Amazing," I said.

"Looks like it, you've got a dreamy look to your face," she said, her tone full of suspicion.

"Yes well, Makimbo and I did get to roll in the hay together," I said, joking.

"Right." Carley nodded just once, but she was clearly not buying it.

"What?" I demanded.

"Nothing." Her tone was innocent, but her expression was far from it.

"Ugh," I grumbled at her, a little incensed, "I need a shower."

Carley didn't need to know about the blue eyed, grumpy Mr Lloyd though I suspected she had that BFF psychic thing going and I wasn't about to encourage her. As noble as Lloyd's cause was, it didn't detract from the fact that he still acted like a first class knob.

## Chapter 6

The next day Carley and I played typical twenty something girls on holiday. We hung out at the pool and ended up with a collection of those little umbrellas and then Carley roped me into having a spa treatment. It was ridiculous really, but she insisted because all the girls in the wedding party were going to get it done before 'the big day'.

Anyway, she thought that I shouldn't miss out.

I'd never been primped beyond getting my hair cut or my eyebrows waxed so this was a whole new experience for me.

"Hope it's a start of a whole bevy of new experiences for you, if you know what I mean," she said, nudging me and doing that eyebrow waggle thing.

I was mortified that she'd even go there in front of the beauticians who were working on our pedicures. Thankfully we also had goop on our faces, so I was saved any further embarrassment from a traitorous blush. It was a wonder said goop didn't melt off with the heat I felt radiating from my skin.

I was further horrified that Carley was getting waxed, and I wasn't talking about her eyebrows either, I mean Ouch! I think I felt more sympathetic pain then she did and flatly refused any more 'sisterly bonding' after witnessing that, even if I did have my eyes tightly closed. Not that later she didn't try to convince me to have a little tidy up 'down there' one day.

"Oh Anna, it's just a bikini wax and saves all that irritation after you shave. Seriously you'll never look back," she said as convincingly as any car salesman trying to sell you a lemon that will fall apart the moment the thing rolls out of the yard. "And," she continued with that glint in her eye, "there's also the bonus that guys love it."

"Ugh." I uttered in exasperation.

Later, back in our room again before dinner, I noticed that Carly seemed a little preoccupied.

"What's up?" I asked her.

After a long and uncomfortable minute watching what looked like she was working up courage to jump off a ledge or something, Carley finally asked me, "Anna, don't you think it's about time you got back up on that horse?"

"I'm not ready." I said, perhaps a little too abruptly. I started picking off a bit of imaginary lint from my Capris that I'd changed into for the evening meal.

"It's been more than three years hon," she reminded me.

"Look, I can tell you're concerned, but I'm alright with my lot, I've got my awesome job, and my little boy, Blue, what else does a girl need?"

She looked at me incredulously as if the answer was obvious. "You should be thinking about more than riding that horse, chick."

I growled in irritation just wanting to stick my fingers in my ears and sing lalalala before I braced myself for the onslaught that I knew was likely to follow.

"C'mon A, you're a freaking stunning woman, shit, it's a wonder you've still got your V card, no-one would believe it, but don't you ever think about having someone in your life?"

"Not really," I shook my head taking a defensive pose by crossing my arms over my chest, "I-It's not as though I haven't looked but..." I sighed and pinched the bridge of my nose. "Just forget it," I said, with a shrug.

"Let me guess. No one comes close to Jayme?" Carley asked.

I sighed, shrugging again.

"Anna, I love you, you know that, right?"

I nodded scraping my bottom teeth over my top lip.

"Good, coz I say this out of love".

She didn't let me interrupt because as soon as my mouth opened, she held up a finger, "Let me say this please," she begged.

This was Carley in full BFF mode, and when Carley was in BFF mode, she was formidable.

"Anna, I've known you for like, forever, and at school you were a loner, I knew there was something up with you in ninth grade after Easter, because you had something that you didn't have before that.

"A spark, I couldn't describe it." She shook her head. "I know you said you had a crush on Jayme the pilot but you know..." She shrugged, "you were fifteen! I couldn't believe that the most level-headed girl I knew, was infatuated by some older guy that... let's face it, the odds were, it would be unrequited right? You said so yourself."

I nodded uncomfortably; she was right. What would a guy nearly twice my age, want with a teenager that couldn't mean anything except a trip to prison?

Biting my lip hard, I remembered the moment that Jayme left me reeling on the Easter of my seventeenth year with my heart ripped out and bleeding all over the concrete floor of Uncle Kyle's hanger...

*-He was later than usual that year. Apparently, he was driving across the country this time around. I was only a couple of days away from returning to school, so I was understandably overjoyed when Uncle Kyle announced that Jayme had just radioed in and said he'd finally turned into our driveway. My heart leapt out of my chest and I honestly didn't know how I was going to survive the next half an hour or so waiting for him.*

*It was a really long driveway.*

*I busied myself by replacing all the inspection panels on the station's Cessna, now that it's hundred hourly service had been completed. Uncle Kyle had his general Aviation Maintenance Engineer's licence which made him able to service all the surrounding station aircraft in the district. It meant that there was barely any downtime during mustering season, we never had to fly engineers in nor ferry aircraft out on dead legs to Kununurra to be serviced. Naturally I learned a little during my stays here and enjoyed helping out.*

*I swept out the building and was just finishing up with the dustpan and brush when I heard the sound of a turbo diesel and the crunch of gravel as a vehicle approached the hanger. Glancing up, I watched a big, flash, midnight blue Ford F350, towing a modified car trailer with a helicopter strapped to it slowly coast in.*

*As it come to a stop, Uncle Kyle pulled at the hanger doors, closing them most of the way and blocking my view - much to my disappointment - before he headed out to meet the object of my affection.*

*I tried to suppress my drumming heart and act casual by distracting myself further, so I made work of meticulously sorting out the spanners and sockets into their corresponding sizes in one of the large red tool trolleys.*

*I turned the moment I heard the shuffling of boots on the concrete floor behind me.*

*He looked just as good as I remembered, all tall and tanned and just Jayme. The butterflies went crazy in my stomach on his approach.*

*Keeping his eyes on the ground, all I could see was the smile on his lips from under the brim of his Akubra.*

*"Hey," I greeted him, unable to stop the corners of my mouth from turning up too.*

*"Hey," he repeated, shoving his hands in his jean's pockets and schooling his expression before looking up at me.*

*There was an awkward silence and I scrambled for something to say. Finding a safe subject, I asked, "So, how'd ya go?"*

*Jayme grabbed his belt buckle, "I recon I went alright," he said. His grin returning.*

*The subject familiarity eased the pregnant tension instantly.*

*I looked down, noting the year in large engraved numbers.*

*"You did it!" I said in amazement.*

*"Yep," he said with a nod, popping the 'p'.*

*I couldn't contain myself and ran to him giving him a huge hug. "That's so cool, you reckon you'll make it a hat trick?" I asked into his neck, breathing him in. He smelled so good, all subtle cologne and man. Just so him.*

*He'd won again at the Nationals and there couldn't have been a better feeling in the world than the one I had at that moment. Jayme's arms wrapped around my waist in an instant and I heard his intake of breath.*

*"I sure hope so, Anna," he said softly before we were interrupted by a shadow falling across the opening of the hanger doors.*

*The shadow belonged to a beautiful raven-haired woman. A citified, skinny jeans, heeled boots, fitted top kind of woman with way too much decoration and spakfiller for out here in the middle of nowhere.*

*Jayme and I let go of each other as though we'd been scorched. The lady slid her oversized sunglasses to the top of her head before putting her hands on her hips and assessing us with a critical look.*

*My heart sank.*

*"Yeah. That's so awesome, bet you'll shoe it in," I said nervously, stepping away.*

*Sliding my hands into the back pockets of my jeans to keep them still, I chanced another look at the sophisticated woman standing at the doors. I must've looked like a dumb kid by comparison.*

*Of course he had a beautiful girlfriend, a real woman.*

*"Honey, can you help me get that luggage out of the car?" She asked, narrowing her eyes at me.*

*"Sure thing Tan," Jayme said turning to face her taking another step away from me.*

*"Oh, hello there," the lady said condescendingly, "you must be the famous Anna that Jayme's mentioned."*

*Her heeled boots clicked on the concrete as she came up to us. Wrapping a possessive arm around Jayme, I watched him swallow and look down at the floor.*

*"I'm Tanya, Jayme's better half," she said with a shrewd smirk offering her hand for me to shake.*

*Nausea swept over me and I thought to say it was a shame that I'd never heard of her before, but I bit my tongue and said, 'pleased to meet you,' instead.*

*I left two days later, and it was the first time I couldn't wait to leave the Station and go back to school...-*

I felt my heart rate and breathing increase and an unwelcome prickling feeling settled itself at the back of my throat. Every muscle was tense, and I curled my fists fighting the urge not to lose it as I thought back to the first time I'd lost him, the time I never really had him in the first place.

But it was nothing like the feeling I got almost exactly a year later, when I lost him again.

"You had four months Hun, four months with him before he..."

"Don't!" I said from between clenched teeth. I was shaking at this point.

"Someone has to."

"I'm not like you! I can't just turn around and be all happy and move on after a few weeks like you're doing, that's not me!"

"And you think that's me?" Carley asked in disbelief, her voice rising an octave.

I shrugged at her.

"Because I assure you it's not Anna!" She said, her eyes welling up with tears.

Shit. What did I just do? Her breakup still so recent and raw. God, I felt like the biggest bitch ever.

"It's not! Blair was my first too you know?" Her voice pitched again with the emotion. "Point is," she sniffed, "is that I saw what it did to you, is doing to you. The spark you had, it died, there's something missing in you, and when Blair did..." She took a deep breath. "What he did. After those first few days I swore I wouldn't let what happened to you happen to me, I was going to get back on the horse. I wasn't going to let that prick waste a single minute more of my time."

"Jayme wasn't a waste of time," I whispered thickly, hurt that she would compare the two men.

"No, I know that, but you've chosen to stop time for three years, I'm not saying you should forget him Anna, but he wouldn't want you to compare the length of time you grieve to how much you loved him, that's just not fair to you. He'd want you to live a happy life with someone you love, being loved."

We both sat quietly for a moment, contemplating.

"Since when did you get so philosophical?" I asked, wiping the corners of my eyes with the hem of my sleeve.

Carley was always the jokester, she rarely took anything too seriously, so this was a bit of a surprise.

"Ever since I was cheated on, it tends to change a girl you know," she said before throwing me a wry grin.

I nodded, "Yeah, I guess it would."

"Anyway, how about we enjoy this holiday like two hot, young chicky's are meant to?" She asked, leaving her funk behind.

I raised an eyebrow at her.

"Oh, come on Anna, live a little, you're gonna be a knock-out at the Gala tomorrow, have one drink just to loosen you up, there'll be dancing, dance with a guy, what do you say?"

I frowned. "I don't know about the drink or the dancing with the guy bit." I shook my head.

"I promise nothing will happen to you." She placed a hand over her heart.

"Why am I not comforted by that Carley?"

"Do you trust me?"

She squinted at me, I hated when people said that, it made me want to not trust them at all, but she was my friend and she'd always been there for me even though there was a continent between us. I couldn't very well say no, could I?

So I nodded.

"Good, you'll have a blast!" She said triumphantly.

There was a long silence, I was still fighting my internal battle.

On the one hand, sticking with my life as I knew it, in my comfort zone but staying stagnant. Even though work at Station to Coast and having Blue were fulfilling, I was for all intents and purposes alone, apart from Pete and his wife Rachael, whom I often thought were there more through obligation. Then there was Carley, who lived half a world away. So really, this was all on me.

On the other hand, there was this pushing my boundaries thing, this trying new stuff thing. Maybe I should be having a crack at this 'having fun' thing.

Should I make an appearance at the Gala night with a bunch of strangers?

It was only one night, right? If it all turned to crap, I didn't know anyone here, I had no ties and I'd be leaving in a few days anyway, right?

Right.

Carley was still looking at me expectantly. "Well?" She said, pressing me.

I rolled my eyes "Okay, okay," I finally acquiesced.

"Really?" She asked with surprise.

I nodded and was crash tackled to the bed before I could even brace myself. It seemed that it was becoming a habit of hers as of late.

"Oh, that's so cool, you won't regret it, I promise, we're going to have so much fun!"

"Can't breathe," I choked out at her surprisingly constrictive hug.

"Shit sorry!" She giggled, sitting up again, "I think this deserves a celebratory drink!" She said, in triumphant victory.

I held my hand up, "Hang on, hang on, could we at least wait till tomorrow before you turn me into a raging alcoholic and let me have a little more time getting used to the idea?"

She pouted of course.

"One lemon lime and bitters coming right up," she said, her face holding a deadpan look as she dragged me up from the bed before herding me out the door.

We ended up at the Hotel Bar. There were about a dozen patrons spread throughout the large area. This was one of the only social zones that had no access to the enclosure area and that was probably for the best. Any interaction between drunk patrons and wild animals was likely a recipe for disaster.

I sipped my lemon lime and bitters while Carley had one of her lolly waters that made her tongue blue.

The ambient mood of the bar was disrupted when a gaggle of chattering women burst through the doors bragging about their day.

The girls swarmed around the bar and ordered a variety of drinks, some making eye contact with Carley and I and smiling with residual excitement.

"You all know each other?" Carley asked the girl next to her, never one for being backwards in coming forwards.

"Yeah, we do... now," she laughed, "we're on one of those under thirty tours, you two going to the Gala tomorrow?"

"Absolutely." Carley grinned.

I nodded staying quiet for now, nervous about interacting with the group of girls that, let's face it, probably went on those tours for a reason and it wasn't just to enjoy each other's company. Not that there was anything wrong with that.

"Great! We'll probably see you there then, there's a dance auction you know?" The girl waggled her eyebrows.

Carley nodded as she puckered her mouth to the rim of her bottle and took a drink.

"I can't wait," the girl said in excitement, "vying for those hot, maybe rich South African bachelors, here's hoping there'll be more than dancing vertically."

Carley grinned at her. "I hear you and Amen sister," she said as she raised her bottle.

Taking the cue, the girl did the same before they clinked their bottles together.

"Hey, maybe we could get you some dance action?" Carley said suggestively before giving me a strong nudge.

"What?" I almost choked on the cube of ice I was sucking on. I dropped it back into my glass, knowing that it might be a little gross to do so but not as gross as coughing up a lung if the damn thing went down the wrong way. "No, no I don't think so, I don't da..."

"I call bullshit, we did deportment classes together at school, and you dance fine, just don't lead when you're with the guy, 'kay?" She winked wickedly at me.

I put another cube of ice in my mouth and crunched down on it in frustration while the girls continued to banter. It seemed as though everybody at the Resort was in a buzz about the Gala and once I actually read the Brochure about it, I saw why.

Apparently, the girl at the bar was right, it was the event of the year in the region. Tables were expensive to buy and were filled with the elite from not only South Africa, but neighbouring Zimbabwe, Mozambique and Botswana. These countries all had interests in the preservation of wildlife, the tourism dollar and shared borders with South Africa. It was as much a networking night as a fundraising night and it also seemed the Mr. Sweet and Friendly was 'offering himself up on a platter' for the dance auction.

Carley's words, not mine.

# Chapter 7

The next morning I was up early. Not one to sleep in, a lifetime of early mornings had me programmed to wake up at a sparrow's fart. Carley however as I discovered, could sleep all bloody day if I didn't take a cattle prod to her... Figuratively speaking of course.

After freshening up and getting dressed, I left Carley with her head under a pillow while I went to go find some breakfast.

Heading up the stairs to the restaurant, I could hear the tell-tale clinking of cutlery and dishes. The smell of a fully cooked breakfast lured me in as I neared the doorway. I wasn't even sure if the place was open yet and when I peered inside, I noticed a group of keepers and other staff members huddled around shovelling bacon, eggs, sausages and all other manner of food into their faces.

It reminded me of breakfast at the station. I smiled at the memory and took a step back from my intrusion. Quite obviously this was the first shift of the day and it was staff only.

Just as I turned to go, I heard a voice call to me from behind.

"Anna, is that you?"

I recognised the voice as that of George and cautiously padded back to the doorway.

"Hi." I said giving everyone in the room a little wave.

"Anna you have good timing I want to show you something." He waved me over as he rose from his seat and gestured for me to follow him to the deck. Opening the accordion doors, we stepped through and I was met with the early sunrise and its foray of soft pastel colours to the east.

"Come, come," he said, guiding me to the edge of the deck and then beyond the barricade that separated the enclosure from the patrons. There was a lone elephant with a calf only about fifty metres away.

"Is that...?" I was squinting in the poor light.

"That's Makimbo and Pragtig," George confirmed at the same time a low rumble reached my ears I assumed was made by the massive female elephant.

"This is good, yes?" I asked.

"Hmm, we are not sure, Pragtig will not let Makimbo out of her sight, Kabri, Pragtig's Mahout is the only one she has let feed Makimbo, so that in itself is not ideal. While Makimbo needs to interact with older elephants in order to learn to be an elephant, Pragtig is not teaching her anything yet, she just seems to touch her and scent her."

I nodded, saddened by George's words while continuing to watch the two animals together. They looked like heaven, but they weren't mother and daughter.

A breeze picked up and swirled around me, I could smell the freshness of the morning and breathed in deeply as the wind tugged at my hair that I had tied into a messy bun.

Pulling out the elastic, my blonde locks tumbled around my shoulders, I re-twisted it atop my head before securing it again. My eyes never left the two elephants as they continued to stand, with Makimo constantly tottering around Pragtig's legs and the bigger elephant touching her with her trunk.

George asked if I wanted to join the crew for breakfast. My hunger had been almost forgotten in the moment but came back with a vengeance at the mention of food. I finally tore my gaze from the endearing scene and nodded in agreement.

With another gust of wind, I had turned and was about to duck under the barrier when we heard an almighty snort. The sound was abrupt enough to make both George and I wheel around in alarm. Rapid, soft but heavy footfalls followed as Pragtig used her ambling gate far more quickly than I could imagine, her ears wide, and trunk up and heading straight for us.

"Whoa," I said as I instinctively backed up from the charging elephant.

Makimo had been left behind in a cloud of dust and in the next moment George had grabbed me by my shirt and pulled me back under the barricade and out of harm's way.

There was a loud trumpet and I stepped back a little more from the intimidating scene. Unable to look away, Pragtig had come right up to the deck and her trunk was desperately trying to reach for me.

"George! Is she alright?" I asked, assuming that she clearly wasn't.

Pragtig was pressed up against the deck breathing heavily. Her trunk was stretched in our direction and I could hear the air rush through her trunk in long, deep breaths.

George was on his radio calling for Kabri and Lloyd. The other staff had also gathered out on the deck, every one of them wide eyed and gaping.

I crouched down to get a little closer to the reaching elephant. "I think she wants to touch me."

"I think so too, but please no closer Anna," he said as Pragtig's tusks clashed loudly with the deck, "I don't want you to be hurt."

"She wouldn't hurt me, would she?" I asked, concerned for the obviously distressed elephant. Behind the ruckus, little Makimbo's handler had managed to entice her away with a bottle while another keeper stood guard with a really big rifle.

"Probably not but she is different from the other elephants, she had a trauma as a six-year old and ever since then, she has not been ridden. She's disturbed Anna and she only trusts Kabri. But she's invaluable to the herd because she brings them in every morning and evening."

"Why does she do that, George?" I looked at the elephant, who had calmed slightly but was still agitated evidenced by her rocking from one front leg to another and her repetitive long rumbles.

"Okay everybody, stop your gawking and get back to work," came the recognisable sound of the boss man himself. His voice filtered over the heads of the crowd, who let him through before most of them slowly dispersed and filed back through the doors.

An older African man accompanied Lloyd's imposing figure. He had grey hair cropped closely to his head in tight curls. Both men were focused intently on the elephant, carefully assessing her body language as they approached. Speaking in low murmurs, they seemed to agree to something with a nod and it took only a moment before the darker skinned man climbed under the barrier and then promptly sat on the deck only a small distance away from Pragtig.

His lips moved, whispering things that I couldn't hear, and reached for her as she came near him, but she backed off, not making contact. Snorting and shaking her head again, her massive ears held forward to attention, she looked and sounded every bit a wild elephant with her agitated stance and her loud rumbles.

Lloyd came to stand behind George and only then did I realise that he was also holding a big rifle that looked similar to the one that the keeper had wielded earlier.

He caught me staring at the firearm and moved the heavy rifle to his other side and furthest away from me, shifting his weight from foot to foot and appeared contrite as if he may have been concerned with my sensibilities.

"Insurance?" I asked nodding to the weapon.

"Hm, what are you doing up here?"

His expression changed suddenly to a look of disgust, as if I weren't worthy of sharing the deck with him. He had his cap on and for the first time I noticed a long scar on his face. It started under the peak, ran over his eyebrow, to his temple and towards his ear.

Not wanting to stare, I looked at my hands, fumbling nervously, "I woke early and..." I didn't even finish before he interrupted.

"You shouldn't be here it's too dangerous," he said abruptly.

I felt like I'd been slapped across the face and quickly backed away from him.

"O - okay," I said with a stutter.

Turning on my heel, I didn't make it three steps before the elephant roared and there was an almighty crack, scaring the shit out of me. I spun around to face the commotion and in turn, stumbled into Lloyd. His arm snaked around my waist sending shivers through my body, making sure to keep me behind him. The grey haired man was trying desperately to calm his elephant because Pragtig had managed to wedge a tusk under the edge of the deck and had punched through the boards.

That had to hurt.

Every available man still on the deck rushed to her aid, trying hard not to yell, but unsuccessfully chanting "Whoa, whoa, easy," and other such words to sooth the distressed animal.

The onslaught of men panicked her, and she wrenched backwards with a crunching sound as three boards splintered leaving a hole large enough for a man to fall through.

Pragtig shook her head vigorously and while everybody was occupied, I walked towards the edge of the deck, staying on the safe side of the barricade. The elephant took advantage on my position and quickly came up to me reaching to touch me.

I tentatively held out my hand.

"Anna no!" I heard Lloyd yell as he aimed the rifle at Pragtig's head. The elephant let out a much quieter rumble - almost like a purring sound - the moment that contact was made and for the third time during my stay, there was only an elephant and me. I didn't know what it was about these creatures, but they completely drew me in.

It felt almost otherworldly, if there were such a thing.

Biting lightly at my bottom lip, I concentrated on Pragtig. "Tembo nzuri," I uttered, caressing her huge trunk.

Crawling through the barricade, I never lost contact with the animal. Pragtig rumbled again as I slid closer to her, crossing my legs Indian style and I fished the pack of mints from my pocket. Shaking out a single mint onto my hand, I passed it to Pragtig.

Amazingly, the finger-like ends of her trunk had no problem taking the tiny pellet from my hand and popping it in her mouth before I was rewarded with another rumble.

"Huko, wewe ni vizuri sasa." I coo'd at her.

Once I knew that the elephant had calmed enough, I stood and turned, only to freeze in my tracks because there, looking on with eyes on stalks, were George and the grey haired man. Lloyd was splitting his attention between eyeing me and sighting the rifle at Pragtig. She had now moved off the edge of the deck and stood looking content for the first time that morning.

"Will you quit pointing that thing at her? She won't hurt me," I said surer than I'd been of anything for some time.

Lloyd shifted his gaze to me, his blue eyes sharp and piercing, before disarming the gun and handing it to George.

"Kabri, go feed Pragtig. George, get her out of here," he said pointing at me, "and secure the area until we get someone to fix that mess," he waved at the broken deck before glaring at me one last time and storming off.

"Kabri is it?" I asked the grey haired man to make sure he was who I thought.

"Yes Miss" he said, verifying my notion.

"Will she be okay?" I asked, gesturing to her.

"I think so, can I please take your jumper?"

I looked at him as though he was crazy.

He smiled and shook his head lightly. "Just so I can move Pragtig to an enclosure, it smells like you and it will help me out, she is calm now that she has finally got what she wants."

"What she wants?" I asked.

"She wanted to meet you."

"Me?" I asked completely baffled. "Why would Pragtig want to meet me?

Kabri closed his eyes for a moment to think of what he would say next and shook his head. "I'm not sure, but she's good now, better. But if you will excuse me, Miss Anna I need to go, please do not say anything about the excitement here this morning," he said with a cheeky wink.

It was definitely warm enough now for the short-sleeved shirt that I wore with my yoga pants and sneakers. Removing my hoody, I subtly took a sniff and didn't find anything offensive or unusual with the scent. Handing the item of clothing to the Mahout and said good-bye to him. I stayed on the deck until I spotted the Kabri join Pragtig below, he allowed the elephant to happily huff my hoody and take it in her trunk. Kabri turned to looked up to where George and I were standing and waved at us. Returning the gesture, I watched him lead her away before George escorted me back inside to ponder over what had just happened.


Translations:

Tembo nzuri - *Beautiful elephant*

Huko, wewe ni vizuri sasa - *There, you're well now.*

## Chapter 8

My stomach growled, reminding me that I had yet to eat but I thought I'd already made enough of a disruption for one day and would come back later.

I didn't get very far, because I was called from the kitchen and after very little argument and apologising on my part, Miss Anna was eating a huge continental breakfast twenty minutes before opening.

I had barely finished when people started flowing through the door, completely oblivious to what had transpired earlier.

Carley called out. "There you are."

I waved her over.

"What are you doing up so early? Wet the bed?" She asked.

I shrugged, feigning a casual air. "I could ask you why you're not sleeping the day away, you know I always get up at the crack," I said, not answering her question and drinking the last of my juice.

"Someone tells me you spent time with that Lloyd fella this morning, care to share?"

"Someone? Who? Martha?" I asked as the waitress took Carley's order.

Carley raised an eyebrow, pressing me to elaborate.

I sighed, holding my hands up before she got too serious with her interrogation. "Alright. He glared at me, asked me what I was doing here, glared at me some more and he left the building in a hurry."

"You were gone for a lot longer than that A," Carley said in a sing-song voice.

I hated it when she did that, it was like she was comparing my account of events with what she saw happen on CCTV or something.

"I woke up early and joined the staff for a bit, they eat at what you consider an unreasonable hour."

"Hmmm," she looked at me suspiciously, "You sure that's all? I hear there may or may not have been an incident with a certain four-legged beasty."

I had to hand it to Carley she was like a dog with a bone.

"I'm surprised that the staff would have such loose tongues." I scowled, before I told her about the elephant damaging the deck, which was why the doors had a sign saying the area was closed until further notice and there was a team already out there getting it fixed before the lunch hour.

I told her I was just a bystander. I didn't tell her about the elephant gun or my apparent pachyderm whispering skills.

That seemed to placate her for now and we spent some of the morning scheduling the day's activities.

We chose to take the minibus that shuttled guests to and from the nearest town a couple of times a day to go shopping for those tea towels and spoons and tacky cards that say, 'wish you were here'.

This was exactly how much care I would put into my gifts, but I did get some cool guy things for the boys at home, they always loved stubby coolers and baseball caps, more so than socks and jocks. They were more of a Christmas thing from a mum anyway, weren't they?

Carley got some accessories for tonight to make us 'pretty' and we bought some snacks for our room too. The town itself was much like any rural town anywhere, where the businesses were mainly based on tourism, with eateries, weekend markets, arts and crafts and booking agencies.

After a couple of hours we were walking down the main street back to the bus stop and passed the local Real Estate Office with posters in the window of not only the local houses up for sale, but also information on the upcoming election.

The real estate agent was running for his own party - always a handy association to have.

There was a picture of the man himself, dressed in all his finery oozing aristocracy, or more accurately ego. 'Vote 1 for Cyrus Veldsmaan,' were the words emblazoned under the picture.

The information indicated that he'd been a lifelong resident of the area, wanting to push new development for landholders that had previously been denied due to the National Parks system currently in place. Development meant jobs for the community and a healthy ongoing economy for the region. It then went on to say what a popular member of society he was and that the best interests of the region were his number one priority, blah, blah, blah.

I sighed, shaking my head. It didn't matter where you were in the world, it seemed beautiful prime land was always gobbled up by large developers and transformed into high density housing.

Money talked.

"What's the bet he's a major land holder that could stand to make millions?" I mumbled cynically under my breath.

"Yeah what better way to line your pockets when you can make the rules to suit yourself. Shonky bastards," Carley said flippantly.

I took another look at the man in the picture and shuddered, noticing his eyes. There was something about them I didn't like. Never trust politicians, salesmen or the tax man was something Uncle Kyle always said.

By the time we got back to the resort, it was well and truly time to get ready for the ball. The lobby was awash with hustle and bustle and poor Martha was looking a little frazzled helping out the two girls on the front desk.

She offered a weary smile as we slipped through the throng of mainly woman and a few 'camp' looking men. Most were carrying those silver brief cases used for makeup and they had garment bags slung over shoulders, so I guessed that these people were part of the entourage of many of the patrons getting ready in-house.

Having lived in Perth since graduating from school, Carley had plenty of opportunity to practice her hair and makeup skills at the hair dressing and beauty salon she worked at. So, it was plainly evident that on this day, she was going to work her magic on me.

An hour later my hair was pulled up on the sides in that messy way that looked neat, and in the way that I could never in a million years replicate. The back was left free and because I had been in hot rollers (don't ask me where she got those, this is Carley we're talking about, she probably had the kitchen sink in her luggage somewhere) it cascaded down my back in soft, layered golden waves. She finished my hair with Swarovski crystal combs. The hair didn't look like mine, it looked like catalogue hair, it looked awesome.

My makeup also looked flawless, and Carley spent time convincing me that it took a heck of a load more skill to make makeup not look like makeup. I just rolled my eyes and let her do her thing. I had to say that the end result was as if I wasn't wearing any at all but at the same time accentuated all my features to advantage.

"Okay you. Just relax, we'll get dressed just before we go." She smiled wickedly and I rose an eyebrow at her sceptically, "What? I don't want you wrinkling the dress," she said matter-of-factly.

I guess that was a valid excuse, but I suspected she was up to no good. Again.

Half an hour before the event started, Carley was finally primped and had far heavier makeup then I, stating that she needed all the help she could get. I argued she was beautiful, hot, and a number of other synonyms that described how attractive she was, and I made her promise to quit putting herself down. I suspected that it may have had something to do with her break up, after all, she was supposed to get dressed up to go to her wedding only a few days ago but instead, she was going to this shin dig a newly single woman. That had to mess with your head.

Her hair was a lot shorter than mine and she also twisted it off her neck leaving some of the ends sticking up artfully.

As she was helping me put on my dress, I was horrified to find that although it was definitely the same bridesmaids dress I fitted only a few weeks ago, that it had been somewhat altered.

I crossed my arms and glared at my 'friend'.

And I use the term friend loosely.

"Carley, um why does there happen to be a split up to my armpit when I'm sure that it only had one to my knee before?"

"Oh, stop exaggerating, you girl, have the best legs in the business, I've just accentuated them a little, that's all, that dress was built to have the alteration done, lucky huh?"

She smiled at me triumphantly, figuring that I wouldn't back out now.

She figured right.

"Lucky she says," I mumbled shaking my head at her.

"Well in any case it's too late to do anything about it now isn't it?" She said as she turned her back on me, "Zip me up?"

"Convenient Carls," I said between clenched teeth.

"I'm not sure I know what you mean."

She looked innocently over her shoulder and winked.

She winked, kill me now.

"Shoes," she pointed a manicured finger at the death traps at the foot of the bed, five- inch peep toe heels in silver to match the clutch and the silver trinkets she picked up today.

"Holy crap," I said as I straightened up. "A girl could get a nose-bleed from up here, you know?" I said as I teetered at my now six-foot, two-inch height."

"Yeah even he'd get turned on by you, I am that good," she said patting her inner stylist on the back.

"He?" I asked.

But. She ignored me.

"Oh just one more thing," she said holding her finger up as she rushed to one of her bags and rummaged around.

I cringed when she held up a small foil packet.

She rolled her eyes at me "Oh come on A, you don't have to use it, but safety first," she said as she reefed my clutch purse from me and had the decency to at least stuff the condom in the little hidden, zippered pocket.

"Agh," I growled, snatching the little bag back from her and turned to open the door.

I heard Carley giggle as she followed me out.

"Don't worry, you'll be fine, lighten up will ya?"

I levelled her with another glare.

"Trust me." She gave me a toothy grin.

"Like I did with the dress?"

"You look fantastic."

"I look like my body is trying to bust out of the dress and my leg is leading the escape," I argued, trying carefully to negotiate the flight of stairs without coming to grief.

Carley laughed. "C'mon, you wear less at work, maybe you could let someone else help your body escape from that dress, I tell you if I weren't straight..." She teased looking me up and down suggestively.

"Shut it," I said from between clenched teeth.

Carley grinned from ear to ear and I was just relieved we'd made it to the lobby without incident.

Martha spotted us in the small crowd meandering over to the grand staircase to the Restaurant.

"Oh my, don't you two look stunning," she said, appraising us with admiration.

Martha was tastefully dressed in a floor length dark green number with long sleeves and a plunging neckline that showed her ample cleavage. Her hair was normally constrained in that severe bun, this time she had softened the look with a looser chignon, she looked lovely.

"Thanks, you look great too Martha," I said, returning the compliment.

I could tell that Carley was starting to get caught up in the building excitement by the way she started to fidget. We scanned the lobby, likely for different reasons and I probably looked as freaked out as I felt.

"Shall we?" Martha asked with a sweep of her hand.

I nodded and took a deep breath. Carley led the way and I concentrated on just putting one foot in front of the other.

"Here, let me." Martha said kindly and linked an arm around mine.

"Thanks," I said, thankful for the lifeline, "these stilts take a bit of getting used to, I'm a steel caps kind of girl."

"Well, I can see why Carley has you wearing these, steel caps simply won't do under your gown dear."

"I guess not," I said, reluctantly agreeing. "I'd probably step on the hem, fall arse over tit and the dress would end up over my head with my backside hanging out! No-one needs to see that." I said, before we both giggled at the thought.

"That's better dear, you were looking decidedly green a minute ago." She patted my hand and steadied me as we ascended the stairs.

"I've never been to anything as fancy as this, I'm not sure what to do," I admitted.

"Just have some fun Anna, you're on holiday, the dinner might be a little stuffy but after that, the party will get started with the auction, and you young'ns can cut loose, word has it this place rocks."

Coming from a woman more than twice my age I could barely contain an outburst and simply shook my head.

"You're allowed to laugh Anna, give yourself permission to have some fun." She said before nudging me towards Carley.

What was with everyone? Was I that much of a stick in the mud?

Carley and I approached the entrance and we settled behind a very tall man. He was in his late forties if I had to guess, with a full head of salt and pepper hair, a little more grey at his temples and he looked immaculate in his suit.

He was accompanied by a young woman with a regal posture, her dark hair beautifully swept into a sophisticated updo. Her gown was gold and so was her jewellery.

She looks like a goddess, I thought to myself.

"She looks like the Gold Logie," Carley hissed under her breath, causing us both to giggle.

Shushing Carley quietly the Logie turned to glare at us. I wondered if I'd actually thought out loud.

Then the large man turned too, and I tried to suppress a gasp, averting my gaze at the sight of his peculiarly coloured eyes.

He appraised us for a moment before sneering and dismissed us by shifting his gaze to Martha.

"Ah Ms. Jarvis," he said with a heavy South African accent, "lovely to see you again."

He smirked mirthlessly rather than smiled. His manner unnerved me in the same way his smirking face on the poster I saw earlier had. It was the Real Estate guy, Cyrus Veldsmaan.

"Darling, doesn't Ms Jarvis look a vision tonight?"

He touched the young woman's elbow before she also gracefully addressed Martha.

"Oh yes Papa, nice to see you again Ms Jarvis, I'm sure you're hoping for a successful night."

She smiled, but I noted false friendliness to her demeanour.

"Yes Gloria," Martha said. Her smile didn't reach her eyes either and her jaw was also a little stiff. "And thank you Cyrus, you look very... handsome, Gloria, lovely as always." Martha said with a nod.

Oh boy, tension much!

I felt decidedly uncomfortable but had no room in which to duck away and people were filing up the stairs behind us creating a bit of a bottleneck.

This Cyrus guy bowed formally to take his compliment.

"Thank you Martha."

His gaze shifted back to Carley and then finally came to rest on me, his stare was penetrating, one eye blue and one eye brown, I almost reeled, but managed to suppress it by blinking a couple of times and taking a small step back under his scrutiny.

"And who are these two beautiful creatures?" He flashed his perfect smile.

"The girls are guests Cyrus, this is Carley and Anna from Australia," she pointed us out with an open palm, "girls, Cyrus owns the game park, Hoogveld located to the South of us," Martha added with a tense smile.

"Pleasure to meet you." He held out his hand. I extended mine which I expected him to shake. Instead he kissed the back of it, his gaze lingering a little longer then was appropriate. He repeated a noticeably shorter interaction with Carley before introducing his date. "Ladies, this is my daughter, Gloria."

After expressing our nice to meet you's, Gloria merely nodded as if looking down her aristocratic nose, even though she was shorter than us both.

"Papa, it's our turn and I want to find Lloyd," Gloria said with a frown while walking to the head of the queue.

"Yes indeed, we seem to be holding up the line, please excuse us," he said with another slight bow before joining his daughter.

Carley scrunched up her nose and teased, "Papa, I want an Oompa Loopa..."

"Shhhh." I interrupted Carley's mocking whisper and with a nudge from my elbow, I glanced at Martha who was now also frowning in the enigmatic pair's wake.

Our names were checked off the list and we were asked to choose from the menu before being given our table numbers. The restaurant had been transformed into a huge ballroom. It shared a wall with the bar to the rear, which I hadn't realised was removable, effectively doubling the space.

Tables were scattered in an organised fashion that maximised capacity. There was a stage with an elegant string quartet playing, their melodic sound, deep and rich complimented the event perfectly. To the right of them was the DJ booth set up to pump out tunes later in the evening and between them was a podium with a microphone.

"I need a drink," Martha said, still looking tense.

"So, does Anna, she needs to relax, I swear she was just about going to leave earlier," Carley added. "Although that Cyrus guy did seem a bit creepy."

Martha screwed up her face and looked as though she was about to say something before thinking twice. "Give me strength," she managed to say tightly from between clenched teeth, before her face softened, "if you'll excuse me, my lovelies," she said pleasantly before leaving us to weave her way through the patrons and towards the bar.

"I wonder what that was about?" I asked curiously.

Carley shrugged. "Don't worry about it, it's got nothing to do with us, we're going to have fun tonight A, so let me buy you a drink," she said as she took my hand and dragged me in the direction Martha had gone.

Finely dressed men and woman milled about the room, and the closer we got to the bar, the more crowded it became. Due to the fact that we weren't escorted, I didn't fail to notice the ogling stares that followed us and Carley ensured me that we were unlikely to have to pay for our drinks tonight.

Lord was she going to be in fine form this evening. After some deliberation, she ordered the 'first round to get us started'

A couple of cocktails were presented appealingly on the long timber bar.

I eyed the questionable liquid in the glass. One wouldn't hurt would it?

As I took a tentative sip, and I was loathed to admit that my drink was really delicious. But it was also full of alcohol and it didn't take long for my knees grow warm and my head to go fuzzy.

Carley was chatting enthusiastically with a guy that had just sat next to her, fluttering her eyelashes and enjoying the attention.

I took another, larger swallow.

"Hey, you might want to slow down there," a voice said from behind and a lanky guy with auburn hair and green eyes sat beside me in a recently vacated seat.

"Yeah I probably should," I said, licking my lips and tasting the sweetness the drink had left behind. I dabbed the corner of my mouth with the napkin provided.

He lowered his voice as he bent his head closer to mine, "Well, pace yourself or I won't be able to dance with you later."

Oh my, he was flirting!

I felt myself blush, but the alcohol had started to affect my brain and made me bold. "Well I'd have to bid on you in order to do that, are you being auctioned this evening?" I asked.

"Like a prized bull," he said with a grin.

That made me giggle.

"Well okay then, I'm Anna."

I held out my hand.

"Jerry," he said, taking my hand.

"Jerry." I'd heard that name before. Then it came to me, "The Vet?" I asked.

"One and the same." He smiled warmly before someone slapped him on the shoulder and slid onto the space beside him.

Jerry turned around, "Hey man, Gloria found you yet?" He asked.

I followed Jerry's exchange, the men fist bumping and the drunken butterflies fluttering madly at the sight of Lloyd.

Stupid alcohol, I thought, internally kicking myself.

"I'm hiding." Lloyd answered wearily, giving the bartender a nod.

Jerry only hummed in understanding or maybe out of sympathy, before changing the subject. "Have you met the lovely Anna?"

A new round of butterflies attempted to take off and regrettably, there was no way for me to avoid the interaction.

Lloyd casually looked past his friend and his eyes froze on me, briefly taking in as much of me as he could with Jerry in the way. "Yes, I have met the lovely Anna, we've bumped into each other before," he said coolly before a bottle of bear was placed in front of him.

"Psht." I uttered, shaking my head at the memory of our first encounter. We had done more than bump into each other, more like he ran into me like a freight train without even apologising. But apart from that, I stayed quiet because I was always told if I didn't have anything nice to say...

"Anna said she's going to bid on me tonight," Jerry boasted, interrupting my rambling thoughts. "Aren't you Anna?" He asked, reaching over to touch my upper arm.

That was news to me, so I raised my eyebrows at him.

He was unperturbed by my questioning look.

"Well," Lloyd took a pull of his beer, "good luck with that." He tilted his head and lifted his beer in a salute and then eyed me, "Anna, pleasure as always."

And then he was gone.

Jerry shrugged.

"Is he always so pleasant?" I asked, feeling emboldened now that Lloyd was gone.

Jerry shook his head. "He's been antsy lately. Ever since we brought in the latest rhino calf."

"It's nice that he loves animals so much and it would normally score a man some brownie points. It's lucky then, that you're not sooo, you know..." - such a bully - I finished internally as I polished off my drink, "anyway you might just get yourself a bid, Jerry."

"Is that right? Well it's good to know I have the advantage over most of the other men here." He gestured in a wide sweep with his hand.

"Oh, how so?" I asked.

He leaned closer and dropped his voice, "Because I'm the lucky guy who's to be bid on by the most beautiful woman in the room."

"Ha!" I burst out loudly at the absurdity. Clamping my hand over my mouth, I looked around the room self-consciously and thankfully I hadn't made a scene.

Jerry was a very pleasant man to be around. If I wasn't careful, I could really get to like this guy.

I cleared my throat and sobered at the thought. "How's the calf?" I asked.

Jerry took my lead and straightened up. A serious expression schooled his features and he went back to Vet mode.

"The calf's still vulnerable to infection, so until her wound closes, it'll be touch and go, but for now she's comfortable and drinking well, I'll need to check on her during the presentation and after that I can let my hair down a bit."

"Presentation?" I asked.

"Mmm," he nodded while he swallowed some of his drink, "Tugs at the heartstrings of the spenders, you know, pictures of what goes on out there, what Lloyd and the Anti-Poaching Foundation he works with have been fighting so hard for."

"Oh, okay I'd like to see that," I said with genuine interest.

Jerry pressed his lips into a line to say something, but we were interrupted by the MC."Ladies and Gentlemen, please take your seats."

"One for the road?" Jerry asked.

I thought for a moment and looked over to where Carley had been, but there was no sign of her, not that I needed her permission, not that she wouldn't encourage me.

I shrugged.

"Sure," I said, with a nod.

# Chapter 9

I checked my table number and Jerry escorted my drink and I through the mêlée of bodies also making their way to their tables. He guided me by my elbow as I tottered towards my seat and being chivalrous and all, he pulled my chair out before assisting me to take a seat.

"You're good Jerry, you love animals and you're a gentleman." I smiled up at him.

He bent to talk in my ear, his warm breath fanning over my cheek. "Just ensuring my bid, Anna," he said, speaking in a low voice.

Damn my constant blush.

Taking a quick sip of my drink, I tried not to spill it when he surprised me by placing a hand on my shoulder. "I'll see you, later," he said, allowing his thumb to briefly stroke my neck before he departed.

I watched after him while he walked to his table, not at all sure how I felt about his touch. It had been years and it was nice, but it was nothing like Jayme's caress.

The thought of Jayme was sobering.

Jerry ended up sitting next to Lloyd, who I watched say something to Jerry before looking my way.

The butterflies triggered my adrenalin and I cursed myself for being caught staring. Quickly averting my gaze I noticed that I was seated with a table full of strangers until Carley plopped into the seat beside me in a very un-lady-like fashion.

"So, where've you been?" I asked her, thankful that I could shift my thoughts, and feeling only slightly guilty that I might have taken it out on her when I didn't hide my accusatory tone.

"Oh, I've been hanging out with Alan." She smiled a little dreamily and was completely oblivious to my flustered state.

"Okay. Who is this Alan you speak of?" I asked, thankful to be let off the hook.

She shrugged, "Just a gorgeous lawyer that I'd like to know better." She grinned, the dreamy look never leaving her face.

"Ah, is that what they're calling it these days?" I raised my brows at her.

"Pot kettle." Carley shot back, mimicking my questioning regard. "I see you were looking pretty cosy with the Vet," she said pointedly.

I may not have been let off the hook after all.

"Touché. But I actually was just 'hanging out' with him," I explained, while I played with the stem of my cocktail glass.

"Sure, sure." Carley teased, not believing a word.

"Whatever you may think. That is not going to happen." I shook my head emphatically.

Carley sighed just as our entrée came out. "Okay A, but I for one am definitely going to enjoy whatever the night brings, so don't wait up," she said with a wink, before tucking into her creamy seafood bisque.

I shook my head at her. Of course she could do what she wanted, as could I. We, after all were both adults. Time to grow up and put on my big girl knickers and reassess what this trip meant to us. Carley needed to let off this head of steam she'd built up and who was I to tell her how to do that? Just so long as she gave me the same courtesy.

I was so out of my element at this 'single and ready to mingle' thing, that it wasn't funny. It appeared so easy for everybody else to pair up regardless if anything meaningful came out of it. I just couldn't get my head around the whole casual dating/sex thing. It just wasn't in my makeup and what I had with Jayme didn't just happen overnight.

To the contrary, it was a long and complicated journey that ended up cut so short, that we hadn't even gotten the chance to know each other well enough for me to see him as anywhere but perched on top of a pedestal before he left me that second time.

My teeth found their place when I felt the memory emerge from the fog...

*-Standing in my cap and gown waiting for my name to be read out at my graduation was taking forever because our names were being read out alphabetically.*

*I scanned the assembly inside the large indoor sports arena of my school again. My eyes landed on my Aunt and Uncle for the umpteenth time and I wondered who they could have been looking for because they'd been doing the same exact thing.*

*They would be whispering between themselves, stopping the moment I caught their eye and I'd only get a nod from Uncle Kyle or a tight lipped smile from Aunt Rose in response. They were clearly worried about something and quite frankly, it was making me more anxious by the minute.*

*My name was finally called out and my nerves almost got the better of me before I pushed myself to walk up to the head-master on stage and retrieve my certificate before taking my place next to the rest of the graduating class.*

*Once the last name was called out and some formal photos were taken, we were introduced again as a class group, and the caps flew through the air in that cliché celebratory tradition. When I caught sight of Jayme, all the applause and cheering seemed to fade into the background. The world literally fell away as I continued to take in the sight of him clapping and smiling proudly at me from the crowd. I found myself being drawn to him despite all the people milling around me, and like a magnet, I made an uninterrupted beeline towards him.*

*Jayme homed in on me too and we stopped only a short distance from one another. I frowned when I noticed his black eye and his busted lip.*

*"What are you doing here and what happened to your face?" I asked, desperately wanting to touch him.*

*"I'm here for you," he said sheepishly, looking nervously around the crowded stadium.*

*"Why?" I asked incredulously, "why would you trouble yourself just for me?" I was bumped by another student and I glanced around noting a few sets of eyes staring at me. They were probably wandering what the meek and mild Anna Stedman was doing talking to a handsome guy, a grown man no less.*

*He was dressed in black slacks and a pale blue button down with the sleeves rolled up, he even had a pair of shiny dress shoes on, but his marred face distracted me from all that.*

*"What happened to you?' I asked again.*

*He shrugged, pushing his hands into his pockets and dropped his eyes to the floor, "I kind of ran into your Uncle Kyle's fist."*

*"What?" I said in alarm. "Let me see," I reached up to hold his face and the moment I touched him, a jolt of energy seared up my arms.*

*His eyes flicked up to meet mine.*

*"Why did he hit you?" I asked horrified, taking a moment to scan the room for the older man. "Why would he do something like that?" Tears brimmed and threatened but I held them back with the anger that was bubbling under the surface.*

*"I came here for you," he said again, "for you, Anna." He took my wrists and removed the gentle hold of his face. Dropping our arms between us, he took hold of my hands.*

*"I don't understand." I must have looked as confused as I felt, because he smiled at me and shook his head.*

*"I thought I'd do the right thing and ask permission to ask you to be with me after graduation, but there is no right way to ask a guardian of a seventeen year old woman if it'd be okay to be with her, so before I could even finish asking him he'd landed two fists on me."*

*He lost me after the bit where he said he asked Uncle Kyle for permission to be with me. "You want to be... with me?"*

*"Yes." He squeezed my hands.*

*"What about..."*

*"Tanya? I ended it as soon as I got back from my first flight after you left last Easter, I thought I could get you out of my system, but as soon I saw you," he shook his head, "I was a goner, I knew there was nothing that could keep me away from you except the physical distance and my morals." He chuckled grimly and then shrugged. "In the*

Thankfully, the MC interrupted my memories, announcing that he hoped we were all enjoying the food thus far and reminding us to dig deep for the auction items - other than the men - that were about to be brought out onto the stage by the staff.

As the evening wore on and the items were bid on and sold, our whole table engaged in the general small talk that you get after introducing yourselves and breaking the ice. Carley got bored after the main course and excused herself to go and find Alan, only to leave me with a table full of relative strangers.

By the time the dessert course came out, it looked as though it was shaping up to be a long night.

"Hey." A voice near my ear had me startle. I snapped my head around to see Jerry standing behind me. "You planning to buy any of that stuff?" He asked gesturing to the stage.

"No, I'm saving my pennies for a dance." I said, joking with him.

"Is that a promise?" He asked optimistically.

"Maybe you'll have to wait and see." I answered, trying not to commit to anything.

"Well, while we wait, how about we go see to my patient?"

"Really? But I'll miss the presentation."

He held out his hand, "I know," he said with a nod, "but surely seeing a baby rhino trumps seeing a graphic and badly recorded documentary?" He asked hopefully.

"Isn't there some rule about guests loitering around the enclosure?" I narrowed my eyes at him.

"Birdie tells me you've already broken the rules," he said in whisper so no one would hear whilst looking around the room for dramatic effect.

I had to giggle at his silliness. He reminded me of Pete. It was refreshing to meet a guy that was so light-hearted and easy to hang around with. With that thought, I reached for his hand. "Well when you put it that way," I finally agreed.

After excusing myself from the others at my table, Jerry helped with my chair and escorted me to the stairs.

"Hang on a minute," I said gripping onto his arm at the top of the landing. I took my shoes off and held them in my hand along with my clutch.

"Well that's better, you know how hard it is trying to feel all manly when your date is almost as tall as you are?" He asked.

I grabbed the hem of my gown to stop me from tripping on it and Jerry threaded his arm through mine to help me down the steps.

"A date huh? Presumptuous much?" I giggled as we walked down the stairs.

"Maybe," Jerry said with a chuckle before making our way towards the exit. "Are you going to be okay on those feet, or do you want me to carry you to the barn?"

"I'll have you know, I've been walking on these feet in the Australian scrub for years, I'll be good as long as I don't step in any elephant shit, because that would be all kinds of awkward." I said, shooting him a pointed look, before we both broke out in hearty laughter.

"You know you're one very unique young woman," Jerry said.

"That's not the first time I've heard that." I said, watching Jerry swipe the card operated door out to the enclosure.

I was pleased that the conversation was easy, I didn't feel completely out of my comfort zone and it was nothing at all like attempting to make conversation with his friend Lloyd, I was just a mess when he was around. I guess the fact that the men were polar opposites in the personality department had something to do with it.

Jerry led me to the Vet area and removed his jacket, he took a lab coat off a hook and handed it to me, before hanging his dinner jacket in its place and retrieving another lab coat for himself.

Then he passed over some crocs of all things.

"Not exactly a fashion statement but these come in handy around the place and are easy to disinfect," he explained placing them in front of my feet.

He unlocked a secure cabinet before he collected some honey, a paraffin gauze box, some padding, gauze bandage and Elastoplast, asking me to hold onto some of it while he scrubbed up.

After following Jerry to the barn, he roused the keeper, who was dozing in the stable next to the heavily bandaged baby rhino. Jerry quietly asked, "Hey Nate, how's the little one?"

"She's good boss, drank all her milk, sleeping, making a mess." He said with a grin.

"Very good, let's have a look at that wound…"

Once Jerry was happy that the wound was looking good, he cleaned it up and re-dressed it. The bullet had lodged itself in the calf's skull between its ears and eye high up on the right temple.

As he worked, he chatted softly. "Poachers use AK47's from a distance because essentially, they're chicken shit and this little one was lucky to have been hit only once, normally they just keep firing until the animal drops or runs off and they track it until they find it from the blood loss."

I was suitably appalled, and it showed.

"It's hard to hear I know, but I can tell you it's harder to see first-hand," he said gathering the soiled dressings and stepping into the breeze way "If this one makes it through, she'll be able to grow up safely and join the breeding herd."

I was deep in thought. We both walked back towards the vet room and I asked. "Is this what the future will be for African wildlife?"

"Who knows," Jerry shrugged, "let's hope not. That's why there are people like Lloyd and the anti-poaching groups out there doing their bit."

Jerry opened the door to the vet area before throwing the dressings in the appropriate waste bin and then headed to the trough to wash his hands.

"What's his deal anyway? He seems to have a permanent chip on his shoulder." It was out of my mouth before I had time to stop it and I promptly clamped my hand over it before apologising profusely.

Jerry feigned a lopsided smile. "It's okay. Lloyd… is complicated," he said seriously, whilst he dried his hands with a paper towel and stood back to give me room to wash off.

"That's something that's not hard to work out, even for me, I mean is he always so…" I left the question open ended.

I pushed the mixer off and took a paper towel to dry mine.

"Anna. You know it's not cool to talk about another guy in the presence of your date?" He came up to me and took the damp paper from me to throw into the bin with his.

I turned red, "Sorry," I said shyly, I wasn't practiced in date protocol, but could certainly see his point, even though I wasn't his date, so I gave him the stink eye. "But I'm not your date."

He grinned wistfully. "That's a great shame."

Jerry was no longer joking. We stayed silent and he helped to remove my lab coat, before he changed out of his and into his dinner jacket.

"Let's get back, I still want to dance with you," he said nodding towards the door.

"I'm not sure I could afford you," I said with a smirk, before gathering the rest of my things.

"You flatter me Anna," he said as he turned off the lights before we stepped outside and he locked the door behind him.

"Not at all, I'm sure a handsome Vet like yourself would be beating the women off with a stick," I said, making our way back up the path to the resort.

"Maybe, but none of them unique like you," he said on approach to the entrance to the main building.

"There's that word again," I said in a sing song voice. "I'm not really sure I should take that as a compliment anymore, it feels like you're saying I have a nice personality or something."

"Well you do." He stopped at the door and turned to face me, "and you're stunning," he said seriously.

I blushed again and was about to open my mouth to say something before he continued. "And you're smart. The perfect package," he said with me shifting uncomfortably. He seemed to read me and his body language also softened, effectively backing off the intensity. "And I've said way too much, but someday Anna, you'll make some lucky man..."

The door beeped and abruptly opened, hitting Jerry in the back with enough force to make him lose his balance and send him hurtling into me. The action caused us both to react by grabbing for each other on instinct in an attempt to stop us crashing to the floor.

"Well, well, well," a familiar and agitated voice cut through the air. Jerry and I scrambled apart like we'd been caught red handed in some sort of secret tryst.

Lloyd continued his tirade. "Nice to see you're getting something out of the night, Jerry. But really, couldn't you at least get her to pay for the privilege for the dance first? You know we need the money," he accused with a snarl.

I swear he was spitting venom. "And you Anna," he emphasised, pointing at me, "are starting to wear out the welcome mat here, how is it that you keep managing to wind up in our restricted areas? No, scrub that," he dismissed, "I think I already know," he seethed, glaring at Jerry in disdain.

"Now, hang on a minute Lloyd, that was uncalled for, you can't talk to Anna that way, she's done nothing wrong, I invited her down here..."

"Of course you did, that much is obvious." He eyed me with the same disgust. "Women like you, you're all the same..."

"Women like me?" I asked in disbelief, my voice raising an octave.

"Whatever," he said turning on his heel, "Jerry, I expect you up there in five, or I'll look for another Vet," he said with his back to us before yanking the door open and striding through.

"What the hell was that? Does he ever get off his high horse?"

"Uh, no... yes," Jerry ran a hand through his hair in frustration "It's... shit, look. It's c..."

"Complicated. Yeah, so I see, but I'm a guest here, does he treat all his guests like that?"

"No!"

"So, it's just me then?"

He grasped the tops of my arms "No, it's not you, look I'm sorry about that, I have no idea what's gotten into him." Jerry shook his head, "well no, that's a lie ..., look I can't tell you, but you have to believe me that Lloyd is a good guy with an enormous amount of pressure to deal with. You have no idea..." he said, pausing before he grabbed the back of his neck in frustration. "Shit, I've already said too much, we need to get back," he reached for the door and held it open for me, "bid on me, buy me, I'll make up the difference."

"What? That's ridiculous, why?" I asked, rushing into the building with him, still on my bare feet.

"Because Lloyd's right about one thing, apart from you, all those women up there are the same, and I'd like to survive this evening intact if you get my drift," he raised a brow. Taking my hand in his haste, he almost dragged me through the lobby and up the stairs.

"Okay then, what makes you think you'll stay intact with me?" I asked while he kept me steady on the landing while I put my shoes on.

"Because you've made it clear that this isn't a date," he said smiling sadly, taking my hand again, before we continued inside.

Escorting me back to my table, he gave my hand one last squeeze before letting go and quickly headed to the stage, where about a dozen other handsome guys stood ready to be bid upon like studs at the sales.

# Chapter 10

Introductions were made with the MC whipping up the crowd, the men receiving applause, whistles and cheering - mostly from the members of what were supposed to be the fairer sex, who were standing on the dance floor and close to the stage for the best vantage.

The women were like rabid dogs, the way they were acting.

I thought it was disgusting.

Taking a deep breath, I pulled my auction number from my clutch and left the table to weave my way into the mass of women.

Scanning the dozen men up on the podium, I noticed that it wasn't just Jerry, who was watching me intently. Lloyd too was glaring at me with repugnance, a look I was starting to get used to, but it left me feeling no less uncomfortable.

I felt a tap on my shoulder and Carley sidled in next to me, giggling like a school-girl and barely making eye contact with me before making goo-goo eyes to whom I assumed was Alan. She was just the familiarity I needed to give me the confidence among the throng of gaggling girls that were vying for prime position.

"Hey," I said to her, and all the while Carley's eyes never left those of the dark haired man on the stage. "So, that's Alan huh?" I asked, giving her a light dig in the ribs.

Her grin got bigger if that were possible and she nodded, "Oh A, he's just..."

"You do realise that we'll only be here for a few more days, don't you?"

Her smile dropped from her face, "Yeah," she said wistfully.

While we watched the auction run its way through the candidates, Carley gave me a quick run-down of her Alan. He was twenty-eight, and the Junior partner in his dad's law firm who represented the Resort, he was good looking with an olive complexion, dark wavy hair and gorgeous aqua marine eyes.

He was going to be pretty popular tonight.

"You're bidding on him then?"

"Well Duh," Carley looked at me like I was an imbecile for even asking, "and I might be staying with him later."

"What?" I asked aghast.

"Well, let's just say that the guy he's supposed to be rooming with, might not be bunking down in the same place tonight," she said with a salacious look on her face.

"Does his buddy know he's got nowhere to sleep?" I asked.

"Na, he'll be fine coz he'll be spending the night with that girl over there," she said, pointing out a short, petite woman who looked as excited as Carley did.

I shook my head, pulling a face and groaning in distaste. "This place is a cesspool," I mumbled under my breath while the excitement in the room increased.

"What?" Carley leaned in closer, not able to hear me due to the noise.

"I said, I think you people need to cool off in the pool."

"Oooh, what a great idea!" She said, bouncing on her toes.

I just shook my head again, noting to make sure the pool was properly chlorinated if I got to use it again.

As the auction continued, I was staggered to find how high the bids went and when Alan came up, I looked at Carley, "Carley, are you sure about this?" I asked, not at all certain if this was going to end up being one of her better ideas on this trip.

"Hell yeah! Who knew that money Blair surrendered would come in so handy?" She said with a cheeky wink.

All bidding started at the reserve of seven thousand rand, which to my calculations was just under a grand in Aussie dollars.

Alan's price had quickly escalated to twelve thousand, six hundred rand and I had to calm Carley down to stop the glaring coming from another girl who was bidding on him from the front row. She also happened to be part of a group of women that included our golden Logie, Gloria.

My excitable friend jumped up and down feverishly when she won the bidding war for the handsome Lawyer at thirteen thousand, one hundred rand.

The group of women continued giving us dirty looks until a few more men were sold.

Finally, Jerry's number came up and bidding started at seven thousand rand, quickly escalating to fourteen thousand rand until a few of the girls pulled out and it was between me and one of Gloria's little hangers on.

Carley nudged me when the bidding got to twenty thousand rand. "What are you doing Stedman?"

"Jerry asked me to bid on his behalf," I shrugged.

"What?" Carley looked surprised.

"And I can see why now," I eyed the girls at the front who were glaring at us again. "Check out those vultures."

"Oh okay, he wants you to keep them off his dick, I get it, he might be a Vet, but he won't want to treat the crustaceans any of those skanky ho-bags might give him."

"Ha! You could be right," I said, raising my hand again after I got the nod from the man himself.

I won the dance at thirty four thousand rand, just under five thousand dollars.

"He'd better be worth it, I'm sure he wouldn't mind you on his dick," Carley said, elbowing me in the ribs.

"You're so gross sometimes." I said screwing my face up but even so, I couldn't help but grin at her verbal expressions. They got cruder the more she drank and was more than able to keep up with the gutter speak from the blokes if I remember correctly.

Lloyd was the last man on the podium and no doubt was favourite to make the top bid, his enigmatic reputation would make him many a woman's target and if the crowd's attention to him was anything to go by, he'd probably start a frenzy.

I left Carley in the thick of it because I needed the bathroom, but I bumped into Martha before I made much headway.

"Hello dear." She said gently, glancing up at the stage.

"Hey Martha," I said, noting she was looking drained. "Big night?"

"Yes, big night," she agreed in a resigned tone, preoccupied by the auction. Turning back to me, she touched my arm. "Come. Let's have a coffee." She suggested.

"I'd love to, thanks, but I was just on my way to powder my nose before the dancing starts, I'll be back though. Promise."

"Of course." Martha said with a distracted nod.

"Everything okay?" I asked, "You look ..." I said not needing to finish my sentence.

She smiled at me sadly. "Oh, I'm sure I will be," she said, looking back to the stage.

I noticed that she was casting a worried and motherly eye over Lloyd, whose bid had already reached fifty thousand rand and was steadily increasing with about half a dozen rich woman vying for him left right and centre. Every bid was countered by non-other than Gloria. I wasn't sure why, but the thought of it repulsed me. The noise increased and the women all sounded like a pack of Hyenas.

"Popular man." I said closer to Martha's ear.

She swallowed hard. "Yes, he appears to be, but he hates it."

"Really? A straight guy that hates female attention?" I asked with raised eyebrows.

"Hmm," she said absently.

After a moment she turned back to me. "I'm sorry dear, I'm just a bit tired, this event takes more out of me every year."

"Well it's a pretty important event, I'm sure that you put everything into it," I said, understanding that these things would take months to prepare.

Martha nodded, swallowing heavily, her eyes were glassy as she kept her gaze on Lloyd. Her concern for him was more than it would have been if he were merely a co-worker.

"And he's like a son to you, isn't he?" I asked.

Martha blinked furiously and rolled her lips inward, biting back her tears before nodding again.

"Oh Martha, I'm so sorry this is none of my damn business, I didn't mean to pry." I put a hand on her shoulder reassuringly.

"Sold! For seventy five thousand rand, to the lovely Gloria Veldsmaan!" The MC called through the room.

Martha's face fell.

She cleared her throat, squared her shoulders and expertly schooled her features and when I followed her gaze, I found that Lloyd was looking right in our direction. His smile was tense, and I could imagine that he was clenching his jaw by the underlying hardness to his features.

He was not a happy man.

Not that I'd ever seen him any different.

I finally excused myself and turned to leave the grand ballroom.

While in the cubicle of the rest room I heard a group of women come in, their giggling echoing in the space like kookaburras.

"They should know by now that daddy would pay anything to make me happy, Erica didn't stand a chance."

Gloria, I thought, as my heart sank.

"And did you see Martha? I thought the old biddy was about to have a stroke," one of the women taunted.

"Yes, it's time for her to retire, and cut Lloydy's apron strings," Gloria said, sounding positively evil, "I'll get to control him soon."

They all giggled again hysterically.

I couldn't take any more, so I flushed and strode out into the wash room. The chatter and giggling stopped "Oh look it's Annie."

"Anna," I corrected them, washing my hands.

They responded with a careless shrug.

"You got yourself the Vet?" One of the girls asked.

I nodded, grabbing a paper towel. "Yep and I'm expected to dance with him, so..." I said, gesturing to the door before throwing the wad.

"He'll expect you to do more than just dance," Gloria said with a snicker, as I took a step towards the exit. "You know that, right?"

I stopped in my tracks, "Right," I said. "Because I paid for the privilege," I added, feeling more annoyed with every word that came out of their mean girl mouths.

"Oh no, because it's tradition," one of the girls smiled knowingly.

My eyes grew wider for a second, but those girls probably registered my momentary shock for the wrong reason, because I knew Jerry wouldn't hassle me, he was supporting the cause, to the tune of more than thirty grand thank you very much. What disturbed me though, was that Gloria was expecting to be with Lloyd tonight.

Even more disturbing was that it pissed me off.

"I can't wait to get the dance over with and... anyway, I'm sure that we'll see you on the floor." Gloria said, smiling wickedly like the witch she truly was.

"Sure," I said dryly. I'd had enough so I made my way out of the bathroom, leaving fits of girly giggles in my wake.

I shook my head in disbelief while I continued to walk away. What was it with these women? It was like high school all over again.

I scanned the room for Martha.

I didn't see her, but my step faltered as soon as I spotted Lloyd. I noticed him before Jerry, even though they were standing together at the bar.

Scolding myself, I pulled my shoulders back, lifted my chin and walked towards the two men.

"There she is, my saviour," Jerry held out a hand as I approached, I took it without hesitation and smiled awkwardly.

Lloyd's jaw tensed, and I looked away. I didn't want to give him the satisfaction of seeing the animosity that he continued to demonstrate.

"There you are darling," said the haughty voice of the one and only Gloria.

I cringed at the sound and felt Jerry squeeze my hand at the same time. I glanced up at the woman, to see her flounce towards Lloyd and then engulf him like a tidal wave devouring a multi-story building.

She grabbed onto his face and surprised him with a peck on the lips.

"Let's get this dance out of the way and then we'll take it somewhere more private, darling," she said, trying to sound sexy as she drew her talon down his chin, his throat and chest before taking his hand and leading him to the dance floor.

"She's not wasting any time," I said under my breath just as the MC asked for our attention.

"Ladies and gentlemen, please clear the floor and let's have a round of applause for our Gala dance couples!" He announced.

Jerry and I strode onto the dance floor with the others and the music started. We began to move and surprisingly, I didn't feel the awkwardness I had expected. Jerry was a hell of a dancer and he led so well, that it was a minimal effort for me.

Carley was completely absorbed by Alan and looked as happy as a clam and they also managed pretty well, considering Carley's state of inebriation.

By comparison, the sight of Lloyd with Gloria pressed up against him like a limpet made me want to throw up. We weren't at a school formal or a seedy night club (not that I'd been to either one but you hear stuff you know?) Not that I cared...Much.

The first song ended. Jerry allowed me to step away slightly, but continued holding onto me. "Another?" He asked hopefully.

I looked down and took a deep breath. "Okay."

"Gees, Anna, your enthusiasm is under whelming, way to make a guy feel good," he said, his voice light and playful.

"Sorry, dancing's just not my thing," I replied, with a shrug while we moved to the music.

"You dance great," He complimented.

"Ta, but still," I said doubtfully.

Someone tapped Jerry on the shoulder. "Jerry, I think you've taken up enough of Anna's time, may I cut in?" A deep voice asked.

My head snapped up and I almost died of shock as Cyrus Veldsmaan loomed over me.

I couldn't discern Jerry's expression, but he wasn't overjoyed, that's for sure.

"Certainly." He bowed slightly giving way to the huge man. Cyrus had at least four inches on me with heels.

I nervously took his hand and placed the other on his shoulder before we started to move around the dance floor.

"So. Anna, you're here on a holiday?"

"Yes sir," I said uncomfortably.

"Please call me Cyrus, Anna," he said, enunciating my name clearly.

I nodded. "Yes, I leave with my friend in a few days."

"What a shame, that leaves you so little time to see more of our beautiful country," he said in a low voice, "You dance wonderfully."

"T-Thanks," I stuttered, my heart thudded in my chest in alarm, was this guy coming on to me?

"You look so much like someone I used to know. The resemblance is uncanny."

I felt like he was almost looking under my skin, and I could barely stop myself from cringing before he spoke again, "Anna, is that short for something?"

I shook my head, "No."

Why was he so interested?

"I've always just been Anna," I said, which was mostly true.

"A beautiful name for a beautiful gir..."

Someone cleared their throat, "Excuse me Cyrus may I cut in?" My body jolted reflexively.

What was it with the steady stream of unpleasant drama this evening?

Even though there was this animosity between us and drama aside, I couldn't have been more relieved when Lloyd asked to dance with me.

I also didn't fail to notice that Cyrus scowled before quickly recovering with a fake smile.

"Of course, Anna, a pleasure, I hope to see you again before you leave?" He said in a questioning tone, his odd coloured eyes holding my gaze.

"Perhaps." I answered, hoping to the contrary. Everything about him screamed danger and I'd be quite happy if this was the last time that I'd see him.

"Lloyd," Cyrus said with a pointed look and light nod, before he took his leave.

I breathed a sigh of relief until I met Lloyd's narrowed glare. "Was he bothering you?" He asked, taking my hand.

I noted the ripple of energy as we touched.

I was stunned speechless, before I tentatively placed my hand on his broad shoulder. Avoiding his eyes, I tried to focus everywhere else but still ended up noticing everything about him.

He was tall, taller than Jerry but not as tall as the massively built Cyrus. His dark suit was tailored and his bow-tie perfectly tied around his neck. His hair was longer than I expected now that it was free of his cap, and it was slightly wavy and looked so soft swept sightly to the side inconspicuously hiding some of the scar on his temple.

"Was. He. Bothering. You?" He said, all but growling in my ear, causing me to scowl. And just like that, there was the manner I'd become so accustomed to.

I was here on a holiday, I was supposed to be enjoying myself, but everywhere I turned, there he was sucking the joy right out of whatever I happened to be doing at the time. It didn't matter how enigmatically attractive he was, I wasn't going to roll over. Not this time.

My foul mood was only dampened by my need not to cause a scene, so from between clenched teeth I hissed, "Not as much as you."

His smirk caused my stomach to whirl, he had some inexplicable ability to girlify me and I inwardly cursed him for it.

"You need to stay away from him," he said, with his lips close to my cheek and his breath fluttering over my neck.

Cue the traitorous goose bumps.

Keeping my voice low, I took back some ground. "And you need to quit ordering me around." I said through clenched teeth.

"I'm looking out for your best interests," he said. His voice held the same low volume as mine.

"My best interests? Why would you be so worried about my best interests? You've made it perfectly clear that you can't stand the sight of me," I said, calling him out and not missing a step of our dance.

"Trust me when I say, it is best that way."

"What does that even mean?"

"It means... it means that you need to lay low until you leave. You're too much of a ... distraction," he mumbled, searching for words that to me, made less sense the more he spoke.

"I don't understand."

"You're not meant to."

"You're nuts, you know that?" I stepped away from him, but he grabbed onto my wrist.

"Ms Stedman, why can't you just do as you're told?" He said. His mouth formed a hard line, his nostrils flared and his glare could have burned ships to the waterline.

"Mr. Staadman," I enunciated crisply, looking around the floor before lowering my voice and hissing from between clenched teeth. "You sir, need to let me go or I'll make a show that would really distract everyone."

He let me go, his face contrite and his hand roughly ran through his hair in frustration. I backed away from him and rubbed my wrist.

Screw him.

My heart was still beating out through my chest. I could hear the pulse in my ears and tried to collect myself.

I found myself heading to the bar. Maybe a drink would take the edge off.

Fuming, I ordered something that Uncle Kyle always had. A whiskey and cola.

I downed it quickly. "Gross," I whispered, pulling a face when the sickly drink burned its way down my throat.

I stared at the empty tumbler for a minute and felt the alcohol warm my knees.

One glass was replaced with another. "There you go ma'am." The barman had placed a cocktail in front of me.

"Oh, thanks but I didn't order that."

"Compliments of Mr Veldsmaan ma'am." He nodded over my shoulder and I followed his gaze to the intimidating giant of a man who lifted his drink and nodded politely at me before continuing the conversation he was having with some other guy.

"What is it?" I asked, lifting the glass.

"Devil's Handshake." The barman answered.

Like someone walking over my grave, I felt an unpleasant shiver run through my body. Nothing at all like the one that Lloyd caused, "Pardon?"

"Tequila, pineapple, ginger, lime juice and sugar syrup, not that you need sweetening up ma'am," the bartender said with a wink.

I blushed, feeling the continued effects from my previous drink. "So, I'm not making a deal with the devil then?"

"No madam, the drink itself is perfectly harmless, but only in moderation of course." He said, with a smile, before glancing over my shoulder again.

I found that I couldn't stop mimicking his move, catching Cyrus' eye and feeling a spike of apprehension. I lifted my glass at him not knowing how else to react and he smiled back almost triumphantly. There was certainly something about these South African men and their arrogance, although Jerry was the exception to the rule and seemed just as down to earth as any Aussie bloke.

Eying my pretty yellow drink, thinking back to what Carley said earlier, I chuckled internally. She was right, getting a drink around here was easy.

I took a deep breath. "What the hell?" I shrugged carelessly to myself, before lifting the glass to my lips to take a sip. "Oh wow."

It wasn't long before Jerry found me and asked to dance again, the lighting had dimmed now that the formalities were over, and it was obvious the party was about to get started. The heavy beat of the doof, doof music was vibrating through the room and the place took on the atmosphere of what I imagined to be a nightclub. After finishing the drink, I was definitely buzzed and had no hesitation in joining him, so long as he was steadying me, and I was able to at least appear a little coordinated.

I did my best to shimmy to the music like the others, but I was pretty sure I sucked. Finding Carley in the crowd, gyrating on... Phil, Peter, no, Alan! That's right. She sure was letting down her hair and having a whale of a time.

I had the feeling I was being watched and sure enough, I caught Lloyd casually leaning back against the bar with his eyes fixed on me.

Shaken, not Stirred I thought of the cliché James Bond analogy. He caught my eye making me realise that my stolen glance had become a stare.

He threw back the rest of his drink and slammed his tumbler back on the bar only to stalk off in his usual lithe manner.

"Pardon?" Jerry asked, noticing my distraction, bringing my attention back to the moment.

I realised I had stopped dancing and I may have spoken out loud. Shaking my head at my gaff, I replied, "Nothing."

After a few more fast beat songs, the music changed and a slow tune started.

"I think I might sit this one out. I need a drink of water." I said, which was only partially true. It was more that I didn't want to get too close and personal in a slow dance.

Jerry nodded in agreement and offered to get some water for us once he'd escorted me back to my table.

While I was waiting, I had nothing better to do than scan the room. Casting an eye over the couples who were slow dancing on the dance floor, I couldn't help but notice the one pair in particular, that I really shouldn't be snooping on.

Gloria had thrown her head back and was laughing in an animated fashion. Lloyd smiled at whatever was so funny and my heart skipped a beat at just how beautiful he looked in that moment while they continued to sway together on the dance floor.

My heart almost stopped when she latched onto his neck like a vampire and for some reason I felt like I wanted to go over there and pull the freaking teeth out of her head. But I settled for glaring daggers at the back of her skull instead.

"Anna?" Jerry said as he placed a hand on my upper arm and a chilled bottle of water on the table next to me.

"Huh?" I asked, tearing my eyes from the dance floor.

"Where were you?" He asked, sitting down next to me, "you were miles away."

But it was too late, I'd already been distracted again. This time by a lip lock and I felt my stomach churn. It was my own fault of course, like a horror smash unfolding in slow motion, I couldn't look away and I was blatantly staring at what was an intimate moment between them regardless of the very public space we were in.

"Anna." Jerry's earnest voice finally drew my attention.

He glanced over to where I'd been giving all my attention and sighed. "You're just not that into this are you?"

I shook my head. "I'm not feeling too great, I think I should probably go," I said, before pushing away from the table.

"You're probably right," he said, sounding resigned and stood to join me. "Let me escort you to your room."

"No. I'll be OK."

"Anna, humour me please. My mother raised me to be a gentleman. Besides, I don't think my ego could take it if you just upped and left me here." He said insistently.

"Oh of course. Sorry. Thanks." I said, just as the penny dropped.

Jerry led me away by the elbow and I got the feeling of multiple eyes following our departure from the thrumming space.

"This is me," I said a few minutes later as we stopped in front of my hotel room door.

"Thank you so much for looking after my manhood tonight," he said humorously. "I'm not sure I would have survived the claws of any of those big city cougars."

We both chuckled at that. "Oh, I'm sure your manhood wouldn't have minded too much," I said, before I looked through my purse for the swipe card to the door. "You're welcome. Thanks for walking me back. Your mother did a good job raising you." I said, with meaning.

His ears tinged with pink and he smiled sheepishly at the compliment. He looked cute that way and if I weren't so messed up, then maybe this evening would be ending a whole lot differently.

"You're very welcome Anna. Good night," he whispered and carefully leaned in to give me a kiss on the cheek.

"Good night Jerry and thanks, I had a good time...With you." I added.

"As did I," he said and bowed politely.

I gave him a smile before opening the door, happy to leave the night behind me. The lock clicked and I attached the chain before I heard the sound of Jerry's footsteps fade down the hallway.

# Chapter 11

I tossed and turned for hours thinking about stuff.

From the dynamics of how the night unfolded, to my building excitement of the Elephant Back Safari that I would join in the morning.

I looked at the bedside clock radio, it was three in the morning and as promised, Carley was quite obviously not coming back anytime soon, which shouldn't really have been any surprise. I took a deep breath and threw the covers back before getting out of bed and pulling open the heavy drapes, and then the sliding glass doors that led out onto the balcony.

I was greeted with a humid breeze and took another deep lungful of air through my nose, relishing the smell of damp earth. Storm clouds flashed brightly with lightning in the distance and I closed my eyes to concentrate and listen to the night sounds.

After I had filtered out the hum of air conditioners, I heard the sounds I was hoping for.

The animals.

I recognised the distant rhythmical roar of a lion and then much closer the familiar rumble of the elephants, quite possibly the resort's own herd and then within it's tropical grounds, the frogs croaked, the crickets chirped and there were also a number of night sounds that I didn't recognise.

Opening my eyes, I looked down onto the gardens. They were as lovely at night as they were in the daylight. Subtly lit by strategically placed lights, giving the whole area an ambient glow with paths criss-crossing through the large grassed areas. The breeze lifted my hair from my shoulders, it felt refreshing even though it wasn't exactly cool and caused my skin to break out in goose bumps.

My peace was interrupted by the sound of raised voices from below.

"Come on Lloyd, you know Papa will stop at nothing, this way we can help each other, surely you can see that?" A female voice I recognised as Gloria's, found its way to my ears.

I peeked over the railing just to be nosy but couldn't see anyone.

"Ha!" Lloyd scoffed in complete disbelief, "and you expect me to believe that you're offering me this-this what did you call it again? Deal of a lifetime out of the goodness of your heart?" He asked, his usual tone of confidence replaced with uncharacteristic alarm.

"Think about it darling, I have Papa eating out of my hand, he gives me everything I ask for, you know that. This way he gets what he wants, you get what you want, Saanastia can continue," she said, almost condescendingly.

"And I... get what I want."

Gloria's voice dripped with seduction with the final words and I felt a stab of anger in my chest that had no business being there.

"We used to be so good together darling, it could be like that again, it would be the perfect solution," she said, as if it really were that simple from her point of view.

"We will never be good together, please don't delude yourself!" Lloyd said with a hiss before he lowered his voice too far for me to hear.

There was a lengthy silence.

"Well, at least think about it and I don't think I'm the one who's deluded." Gloria pointed out, "honestly darling, how long are you going to live on the hope of a ghost? You only have until April and by then, there will be nothing that you can do. It'll be too late to save your precious Saanastia."

"Well until then Gloria," Lloyd said, with a seething tone. "I'll take my chances."

The sound of a pool gate swinging open and then slamming shut preceded Lloyd before he finally came into view. Cursing, he charged across the lawn alongside the pool, roughly pulling at his tie to loosen it from around his neck and then threw it into the water dramatically.

"Think about it sweetheart, I'll be waiting for you," Gloria called after him in a singsong voice, sounding so pretentious that I could imagine the smirk on her face.

Lloyd cursed some more and slammed the second pool gate, before he headed down a path that disappeared into the darkness behind a line of trees.

There was evidently more than a little trouble in paradise, and I had to cringe at the selfish pleasure I felt with the knowledge that Gloria didn't follow Lloyd to where I assumed he'd be for the rest of the night. Whatever they had going on earlier that evening had obviously come to a shuddering halt.

I had to ask myself why that little titbit evoked that reaction in me. My relief that he and Gloria hadn't ended up together gave me a sick sense of satisfaction.

By the same token, I had to remind myself that any time I spent thinking about that man's business, was a complete waste of my own.

Not that I could help it.

In any case, I'd be out of here in a few days, and leaving these complicated troubles behind.

With nothing more to see, I retreated back to the room and to the comfy bed.

This time it didn't take too long to fall asleep.

But my slumber was filled with dreams.

Dreams of Saanastia, of elephants - a large herd thundering over the red dirt. The dust filling the air then the milling of many large tree trunk-like legs, the swirling cloud clearing and the movements slowing before the herd parted for one lone elephant who wore a chain around its front leg.

*-It came up to me and reached out with its trunk. Outstretching my hand to touch it, the feeling was familiar and warm, rough but soft at the same time. The chain fell from its leg and it bowed its giant head in thanks. Holding it's trunk out, my dream-self stepped onto the strong fleshy appendage like it was a platform, and with a quick flick of the head, the elephant had me sailing up over its shoulders and scrambling to get purchase on any part of the wide tabletop back.-*

I remembered the dream in the morning and was shocked by the feelings that it evoked. Even though the actual content of the dream was pretty unrealistic, the underlying symbolism of it wasn't lost on me. To free the elephant from its chains was profound and even though it was just a dream, it felt like some weight had lifted from me and if I was excited about the Elephant Back Safari before, now I'd had the dream it was almost like my soul needed to experience it as much as my body needed air to breath.

Looking through my itinerary, it stated that I needed to pack for an overnight stay at The Elephant Outpost Reserve. Apparently this place was a luxuriously appointed safari tent camp about forty kilometres north of the resort and we would be meeting at the Resort reception at 08:30 hours, before departure to be checked into the tour and to have our bags packed into the vehicle that would be conducting the drive part of our tour.

Carley was also booked for the tour. I waited for her till 08:15 and she still hadn't shown. With her phone going straight to message bank, I figured she was going to be a no show, so I gathered my things and made my way downstairs, where I was greeted by about thirty guests milling around the lobby.

"There you are Anna!" Martha's cheerful voice carried over the crowd.

"Hey Martha, have you seen Carley?" I looked around in the hope that she might appear, "She uh, didn't stay in our room last night."

"No, I think she might have been otherwise occupied with young Alan Rochester," she said with a knowing smile "It's a shame that she is going to miss out on the ride of a lifetime."

"I have a feeling she might disagree with you there, Martha," I said in jest.

We both giggled at the insinuation.

Martha wished me a great time and the group was led out to the animal enclosure and to the mounting yard where the elephants were all moved to stand alongside a raised platform that we would use to literally slide on behind our Mahouts. We were told all the common-sense safety instructions, which George rattled off and we all laughed when he complained that the problem with common sense was that it wasn't all that common, so he needed to state the obvious.

To be kindest to the elephants, no more than two people in total were allowed on at a time. Sitting on the thick padded mat, we could only take minimal supplies in the specially designed backpacks worn by the Mahouts. That way patrons could easily access water, snacks and simple first aid supplies. Lanyards were used to attach mobile phones and camera gear wasn't allowed unless they were worn with a neck strap.

I felt privileged to be put on the lead elephant, Shahara. Tommy, her mahout said that she was the second in charge of the herd and was the only elephant that Pragtig would allow to direct the group.

"So Pragtig will travel with us then? Without her trainer?" I asked Tommy.

"Yes Miss, she will be at our side the entire trip, she knows the way she does not need Kabri, he is driving the bus with the other passengers. He will be at camp in time to look after Pragtig, have no fear."

He grinned and so did I. I was excited to have some more time with my special girl.

A few of the guests squealed when we moved off and I internally rolled my eyes at them. In single file, we started towards the massive double gates that would lead us out into the game park proper for the first time. The slow rocking motion was comfortable to sit to, but it took a little getting used to the great height at which we rode. Tommy said it wasn't unusual for some guests to get a little motion sick, but our lot seemed okay so far.

Pragtig stuck by our side, just like Tommy said she would, and reached for me with her trunk on regular occasions.

"Tembo silly," I touched her briefly before she took her trunk back.

I could hear murmurings from behind me, but it was way too much effort to constantly try to involve myself. I was far more interested in my surroundings, and the fact that I might get to see some or all of the big five in the next thirty-six hours.

I would be forever grateful to Carley for booking this popular tour. A group of approximately thirty would normally be split in two and then half would travel on a four wheel drive bus to take the longer route to the outpost via the plains land, maybe covering a couple of hundred or so kilometres over varying terrain while the other half would travel by elephant on the more direct route. Both groups would stay at the outpost overnight and swap the next day because let's face it, not everyone would think it endearing to sit atop an elephant for two days.

Unlike me.

Along the way, the grassy plains stretched on for miles. I took photos of buffalo, wildebeest, and a variety of antelope that Tommy repeated the names of a number of times as it took me a while to remember them all, because some of them were quite similar at first glance.

It wasn't the first time that I marvelled at the similarities the landscape had with the Kimberly country that I loved so much, with flat plains, red dirt and tall grasses. The most glaring difference were the ranges set to the east. At home random hilly areas consisted of almost barren, rusty coloured ironstone, sparsely covered with the tufty spinifex grasses and maybe a few spindly trees clinging to the rock faces. Here, the hills were mountainous and much greener. Tommy said that there were even pockets of remnant rainforest in the fertile valleys and along the tributaries that fed the rivers, similar to the one where The Elephant Outpost was located.

We came across a wide river that broke our landscape in two. To one side, the vast plains and grass lands as far as the eye could see and on the other, open range that gradually changed to shrubbery and spiky acacia stands, before giving way to foothills with broader leaved trees and then towering mountain ranges, all within only a dozen or so kilometres.

The elephants ate on the foot, stretching out their trunks ahead of them, before expertly wrapping them around a sheaf of grass and tearing it off while they continued to walk and shoving it into their mouths.

Pragtig checked on me after almost every mouthful, it was so cute, and every time she did it, she became braver until I could finally hold the end of her trunk. It felt like it was just she and I there each time we connected. It was a beautiful experience.

"Unataka mint Pragtig?" I said, mumbling under my breath without thinking, before I turned to Tommy and asked, "Can she have a mint Tommy?"

"I heard you the first time Miss." I could hear the smile in his voice.

"Pardon?" I asked him, feeling confused.

"You know Swahili."

"I'm not sure I know what you're talking about, how can I know Swahili? I've never been here before?"

"Swahili is not the prominent language here Miss, Afrikaans is, and you just asked Pragtig if she would like a mint."

"You know Swahili?"

"I am originally from Nairobi, there they speak Swahili," he said, speaking softly.

I was more confused than ever. "I could swear I asked you if she could have a mint."

Tommy chuckled, "Perhaps you are right and Pragtig may have a mint," he said giving his consent.

"Cool, you want one? Does Shahara?" I asked.

"No thank you, I am sure you should be sharing them with your elephant." Tommy said kindly.

I chuckled at the absurdity of it. "I wish she was my elephant, then I could take her home, but somehow, I don't think she'll fit in my hand luggage."

"She can travel with her own trunk, Miss." Tommy said, adding to the corny hilarity.

We both laughed and I gave the mint to my elephant, who delicately took the treat from between my outstretched fingers and popped it in her mouth, relishing it just like she had the other morning.

Tommy guided Shahara with his legs much like one would with horses. He explained that the mahouts on the sanctuary never use bull hooks as they were believed to do more harm than good. Especially with African elephants, who were more sensitive and temperamental than their Asian cousins.

"We take ten years to teach an orphan baby to be safe to use on a tour, with only our bodies and this rope." He traced his hand over the heavy manila rope, which he said he only used when he needed quick changes in direction. All other movements were gradual, and the elephants seemed to know where their mahouts wanted to go without any physical cues in the first place.

They appeared to have amazing partnerships.

I looked down again at the other elephant walking along with us and asked Tommy. "So what about Pragtig?"

"Ah Pragtig, she is very special." He said, looking over his shoulder with a smile.

She was definitely special. I studied her closely. The set of her eyes and ears, her body language, that amazingly dexterous trunk and her movement while she strode alongside us and then noticed she had an ugly scar around her left front leg.

It almost looked like a severe burn. The skin was tighter and smoother than the textured skin around it and covered the thickened granular tissue from the wound. It was just below her knee, had healed long ago and she wasn't lame on it at all.

My dream came to mind in an instant, in it that elephant had a chain wrapped around it's left front leg.

"Tommy, what happened to Pragtig's leg? Was she chained at one time?"

Tommy groaned and he shook his head, "No Miss, she was found as a baby caught in a snare trap," he said, his voice sounding sad.

"Oh no poor love," I said horrified, but relieved that she has quite obviously been nursed back to health, "but I thought she was an orphan."

"She is Miss, her mother stayed with her when the herd moved on and poachers found her by herself and..."

I swallowed the tightness in my throat. "They killed her, didn't they?'

"Yes, miss she ran from them away from her baby, Mr Staadman was too late to save the mother but found Pragtig and managed to save her.

"Lloyd saved her?"

"No Miss, Lloyd's uncle, he ran Saanastia many years ago."

"Oh, I see," I said, but my mind was still on Pragtig's terrible start in life. "I'll never understand how people can do this sort of thing," I whispered, my voice tight with emotion.

Tommy shrugged. "When a man has nothing and he needs to feed his family, he becomes desperate Miss, the elephant is an opportunist, a threat to what little land he may be able to cultivate, the human too is an opportunist, and at the time his family mean more to him than the elephant."

"But surely there are more humane ways to go about it?"

"There are, but they are also more expensive, and one man may not survive against an angry mother elephant."

I sat silent for a long time trying to see both sides of the story and just couldn't reconcile what my mind saw as complete and unnecessary cruelty. Pragtig was lucky, she was rescued and nursed back to health, her treatment must have taken months judging by the size of her scar.

Those thoughts were never far from my mind, but I wanted to learn more about this spectacular, yet hostile country, so I put them to the back of my mind and started taking beautiful photographs instead.

Before I knew it, the rolling foothills that had been in the distance were much closer, familiar looking trees broke up some of the gradually changing landscape. "Those trees Tommy, they're almost like the Boab trees we have in Australia."

"They are Boabab trees. Did you know that our countries were once joined?" He asked, glancing over his shoulder.

"Oh that's right! I remember learning that at school. It's amazing don't you think that thousands of years and kilometres of separation can breed such familiarity?"

"You seem very comfortable here," he said, waving his hand over the landscape.

"It's beautiful Tommy," I said, taking in the view, "just beautiful."

We came nearer the river and the elephants picked up pace.

"They are thirsty," Tommy murmured.

The grasses gave way to red dust and then darker red clay before the banks of the river became damp and sloped down towards the water. The elephants picked their way carefully taking the easiest route to the water's edge. There were a variety of animals on the banks, including a large herd of zebras. My camera was in overdrive now and I did a silly girly squeal as I watched a few hippos surface in the distance, their little ears flicking off the water, their huge mouths opening as if they were yawning, making grunting sounds at each other. I cranked my zoom as far as I could, but I still couldn't get quite close enough for my liking. Not that I wanted to get too close because Tommy informed me that the hippopotamus had the vilest of tempers and killed more people than any other animal in the country.

With the elephant's thirsts fully quenched, we set off to cross the river. The water came almost to our feet so the height of the slowly moving river would have been impossible to pass any other way, even with the huge four-wheel drive bus the other half of the group were on.

The landscape had finally changed from drier open range to lusher grazing, scrub and spiny acacia trees as we meandered through the slightly undulating scenery. Coming up to a dense stand of acacia trees, Tommy abruptly raised a hand, halting the group and then placed a finger over his lips, asking me to stay quiet.

"Giraffe," he whispered.

I followed the direction of his pointed finger and spotted what we had almost walked into. Without taking my eyes off the small herd, I picked up my camera and started to photograph the elegant animals as they browsed on the trees. Their long legs and necks able to reach the abundant greenery that other species couldn't.

Focusing through the lens, I could see their long, prehensile tongues wrapping around the thorny branches to strip off the leaves with expert precision.

It was amazing how Tommy had spotted them, their patchy coats were great camouflage in the dappled light under the trees. Our elephants took advantage of the break and pulled at the green grass chowing down while they waited.

"I can't believe how close we are Tommy." I whispered.

"That is the beauty of riding by elephant Miss," he said in his heavy dialect.

Pragtig rumbled, as she touched me again.

"Yes Tembo, you're the expert guide sweetheart," I said kissing the tip of her truck before letting her go.

Meanwhile the giraffe had finally spotted us and were on alert although not panicked, and quietly walked off deeper into the bush until they were out of sight.

We pressed on through the scrub land and then followed a grassy gully. The acacia trees started to dwindle and other broader leafed species appeared in their place.

Baboons skittered from the ground and through the trees, I scrunched my nose up at their red behinds, I wasn't fond of these guys, I'd heard all about their cunning and immoral behaviour.

We stopped to take photos of a lazy leopard snoozing in the fork of a tree. He looked completely at ease and somewhat comical, draped with his belly flat to the branch, and legs dangling out on either side of him, he was totally oblivious to the world and our intrusion.

It was late afternoon and the gully narrowed into a well-worn track, Tommy said that we would be at the Outpost shortly. The trees closed in over us and the grasses disappeared because there wasn't quite enough light to grow much under the canopy of thick foliage.

The elephants crunched over the leaf litter and twigs as they negotiated their path.

"We are here," Tommy said proudly as the tall trees abruptly stopped at the edge of a clearing.

"Oh my," I said in wonder at the stunning piece of paradise before me.

Pragtig took advantage of our brief pause to touch me, almost as if she was telling me 'isn't it beautiful this is my country,' and then proceeded to trumpet our arrival before leading the way she obviously knew so well.

Spread before us was a massive, very green and closely cropped grassy clearing in a valley that gave way to wetlands, the tall reeds were scattered across the banks of a slowly moving tributary and in the swampy low laying areas where the grass was tall and thick. The entire clearing was a few hundred metres wide and stretched to the forest boundaries and for what could have been kilometres along the watercourse.

This place almost looked prehistoric if it weren't for the presence of a modern looking tent-like town.

"It's like Jurassic Park Tommy," I said while looking around in awe.

"Almost Miss. Only it is the lions and crocodiles that would want to eat you," he said with a cheeky grin.

"Has that ever happened?' I asked, slightly shocked by his admission even though I probably shouldn't have been.

"No, not here, the lions keep their distance and we remove any crocodiles and take them to one of the Crocodile Farms where they display them."

"Oh." I nodded in understanding and thought of how we did our bit to contain crocodile numbers at home. "Where I come from there's a croc egg harvest at laying time. We sell the eggs to farms to grow out and use for meat and hide."

"That must be a dangerous thing to do?" Tommy asked with great interest.

"It is, we do it by helicopter."

Images flooded my mind of our wet season antics. Finding huge messy crocodile nests and ambushing them from the air on a harness with nothing but a plastic crate, a marker pen, and a flimsy wire cage with canvas skirting to protect us.

Crossing the grassy expanse, the sun had already disappeared from view behind the tall timber and undulating surrounds. Our destination was lit with ambient lighting and the scene was picture postcard perfect. I noticed that quite a few four-wheel drive vehicles, including the tour bus had been parked on a level clay hardpan and behind a heavily constructed bush pole and wire fence that surrounded the entire complex.

"The compound is protected from elephants by the fence," Tommy explained, "this is their favourite grazing and wallowing area and they get excited by their play sometimes, if too many come to the clearing they could stampede and destroy the outpost."

"I can imagine."

My eyes were still on stalks while I looked around. The outpost tents weren't simply tents. No, this was luxury Glamping. The tents were raised on elevated wooden floors and connected via similar walkways. They were artfully lit by LED guide lights and flanked by tropical shrubbery. Tommy guided us to a similar mounting area like the one at the resort and I laughed when I found out I wasn't the only one that was stiff and suffering from sea legs.

"Can I help Tommy?" I asked, lagging behind the others, who were setting off after some friendly staff, who were handing out glasses of sparkling wine.

"No Miss, you relax and enjoy, but you can come with us tomorrow morning and maybe watch Pragtig have a bath with the others before we get ready to head back to Saanastia if you like." He said, offering something I could hardly refuse.

"Really?" I asked, not wanting to step over that welcome mat that Lloyd had so politely pointed out.

"Of course Miss," his teeth showed brightly against the ever-fading light, "she normally will only let Kabri wash her, but I think that since you're here you might like to help. Kabri will be here so I will ask him." He grinned at me.

"Are you sure?" I asked in awe.

Tommy nodded.

"Then I'd love to," I said with a huge smile on my face.

"That is good, I will see you on the morning," he smiled, "now you go with the others and let me tend to Shahara."

I nodded again and thanked him before leaving the mounting area and joining the other guests who were enjoying their bubbly and canapés.

After the official welcome, we were then escorted to our rooms - or more accurately, tents - to freshen up before the outdoor feast scheduled that evening.

Inside, they were fitted out like a hotel room, with a King sized bed, and a sitting area. The furniture looked heavy and rustic, even though it was obvious that the craftsmanship was exquisite. Woven grass mats covered the polished wooden floors, the only things missing were communications and a TV, but who needed those things out here anyway?

There were bathrooms too, fully plumbed and the shower spray was soothing to a body that had been sitting on a moving mountain all day.

Once cleaned up and redressed, I consulted the site map and noted where the outdoor meal area was located and stepped outside to find dinner.

Treading the board walks, it only took a few minutes before I came to a large paved area with an open fire pit in the centre which was surrounded by stone benches. Further away from the fire was a number of comfortable looking sitting areas and long tables full of food.

There were already people sitting or milling about, most of them I had seen around the resort and of course I was a little more familiar with those that had been in my group today. They were mostly couples and groups of friends. I was obviously on my own, which was a little awkward, but a girl needs to eat so joined them and made my way towards the buffet table.

"Ah the elephant woman!" A loud male voice called in a British accent, causing the whole crowd to turn their attention towards me.

I was instantly mortified.

"Uh hi?" I waved tentatively with a nervous smile.

Then, a lady standing next to the man who'd called out asked, "It's Anna isn't it?"

I swallowed thickly and nodded.

"We were just talking about you," she said before sipping from her drink and waving me over. "Come, come join us. Ernie, go get the girl a drink. Anna what do you want sweetheart?" She continued busily flailing her free arm around as if she was directing traffic.

"Oh, just a soft drink thanks." I could feel my face flush and my hands didn't know what to do so I just shoved them in my pockets to keep them still.

"Anyway, we were just saying that we all thought it was really odd how you seem to have made friends with that crazy elephant."

For a moment I felt the anger build that someone would call Pragtig crazy, but I knew better, the lady was just an ignorant tourist. I had met them before and I would meet them again, so I sucked it up and smiled. "It's all in the mints."

"Mints?" The woman asked with a cock of her head.

"Um yeah," I said.

Ernie came back with my drink. I glanced at him, "Ta," I said, thanking him before addressing the woman who's name I still didn't know. "I had a pocket full of mints, Pragtig knew I had them," I explained with a shrug.

"See Ernie, I told you that there'd be an explanation," the lady said smugly, slapping the poor man lightly.

"Well," Ernie said, "it's still amazing considering that animal's history Sally."

"What history?" I asked, shifting my gaze between them.

"Oh, we were talking to that handsome Mr. Veldtmaan at the Gala the other night." Sally continued looking like the cat that caught the canary and Ernie simply looked on as though this was his wife's normal behaviour.

This woman, I figured to be a gossip hound and I'm sure that she grew even more smug when I wasn't the only one paying attention to her and I noticed a number of other guests had stopped to listen. "He told me that it was lucky that the beast was even alive, said it was a killer."

"A killer?" My eyes grew wide at the shocking statement.

"Now Sally," her husband warned.

"Well, he didn't say that in so many words, but apparently a man was killed years ago, trampled to death by a herd of elephants. Mr Veldtmaan said it was that elephant who was standing over the body and that it ran off as soon as he got there."

"Sally, Mr. Veldtmaan said himself, no-one was there to witness the actual event," Ernie corrected her.

"Yes, well, that may be true but if you ask me," Sally said looking around her conspicuously with narrowed eyes, before she leaned closer to me and lowered her voice, "That elephant was guilty," she said with a nod as sure as she could be.

I stood there dumbfounded at her words, before we were mercifully interrupted.

"Ladies and Gentlemen, can I have your attention please?" A tall woman with brown hair and dressed in the same uniform that Saanastia used, called us all to attention. "Welcome to The Outpost Elephant Reserve, we trust that you have enjoyed your first leg of the tour and that you have seen at least a couple of the big five on your travels so far."

There were murmurings throughout the crowd and quite a few nodding heads before everyone's attention turned back to the speaker.

"We have a treat for you all, should you be interested for tomorrow. As we speak, trackers are keeping an eye on a large rhinoceros not far from the Outpost."

There were a few Ooo's and Aar's.

"And since the rhino is so close you will all be given the opportunity to observe some of the process that Saanastia applies to help this endangered species. We need to know numbers so if you would be so kind as to put you name down on the manifest, we can then proceed to process you. Unfortunately, for those of you checking out from Saanastia on Friday, you won't be able to attend as you have to meet your travel obligations and this treat will delay our tour. We will not accept any changes of mind after nine o'clock this evening. Thank you and enjoy the rest of your evening."

There was a small round of applause and jovial appreciation at the amazing opportunity that had befallen our group. It was a once in a lifetime event that I certainly would not be missing out on.

# Chapter 12

There was no way I could avoid waking up, the walls of the tent were thin, and I swear that every freaking animal in the jungle woke up at the same time before the sun rose enough to shine its light into the valley.

The air was damp but cool and rather than laying about, I was dressed, had brushed my teeth and hair before tying it into a ponytail in only a few minutes.

Contacts - check, sunnies – check, camera – check, regulation mints – check. I put my boots on at the door, before I made my way out to investigate if there was some human activity within the camp.

I was pleased that there was movement at the camp in the form of staff going about their morning chores and getting the day started.

Hoping to hunt down some breakfast, the tell-tale clinking of dishes led me to the mess tent, cleverly situated not far from the barbeque area, I popped my head in to see that the tables were already set, and a buffet area was clean and ready to take the large variety of provisions for breakfast.

A couple of people were flitting about the room still getting things ready before a third came from behind a partition, wheeling a trolley full of dishes to the buffet area.

"Can I help you?" She asked, spotting me in the doorway.

"Uh, sorry I'm early, force of habit." I smiled hoping I wasn't putting anyone out.

"No trouble at all ma'am, but breakfast won't be ready till seven thirty."

"Okay no problem, I'll just..."

"Hello Miss Mandy," Tommy's voice surprised me from behind.

I turned, giving the friendly man a beaming smile, feeling my excitement rise with anticipation.

After the usual morning greetings, Tommy asked, "Miss Mandy, our young friend here will be joining us this morning, do you have our things ready?"

"Oh yes Tom, of course just one moment," she said brightly.

I turned to Tommy with a questioning look.

He smiled vibrantly.

"You want to spend some time with your elephant before your adventure do you not?" He asked, lifting his eyebrows knowingly.

Surprised and a little confused, I stammered an awkward response. "Oh, I thought that... I didn't think...how did you?..."

"Miss, you may not have the time to join us bathing the elephants however, we shall have our breakfast with them instead and I will have you back before your tour leaves. I promise you," he said, assuring me that he had this.

"Okay, but why...?"

"Here we go," Mandy's return interrupted my query about my favourable treatment when she came back carrying a large picnic basket and handed it to Tommy. We both thanked her, and I walked with him down the boarded deck.

"So, does Kabri know I'm joining you guys?" I asked, stepping off the board-walk and onto the grass.

"Yes, of course, it was his idea," he answered.

"Oh... um Tommy?" I asked quietly, "Why do I seem to be getting all this special treatment?"

"Because, you care enough to deserve it," he stated.

"But the others, they..."

"Are perfectly lovely tourists Miss Anna," Tommy said, "they care, but perhaps more about themselves when they are on holidays. Now come, we need our breakfast."

"So, this special rhino trip, has it ever happened before?" I asked as we came up to one of the boundary gates.

"No, never," Tommy shook his head, "it is purely by chance that the rhino has walked near to the route that the tour takes, it is on the other side of the river for now and we are very fortunate, but we have been waiting for the helicopter to bring Jerry so we can tranquillise it and take off the horns and give the animal a health check."

Closing the gate behind us, we made our way over the grassy expanse, before the land fell away nearer the water course to reveal the herd at peace in a light coloured slightly hollowed out section of the bank, picking at the soil.

"Are they eating dirt?" I asked.

"Yes Miss Anna, the soil is full of minerals, this is another reason the elephants come to the valley, it is where we believe Pragtig came from."

"Oh?"

"She used to come here all the time, Kabri followed her here at one time..." he cleared his throat, "we think she remembered her mother bringing her here with her herd when she was a baby. It was later that Saanastia built the Outpost as it wasn't too far to take people on safari, it has been the biggest single money earner for Saanastia. People come from all over the world to experience our elephant safaris."

"Pragtig sounds like an amazing elephant," I said in wonder.

Saanastia seemed to put an awful lot of responsibility on that animal and I didn't know how I felt about that.

Well. Maybe I did, but I kept my concerns to myself.

"You are right," Tommy agreed.

In front of us the mahouts were lazing about, reclining in the grass and started cheering when they spotted us with their breakfast.

"They are always hungry." Tommy said with a grin before we picked up our pace.

I found it funny to see the boys scrambling in preparation of a good feed.

Water had already been boiled on the fire and the coffee and tea was made in no time. In our basket, we had eggs, bacon and the tomatoes, mushrooms and onions all chopped up and ready to go. Thrown into in a large fry-pan, everything was cooked in the time it took me to set out the croissants, bread rolls and pastries on a large tray that was cleverly included in the basket. A resealable jug of juice, butter and jam followed, and lastly, the tin plates and cutlery were revealed at the bottom of the basket.

"You guys have done this before." I said, when I glanced around at the efficiency with which the boys had put everything together.

"This is the best time of the day and the best way to enjoy it," a mahout called Benjamin said, spooning some of the cooked food onto a plate before passing it to me "ladies first," he said with a grin, eliciting a chuckle from all the boys.

"Thanks," I said and blushed at his gentle manner. I waited until he'd dished out the food evenly down the line of ten or so guys and we helped ourselves to the ingredients from the tray and sat down to eat.

I looked out over the Outpost as the morning continued to unfurl before me, the elephants were chatting to each other, their rumbling easily heard even from this distance. At the water's edge was an array of water birds wading in the shallows, spearing their own breakfast when it came swimming by. Benjamin was right, this was definitely the best way to start the day.

I felt safe thanks to the experienced men that surrounded me, and the fact that each of them had a rifle permanently attached to their side, I guess anyone at this point could be forgiven for forgetting that we were actually in a clearing deep in the confines of an African jungle.

"Where's Kabri?" I asked, after noting his absence.

"He is going over some last-minute details at the camp," Tommy informed me, "and we also need to start getting ready." He got up and dusted himself off.

Everyone followed suit and it wasn't long before we had packed up and I was handed a couple of left over bread rolls, the boys called for the elephants urging me to call Pragtig. To say it was little intimidating to watch a dozen five-ton elephants lumbering towards you was an understatement. As if by magic each mahout had paired with their elephant, feeding them the treats and Pragtig gently took one roll at a time from my hands before tracing my face with her trunk. I could hear and feel her breathing, scenting me before she joined a chorus of purr-like rumbles of contentment. Her trunk sought my hand and I took it with both of mine and rubbed her fondly.

"Come, we go to camp," Tommy said giving the basket to Shahara to carry for him as he led the way.

Following him with trunk in hand, Pragtig and I meandered towards the water's edge to a gravelled area that looked like a wide boat ramp right next to camp where some of the guests had gathered. They peered over the edge while leaning on the railing from the deck above us and had come to watch the elephants bathing. The boys pulled off their shoes and socks before grabbing a stiff broom and leading their elephant into the shallow water.

The water was fairly clear thanks to the bottom of the water course being lined with gravel eroded from the rocky hills nearby.

A radio cracked from Tommy's belt and he talked in quiet tones in Afrikaans before grinning at me, "It is time for you to say goodbye to your Pragtig."

"Oh," I said sadly, hoping for more time with her, she hadn't stopped holding my hand the entire time since she'd first taken it, she kept squeezing me, rumbling softly and I too didn't want to let go just yet. "She'll be back at Saanastia tomorrow right?"

"Yes Miss." He grinned, pearly white teeth on show.

I gazed up at my elephant, missing her already and the rest of world faded, I had eyes only for her, it was just the two of us there, I shut out the mumbling guests watching from above and whispered, "Well then tembo nitawaona kesho ndiyo?" The elephant rumbled and poked at my pocket. "Tembo silly," I took the mints from my pocket and fed one to the massive grey beast.

"I have to go now," I said, before I hugged the thick trunk, giving Pragtig a quick kiss. "Kuishi Pragtig."

Even though I hadn't known this big girl for very long, leaving her there was awful to my heart. It felt the same as having to leave Blue for any length of time and I had to remind myself that there were equally warming experiences to look forward to later that day.

I was escorted by Sarah, one of the female staff members, who helped me through yet another gate not far from the elephant wash zone.

"Kabri is waiting for us in the barbeque area, with the others," she said, in a friendly tone.

"Thanks, I'll just get my stuff out of my room and meet you there." I said, before hurrying to collect my belongings.

Only a few minutes later, I joined the group. Sarah was checking the names off the manifest and I noted with relief that the unpleasant busy body from the previous evening wasn't among the small group of nine.

We were bundled into a beige Landcruiser personnel carrier. An older lady was given the front seat while the rest of us were relegated to the pair of long padded benches in the back. We headed off in a totally different direction to which we'd arrived with the elephants, exiting the valley at its most northern point.

The group was quiet for quite some time, until a small herd of warthogs crossed our path in fright and disappeared into the undergrowth as quickly as they emerged.

"Ugly little critters ain't they?" A guy with a Texas drawl said loudly.

"A face only a mother could love," I said in agreement.

The group visibly relaxed now that the ice had been broken, and everyone started making small talk. Every now and then, Kabri would point out something interesting that we were missing, slowing the vehicle so that we could take pictures, the group oohing and aahing at the sights as we passed them by.

As a consequence, the time flew and before we knew it, it had already been an hour by the time Kabri had negotiated the four-wheel drive comfortably through the jungle and out onto the brighter and less lush grassy plains.

The car could travel far more quickly out on the open country and we followed a dusty, corrugated track that set a hum vibrating through the vehicle, not unlike the infrequently graded roads did back home. We slowed when we came to an intersection of a wider road near the steep banks of the river Kabri said was where Saanastia ended and the public roadway began.

"I was wondering how we would cross the river," a lady said when we turned onto the dirt road, crossed over a long narrow bridge and headed back onto Saanastia property again.

After a few questions from the guests, we were told that it would be at least an hour before we got near the location of the rhino. We had to keep our distance so as to not disturb the animal any more than necessary and until it was knocked out. Only then, could we approach the operation site to see the de-horning.

On the way we saw wildebeest, kudu and even a pride of lions lazily sleeping the morning away under the shade of one of the few sparse acacia trees. Kabri was nice enough to slow down so that we could take photos and gave us exceptional information on all the species.

He drove carefully through a massive herd of zebras, making sure that none of them became upset. They appeared unfazed by the vehicle manoeuvring through the herd and quietly moved aside to let us through. Kabri straightened in his seat and looked as though he was trying to find something, I followed his gaze to whatever that might have been, and noticed his face change from his searching look to one of relief at his recognition, perhaps of a landmark or something. He slowed right down and picked up the CB while we continued to crawl along. The black and white stripes of the continually milling zebra was almost hypnotic, I could see how they could confuse their attackers with herd numbers like this, it was enough to want to close your eyes and block it out. It was amazing how evolution created these sort of defence mechanisms within animals. After all one wouldn't think that such loud and distinct markings could exactly be called camouflage.

"Mobile four, do you copy Boss?" Kabri spoke clearly into the handset.

After a small delay the radio crackled, "Copy that Mobile four, what's your position?" Hearing Lloyd's voice, my heart involuntarily fluttered, and the heat of my adrenalin spread from my chest out to every limb in waves. I looked around at the others to see if I'd been sprung but everybody seemed completely unaware of my reaction, which I was certain would have been blindingly obvious if my inner response was anything to go by. I was so thankful for my apparent casual outward appearance.

"We have just stopped at bend number four and we are approaching the last coordinate boss."

"Good, park up and I'll let you know when it's down, the ETA for the chopper is five minutes, so hold tight."

"Will do." Kabri had found some hot property and pushed a couple of disgruntled zebras from the shade of a tree back to their herd, their grumpy faces showing their displeasure at being moved off their turf so unceremoniously. They got over it pretty quickly though and were grazing with the others only minutes later.

The other guests were chatting among themselves, they were all paired up and I felt the odd one out, not that it was anything new. That led me to an image of Lloyd of all people, an arrogant, bossy, angry, proud, tall and of course incredibly attractive man.

Scolding myself internally, I closed my eyes tightly and warred with the thoughts in my head. I'd probably see him again in the next hour and that damned flutter flowed at the thought, causing me to sigh loudly with the disappointment I had in myself.

I hadn't looked sideways at anyone in three years. There had been a few nice guys that had approached me, good looking and probably great catches that I could have moved on with, none of them though, had stacked up to my idealised version of Jayme.

So, what was causing my heart to betray my good sense at the simple thought of this man?

He was nothing like Jayme.

Nothing.

"Drink?"

The lady next to me, Gwenn, I think her name was, nudged my knee with a cold bottle of water that she'd been passed from the cooler by one of the others.

"You look a little flushed dear," she said with concern, "you drink that, we all need to keep up our fluids."

The icy cold bottle on my heated skin pulled me out of my reverie.

"Thanks." I smiled as I took the bottle from her.

I looked around self-consciously, the others all had a bottle in their hands, windows were open and Kabri had his door open, his rifle at the ready as always. It was hot in the car full of bodies now that it was getting up to the middle of the day, even though we were parked in the shade and I ran the bottle along the back of my neck before opening it and taking a drink.

Gwenn nodded with approval, fanning herself with a Saanastia brochure she had swiped from its holder between the front seats. I was hot admittedly, but unlike the others I was used to it and it wasn't that kind of heat that had me flushed anyway, not that she needed to know that, it was bad enough that I knew it.

"All units, standby." The CB crackled to life at almost the same time the zebra herd suddenly whirled around to stand face on in the direction of a perceived threat, the red dust was kicked into the air. Their heads held high, some snorting, with their big ears pricked on alert, standing to attention and looking eagerly at something far off into the distance.

Then I heard it, the sound as familiar as my own beating heart. Rotors hitting the thick air in the distance and I couldn't help the smile that came to my mouth at the thud that had been an integral part of my life since I was sixteen.

Excitement bubbled within me and then through the group. Kabri closed his door and started the engine. I cleaned my sunglasses and put them back on, scanning the sky for the helicopter now that I couldn't hear it over the diesel motor of the four-wheel drive. I squinted, looking between the two people sitting directly opposite me who were twisted around in their seat also trying to see what was happening.

The red chopper was flying fairly low, the air blurred into a mirage around it before it slowed to a hover and turned slightly to take a clear shot.

"All units, we have a hit." It wasn't Lloyd's voice this time, but it didn't matter.

It was action stations as Kabri carefully drove off.

My heart rate had spiked with the excitement of the event, and by the look of the rest of the group, I wasn't the only one, everybody it seemed was sitting on the edge of their seat.

The helicopter was attempting to land, a large plume of red dust and loose grass kicked up under the machine, startling the zebra into a gallop, kicking up and filling the air with the same fine red dirt. Once we were completely clear of the herd Kabri sped up, bumping over the rough surface and away from one choking dust cloud and towards another, where the helicopter had finally set down.

Arriving at the site, half a dozen people were already working quickly around a giant grey mound lying on the ground.

We had ourselves a rhino.

I spotted Lloyd's strong frame right away, which was easy to do considering he was the only white guy in the group among the sea of khaki clothing.

I forced my eyes away as we came closer to the chopper, the blades were moving slowly, still winding down and only a slight haze of fine bulldust still hung in the air when we finally stopped a short distance away. I spotted Jerry step out of the helicopter, minus its doors with his medical bag in hand.

Kabri opened the rear barn doors of the Landcruiser to let us out and I'm sure I wasn't the only one who was relieved that I could once again stretch my legs and iron out the kinks after spending all morning on an uncomfortable bench seat.

Jerry waved at me as the group walked towards him and I couldn't help but grin at his happy face.

"Direct hit?" I asked.

"Of course," he nodded proudly, "Good to see you again," he said, giving me the once over, before addressing the crowd in a more serious tone. "We need to move quickly folks, please follow me."

The group did as they were told leaving an older man, who I assumed was the pilot sitting in the chopper drinking some water, and a guard standing outside on the lookout.

Once we got nearer to the gathering, Kabri stopped us from moving any closer. Jerry continued to walk straight to the head of the rhino, who had its eyes covered with a wet towel. He checked for the standard eyelid response and then the pulse and breathing with his stethoscope, he gave the nod and Lloyd strode over with a chainsaw. Some of the guys all of which were armed were assisting, one had a nice camera and was taking photos while another took video of the whole procedure. Yet another man had a laptop resting on the animal's rump and was busy taking notes, while a couple of others stood near, to observe everything. Kabri explained that they were new anti-poaching rangers who were also witnessing their first de-horning. They were from an organisation that worked alongside Saanastia, who actively tracked poachers and apprehended them.

The combined project was so much bigger than I'd imagined, and I was completely in awe of it.

Lloyd, looking ever so masculine, even in his baggy khakis, delicately traced a line with a black marker around the base of each horn. Minutes later he started the chainsaw and deftly sliced through the horns before swapping the machine for a large standard hoof file to neaten up the jagged edges. Jerry followed up with the injectable die and was constantly checking the rhino's eye response and other vitals. The other guys busied themselves wetting the animal down to keep body temperature under control and ghosted a scanner over the animal's neck.

"We're searching for an identification chip, if we find one that means that we have treated this animal in the past." Jerry said, while listening for a beep.

When no beep sounded, Jerry's face lit up. "Great stuff, an unadulterated male rhino," he said before loading an applicator with a microchip, confirming that it was in working order and inserting the very large gauge needle deep into the neck and between the shoulder blades of the huge animal.

A few of the guests cringed at the sight while one man looked a little green around the gills thanks to his needle phobia and had to turn away.

The scanner was used again to see if the chip was still working. It made the familiar beep and the guy with the laptop nodded to confirm their success before he punched in some more information. Jerry injected the animal with vitamins and then we were ushered away so that the boys could finish up before the rhino received a dose of anaesthetic antidote.

With all the gear packed away, everyone headed to their respective vehicles leaving only Lloyd and Jerry to complete the job. The injection was made into a vein in one of the animal's ears before Lloyd took the towel from his eyes and both men high tailed it in our direction.

The beast got up surprisingly fast and whirled around to get its bearings and look for any possible threat, creating dust clouds in the process.

Kabri said that rhinos had poor eyesight and they readily charged, which was why the group was positioned down wind. It made sense of course and there were comments on how everything was so well thought out.

With a loud snort as if to protest his undignified new look, the animal wheeled around some more before taking off in the opposite direction, rather elegantly considering his massive bulk.

Once far enough away, Lloyd strode over carrying the two large rhino horns.

"So, you guys are the first tourists that have ever witnessed a de-horn at Saanastia and you are also likely to be the last."

"Why is that?" One of the female guests asked impulsively.

"Because," he inclined his handsome head, his ever-present cap hiding his scar, "what was your name?" He asked with a crooked grin full of charm.

"Julie."

"Because Julie, the likelihood of being in the right place at the right time is almost as frequent as seeing a pig fly, if you were at the Gala presentation, you might remember hearing that these animals are in grave danger. Last night the death count stood at a hundred and ten rhinos for the last year to poachers in South Africa and its eastern neighbours. But this year it's far worse, new figures are showing approximately thirty a month," Lloyd said bitterly.

His passion on his subject matter was so deep that he looked not far away from forgetting or perhaps not caring that he was in polite company.

We were all left overawed and in awkward silence to mill over the information before Lloyd closed his eyes to collect himself and swallowed thickly before looking at me pointedly.

"So who was at the Gala the other night?" He asked.

My heart leapt out of my chest at his accusatory stare.

A few guests raised their hands, which included my own somewhat reluctant attempt.

"So, in that case let's have one of you inform those that weren't able to attend how much these horns are worth?" He lightly tossed the horns in his hands before raising his brow at me "Anna?"

He knew damned well I wasn't there at the time of the presentation.

"Uh," I nervously looked around me stopping my gaze on Jerry who looked a little miffed at Lloyd but was powerless to help, "Thousands?"

"Thousands." He said flatly, taunting me with a nod.

"Fifty thousand per horn," one of the men interrupted, "give or take."

"Ding, ding, ding, yes, sir you are correct," he said as if the man had just won a sideshow prize. The guests who were newly informed, mumbled their amazement, "good to see that at least some of you were paying attention."

The crowd laughed and I felt humiliated, a deep blush of embarrassment flushed from my chest up to the top of my head. What a bastard, I thought shifting uncomfortably and looking at the ground.

"So, let's try again shall we? Anna can you tell us what the horns are made from?"

He was doing this on purpose, and I had no idea why. Jerry took one of the horns, staring his friend right in the eye. Lloyd glared back at him and then scowled before the friendly mask made its return and I watched him shift his weight when I was handed the horn for inspection. It was heavy and had small vertical lines on it from base to tip, giving me a clue.

I sniffed the freshly sawn-off end and knew straight away and a small smile lifted the corners of my lips. "It looks and stinks a bit like horse's hoof, so my guess is it's keratin?" I looked around the group then at Jerry who winked at me with a smile, confirming that my answer was on the money. I couldn't contain my grin, my eyes moved to Lloyd, who's smug look had fallen from his face.

Pride rose in my chest, giving me a strangely triumphant feeling over Lloyd's previous douche bag behaviour.

He cleared his throat, "Well you're right of course," he mumbled reluctantly.

I was tempted to ask him to repeat himself, but he beat me to it by addressing the group.

"So as Anna has so eloquently informed us, rhino horn is made of keratin. Please pass it around," he nodded at me. "Keratin is the same substance that forms a horse's hoof and is also what our fingernails and hair are made from." He said, while the horn made its way through the group.

"Shit! So you're saying that people are paying fifty grand for nail clippings?" One of the men asked dubiously, "man I'm in the wrong business, my wife's a beautician maybe there's something to it after all."

"Thin ice Bruce," his wife said in a warning tone, smacking him lightly on the chest, "and the thought of saving nail clippings is just disgusting," she added, pulling a face.

With us laughing and Lloyd shaking his head at the irony, he waited till the group quietened down. "It'd certainly be good for the rhino if it were only that simple, but it isn't, which is a shame because there are good folks out there convinced that putting all their faith in nail clippings will ward off serious diseases that could kill them."

"So, I'm guessing that biting my own nails isn't like that magic blue pill then?" One of the other men joked.

Bruce laughed boldly when the horn was passed to him at that moment and he placed it over his crotch. "The way I see it is the only way this will ever be an aphrodisiac is if you strap it on." He thrust his hips forward.

"Bruce!"

His wife slapped his shoulder this time and the crowd laughed again as Bruce held up his hands, thoroughly enjoying the attention and his wife's discomfort.

"Boss!" One of the boys yelled urgently from the helicopter causing the entire group to fall silent and shift their attention. The pilot was slumped in his seat clutching his chest, while another man was reaching in to help him.

"Shit!" Lloyd dropped his things and ran over to the drama, the crowd followed like sheep, leaving Jerry and I to pick up Lloyd's things before making our way over too.

"Stay back and give us some room," Lloyd said as he kneeled on the passenger seat to check on his friend. With their conversation muted from within the cockpit, we couldn't make out what was being said.

Kabri ushered the guests back a few steps nearer to Jerry and I.

"What's wrong with him?" One of the women asked.

"If you wait a few minutes we might find out," another snapped as the tension rose within the group.

I could tell the lady was affronted and was about to say something before Lloyd stepped out of the helicopter, his distress evident. "I think he's having a heart attack! Any of you a doctor?"

He searched the crowd, hoping for the best and I nudged Jerry forward.

At the same time, Lloyd must've dawned on the same idea and called the Vet over, before continuing to call out more orders.

"Kabri! You radio base and tell them what's happened and have Martha stand by. Get the guests out of here, take the scenic route if they want it, the rest of us need to take Fred back to base ASAP."

Lloyd turned his attention back to the pilot and with Jerry, he started to try and get Fred out of his seat.

Kabri sprung into action and together with a couple of the other men, acted on Lloyd's orders.

The guests proved somewhat unwilling to get back to the tour vehicle. Some asked what they could do to help, while others lagged behind and looked on helplessly. One person even had to be reprimanded for trying to take footage of the drama on her phone.

I was no exception and as much as I was expecting to be asked to get a move on, I had a gut feeling that I needed to stay back.

Jerry and Lloyd's voices rose as they started to argue over their options while an idea started to form in my head.

"But that'll take too long Lloyd, Fred could be dead by then!" Jerry said fretfully.

"Well then. What do you propose oh wise one?" Lloyd asked sarcastically, the stress clearly evident in his voice.

"We radio an ambulance and take him to the road, then he's not subjected to as much rough ground and we can meet the ambulance on the way."

"Okay do it. You're right, it's our best option." He took his cap off and ran his hand through his hair in frustration, seeing me out of the corner of his eye. He groaned, "What the hell are you staring at?"

"Lloyd," Jerry warned.

As much as my body flinched at his offensive question, I felt my temper start to heat.

"What?" Lloyd asked with the same tone. Turning to the other man, he repeated, "what Jerry? The girl is always were she shouldn't be, every schmuck is constantly allowing her into restricted areas, she's always in the way, putting herself in danger..."

Right, that was it.

I straightened my shoulders and through clenched teeth I accused, "you're such a jerk!"

He swung easily from the chopper and strode closer, glaring at me furiously. "Kabri, come collect your stray!" He called, his eyes never leaving mine, before narrowing them at me as he closed in on me. "Little girl, you are really wearing my patience thin, this is not the time nor the place, I suggest you go with the others while we try to save this man's life," he said ominously, pointing the way with his outstretched arm.

I was at boiling point and I stood my ground, placing my hands on my hips there was no way I would back down. No way that I could.

"You!" I poked him in the chest hard, "have a better option than to drive that poor man anywhere, mate!" I poked him again. "If you'd rather not hear it then fine! But somehow I don't think you'd like that on your conscience when you find out and it's too late for your buddy there!" I pointed through the open side of the helicopter and continued to hold his gaze even though we were both wearing sunglasses.

There was silence except for the rustle of the breeze through the dry grasses. Lloyd's jaw was working, towering over me in a standoff before he drew in a breath through flared nostrils and pinched the bridge of his nose. "Oh, for the love of god," he mumbled.

Taking a deep breath, he managed to compose himself enough and take a step back, "Please," he held out his hands, "do tell before I forcibly remove your ass and dump it in the 'Cruiser myself."

I blinked a couple of times, amazed that Lloyd had backed down, even if he did threaten to manhandle my 'ass'. I let out the breath I didn't even know I was holding, I don't think I'd ever stood up for myself in that way and it was empowering, so I continued while I still had my blood up. "We can get him to hospital in the chopper..."

Lloyd laughed out a mirthless breath. "Fuck my life!" He mumbled under his breath.

"C'mon, you're going," he said impatiently, moving towards me.

I avoided him by stepping aside. "Wait! Will you let me finish?" I asked him.

"By all means," he said acerbically, throwing up his arms in exasperation.

"I'm a helicopter pilot, so we can medivac your guy out!"

Translations:

Tembo, nitawaona kesho ndiyo - *I'll see you tomorrow*

Kuishi Pragtig - *Behave Pragtig*

# Chapter 13

"You're What!?" Lloyd shouted so loudly, that if the rest of the group weren't able to hear our little altercation leading up to his outburst, they sure as heck could now.

Rubbing his neck and glancing around self-consciously, he toned it down and asked, "you're a helicopter pilot?" Followed by, "You can fly this thing?" While hitching a thumb over his shoulder.

"Oh Please." I said, before throwing some of his own words back at him.

"Tell me, what little girl do you know that could identify the model of that thing as you put it," I said, pointing at the chopper, "as a Bell 206 B3 at a glance? I could give you all her damn stats if you like, but since we apparently don't have the time for that, how about we get going?" I said, pushing past him.

Lloyd grabbed me by the arm as I passed, "You better not be messing with me."

A jolt rushed up my arm that was so fierce it caused me to shrug him off abruptly. Shocking as it was, it didn't deter me in the least with my fight mode still in full swing.

The man was long overdue for an attitude adjustment. "Keep your hands off me!" I said icily from between clenched teeth.

Surprisingly, Lloyd stepped back and held up is hands in surrender.

He must have known he'd crossed the line.

Emboldened, I pointed at him. "You might be the one who knows rhinos mate, but I know choppers," I said, thumbing my chest. "I for one am not going to stand around arguing all day when your man there clearly needs our help!"

I whirled around, hoping to leave him standing at least a little dumbstruck.

I might have achieved that judging by all the other eyes that were still fixed wide on me from a distance and by the silence that I left in my wake.

I didn't look back to check.

My blood cooled the moment I saw the poor pilot, who was finding it hard to breath. Once I made it to his side, I touched his shoulder and asked, "It's Fred isn't it?"

He nodded.

"Do you trust me to get you out of here?"

His brows rose in question.

"I've got a few hundred hours on these birds and you know what they say right? Any dimwit can fly them," I said kindly of the forgiving workhorse that was the Bell Jet Ranger.

He smiled despite the pain he was in and nodded again.

"Good. Anything I need to know about her before I get us into the air?" I asked, just wanting to make sure his chopper didn't have any undesirable personality traits. It would suck if things like fuel or other gauges didn't read true once we were already skids up.

Fred closed his eyes and shook his head slightly.

"Good," I said, letting out a long breath, giving his shoulder a light pat, before feeling the heavy responsibility that firmly rested on my own.

But I was in my element and took strength from that before addressing Jerry. "Hey, can you guys get him in the back and keep an eye on him please?"

Jerry nodded and he and Lloyd helped Fred get as comfortable as he could in the rear of the helicopter.

"Mr Staadman, you get to sit up front, I'll need help finding my way," I said, strapping myself into the pilot's seat.

I slid on a headset and proceeded with my pre-start checks.

Within minutes Lloyd had radioed ahead and an ambulance would be on its way to meet us, it would be carrying the vital supplies that Fred needed and take him the rest of the way.

"Belt up folks," I said, noting that Lloyd was still not tied to his seat.

He complied, which gave me a small thrill. He was on my turf now.

The flight controls were free and gave me full range of movement.

I checked throttle, landing light, anti-ice, hydraulics. "Closed. Off. Off. On." I mumbled while correcting dials and buttons and working through my engine start checklist until I engaged the starter.

With the familiar ticking sound of the igniters, the turbine spooled up until it roared, coming to life.

"Alight" I said to myself.

Once the throttle was at full and the blades hit revs, I finished off my checks and when everything looked as it should, I cast an eye over on my passengers one last time, giving a thumbs up to Jerry, before glancing at Lloyd.

He in turn was watching me like a hawk. But it didn't feel like he was checking up on my every move. No, it felt as though he was watching me in awe.

But I didn't have time to think about that.

Glancing around outside to make sure the area was clear, I pulled up on the collective and eased us up into the air until we were well free from treetop height and then pushed the cyclic forwards to encourage the chopper to do the same.

We were on the other side of Saanastia. I found Lloyd was a great navigator and surprisingly easy to communicate with under this sort of pressure. We had a hundred or so kilometres to fly until the open range hit the road, I took the diagonal path which would cut some of the distance out. Thankfully, I remembered that the road was straight along the boundary, so we would inevitably intersect it at some point.

It didn't take long before we were flying as fast as we could with the doors off and towards the lifesaving treatment that Fred required.

Feeling right at home, I relaxed at three hundred feet and snuck a glance over at the man in the co-pilot's seat. He was staring at my hands with fascination. He noticed that I'd turned to him and he gave me a tight-lipped smile.

"Thank you Anna," he said, the worry clearly evident in his voice.

Even with the slight tremor, my name sounded like heaven when it came from his lips, his voice was rich and held a genuine tone even while hearing it through the noise-cancelling headset.

"Hey," I said gently, "we're doing everything we can, okay?"

"I know and... just thank you," he said, continuing to surprise me with his sincerity.

"Romeo Echo Delta, Saanastia, do you read?" Martha's friendly voice was a welcome intrusion.

I smiled. "Saanastia, Romeo Echo Delta, what's the latest Martha?"

"Oh sweetheart, it's so good to hear your voice, I'm on the phone with the hospital and the Ambulance is on its way and ETA at the junction from the main road and the border road is ten minutes."

"Wow that was quick, we have a tailwind but will still be a little longer, any chance we can get them to start driving up the dirt road?"

"Standby Anna." I waited a moment before she was back.

"Anna?"

"Copy."

"That's not a problem dear."

I smiled with relief. "Great, we'll keep an eye out."

"Very good and thank you, Fred's a valued member of the team, we couldn't do it without him," she said, her voice cracking with emotion. "What's his condition?"

"You're very welcome Martha. Standby." I looked at Lloyd who was privy to the whole conversation and already twisted in his seat to get the latest from Jerry.

He nodded a few times and then sat facing forward again. "Hey Martha," his voice was gentle, smooth and calm.

"Lloyd sweetheart," Martha's voice choked up at the sound of his voice.

"Jerry said Fred's hanging in there, okay? He'll fight this, we'll get him sorted."

"I don't know what I'll do if one of you..." and she disconnected, presumably to hide how upset she was.

"Martha?" Lloyd called out in concern.

"Yes lovey?" Martha said, her voice cracking with the emotion.

"We won't let anything happen to him okay?"

"Oh, I know sweetheart, I know everything will work out just fine with you two there," she said in a stronger voice and I kind of felt a little guilty that Jerry seemed to have been forgotten in the mix.

We signed off and Lloyd helped me track our progress, because I was completely unfamiliar with the landscape.

While I was ever grateful for all the remote areas I'd flown over, it didn't help me now. Not having planned the flight meant I was only relying on GPS for a very basic idea of where I was in relation to where I was going. With no distinguishing landmarks and flying at low level, I depended more on Lloyd's intimate knowledge of Saanastia to guide me.

My eyes felt sore from the contacts and even with my sunnies on, the wind in the cabin and the dust that I'd been exposed to earlier was an irritant that I didn't need. I probably should have taken them out before flying, but I wasn't mustering so it wasn't a priority at the time.

Minutes later, the road came up on the GPS just before I got a visual on it. Once we intersected it, I turned the chopper to follow the road south and dropped low.

It would only be a matter of time before we would come across the ambulance.

Finally in the distance, a tell tail plume of dust rose from the flat landscape indicating a vehicle on the road. I really hoped that it was the ambulance.

As it got closer, I spotted the hint of the flashing lights and felt the relief almost immediately. Glancing across the cabin, I noted that the tightness on Lloyds face had eased.

The ambulance slowed, having seen us barrelling towards them at low level and stopped on the side of the road where it waited for us to land. I made a circuit to check for any other vehicles and animals that could be a potential hazard.

After creating another dust storm, we touched down on the road and not far from the van.

Lloyd unbuckled, before hanging up his headset while the chopper blades slowed, and he stepped onto the gravel once it was safe.

He ran to the ambulance carrying a rifle. I hadn't seen him stash it on the floor beside him when he boarded earlier, and I shook my head dubiously.

Carrying firearms was a much more casual affair in these parts. Back home and before I started at STC, one of the station pilots had an accidental discharge from a loosely stowed 308. Unfortunately, it shot out a rotor blade, shearing it off and brought the helicopter down in an uncontrolled spin from only thirty feet up.

It wasn't the spiralling crash that killed the pilot though, it was the fuel tank explosion when the R22 hit the ground and broke up. The pilot was burned alive when his other injuries prevented his escape.

Since that incident, all our rifles were locked in a gun safe attached behind our seats until we needed them and fuel tanks on Robinson Helicopters had been upgraded world-wide.

While I had the down time, I checked over the instruments and looked at the logbook for any notes that I should have read earlier. Thankfully everything seemed to be up to scratch and I stowed the logbook just as Lloyd came back with the EMT's wheeling a gurney.

It was their turn to show their expertise, they quickly placed him on the gurney and the medics hooked him up to oxygen before Fred tapped one of them on the forearm to get her attention. He lifted his head, his face obscured with the mask and looked around until he found me. He gave me thumbs up in thanks before he fell back again and was whisked away.

The pride I felt was overwhelming and my throat tightened. Clearing it I made myself busy and cross-checked the fuel gauges. I only had enough fuel to get back to Saanastia. There should have been at least another hour of fuel on board, plus reserves according to the figures Fred had entered on the flight plan before leaving the airport where RED was based.

I sensed I was being watched. I looked up towards the ambulance, which was being prepared to leave and found Lloyd eyeing me while Jerry was giving a last wave to one of the EMT's before the rear doors were closed.

As soon as Lloyd was sprung, he avoided my gaze looking away and it wasn't long before he returned to the chopper with Jerry.

Once the boys climbed into the cabin, I sat sideways on my seat so I could see Jerry in the back and asked, "so, how's Fred gonna do?"

Jerry shrugged but appeared a little more relaxed now that most of the urgency had dissipated. "They're not really sure, it's still touch and go but his chances are streets better thanks to you. Why didn't you tell me you were a pilot?" He asked, clearly impressed.

I shook my head, not really knowing. I guessed that it just didn't come up.

"You probably didn't ask her, you bonehead," Lloyd said flippantly, before turning around, shoving his headset on and saying, "c'mon, let's get going, we still have things to do."

Jerry and I grinned at each other, before I turned and went through the whole start sequence again.

Descending into Saanastia, there no way that we could miss the number of vans and light trucks parked near the resort building, or the news cameras that were waiting for us on the ground as we landed.

No pressure or anything.

Walking away from the concrete helipad, painted green with a huge, white letter H on the front lawn, I shrunk behind both men, terribly uncomfortable with all the attention. Reporters were calling my name and asking questions left right and centre. It didn't take long for it all to just become a blur.

Thankfully, the boys shielded me and took the brunt of the interrogation, to which they gave no answers and Martha waved us into the relative safety of the building. But it wasn't any quieter in there, because we were welcomed with a huge round of applause, cheers and whistles from the staff. Martha promptly guided us into the privacy of her office.

"How's Fred?" Lloyd asked before the door was even shut.

"Not much news yet," Martha said anxiously, "but he's had an ECG and has been taken for a scan. Whatever happens, he will be going into surgery as soon as they know where the problem is."

Lloyd nodded.

Three chairs were lined up in front of Martha's desk and she gestured us to take them before walking around to her own. "But before we start, does anyone want a drink?"

"I don't know about anyone else, but I could sure use a beer after today," Jerry said wearily, slumping in his seat.

"I could go a beer," Lloyd nodded, wiping his face with his hands before Martha looked to me.

"Just a water please," I said, taking a quick glance around the room.

"You sure you don't want anything stronger?" She asked, "No one would blame you"

"No, No. I'm good, I'm pretty sure I've had my quota already," I grinned sheepishly.

Lloyd gave a light chuckle, so I gave him a sideways look to figure out what was so funny, but he stared ahead, pretending like he hadn't done anything.

I narrowed my eyes at him suspiciously and studied him, taking advantage of the time Martha was using to order the drinks.

Lloyd's profile was just as attractive as the rest of him, a straight nose and high forehead. I was sitting on his left and could see his scar clearly now that he didn't have his cap on. He'd been running his hands through his hair since he'd taken it off at the door and I could see that the injury was far worse than it first appeared. It looked like he'd had a skin graft and his eye had been affected because his eyelid slightly drooped now that he was clearly tired, it was amazing how well he hid it under his cap and behind his sunglasses. It was also amazing I hadn't noticed it the night of the Gala when he had nothing but his hair to hide it under, then again, I also didn't look at him that closely since I was probably too chicken to pull my eyes from the floor when in his presence.

"Weren't you ever told that it's not polite to stare?" He asked.

I gasped at being caught, "s-sorry," I said before looking away.

He was right, it was rude, and he was probably sick of people staring at his scars, after all, they were quite polarising.

I knew what it was like. No excuses.

Thankfully, we were interrupted by a knock on the door, and one of the staff walked into the office with our drinks on a tray.

"Thank you, Judy. That will be all," Martha said with a nod, dismissing the server more formally than I'd ever seen her address anyone. She clasped her hands momentarily watching the door close and then addressed us with a shrewd look on her face.

The boys had already taken long pulls from their bottles.

Lloyd caught Martha's eye and froze. "Uh-oh. I know that look, what have you done Martha?" He asked.

Martha cleared her throat. "Well lady and gentlemen, I may as well jump straight in. What I think we need to do is grab the bull by the horns and turn this unexpected dilemma into something positive for us."

Lloyd swore under his breath, shaking his head and his leg began bouncing in irritation.

The optimism left Martha's face and she levelled a look at the man sitting beside me. "Do you have something to say Lloyd?" She asked, crossing her arms and raising a brow at him.

"Well I was wondering how the fuck that is going to happen now? After everything that we're up against, this just feels like another nail in the coffin, we are down one of our greatest assets. I just can't see the glass half full like you Martha. How long before Fred gets his ass back in that chopper?"

"Well first of all young man, watch your language," Martha said, scolding Lloyd.

I had to look down when the corners of my mouth curled up. I felt Lloyd shift uncomfortably beside me.

"And second, we might be able to get someone else to fill in while Freddy recovers." Martha said, her cheerful demeanour returning.

"But Martha, we took forever to get Fred on board, we simply don't have the time to wait!" Jerry said earnestly, "And he gave his time for cost. We don't have the money to pay a charter that doesn't have a clue what they're doing."

"Well, that might be the case, but we have a really good publicity opportunity here, just look what was waiting for you outside." Martha said with a wave in the general direction of the door.

"How did they get wind of this anyway?" Lloyd asked, unimpressed with the media surprise.

"We don't know, but we think it may have been one of the guests." Martha answered.

I felt my stomach drop in anticipation of what was to come next. "And that's why I agreed for one of the morning shows to come here and do a story on Saanastia and what we do here. I told them that with Fred out of action, that the helicopter is grounded and we were severely compromised. If we accept the exclusive, they have offered the use of the network chopper in the short term until we find someone."

"What channel?" Lloyd asked.

"SABONE."

"Do you think that's a good idea? You know the owner's going up against Veldstmaan in the elections, don't you?"

"Exactly," Martha grinned malevolently, "This will get him some brownie points with the voters and might give us even more sponsorship with the exposure it creates. It will also distract Cyrus, who no doubt will be forced to lift his profile, so he'll need to work harder to keep his nose clean."

I wondered what Martha meant by that, I figured all politicians were crooks. Uncle Kyle said as much every time there was news of elections somewhere in the world, but something told me that Saanastia had a lot riding on the upcoming local appointment and there was far more going on with Mr Veldstmaan then met the eye.

"I feel there's a 'But' in there somewhere." Jerry piped in.

"Well yes, there's always a compromise. They want a cameraman on every flight and exclusive branding."

Lloyd stayed quiet, deep in thought and a smile grew on his face. "Martha you're a f.. freaking genius!" He exclaimed.

"I know, that's why you pay me the big bucks," she gloated proudly, before refocusing and becoming serious again, "in the meantime we have some breathing space to either get Freddy back in the air or find an alternative." She paused wistfully, before shaking it off. "But first things first, you three will be on live television tomorrow morning, to be interviewed by the breakfast show."

"What?!" I said in shock. I shook my head from side to side, "Martha, I don't think that's good idea."

"Anna sweetheart, you're the star of the show, if it weren't for you this wouldn't have been newsworthy, it's you they especially want to interview."

"I-I can't –I" I stuttered, knowing that I was being expertly herded into a corner that I wasn't at all comfortable with.

Lloyd put a hand on my arm and I snapped my eyes to his.

His touch had both excited and calmed me at the same time, I looked down to where his hand came into contact and he rubbed me with his thumb, "Anna," he said softly, causing a traitorous thrill up my spine. "I know it's a big ask but could you please help us out, the future of the organization could hinge around what happens tomorrow.

Please?" He asked me, in a genuinely desperate tone. His eyes pleading with me, his touch and his voice scrambling my thoughts.

I swallowed thickly and eyed firstly Jerry and then Martha.

That proved to be a big mistake.

Huge.

My resolve continued to slip.

I wasn't sure where these people had learned how to make puppy dog eyes like that, but with those hopeful expressions, how could I not agree to this heartfelt request?

Taking a deep breath, I nodded, "Ok, just so long as you guys know I'm probably not gonna be as good on the air as I am in it."

# Chapter 14

Lloyd's smile was my reward, and his relief was evident even if only for a moment. He cleared his throat, squeezing my arm, before he took his hand away and turned back to Martha.

"So what time is all this going to happen?" He asked, getting right back to business.

I stayed fairly quiet for the next fifteen minutes, just trying to absorb what I'd agreed to and only contributing when I was asked something directly as we were briefed.

The more I thought about it, the more anxious I became.

Don't worry. I thought. You're leaving Saturday morning, no one will remember you once you're gone. I repeated it over and over, while I tried to convince myself into looking forward to being on a national television show the next morning.

I'd just have to suck it up for the greater good and then I could bask in the warm fuzzy feeling that apparently happens after a good deed is done.

"... for dinner tomorrow evening?"

"Pardon?" I asked Martha, having been completely distracted with my wayward thoughts and the fact I was starting to feel a little green about the whole thing.

"Where were you dear?" Martha asked.

"Sorry, I guess I'm just tired, it's kind of been a long day," I said.

"Ha!" Jerry blew out in agreement, "that's an understatement."

"What were you saying?" I asked, before a cleverly timed yawn snuck up on me.

"She was asking if you'd like to join us for dinner at the house tomorrow evening, you know, before you head off." Jerry repeated hopefully.

"Oh," I sat up in surprise, "Um" I looked at Lloyd who remained silent and was sitting with his arms crossed in front of his chest.

I wasn't sure if he was also in deep thought, or if he felt that the offer was one step too far.

"I- I don't know, there's no need to go to any trouble, everyone's already bent over backwards and..."

"Nonsense Anna, what you did today trumps all of that. It's the least we can do before you go." Martha looked at me expectantly.

"Yes, and Martha can cook up a storm, she seriously should have been a chef," Jerry said in an encouraging tone, earning an endearing look from the kind woman on the other side of the desk. "Though she also makes the most awesome manager." He grinned.

"Kiss ass," Lloyd said under his breath.

Martha shot Lloyd an ornery frown and then a contrary smile to the other man. "Bless you Jerry, you must be craving my sweet potato pie again my dear, because you know flattery will get you everywhere."

"Yessss!" He said triumphantly, giving his friend a mocking side eye like he was the favourite son or something.

I felt heartened with the dynamic between the three close friends. Martha turned to me. "What do you say Anna, will you and Carley join us at the Homestead?"

"Um can I think about it? I'll just see what Carley wants to do and maybe I can get back to you as soon as I can?" I asked, not wanting to speak for my friend.

"Of course dear, that would be fine," Martha said with a nod.

I glanced at Lloyd and Jerry again. One was still sitting closed off with his arms crossed, appearing tense with one leg bouncing impatiently and the other was looking on with a hopeful and expectant expression on his face.

There was such a stark contrast between these two men, so much so that it had me baffled they'd become friends at all. Both Jerry and Martha were clearly extremely fond of Lloyd who had made my visit here both challenging and exhilarating all at once. Maybe they saw more in him than those fleeting moments of compassion that I'd witnessed during my stay, because for the most part he had acted abhorrently towards me.

Despite that and much to my own disgust, I still found him wildly attractive and it seriously left me questioning my own sanity.

It was therefore a very good thing I was leaving. I could then regroup and get back to my normal life and forget that Lloyd ever existed.

When I returned to my room, Carley wasn't there. Fetching my phone, I remembered that I'd turned it off before I'd even arrived in South Africa. I'd totally forgotten to turn it back on, but being so busy having a holiday and all, I hadn't even given it a second thought.

Oops!

The phone woke up with a series of alerts and I lowered myself onto my bed to sift through the messages.

There were five in total, two from Pete that came the day after I arrived:

How was your flight?

He'd be happy to know that I still hadn't been converted into a fixed wing fan.

You too good to talk now that you're a hoity toity jet setter, Stedman?

I grinned at Pete's dig and made a note to contact him later.

Then there were three from Carley:

Wednesday 10:12am. Hey chick hope you're having fun with the giant grey beasties, I'll be out with Alan for the next two days, he'll be showing me round Joburg.

I smiled at the local slang she used.

Thursday 12:47 pm God this is such a nice city, I could seriously live here and the company's not bad either, call me when you get back.

Shaking my head I sighed. That was quick. I think she might have fallen for the guy.

Thursday 17:28 OMG girl I just saw you on the news! Call me!

I rolled my eyes and dialled her number.

To say that Carley was excited at the prospect of what was to hit the airwaves the following morning was an understatement, she squealed and relayed the story to Alan and then squealed some more. Then she became distracted by her new man and left me to it. It was just as well because I really needed to have a shower before dinner, and I was starving.

Fortunately, Martha had organised room service for me, so I could have a quite night in. She said she'd be at the hospital to be there for Fred until visiting hours ended, he'd had a stent put in and would need Martha to help him with his recuperation post op.

I really admired Martha, she was an amazing woman, and it was lovely of her to think of me when she had her own worries for Fred and everything else she had to deal with.

Grateful and exhausted but no longer hungry, I set my alarm for four thirty the next morning for a bright and early start.

It was early, even by my standards and upon entering the board room, I had to squint until my eyes got used to the bright studio lights.

Lloyd was evidently not a morning person, not that he was really an any time of the day person, but he seemed to save his best brooding for this part of the day.

Damn him, that he managed to look good at this hour, even while he went about his said brooding.

We were having makeup applied and Lloyd continued to mutter while it was being slathered on, causing me to internally giggle at his discomfort.

We were asked to dress up a little, so I put an Aztec print sundress on. One that was normally used at home as my 'town cloths' with a pair of strappy sandals that I'd brought with me and I wore my hair in a high ponytail. Both men wore nice dark slacks with long sleeved shirts, Jerry's was white with a simple black tie while Lloyd's was light blue, going more casual with the first few buttons of his collar undone, showing a sparse peppering of chest hair and with the sleeves rolled to his elbows revealing his strong forearms.

Not that I was secretly checking him out or anything.

It was six in the morning before we were seated comfortably on a large Chesterfield couch in front of a green screen. There were no windows in this room because it was in the centre of the building and on the ground floor under what I think would have been the bar area, but it was beautifully appointed with wooden panelling covering the walls, floor to ceiling. Blue/grey coloured slate covered the floors topped with a massive Persian carpet in deep red, gold, cream and black pile, in the centre of the room stood a long solid dark wood table with at least twenty chairs upholstered in the same colour as the couch.

From where we sat, three cameras surrounded us from different angles and the crew were currently measuring the light and adjusting the diffusers to suit.

Not intimidating at all...

We were hooked up with microphones and the journalist from the show took a seat across from us and it was then that my nerves really started.

It was time and the reporter was led into the segment by the anchors back at the SABONE studio.

"Good morning Jaden, good morning everybody, we've indeed been lucky enough to be invited to talk with our newest heroes at Saanastia, who have become the talk of the region since late yesterday afternoon..."

Fortunately, the first few questions were directed at the boys and their everyday roles.

"...So, this is very good for Saanastia, but also a great mouthpiece for your Rhino and Orphan programs, can you tell us a little about those?"

Lloyd cleared his throat nervously and it surprised me that his usual confident demeanour appeared flawed for once. However, his passion for his cause soon replaced his discomfort once he started to talk.

Most of the things he spoke of were about things I'd heard before, but there was also a lot of additional information that I hadn't. It made me acutely aware that Saanastia wasn't unlike Lloyd in that there was far more to the tourist based wildlife reserve than met the eye.

"So that brings us to the star of the moment," the reporter said turning to me.

I jolted in my seat when a wave of anxiety prickled from the back of my head and down my spine.

"Anna Stedman, the young pilot who just so happened to be on the safari and was brave enough to volunteer to fly a helicopter across an unknown country to medical help. Anna what was going through your mind when you put your hand up to do something so courageous?"

"Uh" was the only sound that came from my mouth. I didn't even realise that my hands were fidgeting until Lloyd gently rubbed his pinky finger inconspicuously on the side of my knee, the skin on skin contact should have had me jump a mile but surprisingly it did the opposite. His calming effect allowed me to gather my thoughts and take a breath.

"To tell you the truth it's something that I did automatically, I happened to be a chopper pilot and we had ourselves a helicopter, I'm sure anyone who found themselves in the similar position would have stepped up."

"You are awfully young though, and you handled it like a seasoned professional. At just twenty years old, how did you find the confidence to take on such a challenge?"

Gees they'd done their homework, it made me feel exposed and I wondered what else they knew about me.

I had to remember why I was doing this, the animals that needed a voice. The media was the best way we could endorse them. I nodded "You're right I am young, but I've had my commercial chopper licence since I was sixteen and have more than fifteen hundred hours under my belt and almost three hundred of them in the same model helicopter as the one that I flew yesterday. I fly in very similar conditions back home so..." I shrugged.

"It wasn't a big deal?" The reporter asked, assuming to finish my line for me.

I didn't want anyone to think I thought nothing of what had happened, but I didn't want to sound arrogant either.

I shook my head. "No, I was going to say that I think we were all extremely lucky the way it turned out. We had the best possible outcome considering the circumstances," I said carefully.

"She was in the right place at the right time," Jerry said right after I finished, and Lloyd's little finger stroked me again. "Our very own angel." Jerry said with admiration.

Then Lloyd's touch was gone in an instant and he crossed his arms in front of him in that familiar closed off manner.

I shook my head doubtfully and with a sheepish smile I said, "Oh, I wouldn't go that far."

"So, Anna, do you have plans to continue where Fred left off, or does he still have a job here?" The reported asked only half-jokingly as she eyed the three of us in turn. "After all, the boys seem to be very fond of you." She sounded almost suggestive in her tone, she was clearly fishing for something that wasn't there and my face heated at the thought.

I chuckled to cover up my embarrassment and glanced at Lloyd, his face was turned to me, but his expression remained neutral. I looked back at the reporter, who was still waiting eagerly for my answer. "No!" I rushed out, shaking my head, "no, I'm just a tourist and I'll be leaving, going back home."

"Come now Nancy," Lloyd said, thankfully taking the heat off me. "You know that the SABONE has generously offered Saanastia their machine until Fred gets back in the air." Lloyd oozed with charm and Nancy fluttered her lashes at him.

"Well I for one think that it's a wonderful cause," she said, smiling sweetly. And I almost gagged.

"Indeed, and we're all extremely grateful for the donation," he said before he continued to schmooze.

There was talk of further donations that the viewers could make directly to Saanastia's cause. It seemed Martha was right on the money when it came to any sort of publicity for the cause and it left me feeling proud to be part of it.

Mercifully, the interview was finally over, and Martha gave us the thumbs up when the cameras stopped rolling. She had organised breakfast for us in the boardroom while the network crew started to pack up the set and once the room was quiet again. She joined us around the long table looking very pleased with herself.

"Well I think that went very well, don't you?" She asked over the rim of her cup, "Anna you were a natural."

I shook my head, disagreeing with her. "Really? I felt like I wanted the floor to swallow me, I was crapping myself."

Martha giggled at my expression. "Well, you didn't look it, you three made a great team and the camera loves you."

Embarrassed by her comment, I averted my eyes to the meal in front of me and shoved a fork full of scrambled eggs into my mouth, Martha was so positive about everything, that it was almost unnerving to me.

Not long after, one of the girls I recognised from the front desk popped her head into the room, "Martha, the phones are starting to ring off the hook."

"Fabulous, just what the doctor ordered." She brushed her hands free of crumbs, finished her coffee and stood from the table. "My turn to work some magic," she said with a smile, before leaving the room.

"Well, that sounds like good news," I stated, looking at each of the two men in turn.

"Yes, this is just what Saanastia needs, you can't buy that sort of publicity." Jerry grinned, winking at me.

Lloyd groaned, "We're still short a Helo long term," he grumbled.

I couldn't help it when the corners of my mouth turned up hearing that term again. Feeling his eyes on me, I was compelled to glance up at Lloyd and not surprisingly, he was glaring at me.

"You find that funny?" He asked.

Not waiting for a response, he proceeded to wiped his mouth, threw down his napkin and left the room without even saying goodbye.

I gave Jerry a cringe face. "Oops" I mouthed quietly, still wondering where Lloyd got stuck on the military term for helicopters that he'd now referenced twice in my presence. It was a bit of an inside joke among us chopper pilots that was often scoffed at. Or, it might have just been an American thing, now I thought about it.

Double oops.

"We'll be okay for now," Jerry assured.

The rest of the morning was spent packing for my flight out the next day and I was just sitting down with a cup of tea when Carley breezed through the door with a number of bags hanging off her arms.

"You're officially famous!" She announced, before she flopped down on the bed next to mine.

"And you are officially nuts. Where are you gonna fit all that stuff Carley?" I asked.

"Meh I'll pay for the extra baggage besides I'm an expert packer. And because I am, I knew to put a bag inside my bag before I left."

Her grin was huge.

"Of course you did," I dead-panned, "so how was your little uh... trip?"

"Oh," she said, reclining back on the mattress with a blissful expression on her face, "I wish I could take Alan back home in my luggage he's just so..."

"Dreamy?" I finished for her.

"Yeah," she said, still with that doe eyed look.

"Oh brother," I said rolling my eyes, "I hate to tell you this Carley, but we are leaving, like, tomorrow. You're gonna need to get him out of your system."

"I'm coming back," she said soberly, sitting up again.

"You're what!?" I asked in surprise, mimicking her and sitting bolt upright.

"I'm getting a working Visa and I'm going to be working for his law firm, it's all been sorted out, we just have to make it happen."

She sat there smiling so wide her face must've been hurting.

I, however sat there agape.

"Carley? Are you sure you're not being just a little premature?" I suggested, stating the obvious and holding my thumb and forefinger only an inch apart.

"Yes! Of course I'm being premature!" She grinned. "But I'll always be kept wondering what if? What if I don't pursue this? What if I regret not trying at least, I mean I'm not marrying the guy for Pete's sake, and there's no way I could do the long-distance thing, I need sausage."

"Ew TMI," I said, cringing at her vulgarity while shaking my head at her.

She loved to gross me out and I don't think there was anything that could wipe the smile off her face at this point.

"So," she said with an outward breath, "enough about me, you and Lloyd looked pretty cosy on the couch this morning."

Her eyebrows waggled up and down suggestively.

"W-What? No!" I said with a stutter. "Where'd you get that idea?"

She grinned at me wickedly.

"Well..." she started.

"Carley," I said, interrupting her with a warning tone, "I think you need to take off your rose-coloured glasses."

"Nope, I know what I saw, and chicka, that man's eyes were on you for longer than what could be considered appropriate and what was happening out of shot huh? You were sitting awful close?" She asked, waggling her eyebrows again.

"You're reading way too much into it." I waved her off. How could she know what Lloyd was doing to my knee?

"I don't think so, but it's okay Anna, your secret is safe with me," she said, tapping the side of her nose with a sly wink.

I narrowed my eyes at her and asked, "Are you on something?"

"No!" She answered incredulously.

"I think you are. I think that all those hormones you've got coursing through your system have clouded your perception of Lloyd Staadman, he does not think of me in that way, he can't even stand to be anywhere near me, ask Jerry, he'll tell you. I mean just this morning he barely even made eye contact with me and then ..." I stopped when I noticed Carley with her bloody all-knowing grin on her face.

"What?" I asked in exasperation.

"You're rambling," she said in a sing-song voice.

"Well, he's an arsehole and he just gets me so...so... Ugh!" I groaned.

"See? You like him." She nodded, dead sure of herself.

"Huh? No way!" I said, shaking my head.

"Oh yes you do! Read my lips Stedman. You. Like. Him," she said again, repeating every word slowly and clearly.

"Now I know you're high."

"No, I'm not. Why else would you get yourself in such a tizz if you didn't like him huh? Makes no sense, you don't go on about that Vet like that," she said raising a brow at me.

"His name's Jerry. And he's sweet," I said truthfully.

Jerry was sweet and Lloyd? Well he... wasn't.

"Whatever, but that's kind of my point. 'Sweet' doesn't fire you up," she said matter of factly, "and believe me you're warming his passion too! Girl, the chemistry this morning? Woo hoo!" She waved her hand around like she'd burnt it. "It was electric and I'm willing to bet that I'm not the only one who's noticed."

I shook my head at her, trying to remain nonchalant even though I was far from it. I admitted - but only to myself - that I thought Lloyd Staadman was attractive, despite his often shitty disposition. But Carley was sorely mistaken if she thought the guy had any feelings toward me that bore any resemblance at all to 'like', no matter how you looked at it.

"Seriously Anna, when he looks at you. Man. It's like he wants to swallow you whole and I don't mean in a bad way," she said, continuing to push the issue.

"You need to back up the truck, just remember you're all loved up at the moment, I'm betting you'd see a spark between the American political parties right now given half the chance."

"Huh? What has that got to do with it?" Carley asked with a confused expression.

I hoped that did the trick to distract her from hounding me.

"Never mind," I said, with a shake of my head and then I asked, "So, are you planning anything tonight?"

"Na, I'm gonna catch some z's, lord knows Alan and I didn't get much sleep the last two days, I think I'll order room service and flake."

"We have a dinner invite from Martha," I said as casually as possible before I went to grab my phone.

She nodded thoughtfully. "Sooo, will it be just Martha?" She asked.

"And Jerry." I said quickly, finding the number Martha gave me.

"And Lloyd?" She eyed me suspiciously.

"Maybe," I said, shrugging her off dismissively. "I don't know."

"Oh, he'll be there trust me," Carley said knowingly and with a sly grin.

That was what I was afraid of.

The number rang, Martha picked up and I proceeded to confirm dinner adding that I'd be the only one joining them that evening.

"Well, that's wonderful dear!" I had to pull the phone from my ear, her exuberance was surprising, "the boys will be so happy to have someone else at the table other than myself," she continued jovially, "are you sure that Carley won't join us?"

Peering inconspicuously at my friend, who was currently laying back on her bed and texting Alan with an eager smile on her face. "Yes, quite sure, she's all... worn out." I replied.

Carley glanced up, giving me the stink eye but she couldn't keep the stern look on her face for long and broke out in a giggle.

"Yes, I imagine so," I could hear the implication in Martha's voice.

"Do you want me to bring anything?" I asked, hoping to change the course of the discussion.

"No, no that won't be necessary, just your beautiful self."

Her kind words caused a confusing flutter of unease in my chest, she was such a nice person to everybody. The friendly familiarity she conveyed, was enough to make anyone feel welcome and even though I'd only known her a week, her demeanour was more like that of a mother figure than a host, which of course I'd missed since my abrupt estrangement from Aunt Rose.

While I had loved Uncle Kyle and Aunt Rose, I could never shake the feeling that they both were somewhat obligated to me, like my presence was perhaps something that had to be accepted all those years ago even though they'd obviously gone to all that trouble of adopting me.

There was something missing from our relationship, they were kind, but always just that bit distant. Especially when I got older and went to boarding school. They cared for me, that much was plain, but the connective parent-child bond was never there like it seemed to be with my limited interactions with the other kids and their parents as I grew up.

For some reason, they never really elaborated on it and I never asked.

Perhaps it was true. Maybe blood was thicker than water and that's what compounded my decision to leave home when I did.

I bit my lip, the pain bringing me back from my musing.

"Alright then, I'll see you all at seven?" I asked.

"That would be perfect, we'll see you in a few hours." She spoke warmly, which caused another wave of unease.

"See you then." I replied before signing off and blowing out a long breath.

I felt Carley's eyes boring into me.

"So?" She asked.

"What?"

"Is he going to be there?"

"Who Lloyd?" I asked, giving myself away the moment my mouth formed an involuntary smile.

She had a ridiculously smug look on her face.

"Told ya," she said, teasing me again and bringing me out of my funk.

I faux frowned at her, "Oh, shut up you."

She giggled, but then became serious and gave me a more pointed look. "Hey. I rang home earlier."

"And?" I prompted, hoping there wasn't anything wrong.

It reminded me that I still needed to call Pete.

I wondered if Carley knew where my thoughts had wondered to earlier, because if she did, it wouldn't be Pete she'd be trying to remind me to touch base with.

"Oh, you know, everyone's fine," she said sarcastically, "I told them we were doing great, they thanked me for ringing 'cause, you know, they were worried." She continued to stare at me intently.

I pulled a face, "I know I should call but.." I said evasively.

"I think it'd be a good idea," she coaxed gently.

She never really raised the responsible card on me, it was the other way around more often than not, but she had a point, even though the call, I knew, would feel like pulling teeth.

I sighed and conceded, "You're right, you're right," I said, holding my hands up to placate her.

Carley nodded, "But I'll be following up on this Stedman it's been way too long."

"Yeah." I said, knowing she was technically on point.

Shaking off my guilt, I looked around the room. I was as organised as I was going to get, with only Carley's things still strewn around. There was nothing stopping me from delaying the inevitable, but I wanted to do it on my own. "Why don't you test your super packing skills and then get that rest, while I go for one last swim and face the music." I suggested.

"Good idea," Carley agreed.

I changed into my bikini and reappeared again minutes later, covered with a light shirt and a sarong.

"Don't be too late I still have to help you get ready for your date," she said with a wink.

I sighed in exasperation, "It's not a date and you know it."

"Maybe not, but I still want you to look your best," she said in a parental tone.

"Yes mum." I turned and took a deep breath before I opened the door.

"A?" Carley called after me.

I looked over my shoulder.

"It'll be okay," she said with a tight smile, probably not really believing it herself.

"Yeah maybe," I said as I stepped out onto the landing. "Catcha later."

I made my way to the pool and contemplated along the way.

The fact was, it hadn't even crossed my mind to contact my aunt and uncle in the past few years, and therein lay the problem. I had convinced myself that the door had shut long ago and was only reminded on occasion by the people closest to me. Those who knew me best.

It was just easier not to think about it. That's why I kept myself so busy in Queensland.

Out of sight, out of mind.

The odd thing was, that ever since Carley had come back into my life, that had changed, and my adoptive home had wound its tendrils into my thoughts more often.

As the years compounded, so too did my fear of the fact that Uncle Kyle and Aunt Rose hadn't tried to contact me either.

Once I settled down into a padded banana lounge, on the wooden deck beside the pool, I thought I'd ease into it a bit and start by calling Pete first.

# Chapter 15

Luckily, we were only seven hours behind Queensland, it was eight in the evening there. I wouldn't be waking anyone up, so I dialled up my brother from another mother.

"Hello stranger," Pete's voice came through the phone.

"Hey Pete, what's new?" I asked, starting with something simple.

"Ugh, you know, same shit different day," he said casually, causing me to chuckle. "You?" He asked.

"It's been... interesting," I said, thinking back over the week's turn of events.

"Oh? How so?" He asked, clearly curious to hear my story.

"How long have you got?"

I told him about my animal encounters, the surprise chopper flight and the appearance on the breakfast show. I didn't tell him about the more unpleasant encounters because I didn't want Pete to go all big brother on me.

"There's no doubt about you Anna, you never do anything by halves do ya?"

"Nope. What would be the fun in that?" I asked, completely deadpan.

"Exactly, and I'm really happy you're finally having some of that, you sound good. Different," he said, and I could almost hear the smile on his face.

"I do? I think you need your ears cleaned out old man, how can I sound different in a week?" I asked in wonder.

"Hey! Enough with the old, I just meant that, I don't know... there's a tone to your voice that sounds..." he was searching for a word, "happy, you know, more zen."

Sniggering I asked, "Is Rach finally getting you in touch with your feminine side Pete?"

"First with the old and now you're questioning my masculinity? I can be perceptive you know."

"Oh right, like that time the guys were trying to give you a clue about Rach's nice rump as she rode coming 'round that last barrel and you commented, and I quote that; 'the horse's hip could have been a little longer.'"

He groaned. "Don't remind me, she never did let me live that down, I was wrong, that horse had a butt like a chamber maid."

He did actually redeem himself that night, when the rodeo ended and he asked her and her 'nice rump' out, much to her pleasure. Apparently, she didn't wear those tight Wranglers for nothing.

I shook my head. "You're a lost cause mate."

"It was a good night," he reminisced.

"Yeah," I said quietly, my teeth grabbing at my lip, before there was a drawn out pause.

That rodeo was the first one I'd been back to since...

The pool gate banged behind me and pulled me from my darkening thoughts.

"Hey! I'm costing you a fortune," Pete said brightly. "Don't be a stranger Anna, and don't get all snobby on me while you rub shoulders with those posh Europeans will ya?"

"Never," I said, smiling again, Pete was an amazing guy. "I miss you."

"Bullshit! Now go have a good time!" He said making me giggle.

"I will."

"Talk soon kiddo. Love ya guts."

"Yeah I love you too, bye."

As I hung up, I was startled by a movement that I caught from the corner of my eye.

Turning, I watched Lloyd's back retreating towards the resort with his as usual, powerful stride.

The gate at the other end of the pool was slammed so hard once he passed through it, that the impact sent a vibration throughout the entire length of the fence. It was a wonder that the gate didn't break off its hinges with the way that man abused it.

I shook my head wondering what the problem was this time.

Was it something I said? Surely not, I think I was starting to get paranoid around him.

Not everything is about you Stedman.

Maybe something had happened to one of the animals. It wouldn't be the first time I'd seen him react so intensely under those circumstances and I almost wouldn't blame him for his behaviour. I wondered how he kept going with all these damaged animals that were purposely injured at the hands of unscrupulous humans. I wasn't sure that I could do it if I were in his place and I almost wished that it was actually something that I had pissed him off with.

My mind went back to the other call I needed to make, I was an expert at procrastinating over this one thing, but I really needed to sort it out one way or another. I pep talked myself for a while longer before I sighed and dialled the Station for the first time in a few years.

"Hidden Valley Bill speaking." I paused a moment.

William was the head stockman and it was a surprise that he had answered the house phone.

"Hey Bill, it's Anna."

"Well blow me down. Young Anna, long time no see." Bill said, clearly equally surprised by my phone call.

"Yeah, sorry about that."

"No problem love, what can I do ya for?" Bill asked in typically Bill-esk fashion.

"Um… Are the old's in?" I asked, squirming uncomfortably in my seat.

"Na love, they've gone on a last-minute vay-cay, I'm looking after the joint."

"Oh, okay then, do you know when they'll be back?" I asked, not knowing whether to be relieved or disappointed with them not being there.

"Na, not exactly, they said they'd be away for about two weeks. D'ya want me to pass on a message?"

"No, that's fine, I'm on holiday too, so I'll call again when I get back home." I said, wondering where Uncle Kyle and Aunt Rose had jetted off too.

"Rightio love, no worries, how are ya keeping anyway?" He asked, genuinely interested.

"I'm pretty good Bill, busy flying up a storm, you know how it is."

"Good, good."

"Well, I'll let you go…" I said after some time.

"Yeah, yeah, no worries love," he said after clearing his throat. He sounded almost as relieved as I felt to end the stilted conversation with a couple of friendly goodbye's.

I sat there for a few minutes, staring at my phone and I decided I was actually relieved at dodging a bullet for the moment. I breathed out a huge sigh through puffed cheeks and put the phone away when I heard the pool gate open and close.

A few other patrons had come into the pool area to cool down from the heat of the afternoon, so I decided to join them and leave Carley to rest undisturbed.

The tables were turned when I'd lost track of time and she rang me.

"Shit." I cursed under my breath before answering the phone.

"I know, I know, I'll be right up," I answered.

She giggled before hanging up on me.

I gathered my things and made my way back to the hotel room.

As soon as I closed the door behind me Carley let fly, "Bloody hell chick, how am I supposed to make you look fit for a dinner date with you taking you sweet time like that?"

I looked at her dubiously and argued, "It's not a date."

She rolled her eyes. "Whatever, you're still going out, and you don't have long."

"I have a whole hour," I pointed out, knowing that I never took long to get ready.

"Exactly, that's almost no time at all, now get in the shower." She pointed to the bathroom.

"Yes, drill Sargent sir."

"I have all your stuff ready in the bathroom." She grinned wickedly.

Uh oh. "What... stuff?" I asked suspiciously

"Just a little something I picked up for you in Joburg," she said flippantly, although she was avoiding any eye contact.

"Why do I get the feeling that I'm not gonna like this?" I asked with a measure of trepidation.

"Oh A, you know I love you right?"

I crossed my arms in front of me to brace myself.

"Well I knew you wouldn't have anything much apart from jeans and shorts and..."

"Gee thanks for pointing out that I dress for practicality," I said sarcastically, scowling at her.

"Don't be like that," Carley said, pouting and matching my gaze in a standoff. "Look, it's a nice dress, that's all."

"That's all?" That didn't help my anxiety, because with Carley you could always expect more.

"Well?" Her brow crinkled while she wrung her hands, "I might have also picked up a sexy matching set of...

"Oh! You have got to be kidding!" I threw my arms up in frustration and whirled around to go see for myself, "I can't believe you would buy me underwear! That's just... just disturbing!" I rambled, flailing my arms about as I entered the bathroom.

Carley followed me and hovered in the doorway. I was imagining some slutty short number with a plunging neckline and a back down to my butt or something.

But it wasn't.

"Oh," I stopped my rant as I took in the grey or as Carley later informed me 'pewter' coloured cocktail dress. It had a high halter neck and an asymmetrical hemline in light, flowy fabric and it wasn't that short at all. I had to admit the dress was really lovely. "I didn't expect something so..."

"Tasteful?" Carley suggested.

I gave a quick laugh, "Yeah, but I was looking for a word that was a bit more diplomatic."

I turned to look at her, feeling chagrined. "Thanks Carley, it's a beautiful dress, but don't you think I might be over dressing? It's dinner at someone's home not a formal event."

"The way I see it, is it's having dinner with senior management of the resort."

"Hmm." I nodded. When she put it that way.

"You have three quarters of an hour, time's a wasting! Chop, chop," she said impatiently, clapping her hands at me in encouragement before she stepped out of the bathroom and closed the door.

After I scrubbed myself to within an inch of my life, I went to get dressed. Wincing a little when I picked up the new lavender underwear set and held the pieces at arm's length to scrutinise them. While Carley had bought boy shorts and not the G-String she would normally go for, there was nothing both to it nor the strapless bra.

They were both lace and very sheer.

The dress had completely distracted me in its sexy conservativeness. Or maybe it was the sneaky way Carley saw her opportunity to high-tail it from the bathroom before I could complain some more.

"Some friend." I said, mumbling sarcastically.

But I was done arguing, no-one was going to see under the dress in any case, so I'd just have to endure it. Slipping on the garments, I had to admit that at least the colour looked great against my skin. I might even go so far as to say that if I imagined the reflection in the mirror was someone else, that it was smoking. But I'd never actually admit to that, so I quickly put a stop to my vain moment and slid into my dress.

The back of the dress wasn't too low at all and hid the bra, I actually managed to do it up easily enough and the ties at my neck hung down between my shoulder blades and didn't annoy me too much.

Carley must've had some sixth sense or something because before I could take another look at myself she knocked on the door to tell me I only had twenty minutes to get to dinner.

Cursing at me for my enthusiasm or lack-there-of, Carley opted to blow dry my hair straight and put it in a stylish high pony-tail. She said it would help to show off my great shoulders.

"I've said it before Carley, I'm built a bit like a brick shithouse, why would I want to show them off?"

She smirked at me and joked. "Because, I think that your delicate bone structure fares just as well as your delicate demeanour around the Saanastia dining table Stedman," she said sarcastically. "Now sit still while I wrap the base," she said, scolding me and when I wriggled, she forcefully held the said shoulders still.

After sliding the same death traps on that I wore to the ball, she rotated her finger indicating I should turn. "Hot!" She grinned proudly.

I was saved from heavy make-up and was only burdened with a little mascara and lip gloss, so I had to hand it to my friend, she had in fact pulled off a Stedman approved outfit even though she had pushed the envelope in a couple of areas.

"Now, you need to go," she grabbed me for a hug while I was still taking it all in.

"I think I'm gonna be sick," I said, feeling my stomach tie up in knots.

"Don't be so negative, it's not like you're having dinner in a lion's den, A."

To my mind, her words sounded fateful.

"I wouldn't be too sure about that," I said dubiously.

She rolled her eyes. "Well look on the bright side, if your night sucks, you don't have to worry how to get home, you're just a quick walk across the lawn and besides," she handed me the silver clutch, "Jerry and Martha are there, right?"

"Yes," I let out a sigh of relief.

"They'll be a nice buffer for you, just don't make it too early, okay hun?"

Somehow, I don't think she was asking.

I nodded, my head was swimming at her logic and her eagerness to get me out the door. She turned me and gave me a gentle shove, "now go or you'll be late."

Then it dawned on me and I rounded on her. "Hang on one minute, why are you so keen to kick me out?" I asked suspiciously.

"Um?" She said, looking coy.

I crossed my arms in front of my chest and started tapping my foot waiting for her answer, "Well?" I prompted.

She had that same guilty look that she used to get in high school.

"Gah Carls!" I said in frustration, "why didn't you just say Alan was coming around?"

She looked surprised that I'd figured it out, but after only a moment, her face dropped and she frowned, looking sad. She sighed, defeated. "Because I didn't want you to think I was skipping out, I'm on holiday with you and..."

I groaned, "It's fine, it's fine," I held my hands up, "you owe me though," I pointed at her.

"I'll make it up to you, promise." She smiled and bounced on the balls of her feet.

I couldn't help but smile right along with her and gave her one last hug.

"I'm sorry I lied. I just didn't want to shove Alan in your face."

"Enough," I dismissed her, "I'll try to lengthen the evening. Just keep away from my bed." I said, puling a face.

"A, you're the best!' She smiled.

"Yeah, yeah you'll keep," I said walking out the door, shaking my head at my friend again as I stepped out of the room.

Walking through the gardens, there was a fresh change to the air. It was strange for this time of the year, being that we were heading towards the warmer months. My heels clicked on the paving bricks and I followed the signs that pointed to the homestead. The trees closed in until I came to an electronic gate that separated the private residence from the hotel grounds with a 'Private Property. No Unauthorised Entry' sign attached to it at eye level.

I took a breath, pressed the button on a small console that sat next to the gate and waited. A moment later, there was a beep and the gate unlatched with a click and I was able to push it open and walk through.

The gate closed behind me and I tracked up the dimly lit path until the trees thinned and opened out onto an expansive lawn, it's borders tastefully lit with up lights and framing an older but spectacular rambling stone homestead reminiscent of stereotypical rich landowners of old. It had many of the features that were also present in the resort and it wouldn't have surprised me if the same person designed or even built both structures. I took my time to take in the large windows and glass doors that lined the front elevation. The façade was brightly lit with authentic looking iron coach lights that were evenly placed along the great walls under the sprawling veranda, and from somewhere in the garden, I could hear the sound of running water, coming maybe from a pond or a fountain beyond this part of the estate.

I hesitated as a pang of nerves prickled through me and used the opportunity to pause for a few minutes to take it all in while I calmed myself.

Before I started telling myself I was being ridiculous, I was alerted by sound of footfalls coming from the path I'd just walked.

The familiar shape of the lanky Vet instantly put me at ease, and I let out a long breath in relief.

"Hey there Anna," he said, obviously in high spirits, his face becoming clearer in the better light.

Aware that eyes swept appreciatively over my form, I felt shy all of a sudden and with a little wave I gave him a rather weak "Hiya."

"You look beautiful," he said, and I held my breath when he approached to lean in and greet me with a kiss to both cheeks.

Dressed in a pair of nice slacks, a dress shirt and a well fitted jacket, he looked very handsome.

I might have to thank Carley for insisting I not go under dressed this evening.

"Thanks. You look not so bad yourself, what have you got there?" I asked, pointing to the bottle he was carrying.

"Oh, just a little something to go with the meal, I couldn't resist and it's Australian." He looked at me optimistically, showing me the label.

The wine was Voyager a drop from non-other than Margaret River.

"Huh," I said, shaking my head at the irony.

"We'd better get inside before they wonder what's keeping us," Jerry nodded across the lawn and towards the house.

Stepping up onto the veranda, our shoes made a racket on the wooden decking loud enough to announce our arrival. I took a closer look around me, timber beams and thick bush poles held up the sharply pitched roof and the ceiling was lined with woven cane rattan.

"Nice huh?" Jerry asked.

"I'll say," I said, agreeing with him completely.

Jerry opened the door for me like a gentleman. "Shall we?" He asked and swept the hand holding the wine bottle towards the interior of the house.

"Thank you, kind sir," I said with a grin and a small curtsey, before I stepped over the threshold and left Jerry chuckling behind me. I slowed in the foyer and waited for him to catch up because I had no idea where I was going.

Jerry led me into the living room. It was sprawling and masculine, with polished wooden floors covered in heavy rugs. It shared the same stone walls from the outside of the house while the secondary walls were smooth plaster.

Dark leather and timber furniture in brown and coffee coloured accents were placed to make the most of the views outside through the full length french doors that also served as every window out onto the veranda. There was no drapery but there were wooden shutters that could be closed in front of the windows for privacy and extra security.

"Hellooo," Jerry called out just as we approached the kitchen area.

"Ah, there you are! I thought I heard someone." Martha called from around the corner.

Rough sawn cabinets were finished smooth with a thick varnish and bordered an opulent kitchen with a huge centre island bench. Both were topped with what could have been granite and hanging from the ceiling was the large pot rack suspended over the island. Stainless appliances gave the kitchen a modern edge to its otherwise rustic look.

"Look who I found." Jerry said as Martha appeared from what looked like a butler's pantry that ran along the rear of the kitchen.

"Hello my sweethearts," she said, greeting us with a delighted look on her face.

She wiped her hands on a towel before striding straight up and giving me a huge hug. I was a little taken back, but if she noticed she didn't show it because in the next second she similarly took hold of Jerry and squeezed the daylights out of him too.

"What did you bring young man?" She asked, looking at the wine bottle in his hands.

"A nice little Australian Chardonnay to go with dinner," Jerry answered.

"Wonderful! You know how we love the quality that comes from Australia!" Martha exclaimed, acknowledging me with a big grin and a wink, before she took the bottle from him.

It was then that Lloyd made his presence known, my heart skipping a beat.

I wasn't sure if it was just me, but I felt that the strange but otherwise joyful dynamic in the room seemed to become more serious all of a sudden.

"Jerry," he said in greeting, the men shaking hands before Lloyd gave me a polite nod. "Miss Stedman."

"Mr. Staadman," I said in kind.

"Lloyd, be a dear and take this out to the table," Martha ordered, interceding the tense moment and handing him the wine bottle.

He silently obeyed.

"Can I help?" I asked stepping forward.

"Thank you Anna, there's another dish there," she said pointing to the island. "Jerry, make yourself useful and grab that tray and I'll be right behind you," she said, easily taking control of the evening.

The dining room was as spacious as the other rooms and housed a long dining table that could comfortably seat ten. Lloyd was busy collecting four wine glasses from the large matching sideboard that sat along a timber-panelled wall decorated with some beautiful enlarged, framed photos of the landscape of what I assume was Saanastia.

Minutes later we were all seated, Jerry sat next to me, Lloyd just across the table next to Martha and all the delicious looking food was within easy reach. There was the clanking of dishes and cutlery as we helped ourselves, politely mumbling to pass this and that.

"Smells amazing, Martha," I said, trying to break the tension in the room.

"I do try," Martha said humbly, spooning a beautiful pesto pasta dish onto her plate. "So Anna, we know that you fly helicopters, but what's your job?" She asked.

I glanced at the others at the table, Jerry was scarfing down his meal while Lloyd sat back to listen albeit with a tight expression on his face, his eyes on his plate.

"Uh," I set my fork down and explained that I worked at Station to Coast, "...for the most part I'm contracted to run my R22 to muster cattle, but when the season is over I'll fly anything from Jet Rangers to my boss's executive AW Power Grand out over the Hinterland and The Great Barrier Reef doing scenic tours and charters."

"Your helicopter?" Jerry asked after swallowing a mouthful, his eyes large in amazement.

I smiled thinking of my other baby, "Yeah sure, doesn't every girl have one?" I asked in an innocent tone.

That was the line I used automatically when someone asked that sort of question.

Martha and Jerry laughed and if I squinted, I might have just been able to see one side of Lloyd's mouth lift for a moment. "Other than my horse, it's the most precious thing I have, the other chopper's belong to Station to Coast, and we have a few that Pete cross hires during peak season too," I rambled.

"Who's Pete?" Martha asked.

"S.T.C.'s owner, my boss." I said, just as Jerry's phone interrupted the conversation.

Jerry excused himself to take the call before leaving the table and we continued to eat in relative silence.

He returned five minutes later.

"Sorry to cut this short, just got a call out to Paladin Ranch, a couple of the white cats have had a scrap and one's got a chunk out of his cheek that needs stitching."

"Ha!" Lloyd blew out a sharp laugh, "Randy bastards," he said, with a smirk before he wiped his mouth with a napkin.

He looked almost relaxed for the first time that evening.

"Yeah," Jerry huffed checking his pockets for everything he needed. "That young one thought he'd try his luck on old Simba and came off second best."

Martha rolled her eyes, and looked at me, "Men, they're all the same," she said, giving me a playful wink, "they're so protective of their girls."

Was she still talking about lions?

"Well, Simba's done me no favours," Jerry said with a shake of his head.

"If I don't see you again," he said, placing a hand on my bare shoulder, "stay safe and look after yourself, won't you?" He asked in a warm tone.

I watched Lloyd's gaze zero in on the contact, the lines of muscle rippled beneath the skin of his jaw and made my heart skip a beat without permission, but he said nothing.

"I'll see you two tomorrow," Jerry said to the other's and then to Lloyd, "and we need to preg-test those rhino's."

"Onto it." Lloyd said with a nod as his friend turned to leave the room.

"And don't forget to save me some of that pie!" Jerry called out to Martha over his shoulder before disappearing from view, causing Martha and I to laugh.

Lloyd pushed back from the table, his chair making a loud scraping sound across the floor.

"Speaking of which, I think I'll serve dessert. Coffee Martha?" She nodded before Lloyd turned to me raising his brows in question, "Miss. Stedman?"

"Thank you." I forced a smile to my lips and he started to gather dishes.

We followed suit, and before long Martha was tending to the delicious looking pie that had been sitting on the bench cooling and shooed me away to wait for them in the sitting room.

Joining me minutes later, we organised the drinks and pie in relative silence.

Martha finally sat next to me on the couch, Lloyd settled in one of the two armchairs and I decided to start a conversation.

"So, how long have you been doing this Lloyd?" I asked, his name giving me a thrill as it came from my lips.

"What? Making coffee?" He asked, with a hint of mirth before looking up from adding the sugar to his cup. The wrinkles around his eyes showing a genuine humour in the exchange.

"No," I chuckled, shaking my head. "The conservation," I said, amending my question.

"'Bout ten years," he answered, taking a sip of coffee and closing his eyes to savour it.

I looked over at Martha for a more expansive answer, and she promptly took my lead. "Saanastia has had close ties to the wildlife since the mid-sixties. Of course, it was a game park back then," she said looking up to convey her serious expression.

"Are you saying that people used to trophy hunt at Saanastia?" I asked wide-eyed.

"Yes dear, they did," she said, "but back then, it wasn't called Saanastia, it was purchased in the early eighties by Lloyd's family and the changes started after that and then the guests started shooting animals with cameras instead of bullets."

"Definitely for the better," I said picking up my plate to try Martha's pie.

"Yes, for the better," Martha brought her cup to her lips.

"Mmmmm, still got it Martha," Lloyd interrupted, spooning the delicious pie into his mouth and effectively ending that line of conversation.

"This is great pie," I said, agreeing between mouthfuls.

Martha beamed with the praise and set about eating her own slice before Lloyd stood and took his empty plate to the kitchen.

"Make sure you leave some for Jerry," Martha said, gently scolding him.

"But there's still heaps left," he said with a whine.

"Not for long young man, I know what you're like," she said, wagging her finger and narrowing her eyes at him.

It was nice to see him let his guard down a little and show something other than business as usual. I imagined that Martha and Lloyd were more like family than co-workers, and for all of Lloyd's moodiness, Martha handled herself with patience, in charge and without Lloyd even knowing it.

We finished our drinks and pie with pleasantries when from not too far away, came the rumble of elephants and I thought of Pragtig. "I think I'm going to miss that sound," I said absently.

Martha smiled, "I'm sure Lloyd could organise for you to say goodbye to Pragtig before you leave."

My heart thundered at the thought, "Seriously?"

I looked from Martha to Lloyd, who was taking a long breath though his nostrils with his eyes shut. I took that to mean it was the last thing that he wanted to do, and I felt deflated in an instant.

Just when I thought Lloyd was starting to warm to me, I didn't want to push my luck.

"Uh no that's okay, please don't go to any trouble, I'm sure you all have more than enough to do, I've already taken more than my fair share of your time. Thanks anyway." I said, effectively eliminating any hope from being able to see Pragtig again, dropping my gaze to the floor despondently.

"Nonsense, Anna, it's no trouble, is it Lloyd?" Martha asked, her tone changing from fondness to authority in a short beat, before she stood and walked over to a credenza along the wall.

I heard Lloyd's sudden intake of breath and braced myself for some sort of angry retort. But instead all that came out was, "Nope no trouble at all."

My head snapped up with his surprising answer to be met with a smile that even blind Freddie could tell was laid on a bit thick.

"You sure?" I asked, "I don't..."

"Nope, it's fine." He cut me off, insisting on the last word.

I sighed to myself in resignation. "Well okay then thanks, I really appreciate it, I don't think I'll get my next animal fix till Vienna." I smiled nervously.

Martha had organised a silver tray topped with crystal tumblers and a matching decanter.

"A nightcap?" She asked.

I shook my head "No thanks, just a water please."

Martha asked, "Soda ok?"

I nodded.

"So you're not going home then?" She asked, before she handed me the soda.

"No, the next stop is Europe, Carley's booked one of those scenic boat cruises on the Rhine. Holland to Hungary," I said with a grin, "and while I'm sure it'll be excellent to see castles and all the other old architecture, I've been hanging out to see the Spanish Riding School."

I abruptly stopped myself from rambling too excitedly and mentally face palmed myself for my word vomit.

"Well I'm sure you'll have a blast, I know I did when I backpacked through Europe with a group of my girlfriends in my youth." Martha's gaze became wistful as she reminisced.

My eyes grew wide. "You backpacked?"

I didn't think I'd ever be brave enough to do that, certainly not in this day and age.

"Yes, but it was a long time ago, I had just graduated from college and even though my girlfriends and I had no money, it was a rich experience that I'll always keep with me."

"I never thought I'd ever travel. I figured that I got enough fly time at home to tide me over. It's only because of Carley that I'm even here anyway," I shrugged, "but I'm glad I did, it's been a real... adventure, not everybody gets to be part of an angel flight while they're on holiday." I picked at some imaginary lint on my dress as I rambled again.

"Oh, how fitting," Martha said warmly, "you were definitely Freddy's angel that day."

I felt the heat climb up my chest and neck and shook my head to disagree.

It wasn't the first time I'd heard that and hearing it again, didn't make it any easier to accept. "I don't know about that Martha. I'm just glad I was there and that it all worked out."

"So are we! Don't sell yourself short Anna," Martha said insistently, adding to my discomfort. "What would we have done if..."

Lloyd interjected over the rumble of elephants, "Martha can't you see you're embarrassing the poor girl?" He asked, appearing somewhat distracted by where the noises were coming from.

They were closer this time.

Then a loud trumpet burst through the night air.

Lloyd jumped up. "What are they going on about?" He asked absently, before making his way to the front door.

His concern showed that this was quite obviously an unusual occurrence.

"I think that's my cue to leave," I said, also standing and tentatively took a few steps in Lloyd's general direction. I peered out through the doors and windows but couldn't see anything beyond the light thrown on the lawn by the house.

Turning to Martha, I thanked her for dinner, and I hoped that I'd given Carley enough time with Alan.

Martha stood. "You're very welcome dear." She said before she hugged me.

Letting me go she called out "Lloyd!" To the man who was almost out the door.

He stopped in his tracks and turned with his brows risen in question.

"Can you be a dear and escort Anna to her room?" The look on her face made it abundantly clear that it wasn't a question. I wasn't sure what Martha was up to, but it was plain that Lloyd wasn't exactly overjoyed with the idea.

He sighed and slumped his shoulders in resignation, "Sure."

Martha walked me to the door before hugging me again fiercely, "I'll see you tomorrow dear."

"You will," I assured before I stepped outside and shivered, I hadn't thought to bring a coat and it was unusually nippy outside.

"Look at you shivering, come, I'll get you a coat," Martha insisted and I followed her back inside. She opened a door that turned out to be a large closet and pulled a beautiful wool coat off its hanger before holding it out for me. I heard Lloyd groan while I shrugged the coat on.

It was a big coat, not Martha's by any stretch of the imagination, the first breath I took while flipping my ponytail out and straightening the collar was heady. This coat was Lloyd's without question, and it smelled divine, his cologne, a hint of leather and everything that was his manly scent.

"Thanks," I whispered hoarsely as I closed the jacket around me. Only my fingertips were visible from the bottom of the sleeves and I must have looked ridiculous in it.

I think I may have sniffed the collar. I couldn't help it, being enveloped in something that Lloyd had worn left me feeling cocooned and safe for some reason.

Martha smiled knowingly. "Goodnight dear."

"Night Martha," I said, as I started out the door again. Lloyd shoved his hands in his pockets and fell into step beside me.

Even though the walk was silent and as tense as I had come to expect, I was surprised that Lloyd was a gentleman enough to open the gate for me.

Stepping through, the elephants made another commotion, Lloyd faltered and looked towards the sound.

"Uh, look, you and I both know that you'd rather be checking on the herd than accompanying me anywhere." He opened his mouth to say something. "No, it's alright, I'm pretty sure I've got it from here." I said, assuring him and I started to shrug off the coat.

"Anna," he put his hands on my arms, immobilising me not just physically but mentally too. He removed his hands and stepped back closing his eyes and shaking his head, "keep the coat, Martha or I will collect it tomorrow."

I nodded, "okay," and wrapped the delicious warmth back around me.

Lloyd hesitated for a moment and then turned quickly without another word, leaving me feeling oddly alone, while I watched his broad back retreat into the darkness.

In my muddled state, I made a decision that would very likely cause me to end up in a world full of hurt.

But only if I got caught.

# Chapter 16

I took off my shoes and followed Lloyd into the shadows.

Along the outside of the Homestead fence and behind some shrubbery, the lawn soon gave way to dirt and leaf litter. I couldn't hear Lloyd's footsteps, so I figured that he wouldn't be able to hear mine either, but I picked my way carefully through the under growth regardless.

By the time the shrubbery cleared I smelled the dust in the air and then I found myself standing in the clearing of a well-worn track that was obviously used by vehicles to get around the resort and sanctuary grounds. There was enough light from the moon to be able to see my way, and I easily made out the tall-electrified fence that protected the resort and ran along the opposite side of the track that I was standing on. Not knowing where Lloyd went, I listened carefully for any sounds to indicate his direction.

I let my breathing grow quiet before a steady rumble echoed through the night as well as another sound of a gently putting diesel motor. I smiled and turned away from the resort and towards the sound.

A huge three-sided shed loomed up ahead. It was softly lit and I could just make out Lloyd sliding a huge square bale of hay onto the forks of a large four-wheel drive John Deer tractor. Once the big green machine was loaded, Lloyd drove it across a vast hard stand and out of sight.

I followed on, feeling every bit of gravel under foot, keeping the tractor's red tail-lights in my sight without getting too close. Eventually I came to a complex of oversized stock yards and stopped to observe from a distance.

The tractor drove into a long race that served as a gate-lock to the various yards and paddocks.

I waited for Lloyd to return and crouched down as he passed by on his way back.

The area was left quiet except for the sounds of the elephant herd tucking into their hay. There was a little tussling until they settled and then all that could be heard, was the ripping of hay from the bale, the loud chewing and the occasional contented purr like groans.

There was no better sound and I had always loved to stick around at the stables with Blue if I had the time and listen to his contented munching.

In the dim light, I slowly made my way towards the herd and came as close as the fence would allow.

One of the elephants snorted, then rumbled and another answered making its way to the heavy gage steel fence to meet me.

Pragtig had sprung me and I couldn't have been happier.

"Hey Tembo," I whispered.

I was rewarded with an answering rumble. Her trunk reached for me and I stroked it without hesitation, I blew into the end of it she huffed my breath before she started feeling my face.

There was something to be said for these intelligent animals. They were so big and could undoubtedly be dangerous enough to kill a man without even trying. But here I was with a six ton elephant gently caressing my face, as if to remember me by touch. Her breath smelt like the sweet hay she'd been eating. I dug around in my small clutch and fished out the mints.

"Moja kwa wewe", she neatly whisked a mint out of my hand, "na moja kwa ajili yangu." I said, popping another into my mouth.

When Pragtig had her fill of my face she started on my neck and then further down. Trailing her trunk over Lloyd's coat, I heard her take a deep whiff, the air rushing up the long appendage for her to analyse.

"Yeye harufu nzuri haina yeye Pragtig?" I mumbled, "Mtu hivyo shauku Saanastia hii lakini hivyo hasira juu ya maisha, kufikiria ambao angekuwa kama angeweza kuchanganya hiyo na alimpenda maisha. Sasa kwa kuwa itakuwa ni kitu. "

"What am I even saying Pragtig? Maybe I should take my own advice. Now that would be something." I said, shaking my head at my musings.

There was a rumble from my elephant as if she was in agreement.

I spotted a plastic feed bucket under a tap just beyond an elephant's reach, but it was not out of mine.

So, I fetched it and turned it over for something to sit on.

I wasn't sure how long I'd been there but there was movement at the hay bale and the elephants seemed to have had their fill and started to move off.

They disappeared from view, but Pragtig stayed with me with her trunk checking on me every so often.

"Je, si unataka kula kitu wewe silly tembo?" I asked her, "Familia yako wameondoka wewe mengi," I said squinting through the dim light, only to see what was once a four foot by eight foot tightly packed bale, that had now become a much reduced and messy stack of hay.

"I won't leave you tonight, I promise," I said to her quietly.

After another half hour it was clear that Pragtig wasn't going to leave my side. The other elephants had long since gone and their rumblings were now quite far away. So, I did something that wasn't my best idea ever for the second time that evening.

I couldn't help myself for some reason. I knew I'd be okay with Pragtig and I squeezed through the railings and made my way towards the hay with Pragtig's trunk in my hand.

"He's so gonna kill me," I mumbled to myself as I thought about Lloyd's wool coat. The hay was still clean, so I wrapped the coat tightly around me and lowered myself into its softness. I hoped I didn't end up with an itch.

That would totally suck.

And it would serve me right.

Pragtig settled immediately and started shoving hay into her mouth.

I grinned at myself and relaxed with the sound and before I knew it, I had fallen asleep.

*-Sweet green lawn turned to arid savannah, there was chaos as the herd of grey milled around me. The dust thick in the air, choking my airways and hurting my eyes. A strong trunk wrapped around me and effortlessly took me off my feet, rescuing me from being trampled from the group of massive elephants.*

*The world was a blur in the rush, the tears wet on my face, streaked and muddy as I clung on to my elephant for dear life.*

*The air cleared and the canopy overhead cooled the relentless heat from the sun. We crashed through the thick vegetation and only then did we slow down enough for the landscape come into focus and for me to see which way was up. I scrambled behind massive ears to settle astride the broad neck.*

*My heart slowing, I slumped forward, exhausted, feeling the familiar soft but tough, wrinkled hide of my elephant, I held onto my elephant, my hero, and my saviour.*

*Then I heard them and from distance they were calling my name...-*

"Anna," I felt something gently stroke my cheek, a rumble from an elephant and the fabric of my bad dream ripped to shreds.

Startled, my breath heaved as I tried to catch it. Frantically I looked around confused and wondering where the hell I was before the cotton wool feeling within my head cleared enough for me to remember.

My eyes were forced to focus onto the figure crouched in front of me.

Lloyd!

Sitting abruptly upright, I gasped and if I thought my heart couldn't beat any harder, I could feel the thing thumping in my neck and hear it in my ears. My head was still a little woozy and my body unstable. It was therefore a comfort when I felt Lloyd's hands on my shoulders to steady me.

I recognised the expression on his face. It was the same one he had when Fred had his turn for the worse.

It was concern.

Concern and also relief.

It was short lived though. His furrowed brow made an appearance from under the ever-present cap and the typical stern set to his jaw returned after taking in a long breath through flared nostrils.

It looked as though he was warring with himself. He shook his head before closing his eyes and whispered carefully. "Would you mind telling me what you're doing here?"

His softly spoken voice was almost worse than if he were to do his nut.

I was in so much trouble and what's more, I knew I had asked for it.

"Uh, I fell asleep?" I said weakly. I regretted the words as soon as they left my mouth and I sounded like a clueless little girl, even to my own ears.

But his touch was too distracting on top of my freshly woken state and I just couldn't think straight with him that close.

He scoffed loudly before his hands slid up my neck to cradle the sides of my face, so that I had no choice but to pay attention and look him in the eye.

I was shocked by the sensation it caused, my eyelids shot open taking in the frown that had formed on his handsome features, his ice blue eyes darted all over my now flushed face and his expression was one of utter disbelief.

"You. Fell. Asleep?" He repeated in an incredulous tone.

I sat rock still staring straight at him, bracing myself for his inevitable onslaught, but before I could answer, his still quiet tone endured, "what were you thinking Anna?"

I could see the turbulence hidden beneath his controlled facade.

"Don't you know you could have been trampled in your sleep or worse?" He asked fretfully.

It wasn't until he wiped at my cheeks with his thumbs that I realised that tears were the source to his unusually tentative behaviour.

My tears.

Finally, I remembered snippets of my dream, I sniffed, "I had a nightmare...I think." I said gulping back an unwelcome sob as I drew back from his touch before wiping my face with the back of my hands.

Lloyd nodded and he swallowed thickly before plucking some hay from my hair. His demeanour was confusing the hell out of me.

I swallowed back another unwelcome sob. "I- I'm okay," I said, with a stutter, "and besides, Pragtig was watching over me."

I internally reprimanded myself. Ugh! Again with the immature air that was so unlike me. I winced at the thought.

Immature was exactly the way I had behaved. It would never have crossed my mind to camp near any of the river's back home for example, I'd be in crocodile country, they would love me... for breakfast.

Why, oh why did I think it was a good idea to camp with a herd of African Elephants?

I obviously wasn't thinking very clearly and I seemed to have lost any ability to do that from the moment I stepped foot on Saanastia.

"I'm sorry." I said and looking into his eyes.

I truly was and I was so, so confused.

"Boss!" A familiar voice called out, interrupting us.

We both flinched, Lloyd rocking back to put some distance between us.

Kabri had found us and had stopped to wait as he casually leaned on the fence.

"It's alright, she's okay!" Lloyd called out, collecting a rifle before he rose to his feet.

I missed his close proximity, but at the same time dreaded what was to come.

I wiped my face free from what was left of my tears and took his out-stretched hand so that he could help me up.

Pragtig reached for me too, touching me again to check in like she often did. The touch triggered flashes of the dream I had and was making it hard for me to focus.

Clearing my throat, I stepped back from Lloyd and tried to smooth my hair and brush myself off. Then I came to realise that there was hay stuck to Lloyd's beautiful wool coat.

I had a feeling that it would happen so it shouldn't have been a surprise, but I was still mortified.

"I'm so sorry about the coat," I said, while I tried to pick some of it off. Some seed heads had buried into the warm fabric and would need careful removal, "I'll pay for the damage," I promised, distracted again when the dream images intruded.

I continued to pluck at the coat absently.

"Stop, just stop!" Lloyd said, and I obeyed. "Forget about the coat. Miss Stedman, Don't you realise that we've just spent hours looking for you?" He asked earnestly.

"Uh..." I uttered while my mind continued to swim in its bewilderment and the red flared on my skin from my embarrassment.

And there it was. Finally his displeasure boiled over, if the shoe had been on the other foot, I'd have felt pretty pissed too and to be fair I absolutely deserved what came to follow.

"I'm sorry," I whispered to him again, not that it would do any good.

"Yes, I know you're sorry," he said, reaching for me and leading me towards the fence by my wrist. "I'm sorry too, I'm sorry that everyone's actions over the last week led you to believe that you could take this sort of liberty. If you weren't already leaving today, I'd kick you out myself. You put yourself in danger, wasted precious resources and you had Martha and your friend frantic, do you know that?"

He didn't give me a chance to respond. Not that I had anything to say, there was no defence for my behaviour. What I did last night was something a kid would do, to throw caution to the wind and be damned with the consequences.

I don't know what had come over me and Lloyd was right.

"Please Anna," we stopped before we got to the fence, "can you do me a favour and stay out of trouble just long enough so that your boyfriend and your parents get to see you again?"

**I froze and felt the nausea in my throat. I tried to keep the memories at bay by biting down hard on my lip, but it was no use...**

*-I had been living with Jayme since New Year. It may have seemed a little fast, but what was the point in a long distance relationship? We agreed that if it didn't work out, I could always return home to the station. Even though that meant I'd have to swallow my pride and go back with my tail between my legs.*

*I, in all my wisdom, was of course confident that would never happen.*

*I was employed with his company Station to Coast Helicopters and Jayme taught me everything I knew, and I wasn't just talking about flying helicopters.*

*But Jayme was a man of his word; when he promised to spare Uncle Kyle from having to pummel him again for taking his nieces' virtue before her eighteenth, he meant it.*

*Crazy I know since I was legal at sixteen, but Jayme took it seriously, much to the frustration of both of us.*

*That year my eighteenth birthday fell on the night of Rodeo Finals, and I guess in a way there could have been no better celebration, whether Jayme won his third buckle or not. This year if he rode well enough and with a bit of luck thrown in, that hat-trick would give him an as good as a guaranteed seat on the American bull riding circuit where it could make lucrative careers and some men millionaires. Jayme had even organised a passport for me so that I would be right to go with him in case things happened quickly.*

*The stadium was packed and Jayme was up. We rested our foreheads together like we always did when we needed connection.*

*He kissed me with everything he had, and I was dizzy when he finally let go of my mouth. "I love you baby."*

*"I love you too," I said, trying to catch my breath and smiling as big as he was with the excitement of what was to come.*

*"C'mon ya Pussy!" Pete shouted from up in the chutes, I just shook my head and after one last peck before we exchanged his Akubra for the stack hat I was holding, Jayme was gone.*

*I settled in my usual spot close to the action and watched Jayme go through his routine. Carefully fitting his helmet that had a full-face guard, checking and rechecking the straps on both it and the body protector three times before putting his glove on and taping it. Before he climbed the chute, he looked for me, blew me a kiss and popped in his mouth-guard.*

*I smiled at him and returned his gesture. It was the same every time I'd come to see him ride.*

*He climbed over the chute and lowered himself onto the broad back of the eleven hundred kilo bull, testing the grip on his glove three times before he tied himself in. One more check of his helmet and then came the nod. The buzzer sounded and the chute was opened.*

*With the roar of the crowd, the bull was already five feet in the air before the first second passed. Jayme had drawn the rankest bull for the night, one that no cowboy had been able to sit eight seconds to for its last six rides.*

*On the speakers, ACDC's Thunderstruck rocked the stadium, it was the bull's namesake and the crowd went wild. The bull spun around and twisted and bucked to try and get him off, but Jayme stayed on.*

*Every second was a second closer, the dust rose, and the slobber was flung from the bull's mouth in anger, this beast knew his job and he was mad as hell that this human was still on board.*

*At eight seconds the crowd erupted and stood on their feet cheering Jayme on, me included. Happy tears welled in my eyes, everyone knew he had it in the bag and the ride was faultless. He had his hat-trick, Three-time Australian National Champion bull rider, I was so happy I could burst.*

*But then everything slowed down, and the world fell away.*

*The cheering stopped and the bull continued to buck. Jayme's rope hand was stuck, his hand was jammed, and he couldn't free himself. He was being flung like a rag doll from one side of the bull to the other and all the while Jayme was frantically trying to undo himself.*

*My hands and my heart went to my mouth as he was finally ejected only to be thrown into the bulls' path. I watched in horror when he didn't try to get up, he didn't try to get out of the way and he didn't even try to roll into a ball, his reflexes were always so quick, he was still flat on his back, motionless.*

*"No! No! No!" I shouted.*

*I climbed up onto the arena fence, not thinking of the danger I'd put myself in with the bull still loose. I was halfway over, when the crowd gasped, everything fell silent and I watched on helplessly.*

*The bull had bucked right over the top of Jayme completely ignoring the clown and the pickup riders trying to distract him from his target. What happened next was the thing that nightmares were made of.*

*The bull put a foot right through Jayme's face guard, the small steel cage was no match for the combined weight and velocity that it was subjected to.-*

TRANSLATION:

Moja kwa wewe - **One for you**

na moja kwa ajili yangu - **and one for me**

Yeye harufu nzuri haina yeye Pragtig - **He smells good doesn't he Pragtig**

Mtu hivyo shauku Saanastia hii lakini hivyo hasira juu ya maisha, kufikiria ambao angekuwa kama angeweza kuchanganya hiyo na alimpenda maisha. Sasa kwa kuwa itakuwa ni kitu - **A man so passionate about Saanastia but so angry about life, imagine who he'd be if he could combine that and love life. Now that would be something**

Je, si unataka kula kitu wewe silly tembo - **Don't you want to eat something you silly elephant**

Familia yako wameondoka wewe mengi - **Your family have left you plenty**

# Chapter 17

I tasted the blood on the inside of my mouth where my lower teeth had cut through the delicate flesh.

"...Anna?"

Rolling my lips into my mouth, I swallowed down the iron taste, shaking my head and taking a long breath though my nose to clear the thoughts and emotions that rose from reliving the heartbreak of Jayme's death yet again.

"Anna. Did you hear me?" Lloyd shook me gently. "Are you ok?" He asked, the worry clearly evident in his tone.

"Yeah," I answered vaguely, nodding my head. Pragtig nudged me with her trunk, "I heard you."

Giving the elephant a rub, before I wrapped my arms around her trunk for one last hug to say goodbye. "If only I had parents and a boyfriend to go home to, hey Pragtig?" I said into her trunk quietly and under my breath.

"What was that?" Lloyd asked.

I wasn't about to repeat myself, so I turned away from him.

"Thank you for the coat," I said quietly, before I shrugged out of it and hung it over a rail. "Please send the bill to my account."

Squeezing through the fence, Kabri, who had been standing there awkwardly handed me the shoes I'd left there earlier.

I thanked him.

Lloyd insisted that Kabri escort me back. I didn't argue with him and he was left standing there looking on with Pragtig giving a loud snort in agitation.

The sun had just risen over trees and it wasn't until I thanked Kabri for dropping me off in the pool area, that I finally managed to see though the haze in my mind. I checked my phone and kicked myself again when I saw the umpteen messages I'd missed and that I'd managed to flick it on silent without knowing. So, the first thing I did was text Carley and let her know that I was both sorry and okay and that I needed to have a little more time to myself.

After a little while and when I managed to collect my thoughts somewhat, it dawned on me that the last week had made the last three years of my life pale by comparison.

And while I didn't want to be living on a knife edge every minute, this was the first time in my life that I actually felt there was something missing and that I couldn't go on like I had been, just marking time and treading water. I needed more purpose then just zooming around in a flying egg beater.

Of course, I had Pete and Rach and I imagined they were like family; they were my connection with Jayme, but I wasn't so sure if that was the best thing anymore and they weren't blood.

Then there was Uncle Kyle and Aunt Rose, but things went south there in the naivety of my youth. They were my adoptive parents. What did they mean to me and did I love them like a daughter would?

I just couldn't be sure.

Of course I had a bond with them. Aside from our isolated life on the station I knew nothing of them outside of that. It just never came up. I was always so busy helping them run the place when I was there and when I wasn't, I was at boarding school, so I guess I didn't really know any better.

I was a content kid for the most part, only becoming 'difficult' for want of a better word when Jayme crossed my path.

So, who were they then? Who were my adoptive parents? Why hadn't it ever been an issue? And why was it an issue now?

I wasn't sure how long I'd been there going over it again and again, but I was saved from it all when I heard Carley call out, "There you are!"

Looking up from my reverie, there she was bounding across the grass with Alan strolling some distance behind her with his hands in the pockets of his khakis.

"Hey! You look like you've... just had a roll in the hay," she said giggling at her own humour.

"Thank you, captain obvious," I said to her, only just registering what I must look like.

"You know you had us all so bloody worried, A." She said, flopping down on the bench beside me.

"Sorry, the night kind of ended early and you guys were... you know and I..." I said with a shrug, "needed to find something to do."

"So, you thought it was a good idea to sleep out there in the wilds of Africa?" She asked.

I stared at her and blinked, thinking back over the hours that led me to this.

"Agh" she threw her arms up in exasperation "Only you, Anna only you," she said before wrapping her said arms around me tightly. "Don't you ever do that to me again!"

Alan sauntered up to us.

"Hi Alan," I said waving sheepishly, difficult to do while Carley still had my arms pinned to my side.

"What is it about you Aussie girls" he shook his head, "that turns our whole world on its head the moment you set foot in it?"

"What can I say," I said, when Carley let me go, wrinkling her nose, "it's a gift."

Alan gave me a jovial look and Carley smiled up at him briefly before turning back to me.

"Anna you smell like a barn," she said, screwing up her face dramatically. "Alan's gonna go finish some business in town so he'll be giving us a lift to the airport."

She stood up and went straight to Alan's side. He wrapped his arm around her and kissed her temple.

"Cool." I nodded, "good to see you've got it all worked out." I got up, realising how stiff I actually was from my impromptu overnight camp.

I stretched and my joints cracked, one long hot shower coming up, I thought to myself and the three of us trudged back to the resort.

Carley sent Alan away to get some food for me while we continued our way back up to our room and once there, Carley whirled on me and asked simply, "What's going on with you lately?"

I shrugged, "I dunno," I said with a sigh, "This place Carley... I don't know what it is but there's something about it. It's making me dream again, feel stuff, something about it just sweeps me away," I replied wistfully.

"I bet it's not just this place that's sweeping you away." Carley said, mumbling under her breath, before giving me a pointed look.

"What?" I asked, having some idea what she said, but preferring to remain wilfully ignorant. What would be the point investing in that train of thought anyway?

"Never mind," she said, knowingly.

I grumbled, shaking my head at her, before I pushed past her and headed to the bathroom. I took the opportunity to fill her in on my phone call with Pete and that I had actually made the effort to call Hidden Valley and questioned what the chances where that the old's happened to be on holiday too.

I also apologised again for worrying her at that hour of the morning while she helped me pull the remaining hay from my hair.

"Well, if nothing else, you won't forget this place in a hurry," Carley said convincingly.

"You can say that again but seriously, I think Lloyd was right, I feel like I've been a freaking magnet for drama ever since I've been here," I sighed.

Carley chuckled, shaking her head and said, "Well, think about it this way when you average it over your lifetime, I think it about evens out in the grand scheme of things."

I nodded but couldn't shake that feeling I hadn't reached my quota yet.

"There you go, I think that's all of it," she said, pulling that last bit of crap out of my hair.

She left me to it and before too long, I was squeaky clean, fed and we had about an hour to kill before it was time for us to make tracks.

Carley and Alan were all over each other and I was starting to get thoroughly nauseated by it, "Ugh, I'll wait for you downstairs," I said, scooting around the room to gather my things.

"Sorry," they both said at once, while I opened the door and rolled my luggage out into the hall.

I smirked at them and shook my head doubtfully. "No you're not."

They didn't deny it.

"I'll see you in a bit, don't get too carried away," but before I even made it through the door, they were at it again. I let out a sigh of exasperation before closing the door behind me with a soft click.

A movement caught my attention through the huge windows, there was a man in a harness washing them from outside. I caught his eye and we waved at each other before I cast my eye over the landscape beyond. Unfortunately there were no elephants to be seen.

Tearing my eyes from the scene and admonishing myself for my heart's involuntary wistful flutter, I forced myself to turn away and make my way downstairs.

Wheeling my luggage, I took the elevator for the first time and headed to reception asking them if they wouldn't mind looking after my bags while I filled in my last hour.

"Sure, just bring them around here," the girl said from behind the reception desk. She had two of her fingers in a splint and I surmised that she was the one who slammed her fingers in a car door the other day and I winced thinking about it.

"Thanks, Natalie," I said after reading her name-tag, "Does Martha happen to be in?" I asked, still needing to apologise to her.

"She's out at the moment but should be back soon." Natalia smiled warmly.

"Thanks, I'll check in again shortly." I said not wanting to miss her. "Is the restaurant open?" I asked, wanting to stay close.

"The café section is open all day, I'll let Martha know where to find you as soon as she gets back if you like, it's Anna, isn't it?" Natalie asked, scribbling on a notepad.

"Um, yeah," I said, smiling nervously, "I guess my reputation precedes me," I said coyly, dropping my eyes to the floor.

"You have made quite an impression around here," she agreed knowingly.

I cringed at the thought that I might be the subject of entertainment during the staff breaks for some time to come.

"You did amazing the other day, getting Fred out safely, I don't think something like that will be forgotten in a hurry. You're like, my hero," she said with complete sincerity.

"Oh man," I felt the heat burn my face, as I was rendered speechless with her compliment.

"Seriously, you go girl, I always wanted to be a mechanic, but my mum almost had a conniption, so here I am," she said and then held up her hand, "and I'm a klutz." Leaning forward and dropping her voice, "I got this when I was fixing my boyfriend's car and the wrench slipped. Shhhh" she said placing her index finger over her lips.

"You could still be a mechanic, it's never too late you know," I said, encouraging her. "We can do almost anything, the bumps and bruises just give you character."

The phone rang, Natalie smiled and mouthed her thanks before she answered it. I gave her a wink and took my leave to go upstairs.

I bought a hot chocolate and a muffin before sitting out in the alfresco area overlooking the animal enclosure. With no trace of the elephants, there was only the rhythmical clanking sound of the large water cannons wetting down the enclosure and the expansive home paddock.

The air smelt delicious, like the ozone after it rains, it wasn't the first time that I had a pang of longing over this place and it probably wouldn't be the last.

It also wasn't the first time I compared it to how I remembered Hidden Valley. North West Queensland didn't have that same draw for some reason, it was beautiful in its own right, but didn't hold onto my heart the way the Kimberley did. Hidden Valley was my sort of country, this was my sort of country.

I wasn't sure how long I'd been staring out over the landscape beyond the fence line, when Martha dragged a chair from under the table before sitting down.

"Natalie said you were looking for me?" Martha asked.

"Yeah" I said, looking back out to the grassy plains before pulling my gaze away and focussing my attention back on Martha.

I smiled as she tucked into a slice of mud cake and I thought I'd take advantage while she still had her mouth full.

"I'm sorry I made such a nuisance of myself this morning, I didn't mean to fall asleep and..."

Martha waved me off trying to swallow her cake too quickly, so she took a sip of coffee to wash it down and used the napkin to dab at the corners of her mouth. "While it may not have been ideal dear, in the end there was no harm done and you got some time with Pragtig."

The memory brought a smile to my face. "She's amazing," I breathed.

"Yes, she is," she said reaching over to pat my hand.

"I'm so going to miss her." I looked out over the enclosure, "I'm going to miss this whole place, it's been life changing."

"Oh? How so?" Martha asked.

"Martha, my life has stood still for three years since my boyfriend died."

There. I said it.

"Oh sweetheart," Martha's eyes grew wide and she looked devastated, but I dismissed her with a wave of my hand, I didn't need her sympathy although I did need to continue.

I ran my finger along the rim of my empty mug and took a deep breath, "I've never really talked about it outside of the people who needed to know. I've been going through the motions, doing the same thing day in day out, I used to have all these dreams you know?"

Martha nodded but stayed quiet.

"When I get home, I'm going to do some soul searching, I don't think I want to still be doing the same thing for another three years." I said, admitting it more to myself. Martha had this knack for making me feel at ease and drawing stuff out of me that even Carley couldn't.

"Well good for you," Martha gave me some encouragement, before reaching out and patting my forearm. "What do you think you want to do?"

I shrugged. "I have no bloody idea, maybe I'll do something with animals, go to Uni, I have no clue where to start but I definitely want to do something more meaningful then ferrying tourists or chasing cows."

"You don't want to fly anymore?"

"Oh no, there's no danger of me giving that up," I grinned, "choppers are in my blood now and maybe I'll have to sell mine to fund the next step if I need to, but I recon I'll still fly enough hours to keep current and stay sane." I chuckled a little.

"Well you're young, you have plenty of time to figure it out."

"Hmmm," I hummed, checking the time on my phone, "Carley will be surfacing soon...I hope."

"Yes, her and Alan, have certainly hit it off," Martha agreed.

"Yeah, she's coming back you know," Martha nodded, obviously having heard, I laughed, shaking my head, "sometimes I wish I had her confident attitude. She doesn't hesitate." I said before I noticed Martha looking up over my head. Announcing his arrival by clearing his throat, I froze knowing exactly who was standing behind me.

"Lloyd darling!" Martha's face lit up.

I turned my head and nodded at him with a tight smile.

"Anna." Lloyd acknowledged with a curt nod of his own.

He was standing with his hands shoved in the pockets of his work pants, he had on a black T-shirt with an open camouflage long sleeved shirt over the top and his usual peaked cap pulled down low, "Natalie sent me, our ten o'clock's arrived early." He mumbled.

"Oh my," Martha stood and looked at her watch, "he's keen," she turned to me, her eyes alight with excitement, "our new pilot," she explained.

I nodded and stood with Martha. It was almost time to go anyway. "Thanks for your hospitality, I-I'm sorry I was any trouble it wasn't my in..."

"Anna dear, stop that, it's been a pleasure, really," she said opening her arms for a hug.

She gave such nice hugs, it was odd since I didn't really know her, but I think I would probably miss her.

"You look after yourself okay?" I nodded on her shoulder, catching Lloyd's blue gaze, before he looked away, rocking on the balls of his feet impatiently.

"I hope you find your pilot." I said while I collected my backpack that also served as hand luggage.

Glancing at Lloyd, I forced a nervous smile on my face before my eyes settled more comfortably on Martha and I pointed to the exit. "Well then, I'll just..."

I felt Lloyd touch my elbow, "Can I talk to you a moment?"

My eyes found Martha for support, she smiled broadly and nodded.

"Sure." I said.

"Maybe you'll visit us again?" Martha asked hopefully, her eyes glassy.

I shrugged, "maybe, you just never know."

Martha smiled wistfully and rubbed the top of my arm, "Well, I certainly hope so, Lloyd I'll see you downstairs."

I watched her until she disappeared from sight through the restaurant doors, delaying the inevitable for as long as I could.

"Anna."

Lloyds voice sounded deep, I always got a rush when he spoke my name, even in anger, which was more often than not. I took a deep breath and braced myself before facing him.

He waited a moment to collect his thoughts, shifting uneasily and licking his full lips, I couldn't help but stare at his mouth as he worked up to talking.

"Uh," he sighed as he removed his cap, to run his free hand through his hair before replacing it. Looking everywhere but my face he said, "about what I said earlier, I-I had no idea and..." he blew out a frustrated breath, "and I'm sorry."

He had heard after all.

I nodded my acceptance. "You were right though." I said.

He quit avoiding my gaze and raised his eyebrows in question.

"I shouldn't have put myself in that position, I don't know what has gotten into me while I've been here, I'm never so... defiant. Ever."

He quirked an eyebrow at me in surprise and I could tell he was fighting a losing battle with the corners of his mouth.

"I find that very hard to believe Ms Stedman, you have been just about the most unruly woman I've ever met."

I stifled a laugh, "Yeah well, believe it. This place..." I said looking out over the view again and shaking my head. "I don't know, it sounds lame but there's something about it, maybe it's in the water," I joked.

Since we both had somewhere to be, we simultaneously made the move to head off.

I was shocked when I heard him laugh, "Well, for what it's worth," he reached over and touched my elbow again. I stopped and turned, "I really am sorry about what I said and..." He paused, "thanks again for the other day. With Fred. You were amazing out there."

He was so close, and he had me stunned like a roo in headlights.

"No problem, it's fine..." I said before my words faded and I was left staring at him a beat longer than what would have been considered appropriate.

Lloyd was first to snap out of it and he nodded towards the restaurant exit and said, "C'mon, I'll walk you out."

I nodded, tickled pink that Lloyd and I might actually be parting on better terms. We walked out together till we made it to the landing.

Lloyd stopped suddenly in his tracks.

"Shit," I heard him hiss under his breath.

Following his glare to the floor below, I recognised the hulking frame of Cyrus Veldsmaan. Lloyd pinched the bridge of his nose before taking a deep breath and trudging down the stairs. I descended behind him, concentrating on where I was putting my feet. One - to make sure I didn't make an idiot of myself and two - so I could avoid eye contact with Cyrus, who was a really intimidating man that I had decided I wouldn't feel terrible for not saying my farewells to.

I was fully intending to go my separate way as soon as I hit the bottom of the stairs, but unfortunately Cyrus had a different plan and deliberately stepped into my path.

Coming to a halt in front of him, I glanced to Lloyd with a questioning look who in turn appeared undeniably apologetic.

"Ah the beautiful Anna." He said, making it impossible for me to avoid any sort of interaction with him.

"Mr Veldsmaan, how nice to see you again," I said.

I forced a smile before I decided to thrust a hand out for him to shake and keep things politely formal.

"Anna, that will simply not do," he said, stepping in, and placing his hands on my upper arms.

Looking at me closely with his narrowed eyes, one blue and one brown. It was quite disconcerting – more due to his proximity than his rare condition - and I wanted to reel back, but he held me fast. Quickly drawing me in, he kissed me on both cheeks before I knew what was happening.

I was left blinking dumbly and struggled to keep the shock from my face as he beamed arrogantly at me, but I noted the underlying ire that subtly radiated from him.

"Now I have kissed a real life hero!" He continued in a boisterous fashion and loosening his hold.

I cut off a nervous laugh. "It was nothing really," I said, trying to play it down and took the opportunity to step back to put some distance between us.

Feeling the tension thick in the air, I glanced between the two men, who were now eyeing each other off like a pair of dominant bulls.

"I beg to differ Anna," he said, keeping his eyes firmly on Lloyd, "You have certainly made a substantial impact on Saanastia. Hasn't she my boy?" He asked in a somewhat malevolent tone.

"Hm," Lloyd uttered, his mouth forming a lopsided, wry smile and not agreeing either way, "to what do we owe the pleasure, Cyrus?" He asked, clearly not meaning a word.

Cyrus shrugged casually and guffawed. "Oh nothing too alarming boy!"

The outburst garnered the attention of a few patrons and I noticed Lloyd bristle.

"I heard Anna was leaving today and just wanted to say goodbye in person, that's all," Cyrus said feigning innocence.

"I appreciate your neighbourly consideration Cyrus," Lloyd said with a suspicious drawl, "but I'm sure Ms Stedman would prefer leaving without all the fanfare."

"Well, I think it's a little late for that don't you think Lloyd?" Cyrus asked in a mocking tone.

Lloyd didn't answer, but did continue to glare, I could hear the acid in their words. There was certainly no love lost between these two.

I had to wonder what was with all of Cyrus' theatrics?

Whatever it was, coupled with what I'd overheard the other night on the balcony, Saanastia was definitely under some sort of peril, and I was willing to bet that Cyrus was up to his neck in it.

I shook my head, irritated at myself. None of your business Stedman. Why did I even care? I was leaving in a few short minutes and this drama would soon be behind me. It wasn't a secret that much of Africa had its issues but to see some of them right under my nose made it all too real.

"Hey chicka, time to go!" Carley and Alan walked past the reception desk to drop off the room keys.

"Be there in a sec!" I called, before turning back to the two men, "Um, I guess that's my cue to go."

"Yes, yes, it has been a pleasure to see you again young lady, I hope that you enjoyed your adventure and that you continue to have safe travels," Cyrus said oddly.

His strange manner didn't sit right with me, and I couldn't wait to take my leave. "Thanks and bye," I said.

"Seeya," I said, offering an innocuous farewell to Lloyd.

Lloyd gave me a quick nod before I headed towards the reception desk to join my two friends.

I couldn't help but look over my shoulder one more time, Lloyd continued to stay rigid and Cyrus looked like the smug bastard he was, murmuring something that I couldn't hear, before Lloyd ushered Cyrus away and the two men headed towards the boardroom.

"What was all that about? You been holding out on me Stedman?" Carley asked, raising a brow at me suspiciously.

"I really have no idea Carley," I shook my head.

# Chapter 18

It was Autumn in Europe, so I had assumed that the weather would still be fair most of the time, probably a bit like a Perth winter. Jeans and jacket weather, so I packed accordingly.

We would be sailing on one of those scenic boat cruises and once we boarded and set our things down in our room, we took an organised tour of Amsterdam.

The canals in Amsterdam were lined with houseboats. I couldn't for the life of me understand how anyone would want to live on one forever and a day and not actually go anywhere. They were cute, brightly decorated boats in all shapes and sizes, like a floating caravan that became frozen in through the winter. But for all the tight living that seemed to be the norm for this city, the pastries in the cafés and on the board-walks more than made up for it. If only for one short day.

My eyes just about dropped out of my head when I was told that a few of the oldest buildings were built of foundations made on hide, and I mean leather, the cow skin kind!

After the tour and dodging the almost exclusive bicycle traffic on the way back to the ship, we made it in plenty of time for our induction and set off from the dock in the late afternoon heading inland on the mighty Rhine River.

The landscape started out with flat as a tack farmland, dotted with the dairy herds of Friesian cows grazing the green pastures.

In between, we came across a couple of towns and near the end of the day, we finally saw some of those cliché Dutch windmills, which weren't actually as common as I expected them to be.

Much to my pleasure, the boat had a couple of restaurants on board and the food was divine. We had our first delicious meal watching the landscape pass.

Being on holiday proved to make me somewhat inactive for the most part, I was a fit woman, and worked out a few times a week, so I was stoked that there was a running track on the sun deck and a gym where I could spend some time on my own without Carley's increasingly mopey face.

She missed Alan like crazy and when she wasn't occupied with the tour, she chucked a sad, which really did my head in.

Pay back's a bitch I guess, but at least I could get away from it and think about my own longings while I ran around the track.

I could imagine two mopey women together would only lead to a shitty holiday and I was determined to enjoy it, regardless of what I assumed was me just being homesick.

The entire tour shaped up to be second to none and our time was split between cruising on the water and exploring the various sights on land.

Germany was amazing and after eating up a storm at the perfectly preserved medieval town of Rothenburg and Marksburg Castle in Cologne, it was like we'd travelled back in time while continuing to discover the myriad of impressive castles that jutted out from the hilly landscape.

And I had no idea that there were so many vineyards in the area. The vines were ancient and I wondered how the wine fared against the Aussie stuff - just out of interest. It turned out that many decades ago some of the variety of these vines had actually made their way down under.

History abounded as we continued on and then we finally got to Vienna.

We were treated to the dulcet tones of a concert at the 'Majestic Palais Liechtenstein, featuring the music of Strauss and Mozart'... that's what the brochure said anyway. I wasn't a music buff, but it was nice and a great excuse for Carley to dress me up again. She was pretty smug about packing that damn bridesmaids dress that's for sure. I think I'd be wearing it out at this rate.

"Isn't there some rule about never wearing stuff like this more than once?" I asked her.

"Psht. Pu-lease, you're on a different continent, so it doesn't count and you're wearing the bolero over the top, it's a different look." She waved her hand at me as I slipped on my equally worn-in silver heels. The bolero was gorgeous, she picked it up when we were left to our own devices in Cologne, I swear the girl should have made Paris her destination.

But it was the Spanish Riding School that I was really looking forward to, watching the parade of highly trained classical Lipizzaner stallions had me transfixed as their handlers recreated the movements and airs above ground. These movements were reminiscent of wartime, when the horse was as important as any weapon in a country's defence.

The indoor ménage was beautiful, built in marble with grand columns and fancy galleries where society's upper class once sat, there was even a huge chandelier strung from the ornately carved ceiling.

I couldn't help but wonder though if these horses were ever given the opportunity to just be horses or were allowed their head and gallop in an open area, like Blue and I did back home.

I missed Blue a little bit more after that.

Our last stop was Budapest, in fact two cities separated by the Danube River, and I got my horse fix here too, because the streets were crawling -

relatively speaking that is, with horse drawn carriages. Though, I don't know if I would have left the driver's seat and just let a pair of horses stand around untied in a public street, but each to their own I guess.

It was the last night of our time away and we were back in a standard hotel room, ready to leave for the airport early the following morning.

"I think I need a holiday from my holiday A," Carley said later when we retired to our beds.

"I know, right?" I said.

"Hey Carley?" I asked a few minutes later, looking away from the telly to where she was reclining on her bed, her eyes heavy.

"Hmm?" She turned toward me, snuggling into her pillow.

"Thanks," I said sincerely.

"Eh," she said, waving me off.

"No really, it's really given me something to think about, there's more stuff out there I want to do with my life. The trip, it's given me a new lease or something..." I sighed thinking of my African experience in particular.

Carley smiled. "Time to kick-start your life Stedman, and I'm stoked, really. You are meant for more than just flying those whirligigs day in day out."

"I'm not giving up flying!" I said, only mildly affronted.

"No, but you don't need to live and breathe it every waking moment either, I'm glad you're finally seeing that."

I nodded. "And you?" I asked

"I'll be back on a plane ASAP," she said with conviction.

"So, you're really going back? Are you sure?" I asked her, wondering if moving so fast was a good idea.

Then I told myself to shut it. As if I was anywhere near qualified to question that.

"Uh-huh." Carley yawned inelegantly. "Life's too short Anna, what if Alan's the one?"

"What if he isn't?" I said, blurting it out before I could stop myself.

Carley blew out a frustrated breath. "Seriously Anna. You've got stop over thinking things girl and go with your heart sometimes. I'd hate myself if I ended up wondering for the rest of my life what if and miss out on what could've been the best thing that ever happened to me."

Carley pulled the covers tightly under her chin, "Now. Go to sleep," she said, with finality in her tone.

Easier said than done.

# Chapter 19

The long flight back to Oz was uneventful and we went our separate ways once we reached Perth saying our final goodbyes before I headed back to Queensland, my life and my not so little boy, Blue.

The first thing I did was sleep thanks to my jet lag.

The second thing I did was saddle up, go on a long trail ride and hitting the beach to blow away the cobwebs, followed by getting my stuff together for a two-week stint on Umbar Station, which was about three hundred clicks inland from Mackay.

I had two days to myself before I had to show my face at work, so once I had sufficiently caught up with my life, I decided to get the third thing out of the way and call Hidden Valley again.

I wasn't sure how long I stared at my phone, but I sure was procrastinating over it as per usual. I took a deep breath and pressed the connect button, a surge of apprehension prickled through me while I waited.

"Hidden Valley," Aunt Rose answered the phone.

I felt with some relief that it wasn't my Uncle, but I still had the need to pause and collect my thoughts.

"Hello?" She asked again after I took a beat too long.

"Hey." I managed to squeak out.

"Anna?"

Her voice set off another wave of butterflies.

"Yeah, yeah it's me." I nodded, knowing she couldn't see me.

It was her turn to pause but I waited it out. I actually half expected her to hang up.

"Are you okay?" She asked.

"Of course," I answered. "Don't worry, I don't want anything, I just thought it might be time to bury the hatchet," I added, perhaps a little too quickly before thinking how that would sound.

"Anna," she said with another pause.

I could hear her take a deep breath and then let it out slowly.

"I am glad you rang. What I meant to say was how are you? I heard from Bill that you called the other day?"

"Yeah," I continued with the stilted conversation, "He said you were away? Apparently, we were both on holiday at the same time."

"Yes," she said quietly before she rushed out, "Oh you know me Anna, I climb the walls here sometimes and I needed a little time away in the big smoke."

"Yeah, you're lucky Uncle Kyle agreed to it at this time of the year, how'd you manage that?" I asked knowing they were wrapping up cattle season, ready for the wet.

"I can be pretty persuasive, and Bill has really stepped up over the last few years, he's been taking on more of a management role."

"I see," I paused again. "Are you guys thinking of moving on or something?"

"Not really, but we're not getting any younger you know," Aunt Rose said, warming a little.

"I guess." I said, having to agree. It was pretty hard work on the station, so it was understandable that they'd want to take it back a notch.

"Hey," Rose said, "I, uh... I heard about Jayme, I'm really sorry about that. You know how the bush telegraph is," she said awkwardly.

She knew?... They knew? ... Yet I never heard from them when they found out?

That knowledge went down like a lead balloon and I wasn't particularly overjoyed how this conversation was going but knew that I needed to make some sort of effort. I wasn't going to be the one to continue being stubborn about it because I knew I'd done enough of that over the years.

However, I did want to change the subject.

"Uh, yeah. Cheers for that," I said dismissively, not wanting to dwell. "Is Uncle Kyle there?" I asked.

"No, no," she took a moment, "he's out with Bill... But I'll let him know you called, if you want?" Her words were tentative.

"Sure, yeah, do that," I said, happy to leave the ball in their court.

"Okay." Aunt Rose said, not exactly spilling over with enthusiasm about it but then again, I wasn't overly surprised by that.

After another long pause I said, "Alright then, well, I guess I better go."

"Thanks, for ringing Anna," Aunt Rose said, actually sounding genuine.

"Yeah, sure... bye then," I hung up not completely sure of what to make of it all.

I took a deep breath and stared at my phone for a bit. I was still miffed that they had never gotten in touch with me when they knew that Jayme had passed away, there wasn't even a note of condolence of any sort.

Maybe I should have told them myself... But I was young and dumb.

Would've, could've, should've. But didn't.

I sighed again.

Nothing it seemed, had really changed, not my feelings, not my indifference, nor theirs.

We'd see if I'd get a call from Uncle Kyle. Not that it mattered as much to me anymore, I'd held out the olive branch, and while it could have gone a lot worse, I certainly didn't feel that the call was exactly a welcome back to the family kind of interaction either.

So be it. I'd just get on with my life, work for Pete for the moment and see where I'd go from there.

The next morning my workplace had already started as I arrived at the STC car park. A Cessna 206 Stationair spluttered to life on the other side of the mesh fence and gave me the signal that I had to get my head back in the game. I pulled my duffle bag from the back of the Ute and I headed towards the hangar, trying to pull myself together.

It would be business as usual.

The huge hangar doors were already cracked open just enough to squeeze through and there she was. My chopper was painted the same blue as the colour of my horse's eye, icy cool with his show name 'Blue Contact' written on the side. It connected the two most precious things in my life.

Jayme's name had joined Blue's with the dates he both entered and left my life. I pulled the covers off the small bulbous cabin, before levering the dolly under the skids. Once I pushed the hangar doors a few metres apart, I towed the R22 out and parked her up. She weighed less then Blue wringing wet, so even a mere slip of a girl had no problem pulling her around the tarmac.

I felt the routine relax me and my mind replaced my wayward thoughts with the job at hand. This was where I felt familiarity.

The fuel truck was spot on time and came alongside to fill up the R22 before I headed to the office to file a flight plan.

Pete looked up from his desk and grinned. "Anna Spanna! How ya hanging?" He asked sliding his chair back, standing and opening his arms for a hug.

"Anna Spanna? Really?" I asked, before being engulfed in a hug, laughing together.

Letting go of one another, I answered with another silly, corresponding question. "How about low and a little to the left?" Leaving Pete to chuckle some more before we both sat down and I filed my plan.

It felt good to be at work again, get some dirt under my nails and some flight hours in.

On the way out to Umbar, the lush hinterland gave way to more arid country once I flew over the Great Divide. Dark green became light green, then yellow and finally red dirt, the familiarity calming me as it was similar to Kimberley country in colour, but the vegetation was different and it was missing that special something.

Saanastia had that something too, something that was never far from my thoughts.

Three hours later, I was refuelling again at Umbar Station's airstrip. There was no driveway service this time, all I had was a two hundred litre drum, a hand pump and some muscle.

It was all part of the job.

Shaun, the station manager gave me the last camp coordinates and I was off to find me some moo cows.

For a relatively cheap machine - comparatively speaking - The Robinson R22 were pretty much designed to be like the buzz box of the helicopter industry. Simple, reliable and then chuck it out before it wore out and cost too much to patch together. You could buy a good one for a couple of hundred thousand and you could even pick the things up for under fifty, but they were almost guaranteed to be timed-out.

However, I had a good one, I bought it with only a couple of hundred hours on the dial and it was still a few years away from costing me big money for its 2200hr rebuild with the conservative three hundred hours a year it was getting now. The R22 was the backbone of the aerial mustering industry, there was nothing as manoeuvrable or as tough.

They would put up with a lifetime of hard flying and not have continual downtime for regular scheduled maintenance or constant breakdowns, even though 'technically' they weren't designed for it.

So that's how the next two weeks unfolded, up at a sparrow's fart and buzz like an annoying bot fly for half a day. The rest of it was spent either setting up camp or doing those odd jobs that made the station turn over. It was hot, dirty work and every night, I got to camp more than eager to eat, clean up and be nestled in a swag under the stars or spend the night in the donga back at the homestead by nine.

I don't know if it was the red country, the clean air, the night sounds or what, but every morning that I woke from sleeping under the stars, I'd vaguely remember that I'd been dreaming of Saanastia, of Pragtig and that man with the icy eyed glare.

The longer I stayed at Umbar, the keener I became to get back to STC, and for the life of me I couldn't figure out why, I was always happiest out in the bush.

By the time my stint was up, and the last truck had left the yards, I was champing at the bit to get back to base and wasted no time in packing and refuelling before I hit the hay that evening. That way I was ready to leave at first light.

The next morning, I didn't even have breakfast and was starving by the time I landed at STC.

Being due for a hundred hourly, I left the chopper on the tarmac and I'd wait to wash her until the engineer had finished with his greasy mitts.

Needing to clean myself up a little more thoroughly after roughing it for the last two weeks, I went home. I might have been comfortable with lukewarm bush showers in the tropics, only armed with a razor and a bar of soap, but I still enjoyed a long soak in a tub every now and then with all the options.

By the time the water had turned my hands to prunes, it didn't have quite the effect on me that I had hoped, and I still didn't feel quite myself. At first, I put it down to feeling homesick, but that wasn't it because I was still feeling it and I was in fact at home.

I had too much time on my hands in the few days I had off and I kept thinking of Aunt Rose and Uncle Kyle, (who, incidentally, hadn't called yet) about Africa and where the heck I was heading. It seemed that my compass was unserviceable for the moment and the needle was spinning around aimlessly. Only Blue lifted me from my funk for a few hours every day.

"Hey there Anna, why the long face," Pete interrupted my thoughts when I was back at work again a few days later.

Pete, my caring brother from another mother - and father.

I sighed and shrugged and must've looked like I was twelve or something. "Nothin'," I said.

"You've been quieter than normal lately, so don't give me nothin'. Did something happen while you were away that's got ya all tied in a knot?" He asked, ever observant.

Yes.

I shrugged again and then my stomach rumbled, causing me only mild mortification, because it echoed through the whole office.

Pete grinned, "How about you let me get this paperwork sorted and then I'll take you out to eat, can't have my pilots starving and fainting on me, now can I?"

"Psh," I huffed at him, "I do not faint Pete."

"Well, too bad I'm feeding you anyway and while I'm doing that, you can tell me all about this holiday you went on okay?" He glared at me pointedly.

He wasn't really asking.

"Do I have to?" I said with a whine.

"Yep," he said giving me a look that left no room for argument.

"You're not gonna let it go, are you?" I asked.

"Nope," he said, popping the p.

I sighed, "Okay then."

Half an hour later we were at the airport café and I was telling him about everything we saw while boating through Europe.

"Hang on a sec, back up the truck Stedman, where's that excitement I heard in your voice when you were talking about Africa and you sounded just as worked up as you did that time you nailed your tail rotor strike training?" He asked, sitting back and eyeing me expectantly.

I made myself busy pretending to be fascinated with my paper serviette and contemplating how, or even if I was going to say what was really on my mind. After Pete patiently waited for me, I drew a deep breath and let it out again in a low whistle, shaking my head as my memories flooded my mind.

"Anna?" Pete asked again.

My face twisted in the discomfort of what I was about to reveal, "I don't know Pete. I mean the stuff that happened there was really life altering. I think… and please don't take this the wrong way, because I'll always love Jay with all my heart, but I think I'm ready to move on, you know?" I explained, raising my gaze to gauge Pete's reaction.

"Wow." Pete sat in amazement. "That's," he paused, "intense," he said nodding in contemplation, looking down at his drink can, which he'd started to turn on its end.

"It's good though." He nodded again, "Real good," he said in an agreeable tone even though he was clearly taken back.

We sat quietly while Pete continued to mull over the news.

Then he straightened and asked, "So, what brought on this epiphany?"

Then I saw a lightbulb go off, when his serious expression turned into one of mirth.

"Anna did you meet a boy?" He asked drawing out the 'oy' with a goading smile.

Shit.

I knew that it was written all over my face, my traitorous blush warmed me from the tip of my head and down to my chest at the mere thought of him.

"It's nothing and it's not as if I'll ever go back there," I mumbled under my breath.

"Oh, I can tell it's not nothing, you've got to remember, I've seen that look on you before," he said emphatically.

Double shit.

He saw through me and everything that I felt. He was one hundred per cent right. Every time I thought about my stay in South Africa, there was this overwhelming connection with every experience I had there. The animals, the land and the beautiful people, and of course Lloyd. I sat a moment and gave a deep sigh in surrender, blowing some stray hair from the front of my face and slumped back in my chair.

"I'm so screwed. That place, it's like it owns me Pete," I said, admitting it out loud for the first time.

"Hm," he hummed, looking thoughtful before glancing at his watch. His eyes grew wide and I knew from that, that we were mercifully late. "You haven't heard the end of this, but right now I own your arse and we've got work to do," he said, getting ready to leave.

I followed suit before getting back to work.

The rest of the day was spent cleaning the hanger until my chopper was ready for a spit and polish, and then I could put her away.

"Plugs in number four were a bit wet Anna, nothing drastic, just check 'em again after your next flight and give me a heads up, I've ordered a new set of rings just in case, so I can change 'em when they get in, it'll probably be okay till the next hundred but..."

"We don't want to drop a cylinder."

He smiled with a wink, Baz didn't cut corners, one cylinder down could mean death at fifty feet and full power, it wasn't worth mucking around with.

"Alright. Now I gotta work on that piece of shit," he nodded fondly at STC's new acquisition, an amphibious De Havilland Beaver, AKA 'The Oil Boat' as he liked to call it.

It was a pet project that he and Pete were restoring. They wanted to branch out and be able get tourists out to islands that were too far for the choppers to fly. There were no runways out there so float planes were the only way to go, but this thing was older than him and I couldn't for the life of me work out why he didn't buy a Grand Caravan or something, I think the silly bugger was a sucker for the grand old birds of the sky.

By the time I'd safely put one baby to bed, it was time to go, and feed my other baby. I needed to spoil the lad with cuddles and the mints he loved so much. I didn't school Blue much anymore, he did everything I asked of him and I just wanted to enjoy our time together now by hitting the trail.

I noted that we were having a full moon that evening, so I decided to go out on a ride that would probably take me longer to get back than the sunlight we had left in the day. There was something to be said for riding at night, there was a special kind of peace that came with it, a trust in my surroundings and also in Blue.

Even with the moon to guide me, I relied on him to look after me. Horses had far better night vision than humans and as always, he never put a foot wrong, not even when a mob of kangaroos bounded off almost from right under our noses.

I sat down with Blue after I gave him his feed and just listened to him eating contently as the crickets, the flying foxes and the frogs made their sounds through anything but the quiet evening.

My phone rang.

Blue raised his head from the feed bucket for a moment to look at his flailing owner, who was scrambling around on his yard floor.

I finally pulled the phone from my jeans and looked at the screen.

After all that, it was an unknown number, but I took the chance and answered it anyway.

"Hello Anna speaking."

Nothing.

"Hello?"

"Anna?" There was a time delay.

"Yes."

"Oh Anna, it's Martha."

# Chapter 20

In the time it took Martha to say those few words, my heart started crashing in my ears. I was both secretly elated that Martha was calling and yet alarmed at the same time by her anxious tone.

"Martha? What's wrong?" I asked, sitting to attention.

"Oh Anna, it's so good to hear your voice sweetheart," Martha said, while her own voice was still pinched but sounding marginally relieved. "How are you dear?" She asked.

"Uh good?" I answered, making it sound more like a question, still a little taken back that she'd called.

After a beat I repeated "Good," again, sounding more sure of myself.

The line was quiet for what seems like ages. "Martha?" I asked, making sure she was still on the line.

"Anna honey, I have some news," she said, her grave tone caused my heart to sink. "It's Pragtig, we've run out of your scent and she won't eat, she's fretting and losing too much weight, and they think that they'll need to make a decision one way or the other soon." All her words running into one another.

"Slow down Martha." I stood up and started to head towards Blue's yard gate. "Are you saying that she might be put down?"

"Y-yes," she said, letting out a stifled sob.

"I see." I breathed out, running my free hand over my face. "And it's really that bad?"

"I'm afraid so, but it's not just Pragtig that's at stake, we rely on her to bring the herd in, Lloyd's worried that the very essence of our Elephant Back Tours are at risk," she said sadly.

The very mention of Lloyd's name sent a flutter through my chest.

"And we've got nothing of yours left that we can use to get her to settle, we used the last bit of your bed sheet a week ago," Martha said, admitting the lengths they had been to.

"Bedsheets? Martha that's kind of... weird," I said screwing up my face.

"It was Kabri's idea. Do you know how hard it was to find those before they were sent away for laundry?" Martha asked, her words quite ridiculous if they weren't so serious.

"Dare I ask?"

"Pragtig sniffed them out of course," Martha said, chuckling humourlessly before she went quiet and then sighed. "Anna, now that she has nothing to scent, we've had to yard her."

"Oh?"

"She started to get disruptive, pacing, roaring, rocking from foot to foot, all in front of the patrons at the restaurant deck, she was beside herself and it's not something that fosters confidence in ecotourism when your animals are clearly suffering..." Martha paused. "We've had no choice but to confine her, it's awful Anna, we think she's going mad. Now she just stands there with her head in a corner up against the barn wall."

A lump formed in my throat, the thought of an animal being so stressed that it would stop eating and stand miserably in a corner was heartbreaking.

"Gosh, I'm so sorry to hear that Martha, I wish there was something I could do, I could send some of my stuff, would that help?"

"That's very sweet dear but, it's only a band aid, even while she had your scent she was off her food, we had to bring hay to her because she wouldn't leave the resort enclosure to forage."

"So, what about the rest of the herd?" I asked suspecting that the wheels had fallen off more than just Pragtig's wagon.

"Well..." Martha started just as I reached my car.

I climbed into the cab and made myself comfortable, settling back into the driver's seat while Martha explained.

I was right, the entire herd dynamic had changed, the new Alpha female Shahara was in charge now that Pragtig had been separated. The staff were stretched even further, they had to close the herd off from free range foraging because they really didn't have any reason to come in and the keepers had to hand feed so that the elephants would be close enough to be convenient for tours.

This was a mess that was wholly created by my visit.

Guilt racked me, there had to be something..."Could you make an appeal to the public? Surely you could get support from those who want to feel warm and fuzzy?" I asked.

"We've looked into that Anna, those elephants aren't part of the rescue centre, they are part of a commercial venture for the resort. I just don't know how long we can go on for before we have to shut up shop, bleeding hearts publicity only gets you so far."

"Well what happened to all that good publicity that you guys got from the rescue?"

"I'm afraid support for that is already waning, we are yesterday's news. Freddy needs to pass a medical and that can't be done until he's recovered. Even then there's no guarantee he'll pass, so he's been grounded indefinitely. And the chopper we have on loan is only a temporary measure and subject to scheduling.

"Lloyd almost had a conniption when we lost a baby elephant to its snare injuries because we couldn't get Jerry out in time before infection set in. The trackers followed it for three days, before the baby finally succumbed and they had to shoot it before the lions got to it."

"I see," I said, in a whisper, feeling totally overwhelmed and helpless by the horrible set of events.

"Martha, why did you really call me? You're the ideas woman, I'm just a simple girl that lives half a world away."

"Anna, you're a chopper pilot with a penchant for big beasts."

"What has that got to do w..."

"Sweetheart for an intelligent girl, you're not being very perceptive," she said gently.

But I was perceptive, I could see where this was heading, but I didn't dare to let my thoughts go there.

"We need you." Martha said in a shaky voice.

"Huh," I uttered under my breath as the realisation hit.

There it was, I was unable to avoid those thoughts any longer.

"We need you," she said again, with conviction, "we need a pilot and we need someone who's good with animals, with Pragtig, to be more specific and you, my dear, are the only person that fits the bill as far as we're concerned."

"We?" I asked, as the enormity of the situation sunk in. "Who's we?"

"Yes we, it was Jerry that planted the seed."

"Hm," I hummed. "I'll need to wrap things up here, I can't just up and leave," I said, feeling torn. I was hesitant to entertain the thought of leaving and equally hesitant not to.

"You said you were ready for something new, this is the perfect opportunity," Martha said, starting to use her magical powers of persuasion.

Was it?

Was this the perfect opportunity?

"Please honey, will you at least consider it? I know it's a big ask, but I'm not above begging here, we're really quite desperate at this point," she said, leaving me with no doubt that they were by the sound of the urgency in her voice.

I leaned back into the head rest. "If you're trying to pull at my heartstrings, they're strumming a tune now."

"I'm not above playing dirty dear."

"I can see that. Look, I will think about it okay?" I'm sure I heard a suppressed squeal through the speaker "But aren't you forgetting a few things?"

"And what might they be?"

"Well for one, there's my Visa and then there's also Blue, my horse, a... and what about Lloyd?" I asked with a stutter. "How would that go down if I showed my face? I'm sure he was pretty relieved that I was finally out of there Martha."

"Honey, all those things can be managed. Let me handle Lloyd, he might be the heart that pumps the blood through Saanastia, but I'm the head that's in control of its best interests. Besides I'm not sure that Lloyd has a better idea, or he'd have had it already.

"And as to the little issue with you being able to work here, don't you worry your pretty head over it, I'll sort something out," she said confidently.

"But..." My argument seemed to rapidly be losing the wind in its sails.

"You've made some good points my dear," she said, cutting me off.

I could almost hear the triumph in her voice.

I sighed heavily with the weight of the position I found myself in.

"Anna. I understand that you feel blind-sided, but what if this is a solution for all of us? What if we can both get something out of it?" She asked, giving me more food for thought.

"Hmmm," I said, while the myriad of thoughts waged battle with the misgivings in my head.

"Anna dear, all I ask is that you keep an open mind, just until I can get a proposal together that you can live with, what do you say?" She asked.

"I say you drive a hard bargain."

Martha paused for a moment. "How about you sleep on it and I'll get back to you as soon as I can. Do we have a deal?"

I sighed, could this be just the thing I needed to move on? I'd be lying if I wasn't excited about the prospect of what this could mean for me, but I was naturally cautious of following my heart and jumping in with two feet. I'd done that before and that didn't go too well.

I tried to push down the thrill I felt bubbling beneath the surface, "Okay Martha, you have a deal."

I heard a sigh of relief. "Thank you."

"Don't thank me yet, Martha I haven't done anything," I said, cautioning her.

"You will, I can feel it in my bones," Martha said, prophetically.

Shaking my head, I had to admire Martha's enthusiasm, "Well, we'll see. Goodnight Martha," I said with finality.

"Goodnight dear," she said, her voice sounding much lighter now, than earlier in our conversation.

Of course over the next couple of days, I was pretty distracted by my thoughts, I made a couple of silly rookie mistakes – nothing serious, just general inefficiency but the boys did notice, because they kept asking me if I was alright.

Chris just shook his head in disappointment, eventually mocking me in a sing-song voice, "those who don't use their heads must use their legs," and drawing out the e's when I had forgotten to bring in a set of logbooks in from the chopper I'd flown that morning.

I scowled at him and not more than a few minutes later, I was caught daydreaming again.

"Here," Chris said, catching my attention shoving a stack of amendments at me, "update these if you're gonna space out like that on company time."

I blinked a few times before narrowing my eyes at him and quietly cursed Pete, who still insisted to do some things old school.

But ultimately, I had to admit Chris was right.

Get it together Stedman.

"Cheers," I said, sarcastically before I spent the rest of the afternoon updating hard copy manuals.

It wasn't until I was eating a chicken salad that evening that I finally received the call I'd been expecting.

"So, what do you have for me?" I asked after the normal salutations.

"Well dear I think what I've come up with will both serve us well and also takes into consideration, your ties in Australia. What do you think of a trial Anna?"

"A trial, how long?" I asked cautiously.

"Well... I was hoping I could snaffle you for three, maybe four months," she asked tentatively, her voice rising an octave when her statement ended more like a question.

I let out a long breath, repeating, "three or four months, three or four months," mentally scrolling through a list of work that I had at STC.

"If I agree Martha, how do we get around the Visa at such short notice?"

"You know the saying it's not what you know...?"

"...But who you know," I finished with her, nodding in agreement, "right," I said, knowing it was probably better not to ask too many questions.

Martha chuckled. "You could live here at the main house, all utilities and food included. I have the chopper lined up ready to go thanks to Freddy and you'll be paid what you get now."

"What about my horse Martha?" I asked.

I couldn't in all conscience go traipsing over to the other side of the world for Pragtig and leave Blue by the wayside. That would be pretty hypocritical.

"Ah yes well, it wouldn't be viable to have him here obviously and I knew he would be the clincher in this deal hon, which is why I thought a trial would be the best way to buy some time while we way up our future options, we will pay for his upkeep in Australia until you decide to go back home."

"I see," I said, realising that there were always compromises to be made and some of us had to make more than others.

"Oh, I know it's not ideal Anna, but it's only for a little whi..."

"No, no, I was just thinking about the expenses, are you sure you'll be able to cover it?"

"Anna dear, with you we'll be in a better position than without. The elephants will be back on track and the boys can finally get back to their jobs properly. Believe you me," Martha said convincingly.

"No pressure or anything huh?" I said cynically.

"None at all dear," Martha said and the hint of irony to her tone was not lost on me. "Ultimately it is your decision of course. I know you need a few days, but I do need an answer soon sweet," then her voice became soft, "I'm not sure you realise just how integral a piece in our puzzle you have potentially become, Anna."

My head reeled at the implication. Little did she know just how guilty I felt.

Despite that, I still needed to weigh it all up very carefully before making a rash decision that I might learn to regret.

"I need to think this over." I said seriously.

"Yes dear, you do that. I'll leave you to it," she said, making me groan at the enormous decision I had to make.

"Gee thanks," I said, mumbling sarcastically.

"I know you'll make the right judgement Anna." Martha said, clearly certain of which way I was leaning.

"I hope so," I said, not quite sharing her same confidence. "I'll talk to you later."

"Soon. Bye dear," she said before I ended the call.

Slumping back in my seat, I blew out a deep breath. What was I going to do?

What was it they said?

Be careful what you wish for.

It took ages for me to get to sleep that night. The thoughts that were rattling around inside my head not giving me a moment's peace until finally, well after two in the morning, exhaustion took over.

And I dreamed in sound. The voices of a kind man and a little girl.

*-"Climb down off that elephant this instant!"*

*"No, you will shoot her!"*

*"Why would I do that? She is a good elephant!"*

*"You have a gun!"*

*"Sweet one, I always have a gun, now don't be silly, we need to leave now, please come down from there, mama needs you ready.*

*Essnass will give you a bath, you look like you have wallowed with the Hippos."*

*"You won't kill her? Are you not angry with her?"*

*"Only a little. At both of you. I do not want you two running off like that again, you had us very worried."*

*"She is my best friend she would never hurt me!"*

*"No, she loves you. I think she would do anything for you. Even set us on a wild goose chase, now come."*

*"She's my elephant, she's beautiful."*

*"She is, that's why you named her Pragtig."-*

I sat bolt upright in bed, my heart beating wildly and trying to catch my breath, I rubbed my face, trying to wake up and felt wetness there, was I crying?

I was hot too, so hot that I was sweating "Pragtig," I whispered whilst I let out a breath. Peeling back the covers, I swung my legs over the edge of the bed.

The cool floor tiles felt like heaven to my feet while I sat there contemplating my dream.

I had a cool shower and once I felt more comfortable, I went back to bed, but couldn't get back to sleep until it was almost time to get up again.

Typical.

"Blimey Anna, you look like shit," Pete said before I dropped into my seat at the office.

"Gee thanks Pete, just what a girl wants to hear first thing in the morning, you say that to Rach when she's had a rough night?" I asked, raising a brow at him.

"Psht, 'course not, she'd have my balls," he said, squirming in his seat.

"Uh huh," I said, mumbling humourlessly and I started the day by sorting the company mail. "Maybe it'd be best that you keep a wide berth from me then," I said, pulling out my trusty pocket-knife and enjoying the sudden wide eyes and audible gulp from Pete after I flicked the blade and used it as a letter opener.

"Noted," Pete said playing along some more when he stepped back covering his crotch.

Changing the subject, he asked,"So, you right to fly?"

"Why? I thought I had desk duty today," I said, holding up an envelope for emphasis.

"Chris called in sick, bad seafood or something," he shrugged, "we've got three guys to take out on a bit of a hush-hush project this side of Moorrinya. We'll need you as soon as they touch down at three this arvo."

"Cool, should be okay to go. Why's it on the down low?"

Pete grinned knowingly. "Because my dear Anna, if we do a good job this arvo, there could be a very lucrative contract that we could be exclusive to."

"Oh. That does sound interesting. Do tell," I said, giving him my undivided attention.

"If it works out, this place you're going to today might make us the sole operator to fly into and out of the area. That could mean daily flights of up to a dozen people at a time, and maybe more down the track, we'll need to expand to accommodate them once they get a strip in, but with a contract, the banks will probably let us get a Caravan or a King Air or something. It could be just the shot in the arm I've been hoping for."

"Oh," I said nodding in understanding, "Fixed wing huh?"

"Yep, why so sceptical Anna?" Pete asked, beaming at me, his bright eyes sparkling with the prospect.

"I just never thought I'd ever see the day…" I said, shaking my head in mild disbelief, my tone teasing.

"Yeah, yeah," he continued to grin, looking like a fresh faced boy telling his parents about this awesome thing that his imagination conjured up, "It could be huge for us. Anyway," he paused in mid thought before focusing back on me. "How about you make like Blue and bolt."

"Hey! Blue does not bolt!" I said in mock indignation.

"Whatever, just go home and get a few more hours, I don't think you'll be back before eight tonight, it's a fair trip and…"

I tuned all my attention to him abruptly.

"So I'm taking TAJ then?" My voice rose an octave giving away my sudden excitement.

"You are," he said looking out for my reaction.

"Cool," I bounced in my seat, grinning like a loon.

Pete used his personal ride, an Agusta Westland 109 Grand that we fondly called the Taj Mahal thanks to its rego and the way the bird was decked out. We used TAJ mainly for VIP's, high end tours and on rare occasions for night flying when all our other IFR choppers were unavailable. Pete was normally the only one apart from Chris who flew it, but seeing as Pete was overnighting tonight at Charters Towers and Chris was barfing his guts up, I was the only other pilot left who was endorsed to fly it. She was a beautiful, twin engine, four bladed, luxuriously appointed limousine of the skies. With leather interior, LED lights throughout, club seating, bar, in-flight entertainment, a glass cockpit, retractable landing gear, you name it, she had it.

"Thought that'd make you happy," Pete said with a wink.

Obviously, I was pretty hopeless at hiding my excitement, now made worse, my hands flying to my cheeks to try and hide my now out of control smile.

"Now scoot," Pete said playfully. "You need to rest up if you're gonna have enough hours to get back this evening." He turned me around by the shoulders and gently pushed me to give me a move on.

Of course, I wouldn't be able to rest in the strictest sense, I just couldn't be on duty, so I went for a ride on Blue instead. It was always the best therapy for anything that ailed me, including insomnia.

I still had an hour and a half after I came back home and showered, so I took a nanna nap and was at the airport completely refreshed with my flight plan made by 1500.

While I was walking around the Grand doing my pre-flight, I heard a group of men laughing and talking loudly before they even made it to the small grassed area in front of the STC office.

"Helloooo beautiful." I heard one of the men say in front of his mates, his voice, carrying with the wind, was clearly not meant for my ears.

Then again, he could have been talking about the Grand too. She sure was pretty.

I sighed at myself, this sort of thing happened on occasion and for the most part, if I was friendly, professional and on rare occasion even slightly flirty, the flight was pleasant. I became pretty good at reading which way I needed go to be able to keep everybody happy. It was 'good business' as Pete used to say.

The boys didn't really get that so much from our female passengers, but that might have been more to do with those standard navy dress shorts on hairy-legged dudes not having quite the same appeal as they did on a woman.

My guests waited for me behind the fence before I made my way over to them and introduced myself to the man in charge. I tried to ignore the creepy way Project Manager, Dimitri Petracov placed a hand on the small of my back while he acquainted me with the other two men. Design Engineer Samual Craig and Geologist Lou Chen.

Worming my way from Mr Petracov's touch, I escorted the three men towards the chopper and then helped get everybody settled in the back like a good host before I seated myself and started the ignition sequence.

The club seating in the chopper meant that the three were in their own little compartment, and like a Limo screen, there was a bulkhead right behind the front seats with limited visual access. There were also the six noise cancelling headsets, one for every seat that provided the privacy for passengers to talk among themselves on the intercom. If they had any questions, or if I needed to inform them of something, we could each press a button and have a word. Somewhat surprisingly, I wasn't called upon and left to my own devices throughout the flight.

The chopper cruised at about 290km/h, so it was about an hour before I was making a circuit to assess the small clearing that had been made close to the bush camp not far from it.

Selecting gear down, I landed the Grand a few minutes later and waited for her to wind down while stowing headsets and unbuckling seatbelts. Outside, the heat was more intense on the edge of the desert but naturally drier than on the coast, which made it somewhat bearable.

Helping the guys unload their packs and among a little mumbling, Petracov suggested the other two go on ahead and he'd catch them up. Once they were out of earshot, he rounded on me.

He looked at the ground and with a smirk on his face, he took a couple of steps towards me.

"Captain Anna," he said, raking his leery eyes up my body, before they settled on my face. He took one last step that was way too far into my professional bubble and caused me to step back.

"Mr Petracov," I said with a nod, making sure that I stayed polite, but cool.

"Dimitri," he said.

"Pardon?" I asked

"Please call me Dimitri," he repeated in a low voice.

I swallowed. "Uh, I'm sorry sir, I don't think that would be appropriate, I don't know you w…"

"That could be remedied Anna."

He gave me a piercing glare that caused me to take another step back and a little closer to the Grand.

"Heeeey," he drew out, "don't be like that, I'm just wanting to get to know you better."

"Uh," I uttered nervously, my heart beating hard now and my body on full alert. I reached back to feel for the handle of the pilot door.

But it did me no good, Petracov had positioned me between the door and himself, leaving me no room to swing it open.

"Anna, you're obviously a very intelligent young woman," he stated with a tilt of his head and the edge of self-assurance in his voice.

"Uh thanks?" I said, at a loss of anything else to say.

He gave me a cocky smile. "Peter is very fond of you, isn't he? Like a big brother?"

I nodded nervously, watching a hand reach forward and feeling his fingers take a stray lock of hair that had worked its way free of my ponytail before he proceeded to tuck it behind my ear.

I looked down and squeezed my eyes shut - just wanting to avoid him and his rakish stare.

This couldn't be happening.

"Look at me Anna," he said, his tone leaving no room for me to question him.

I did as he asked but kept my head low, he had already ducked his head to catch my eye and smiled a smarmy lopsided grin before taking a quick breath.

"You know, you can help Peter to secure that contract Anna, it was a stroke of luck that he had the machine that we needed at such short notice today and that will stand him in good stead, but there are a few other companies that are already set up to supply us with what we need going forward, which puts him at a disadvantage."

"I don't understand, w-what difference could I make?" I asked, already dreading the answer.

He ran his eyes over me again, causing me to squirm uncomfortably.

"Well," he said, clearly enjoying my discomfort, "I'm having to move to Mackay from Brisbane so that I can fly to site every day until there are some better facilities out here. I don't know anyone here Anna, and I think it would be very nice to get to know you." He said, smiling more sincerely this time.

I swallowed, my eyes closing at what was obviously a seedy proposition that he actually thought was a sure thing.

"I don't think..." I said shaking my head.

"Shhh, I think you would love to see Peter do well, hmmm?"

His lascivious expression was back and the bastard was bold enough to run the backs of his fingers down my arm.

I scanned the area around us, hoping that someone would be near enough so I could draw some attention to us but it seemed that I was clean out of luck, so I nodded instead imploring the powers that be to let this be over if I just went along with his game.

"Good girl," he said like I was some pet. "And don't worry beautiful, I'll be sure to make it worth your while too." I stared at him in utter disbelief.

"So curious I see," he said, narrowing his eyes at me even though I was pretty sure he could tell I was no such thing. "Peter hasn't told you what this place is yet?"

"No," I said in hoarse whisper, shaking my head as I looked around at the rusty coloured ironstone rock. "Iron Ore?"

He threw his head back to laugh, "Oh Anna, Don't you think that the pretty sparkling stones mined here would look so much better on you than something made from humble steel?" He asked grinning confidently and looming closer.

Unbelievable.

This was not only an indecent proposal, but Petracov thought that he could both blackmail me and buy me with diamonds like some whore. My stomach churned and I tried to think of a way to get out of this without compromising both myself or Pete.

Petracov waited for my reaction and leaned in to whisper in my ear. "What do you say Anna? Diamonds might just become your best friend if you play your cards right," He said shamelessly, before stepping away and leaving me feeling physically sick.

I had always loved my job and although there had been moments that were challenging, that never changed. But right now I could categorically say that this was the first time in my flying career that I really hated it. No one should be made to feel like I felt right now.

"I'll tell you what sweetheart," he said shoving his hands in his pockets, "why don't you run along and have a little think about it. Let me know when you pick us up again? Hm?"

In order for me to extricate myself from the jam I found myself in, I had to literally remove myself from the equation, it would at least give Pete a fair chance at getting the contract without me influencing the outcome. Then I could also avoid the shame, the guilt and a host of other nouns that would be firmly heaped atop my shoulders, whether I agreed to Petracov's proposition or not.

I took a deep breath and gathered all the courage that I could muster. "That won't be necessary Mr Petracov..." I said, my voice wavering.

"Dimitri," he said reminding me, a malevolent grin spreading over his face, "I like a woman that can see it my way, it makes things... you know, easy."

"I think you misunderstand me, Dimitri," I said, my confidence rising as my thoughts became more definitive, "you see, I'm leaving Station to Coast." My words were laced with mock innocence.

Both of Petracovt's eyebrows shot towards his hairline. "Well," he said, pausing for a moment as he thought, "no matter, I'm sure we can still..."

"No, Mr Petracov," I cut him off with a more formidable tone, "I'm leaving Mackay, so that makes any further discussion on any uh... future arrangement a moot point," I said choosing my words carefully so that they couldn't be misconstrued.

He took a moment before he finally recoiled in surprise. "What?"

"I have a new job lined up, for a while now, so I'm sorry Mr Petracov, I'm afraid I won't be able to assist you," I said, reiterating.

He clenched his jaw and I became a little worried at the sudden reddening of his face. But as quickly as he coloured, the colour drained until he quietly nodded and stepped back as the news sunk in.

"Now, if you'll excuse me, I really need to be getting back, have a nice day Mr Petracov," I said, smiling politely.

Internally I was still shaken... even though I was secretly fist bumping myself that I'd found the strength and dodged a bullet.

Or had I?

Now all I needed to do was find the same strength to tell Pete.

# Chapter 21

Turns out Pete was surprisingly good about the life changing news I had for him.

When I finally informed him that I'd been 'poached' for want of a better word, he asked all the right questions.

What brought this on?

Are you sure about this?

Is this because of that boy?

I only told him what he needed to know because there were multiple answers for any one of those questions.

A change is as good as a holiday... and an elephant.

Yes... no.

No, go back to answer number one - I may or may not have turned red and faltered a little when I answered that one, which may in turn have belied that answer.

"Awwww sparrow, you're finally leaving the nest," Pete said teasing me, dabbing at a non-existent tear for added dramatic effect.

"Oh shut up you," I said, grumbling at him, because it was all I could do to keep my real tears at bay.

Martha was as predicted, delighted with my news and after giving her the information she needed, she worked her magic and fixed things so that in only a few short weeks, I'd be retracing the same steps I'd taken only months earlier.

I managed to avoid picking up Mr Petracov and his cronies only a few days after I had dropped them off because luckily, Pete took on the flight himself. I was pretty sure he was non-the wiser about what went down that fateful day, judging by his happy demeanour when he returned. He was full of smiles as he entered the office after seeing the men off at the main terminal for their connecting flight.

It would remain to be seen who would be awarded that lucrative contract once all the tenders were sent in.

When the day to leave finally came, I was again standing in the main terminal just as I had done not so long ago, only this time, both Pete and Rach where there to see me off. Rach, was a lovely lady, but we didn't run in the same circles any longer. She was still right into the rodeo scene and I, well I wasn't.

We simply didn't have enough else in common to develop anything outside of Pete's and my world at the airport.

She shocked me when she started to look like the floodgates were going to open. She did that whole looking up and fanning her face thing and no amount of jovial banter on Pete's behalf stopped his eyes becoming glassy either, which meant that I just couldn't look at either of them. Especially after our final embrace and I backed out of Pete's arms. Not wanting to make eye contact, I turned abruptly and kept my head down after he told me to look after myself and to be good.

"Always am Pete," I said, having to clear my throat as I croaked out the words.

Pulling my shoulders back, I took a deep breath and walked away without looking back at either of them for fear that I'd fall apart.

Like I had at the stables earlier.

While no one else was around, I balled my eyes out into Blue's mane as I farewelled him with an hour long (or so it seemed) hug around his cresty neck, feeding him carrots and apples and mints to make up for my absence.

That bloody horse was the one that I felt I was leaving behind, I was responsible for him and I knew that even though I was leaving him with people who were amazing at their job, they could never look after him the way I could. The only reason I had even considered stepping foot on the plane was that I'd be back. A proper spell for him in a big paddock with a herd of geldings would probably be good for him.

At least that's what I told myself anyway.

So, there I was, almost like déjà vu except it wasn't, on my way to a place that was so foreign but somehow so familiar to me. Had it been anywhere else, I would have seriously doubted that I'd have entertained the move I was making now.

I managed to sleep a little but was still dog tired when we finally touched down in Johannesburg after the change-over in Perth.

I looked out for the shuttle bus and as soon as I approached, the driver recognised me with a huge gleaming smile.

"Miss Anna, you are back; it is so good that you have returned," He said, and I was thankful that he reminded me that his name was Tommy. He was filling in for the usual driver, who had the day off.

"Thanks, I'm excited to be back." I said to the Mahout.

It seemed that word had got around.

Tommy smiled again and started to stow the passenger luggage in the trailer behind the bus. I took the opportunity to board and get as comfortable as I could for the last leg of my journey.

As we travelled closer toward Saanastia, my weariness faded as thoughts of what was to come started to enter my mind. I sat at attention, watching the long stretches of South African bush, with its red soil, tall grasses and sparse acacias gradually morph into suburbia and back again as we passed through the towns and villages.

Even though Pragtig had been at the forefront of my thoughts ever since Martha had informed me of her plight. Now that I was finally here, the pictures of a huge grey elephant became more and more prevalent in my mind as the landscape flashed by.

It was getting to the point that I was starting to get anxious about her state of well-being.

Finally, the tall electric fence that marked our arrival at Saanastia caused me to take a deep breath in an attempt to quell another wave of nervousness from crashing over me.

I had no such luck.

I moved to the edge of my seat, keeping an even closer eye to any details that I may have missed the last time that I was here while passing the familiar landmarks and all the time thinking of that elephant.

I couldn't help the feeling of relief when we slowed and turned to enter Saanastia's long driveway. We drove past the camp ground and up to that large stone walled building that would be part of my home for the next few months.

There, at the main entrance was Martha, looking so terribly worried that I was up and rushing to the front of the bus before it had even rolled to a stop. She surged forward the moment her red rimmed eyes met with mine and the driver, not missing our exchange quickly opened the door for me to rush out.

Meeting me stride for stride, with Martha's face ashen, I felt my gut twist the closer we got and I had to ask. "Is she still alive?"

My throat constricted around the words with the effort to keep my tears at bay and Martha suddenly burst into tears before engulfing me in a tight embrace.

"Oh Anna, thank god you're here, come quick, she went down about ten minutes ago and they can't get her up."

With the same ferocity of her hug, she grabbed my hand and dragged me through the building, ducking and weaving through a few small groups of curious onlookers.

"Once Lloyd gets back, we'll have no choice but to tell him," she said, fumbling with the card when attempting to unlock the door.

I'd never seen Martha this way, she was always so calm, even when she had every right not to be.

The door finally pinged and I followed her into the animal enclosure.

"Now that she's down I fear we're already too late."

"Too late?" My voice pitched an octave.

"Sweetheart, if we can't get her up, her weight will crush her organs."

Her steps quickened into a run until we got to the back of elephant barn and stepped outside again to a series of solid yards that I hadn't seen before.

I heard a commotion coming from the very far end of the lane way.

"Come," Martha grabbed at my hand again showing me the way.

"How is she Joseph?" Martha asked bleakly and was slightly out of breath as we pulled up at the last yard and to one of the sweaty men who acknowledged our arrival by opening the gate.

He however didn't answer, he didn't say anything.

He didn't need to, because his silence was deafening.

There was Pragtig, laying on her stomach, up against the far rails of the yard with her front feet in front of her and with three men trying desperately to move her.

"We are trying missus, we are trying, but we are not strong enough, ten men are not strong enough, we need her up or to put her on her side, because like this…" he took off his cap and wiped his brow, "she doesn't have much time." He said shaking his head slowly.

I felt my heart rip in two.

The men had quit struggling with their impossible mission and were all puffing and panting from their efforts. I feared I was too late, I looked up at Martha for an answer, my chin starting to quiver, hoping desperately that she'd have some sort of answer.

But I knew that the opposite was true.

Martha looked completely dejected, for a moment at least, until she straightened her shoulders, sucked in a deep breath and fixed a strong gaze on me.

I stood there feeling the cool wetness of silent tears running down my face and then Martha's warm hands upon my shoulders.

"I think it best if you go to her Anna," she said nodding in encouragement.

I blinked rapidly and wiped at my tears. Agreeing soundlessly with a nod of my own, I made a move towards my elephant.

I noticed for the first time that Kabri was there.

"Miss Anna," he breathed out on approach, before grabbing both my hands and giving them a heartfelt squeeze. The desolation was clearly evident on his features. "Thank you for coming back to us," he continued on, puzzling me with the familial nature of his words.

He led me to the hulking mass slumped up against the great steel bars of the yard.

There lay Pragtig. A once magnificent beast, now such a pathetic sight. Her spine and hipbones jutting out, her ribs on which you could play a tune. Her head rested on her tusks and between her front legs, the hollows so prominent above her eyes.

She was seemingly totally oblivious of her surroundings, her eyes dull and lifeless. A bale of lucerne hay sat in the opposite corner yard as was a blue plastic feeder, half full of nutritious pellets. Both of which appeared to be untouched.

I reeled at her emaciated appearance.

"Oh Pragtig," I whispered "Umefanya nini na wewe mwenyewe mpenzi wangu," I said laying a hand on the thick hide of her side, her breaths were slow and laboured with the effort to expand her lungs.

"Tafadhali amka," I said quietly, running my hand over her bony shoulder.

Nothing, there was no reaction, "Tafadhali?" I begged as she lay prostrate.

"Tafadhali Pragtig, unahitaji kupata up!" I said with more strength, stepping over one of her legs before crouching down next to her head. "Tafadhali" I begged again, and again, over and over, each time crawling closer to her. Picking up the end of her heavy trunk, I held it to my chest and stroked it gently.

The tears were rolling down my cheeks now, the guilt gripping me as the life continued to flow out of this most majestic of animals I'd ever been privileged to be graced by.

If only I hadn't been so bloody nosy. If only I hadn't been so enamoured by her. If only I just hadn't come here in the first place, then none of this would be happening now.

This was all my fault.

Kissing the end of her trunk, that no elephant could live without, I felt the warmth of her breath struggling to course through it.

I blew into the end hoping that the scent laced air that gave me life, would trigger something to save hers.

"C'mon girl, please get up for me, I'm sorry Pragtig, so sorry that I put you here. Sorry I can't save you, so sorry, so sorry," I repeated, hugging her trunk to me.

"C'mon Martha, we've waited long enough," I heard from afar.

"Just a little longer Lloyd love, please," Martha begged.

"Martha," Lloyd said in a warning tone, his voice was strong, but held a tone that indicated the same devastation that everybody felt.

We had run out of time and Lloyd had run out of patience and excuses to put off the inevitable. My heart skipped a beat, partially from fear and much to my disappointment also from the excitement of seeing him again.

"I've given that animal more time than is humane," Lloyd said determinedly.

"I know dear but..." Martha said, trying to stall him.

"Dammit Martha, what have you been up to?" Lloyd asked.

Lloyd was onto her and I could hear his footsteps coming close.

"Lloyd!" Martha's voice carried down the lane way, "Shit," she hissed before I heard her break into a run after him.

I braced myself.

"Please Pragtig, please!" I begged again in desperation, just as Lloyd finally made it to the huge steel gate.

I whirled around knowing that Pragtig's life now lay completely in my hands and also at Lloyd's mercy.

Lloyd looked as handsome as he always did, all hard planes and angular features, his usual rigid expression disappeared for a fleeting moment before his brows knitted together, "What the hell are you doing here?!" He asked, handing a big gun to one of the other men.

"Lloyd," Martha touched his shoulder hesitantly.

He shrugged her off as he turned to glare at her, "You!" He pointed and she flinched at his wrath. "How could you?"

"I-I wanted to give Pragtig one last chance, I had a hunch," she said, squaring her shoulders.

Lloyd gave Martha an uncompromising glare.

"Well you have to admit, my hunches are usually pretty good," Martha said, arguing a valid point.

"Martha," he sighed in exasperation, pinching the bridge of his nose and tamping down his utter infuriation. "That bloody elephant has had more chances than any other. Every chance we've given her, she's been non-responsive! It's just cruel to keep this going, what makes you think she can help?" Lloyd asked, hiking a thumb over his shoulder before propping both hands on his hips while he waited for Martha to answer.

"Lloyd," Martha said in a placating tone, "Anna's here now, so what could it hurt?"

"What could it hurt? What could it hurt?!" Lloyd repeated her words in exasperation. "What good would it do Martha?" He asked with a pained pitch to his voice.

After a short standoff with Martha, Lloyd turned and took the rifle back. "Get the girl out of here, the last thing I need is another emotional female around to make things worse than they already are." He said dismissively.

My first thought was bastard.

But the second made it plainly clear to me that Lloyd was just as affected as any one of the people involved by this awful situation. The only difference was in our personal reactions and everybody was at a loss as to what more could be done at this point in time.

I scanned the group of proud African men all of which were solemnly quiet. Their liquid brown eyes glazed, and their usual bright, white smiles hidden from view.

Lloyd converted his sorrow into anger and upon taking a closer look - a rare thing for me to do because he intimidated me in more ways than one - showed that his eyes most certainly belied that anger. They had dark circles under them, and he carried an extra layer of darkness with him. He looked physically and emotionally wrecked.

And Martha, who I'd always thought of as the most optimistic person I'd ever met, looked completely defeated. "At least give Anna a few more minutes, she has come a long way," she said despondently.

Lloyd glanced at me.

Sighing, he scrubbed his hand over his face and finally said, "You have five minutes Anna." He briefly glanced into my eyes before turning on his heel and striding away.

Martha blew out a sigh with puffed cheeks at the small reprieve.

"Thanks, Martha," I said with a sigh, before kissing the end of Pragtig's trunk.

Martha nodded with a tight brief smile.

Pragtig's trunk twitched suddenly, before lifting of its own accord and whiffing in my breath. She vibrated beneath me, a rumble so low that I could barely hear it, but it was there. I sat back and glanced wide eyed at Martha, "She rumbled," my voice cracked, Martha's hands flew to her mouth.

"Come on girl," I shifted to stand and heard a strange squeak, before she stirred slightly.

"Pragtig, come on baby," I squatted beside her head, touching her again, "up you get. I promise if you get up, I'll stay, I'll never leave you again, but you need to get up. Please!" I begged her, a sob of desperation escaped me before I could stop it.

Her ears moved and I decided to step back to give her room, there were more short squeaks and her rumbles became more audible. There were mumbles from the few men standing around the yard and Martha? Well her eyes where shiny and wide, her hands still up over her mouth in hopeful trepidation.

"Look. She is crying," Kabri said.

"Of course, I'm bloody crying!" I wailed.

"Yes, No... Miss Anna, I mean Pragtig. She is crying."

I looked more closely at my elephant, she wasn't crying in the human sense and not that I expected that, but it didn't stop me from searching for the human element.

"The squeaks are the sound you hear when they grieve for a lost herd member," Kabri continued, "It has been seen, that if an elephant died on a migration route for example, that the herd will stop to pay respect to the bones when they pass again, even for years thereafter. Studies say short squeaks could be the sounds of their sorrow."

I looked back to where my elephant lay, whatever the studies say, they weren't going to make any difference to Pragtig's fate if she didn't get up.

The sound of ominous footsteps made their way back down the lane way, my heart plummeted again, knowing full well that my girl had only a few minutes to live.

I watched Lloyd come into view, his jaw clenched, his eyes focused on the floor before him, that big gun held to his side, muzzle down.

Slowing to a stop Lloyd stroked the stubble on his face, "Uh, best you two leave now, you don't need to see this."

Nodding, I took in the sight of the prone elephant one last time. With Martha giving me a strained "C'mon love," before she sucked in a shuddering breath and wrapping an arm around my shoulders to guide me away from the miserable scene.

My chin quivered as I walked away, not being able to hold it in any longer, the sorrow was too much and the uncontrollable sobs finally escaped, racking my body in a way I couldn't remember ever experiencing. Feeling Martha's arm hold me tighter, she too was caught up in the despair and wept quietly.

I'd dropped many animals in my short life, whether it was a beast to butcher for our own consumption or to put out of its misery. Thankfully, I had never had to draw the line for animals I'd known, those faces I'd come to love, and I wasn't sure that I'd ever be able to do that knowing how I felt at this moment.

Martha led me down the long lane way towards the barn. Arm in arm, we leaned on one another, our tears flowing freely. The atmosphere around us fell eerily silent but for our footsteps and the sounds of our grief.

I expected the sharp sound of the gunshot to pierce through the air, but it never came and before we exited the building, an almighty trumpet reverberated through the air before a series of crashes and bangs and general ruckus erupted from behind us.

"Anna!" Lloyd called, his voice breaking through the loud noises, stopping Martha and I in our tracks.

Simultaneously, we looked at each other wide eyed and in disbelief. I wasn't going to waste a moment longer.

I turned and sprinted back towards the yards.

My Beautiful was standing.


TRANSLATION:

Umefanya nini na wewe mwenyewe mpenzi wangu - *What have you done to yourself my darling*

Tafadhali amka - *Please get up*

Tafadhali - *Please*

Tafadhali Pragtig, unahitaji kupata up! - *Please, Pragtig, you need to get up*

# Chapter 22

I camped next to Pragtig for the first week until she was strong enough to cope with me finally leaving her for some period of the day and that eventually morphed into overnight and then became a visit twice a day, before and after work. The process took about a month, but we needed to take it slowly in order for me to be able to work away from the resort and not have her regress.

She needed to know I'd come back.

I also took that time to research anything I needed to know to finally be able do the other thing I came here for... to fly.

From there, it was a couple of weeks before Pragtig was allowed out into a larger enclosure, always with her herd right next to her to keep her company through the rails.

It had been some time since the group had been out on the open range, but we couldn't risk isolating Pragtig completely from them. The days that there were elephant back trails, I stayed with her just in case, and she didn't seem to miss them from what we could observe. She just ate like a horse - well an elephant in this case. Every day she was getting stronger and every day, she became more confident in herself again.

Being able to sleep in a proper bed regularly was seriously underrated so I was assigned to one of the self-contained suites.

It was an interesting set up. The homestead had a whole private wing that hadn't been used for years. The mere act of glancing towards the connecting door was enough for Lloyd to make it perfectly clear that that part of the house was strictly off limits. Whether that was through respect, or some other reason I wasn't privy to, but his reactions naturally made me insanely curious to find out.

The guest suites were on the opposite side of the building and were joined by a wide hallway and it was set up similarly to a hotel.

They had been used for staff in the past and when Saanastia was still considered to be out in the middle of nowhere.

Now with so many small towns popping up and expanding all along the highway leading to the property, everyone had their own houses near enough to use their various methods of transport to get from place to place more reliably.

As a consequence of the urbanisation, it had left only Lloyd and Martha residing at the homestead on a more permanent basis and the spare suites were used in the event staff needed to overnight for any reason.

Each suite was laid out with a large comfy bed, a compact lounge and entertainment area, kitchenette and of course, a bathroom.

I settled in as well as could be expected and from there a routine of sorts started to come together. Everyone shared the duties in the house and Martha had made a schedule that kept everybody honest.

Lloyd had barely spoken a word to me until I'd moved in and even then, it was really only when something needed to be said. Not that I expected to sit down idly chit-chatting over coffee and cake or anything on a daily basis.

He said nothing to my face regarding my re-appearance and for now I just wanted to lay low and carry my weight to prove myself.

So, I spent time familiarising myself with Saanastia by way of a general induction, helping anywhere and everywhere that needed an extra hand. That could be anything from filing to laundry, to poo duty.

I also had to jump through a few hoops to get my pilot's licence sorted so I could officially fly commercially within this vast country. After having passed the medical, the only thing left to do was to take a flight test with an instructor.

And when that day came and I was finally heading to the closest airstrip near Saanastia, I was super eager to have the said test and then pick up the helicopter and fly it back to base.

Luckily there was no short straw for who would drive me to the small airstrip where Fred kept the bird, because Martha was more than happy to take me.

"So… You and Fred huh?" I asked, teasing her and waggling my eyebrows like I remember Carley used to.

Martha blushed, "He's a wonderful man, Anna," she said smiling briefly.

Her smile turned into a frown, "He's a bit lost now with what to do with himself though, he loved flying and now that he's grounded…" she said, the words trailing off with a shake of her head.

"I totally get that Martha, believe me, flying gets into your blood, I don't know what I'd do if I couldn't fly at least some of the time but I'm sure when Fred's ready, that you guys will come up with something… easy for me to say, I guess…" I shrugged.

"I'm sure you're right dear, there's plenty of life in the old boy yet," she said with a grin.

"Bet only you could get away with saying that!" I said, knowing she probably had his heart as much as he had hers.

"Saying what?" She asked in mock innocence before we both burst into giggles.

The rest of the ride was non-eventful as we made small talk along the way.

Twenty minutes later we turned off the main road and stopped at a tall mesh gate with a sign indicating we were entering a regional airport and to watch for low flying aircraft. Right on cue an old Piper Scenica flew by on take-off at a hundred feet to our right, clearing the border fence and soaring its way into open airspace.

Once through the gate - which wasn't locked - we followed a dirt road, passing the low shrubs and grasses before they gave way to a neatly mowed expanse of open space. Ahead of us, the road opened out to a parking lot and a couple of rows of small hangars facing each other across an apron and taxiway. Flanking the fence was a building that looked like a small terminal or maybe a clubhouse and to the right of that lay the dirt airstrip that closely resembled any outback runway in Australia.

We parked up at the front of the main building and I followed Martha through the gate that led to the tarmac and over to one of a few open hangars.

"Helloooo," Martha sang out as we neared the hangar doors, revealing the red Jet Ranger just as I remembered her, except this time she had her doors on.

Squinting into the comparative darkness, a voice called out to us. "Ahoy there!"

Fred walked towards us, returning some tools back to a large, red upright toolbox with a clatter.

"Martha darling," he said endearingly, taking hold of her upper arms and kissing her on both cheeks before giving her a warm hug.

Fred turned to me with open arms, "Sweet Anna, my angel," he said repeating the gesture, "How are you my girl?" He grinned, before holding me at arm's length to see for himself.

"Good, good." I smiled back at him. "Just sorry to hear about your ticker mate, how are you feeling otherwise?" I asked.

His smile dropped for a moment before the corners of his mouth lifted again and he shrugged. "Agh you know how it is. A bit of a blow that I can't fly commercially anymore," he said reservedly, rocking back on his heels. "But I'll still keep my private hours up enough to stay current once I get the all clear," he said more brightly.

I nodded in understanding. "So you'll be visiting on occasion then?"

"Of course!" He smiled looking at Martha. "Try and keep me away! Have to keep an eye on this one, make sure she's doing it properly!" He said teasingly, while shooting me a cheeky wink.

"Hey!" Martha said in protest.

Their banter was too adorable.

Fred cleared his throat and gave his apology. He wrapped an arm around his lady and gave her an affectionate squeeze.

"Anyway," he said. "It makes it all better knowing that RED here can still be of use."

"It's a good thing you're doing Fred, not many people would be so generous." I pointed out.

"Eh," he said with a bashful shrug. "Sometimes it's not all about what you can get, but what you can give, I could have sold the chopper and sat pretty for a while, but Saanastia needs it more than I do right now. This thing," he patted his chest, "helped me to see what's really important, you know?" He asked, looking warmly at Martha again.

She returned his gaze tenderly and pecked him on the lips.

As cute as they were, I felt just a wee bit awkward watching two 'mature' adults, acting like love-birds and looked away.

I was saved from any further unease by the appearance of my instructor, who introduced himself as Guy DeReymaar, a middle aged, balding man with a mild beer gut.

I'd studied and already completed all the written components of the South African endorsement, and all that remained was the competency test before I was given an official stamp of approval.

Having made myself familiar with the regional maps, I had a good idea of where I was flying today, and after a brief pre-flight, I had a very thorough flight check including some emergency drills and some practice on my sling/longline rating and then I was deemed safe to fly.

After a congratulatory handshake to seal the deal, I caught Fred and Martha's eye and gave them a double thumbs up while shutting down the chopper.

"How'd she do, Guy?" Fred asked as we approached the couple.

A grin grew on Guy's face, "I don't think I really need to tell you she aced it Fred, she is a mighty pilot," he said before we started walking towards the main building.

I felt the heat in my cheeks, before he turned to me, "When you're done with following fence lines, you call me, ok?" He gave me his card.

"Um, thanks?" I said feeling mildly embarrassed.

"Uh uh, no you don't young lady, you're mine," Martha grumbled in jest causing everyone to laugh at her possessiveness.

"Don't worry Martha, I'm not going anywhere," I said assuring her.

"Seems like I've lost out there." Guy conceded.

"Anna is one very popular lady at Saanastia," Fred added, my colour rising again on our approach to the club house.

Guy opened one of the glass doors to let us through "I have no doubt," he said with a smile before we picked out a comfy lounge area to sit at.

"And on that note, I better get your paperwork filled in," he said, taking a seat before rummaging through his briefcase while Martha and Fred organised refreshments.

I received temporary dispensation and would receive my newly amended licence in the following week.

It wasn't long before we wrapped up and then Guy bid us goodbye, leaving Fred, Martha and I to it.

Fred mentioned that everything I needed was at Saanastia now that RED was going to be based there. I had of course already figured the containers and makeshift hangar that had been set up near the helipad were for the chopper.

The containers had tools, machinery and stores of spare parts and liquids that were needed for any maintenance that might be needed. I could handle the basic stuff like the regular compressor washes and when scheduled maintenance came up, Fred was licensed to do it and he would happily service the chopper.

Later, back at the hangar I said goodbye to Martha, who was ecstatic that another piece of her plan was slotting into place.

"I'll see you at home," she said offhandedly.

"Yeah." I said, struck by her words before I climbed into the chopper that had been waiting patiently on the apron in front of the hangar.

Home. Where was that now? I thought to myself while I buckled up the harness.

In the time I'd been here, even with the often menial chores I'd get assigned to on a regular basis, I realised that Saanastia had felt like home. It felt that way right from the time I'd first stepped foot on its soil with Carley and it felt more so for every day that I stayed.

When I thought about 'home', all I wanted to do was kick this three-month trial to the kerb. If only it wasn't for my old mate, Blue, I'd be completely committed to this new path in my life without question.

I thought myself ridiculous while I pondered my dilemma, I was essentially that silly little girl who thought nothing in the world was as important as her bond with her unicorn dream pony.

If only I could have my cake and eat it too.

But that wasn't real life. Real life meant compromise and I knew that better than anyone. One day soon, I'd have to put my big girl pants on and start to adult a bit. Either way I'd have to sacrifice something.

No, this trial needed to take its course. I dreaded the day that it would inevitably end and I'd be forced to make a decision.

"Fly safe Anna," Fred said, interrupting my see-sawing thoughts.

"Always do Fred," I assured him.

"I'll see you soon, you'll look after RED won't you?"

"Like my own," I said, assuring him.

"I put her cover in the back," he said, gesturing to the rear of the machine.

"Don't worry Fred," I said, knowing he was stalling.

"You're an angel," he grinned.

"You said that already." I reminded him.

"Well, it's the truth," he said, his hand finding its way to his chest. Whether he knew he did it or not was anybody's guess.

I gave him a tight smile, "You don't have to feel indebted to me you know."

"I know, but it's fun seeing you squirm." He winked and right on cue I felt another wave of heat flush my cheeks.

"Cheeky bugger. Can I go now?" I asked, pretending to be done with being the brunt of Fred's amusement, because it was really good to see him doing so well.

Grinning like a Cheshire Cat and clearly enjoying my embarrassment, he waved a path for me to the sky. "Absolutely, be my guest, Anna." He closed RED's door on me and turned to make his way back to Martha.

Minutes later I gave a final wave to two beautiful people who were standing arm in arm again. I lifted off, rotated the chopper 360 degrees and made my way to Saanastia.

Back home.

Admiring the bird's eye view of the green lawns and the beautiful gardens, the rustic stone resort and the elephant barn, the homestead and its various sheds, yards and other outbuildings, Saanastia was a sight to behold.

I closed in to land on the big H that was painted on Saanastia's helipad. A few of the boys emerged as I shut the chopper down and I spent the next half an hour showing them how to load the chopper onto its dolly and push it into a temporary hangar made out of a domed tubular frame, covered in heavy taught liner fabric that spanned between the two forty-foot containers.

The Jet Ranger was quite a bit heavier than my R22, so I thanked my helpers and as always, their big welcoming smiles beamed back at me.

Finally, I covered the cabin and any holes and probes to stop the insects and birds from nesting.

RED was finally available for an overdue supply run that we had scheduled for the following day.

Before I knew it, it was late afternoon and I really wanted to see my elephant.

She was happily munching away and was well on her way to putting weight on again. Pretty soon she'd be fit enough to reintroduce to the herd, but then we might have a new dilemma to contend with, because we didn't have any guarantee that the herd dynamic would go back to how it was prior to Pragtig leaving it. There were so many layers to my life now and gone was the simplicity I used to live by.

"Hey Kabri," I announced myself picking up a second muck rake ready to help him clean the yard. As always, he had a rifle strapped to his body and the instruction was to never enter Pragtig's enclosure without at least one person being armed because we just couldn't be absolutely sure of her anymore. Time would tell once the routine started to get back to normal.

"Hello Miss Anna," he greeted warmly, "Come in, come in." He encouraged, waving me over.

"How is she today Kabri?" I asked, starting to pick up poo and transferring it to a trailer attached to an ATV.

"She is well and getting better every day," he answered adding to the load, while Pragtig shoved another trunk full of hay into her mouth and ambled over to say hello. Her trunk found one of my hands and she grabbed on, so I had to stop what I was doing.

"What is it?" I asked her, propping the fork against the trailer and rubbed her hide. Rumbling, she deftly slid her truck out from between my hands and prodded the pocket at my hip.

"Oh, I see how it is, you only love me for my mints now," which of course prompted me to produce the little packet for her. "Wait a minute" I held my finger up to ask her to her to hold off, and she politely took a step back before I fed her the mint, "good girl," I rubbed her trunk again.

Kabri grinned when I caught him looking at our interaction. I joined him in a smile, thoroughly enjoying these moments.

This had become somewhat of a routine for us of late, that if she begged for a treat, I'd quietly back her off so she wouldn't get rude about it and learn that she'd have to work a little harder for it. With Kabri's help initially, we made up short lessons where he'd help me to practice moving her around me to keep her spatially aware while I was with her. I used the same principle as I did with Blue.

Being so much bigger, I needed to use a long piece of bamboo to tap her body where I couldn't reach and give a command. The positive lure of a piece of fruit or a cuddle made it quite easy for me and pretty soon I could inspect her feet and lay her down. My goal was to be able to point and give a voice command and then wean her off the treats with a rub and a "good girl".

She wouldn't leave my side and became my extremely large shadow while I cleaned her yard. This meant I'd have to do my bit and be aware of her too or I could easily get hurt if I allowed her to get distracted and take her eyes off me.

My last job of the day was to prepare her evening concentrate feed, which was made up of nutritious pellets that were likely very similar to the feed I gave Blue twice a day. Bidding a farewell to my girl by wrapping my arms around her massive trunk, I left the yard, and said goodbye to Kabri before I went to find my own dinner.

Back at the homestead, I showered and made my way to the kitchen to see if Martha needed help. But surprisingly, it was Lloyd who was looking in the fridge to see what could be rustled up.

"Where's Martha?" I asked, retying my hair into a messy bun.

"Martha and Fred are having a date night," he mumbled monotonously.

"Naw, they're so cute, they make me want to hurl," I said, cooing sarcastically. "Do you want a hand with anything here?"

"Na, I'm beat, I'll just go and fix a sandwich and then hit the hay, it's going to be another big day tomorrow. You make what you want."

I opted to do the same, because I wasn't going to cook a full-on meal for just myself. I waited for Lloyd to finish with the fridge, so I could take my turn.

After a bit of a fossick, I managed to discover enough ingredients to make myself a really substantial chicken BLT. All I needed to do was fry the bacon, so I started pulling out everything that I needed.

I felt Lloyd's eyes on me and glanced at him, "What?" I asked self-consciously.

"That looks a million times better than what I had in mind," he said looking at the simple cheese and tomato he'd been planning to prepare.

"Is that your way of saying you'd like to have one too, Mr Staadman?" I asked him playfully, testing the waters to see if he'd at least be somewhat receptive to my friendly interaction with him.

He had the rare grace to look sheepish and then an even rarer crooked grin formed on his face "maybe?" He said quirking an eyebrow, all of which sent me into a spin to which I had to internally scold myself.

"Okay then," I said, struggling to unscramble my thoughts, "why don't you cook this," I handed him the packet of bacon rashers, free range, I noted, "and I'll put the rest together."

We worked in companionable silence, the room filling with the delicious smell of frying bacon, while I prepared the large slices of toasted sourdough bread, spread with mayo, relish, sliced avocado, shredded chicken, lettuce, cheese and tomato. When Lloyd had sufficiently crisped the bacon to perfection, I asked him to set it aside on a paper towel to drain while we cleaned up after ourselves.

Sliding the completed sandwich towards him, his eyes eagerly consumed it before he'd even laid a hand on it. "Can. Not. Wait to sink my teeth into that," he said, rubbing his hands together eagerly.

"Well, don't let me stop you," I said, urging him with a sweep of my hand at his plate.

I watched him as he picked up the stacked bread and brought it to his mouth. Staring intently at me as he bit into it, I watched him unashamedly and his reaction as he started to chew was like a train wreck. I just couldn't look away, his eyes rolled back before the lids closed and he let out a long groan. I thought that had to be one of the most erotic things I'd ever seen.

And that was exactly the thought that I needed to stop my incessant staring.

"Well, I think that's my cue to give you two a bit of privacy," I said gathering my own meal before I started to leave.

He placed his food back onto the plate and swallowed. He nodded and shrugged. "Hm. Not bad at all," he said, downplaying his actions.

"Not bad he says."

With that he grinned impishly, before following me out of the main room. He turned off all but the soft glow of a free-standing light next to one of the couches.

"Let's just say that you cook as good as you fly," he said, with a wink before he lifted his plate, "thanks Anna."

I did not expect that.

All I could manage was a shy, "you're welcome," and my heart swelled more than I wanted to admit.

Walking down the hall, Lloyd stopped at his room. "Be ready to fly by 0800," he said, without making eye contact and opened the door.

His words stopped my giddy state of mind in its tracks and I frowned at his retreating back before the door clicked shut, leaving me and my 'not bad at all' sandwich to ponder in the hallway.

I should have known that Lloyd's pleasant demeanour was too good to be true.

Sitting on the couch, watching telly with my dinner and a cup of tea, I was interrupted by a text message.

Glancing at the screen, I smiled when it showed that it was Carley.

Carley: Guess where I am?

"Oops," I said to myself. With getting caught up in the crazy goings on that led to my sudden departure from my homeland, I may have forgotten to tell her where I had ended up.

Judging by her ongoing intentions since she'd met Alan, I could deduce that Carley may not be as far away from me as she might have thought.

Anna: I'm guessing that you're not in Perth ;)

Carley: I didn't ask you to guess where I'm not Stedman :/

Anna: Well, I sure hope you're not going to knock on my door at home.

Carley: Grr... I'm dying to know what you mean by that, but we'll get to you in a sec.... anyway, about me.

Anna: Well, if you're not "home" I'd say you're sitting on Alan's lap.

Carley: You're good, you're good! *squeal Oh Anna! I'm, sooooo happy!

Anna: I think you guys should visit.

Carley: ?

Anna: I might be "just down the road from you."

My phone rang.

I swiped the screen.

"What the hell Stedman!?"

I had to pull the phone away from my ear and then spent the next ten or so minutes filling her in on how I came to be here.

"Just so I'm clear. You're telling me you're just there for the whirligig and for that behemoth, are you sure there's not more to it than that?"

"No!" I said a little too loudly, pausing for a moment to listen if I'd disturbed anyone, "I mean yes, I'm sure" I snapped, keeping my voice down.

Carley giggled, "Sure, you're sure, A."

I fumed silently at her insinuation... whatever it may have been.

"Look, Carley, I have a big day tomorrow, how about we catch up next time we're both free?" I asked, hoping to divert her train of thought.

"What a great idea!" She exclaimed, causing me to put some distance between me and the phone again.

I explained that I couldn't really leave overnight until Pragtig was more emotionally stable, which would be re-evaluated once she was back with the herd.

"No problem, we'll come to you instead!" She said, continuing with her boundless enthusiasm.

From there, we made plans and I'd be seeing her again on my next day off. Both her and Alan would stay at the resort for the corresponding weekend, so it would almost be like the holiday all over again.

I finished my tea, had a shower and went to bed, contemplating how life seemed to happen to me lately.

# Chapter 23

The morning was already heating up by the time I'd started prep at 0700. I'd been given a number of uniforms, the same as all the keepers that worked with the animals, so I definitely looked the part of a safari pilot. I heaved the chopper out of its shelter and onto the helipad. Luckily there was a concrete pathway and once I had her rolling, she wasn't too hard to move. Had there been grass or gravel between the two areas, then I'd have had no hope hauling her back and forth by myself.

Halfway between the hangar and the helipad stood a fuel tank on a tall stand filled with JetA1. I was really impressed with the set up considering that there was nothing but the helipad here when I last landed at Saanastia. Fred had made sure he had everything covered.

With the gravity feed, it didn't take too long to fuel up.

Similarly, to mustering on a station, I didn't have to worry about flight plans if I started from and then stayed on Saanastia property, so I used the remaining time cleaning the windows and doing the pre-flight.

The humidity was higher now that the build-up to the wet was closer than when I was here previously. I wiped my brow and had just replaced my aviators before I heard the footsteps of my passenger for the day.

Traitorous butterflies flapped about in my stomach and I couldn't help but to watch Lloyd swagger towards me. He carried a pack on one shoulder and a heavy gauge net was thrown over the other.

"Good morning," I said, offering a friendly greeting to start the day.

"Morning," he muttered, dropping his pack on the ground without missing a beat and continuing towards the makeshift hangar. By the time he came back, one of the boys, George as it turned out, had wheeled a trolley over with a few boxes to join Lloyd's discarded bag.

"Good morning Miss Anna, Mr Lloyd would like these loaded for Camp Foxtrot today please." He smiled brightly. Every camp was identified by the phonetic alphabet.

I grinned, "Morning George, have you got a final weight for me?"

"Yes Miss." He handed me a slip of paper.

"Thanks George, we'll see if we can get it all on, can you help me take out the back seats please?"

George agreed cheerfully and within ten minutes, the seats were slid off their rails and I left him to take them back to the storage container. After a few calculations we were well within our limits and I loaded the boxes on board. It looked to be general food supplies and toiletries. I covered them with a cargo net and tied it all down safely.

I said goodbye to George and sat myself in the pilot's seat while Lloyd was rummaging around in his pack.

"I've got something for you. A two-way," he said handing the walkie to me, "Clip it to your belt, it could be your lifeline if you're by yourself away from the helo and will be good for at least three miles. Further if you go higher. We mainly use them for operational coms, like the day we did the de-horning. You're responsible to keep it charged."

"Cheers," I said noting the channel before I clipped it to my belt.

"It's pre-set for Saanastia's own channel, memorise it and use it on RED's radio when you're flying."

I automatically glanced and pointed at the second UHF in the dash and noted that it had already been set.

"You shouldn't need to worry about any others not copying, there is always someone with their ears on. Whenever you go up, just treat the channel as your own personal traffic control inside the property to let everyone know where you're at, every ground base has a UHF so, you should be covered."

By the time he'd finished his spiel, he'd zipped the pack up again, stowed it and parked up beside me.

"Any questions?" He asked while he buckled in and reached for his headset.

"Nope, all good," I answered. This was the same sort of system I'd used before, so it wasn't new to me.

"Alright then, let's get out of here, head east and I'll show you any camps that come up along the way, you'd have noticed Fred's maps and the GPS," he said, pointing to the monitor in the dash, "have already been marked but, they can be fairly easily missed from the air, because we try to make them as inconspicuous as possible. Once you get your eye in on what you're looking for, you'll find them easily enough."

I nodded before I ran through my checklist, started RED and a few minutes later we were airborne and headed east until we hit the border fence and from there, we simply followed it.

The day was spent in relative silence as far as casual conversation went, but every time there was something important to point out, Lloyd spoke freely and informatively.

The most exciting part of the day was seeing the herds of game just being in their element. The day itself was uneventful and we would check the other parts of the property as needed. Halfway through, we set down at Camp Foxtrot and refuelled RED. We had lunch with a group of female rangers that weren't employed by Saanastia but were part of an anti-poaching team that worked alongside its interests. They simply passed through from camp to camp and were a little bit of added insurance for the wildlife on the property. Long ago, Lloyd had agreed to share any camp facilities to make things run more efficiently and comfortably for both organisations. I helped Lloyd offload the supplies that were gratefully received and then we were on our way again.

By the time we'd landed at 1500hrs, we'd travelled almost 1200 km and only covered a fraction of the property. Lloyd left me to put RED to bed and asked if I could have her fuelled and as flight ready as possible in case we needed to take off in a hurry.

The rest of the day was spent wherever I was needed and with my elephant until it was time to head back to the homestead again.

I hadn't seen Martha since the previous morning and upon my entry into the kitchen, I could hear her humming away merrily. That in itself put a smile on my face after what had already been a good day.

"Hey Martha," I greeted on my approach.

"Anna sweetheart!" She beamed at me.

"WOW, that good is it?" I chuckled. "What has you so chipper this evening?"

"Oh, you know, a little bit of this and a little bit of that," she answered.

I narrowed my eyes at her in suspicion, "Uh huh? That sounds suss, what are you up to?"

"Up to? Whatever do you mean dear?" She looked at me with wide eyed innocence, "I'm merely just happy that everything seems to be working out. Pragtig will be well enough to put back with the herd this week, you are settling in wonderfully and Lloyd seems more relaxed than he's been in such a long time."

I decided that it was reason enough and I asked if she wanted a hand getting the meal ready, but she shooed me off and told me to come back after I'd freshened up, which likely translated to: you stink and you're a grot, have a wash.

I could be forgiven for thinking I might have been lulled into a false sense that these calm, happy, easy going few weeks could stretch out forever, but I knew full well how quickly and easily that could change.

# Chapter 24

Carley and Alan arrived on Friday evening for their weekend stay and it was wonderful to catch up with them and do something that was outside of work. Carley made reservations for Saturday night at a local restaurant in town. I hadn't left the property at all in the time I'd been back, except to join Martha for the occasional weekly shopping trip, so I was looking forward to it.

The couple had a car, so we didn't have to trouble anyone to borrow a set of wheels.

When it was time to leave, we headed into town. It was the first time that I'd ventured away from the main shopping precinct and we found ourselves at a high-end golf course and country club on the outskirts of the settlement. Walking towards the building, we were surrounded by green fairways and stands of trees. The afternoon's thunder clouds were building in the distance and it would likely rain before our evening ended.

The buildings had very traditional looking grass thatch roofs and the walls were mud rendered, in keeping with the traditional theme.

Through the French doors, there were polished wooden floors and the ceiling was amazing. There were many timbers to support it, their criss-crossing nature adding to the appeal of the natural beauty of the style. Hanging from the rafters was the tasteful modern lighting and gently turning ceiling fans. The thatch was able to be seen from underneath, tightly and neatly bound in rows and supported by narrow stringers.

The décor in solid wood, finished off the look beautifully.

Different sized tables were strewn through the main reception room and a long bar was built to one side. Opposite to the bar there was a glass wall in French style windows and doors, overlooking the gardens and a beautiful view.

The place was well filled, we had a reservation that ensured a good seat overlooking the gardens and the green beyond. Alan was great and I didn't feel third wheel-ish at all with the couple. We ordered, and while we waited, we wasted no time catching up.

Carley had organised a working Visa almost as quickly as mine, thanks to Alan's help and she was lending a hand at the family law firm until she found her feet. Since their relationship developed so quickly, I wasn't entirely sure where said feet would take her and only time would tell. Not that it mattered for the moment, because she was ecstatically happy right now and I wouldn't be the one to begrudge her that.

Our meal arrived, we opted to have a banquet, which included a range of cultural stew like dishes set in the middle of the table. A plate piled high with flat bread called chapatti was our cutlery. The technique was to tear off a piece, and "pinch" up a portion of the dish. It was also good for mopping up the last dregs. The spices used in the variety of dishes were super yum if not a little hot, but there was a yogurt dish included to quell the heat, which also complemented the spicy food. I thoroughly enjoyed the experience and imagined eating this way with a large group of great people, out under the stars and around a campfire.

Alan was clearly thrilled that Carley was finally with him, he couldn't keep his eyes (or hands) off her and the meal was ideal for the both of them to feed each other, which was kind of sweet and kind of gross at the same time, to the point that sometimes I just had to look away.

For dessert, the love birds shared a serving of koeksisters - pastry twists smothered in a thick syrup - and I had a refreshing guava ice cream.

Alan excused himself to go to the 'little boy's room' - his words, not mine, but it did sound charming in a South African accent - and asked what drinks we wanted while he was up. I ordered my usual lemon, lime and bitters and Carley asked for a rum and coke.

Once we were alone, my friend couldn't wait for two seconds before she got 'that' look on her face and went straight for the jugular. "So," she leaned forward on the table, "How's your thing with Lloyd going?"

"Thing? What thing?" I asked, taking a sip of water.

"From the brief moments I've seen you guys near one another, that glint in his eye hasn't changed since the last time we were here, he still looks like he wants to ravish you every time he sets sight on you."

I almost choked on my water, "Carley, you've got one thing right, nothing has changed, but I've never seen him looking at me like that," I said before I cleared my throat some more.

"That's because you're always looking everywhere else but at him. Trust me, in doing that, it gives him more time to ogle you. He's not even aware that he does it unless you chance a glance at him, he's completely oblivious to it at any other time, you're like a magnet to him," she said knowingly.

Alan returned with the drinks leaving our conversation hanging and me of course overthinking, but at least the conversation changed to more general banter until it was time to leave.

We were just paying for our meal at the counter, when our attention was turned to a loud gaggle of women making their presence known as soon as they burst through the doors, accompanied by an ominous flash of lightning that silhouetted their form and added to the dramatic entrance.

Many of the guests also craned their heads toward the group who had the grace to quieten down once they realised that all eyes had landed on them.

They looked like they were just beaten by the rain and although slightly damp, they didn't seem too perturbed by their state.

Carley leaned into me and stage whispered, "Isn't that the Logie girl from the gala? What's her name again? And her hangers on?"

I nodded and right on cue, the woman in question caught my eye, the smile dropping off her face, before recovering quickly and returning her attention back to her friends.

"Gloria Veldsmaan," Alan said under his breath, not looking the least bit impressed.

"That's it!" Carley said, her memory jogged before we made the move to leave.

We passed the women as they waited to be seated, Alan nodded in acknowledgement, muttering Gloria's name and the woman mirrored him in kind. Carley and I stayed quiet and I kept my eyes downcast.

I felt the group's eyes follow us out, murmuring among themselves and then bursting into laughter the moment the large doors closed behind us.

"Bitches," Carley said from between her teeth, taking a hold of Alan's hand as we walked to the car. The storm had almost passed, with only light rain remaining and the occasional lightning flashing from a distance. We had to pick our way through the puddles to the car, the water dripped from the trees in the parking lot and everything felt fresh and washed free of the red dust.

Alan's tension continued once we were seated in the car and he sighed a few times as we drove back to Saanastia. "Don't know how she sleeps at night," he grumbled under his breath.

"She's a self-entitled brat, that's for sure," Carley added in support, indicating she clearly wasn't privy to the goings on between Gloria's family and Saanastia, and Alan wouldn't have told her of course, because he was bound by client confidentiality.

But I wasn't.

"I don't think that's what Alan's talking about Carley."

"What do you mean by that?" She asked.

"I'm not entirely sure, I might be putting two and two together and coming up with five. But remember that weird send-off that her dad gave me?"

Carley nodded.

"Well, with that and a few other things I've picked up on, I'm pretty sure that Gloria's father has something on Saanastia."

"Really? Wonder what it could be?" Carley asked.

"Well, let's not speculate," Alan suggested, "All I can say is that there's a long history between the Veldsmaan's and the Staadman's and that's no secret," he revealed.

"Care to share?" I prompted.

Carley squealed and clapped her hands in excitement, "Ooo I do love a bit of murder and intrigue," she announced dramatically, before she gasped, realising what she'd just said. "Shit, that didn't come out right, there's no murder is there?" She touched Alan's arm, "I hope not anyway," she said back peddling.

"Well there's plenty of intrigue that's for sure and tragedy. It's still talked about today and it's some story, let me tell you," Alan said, effectively dangling a carrot for us.

"Well. Don't let us stop you!" Carley exclaimed, prompting him excitedly.

"Just remember, it was about twenty-five years ago and has been told and retold, so it's become a bit of local folklore around here. There are official transcripts that are a matter of public record, but that never stopped anyone from getting in the way of a good story.

"I think that my rendition will be fairly on point, since our firm acts on behalf of Saanastia and it's kind of my business to represent the truth," he said, with the barest hint of mockery.

I scoffed at him.

Alan glanced at me in the rear vision mirror, the small creases appearing at the corners of his eyes, "Well client's version of the truth in any case," he amended, the grin evident in his tone before he went on to tell his version of the legend of Saanastia.

Saanastia was purchased by Lloyd's uncle and aunt along with his parents, who were silent partners. The property was originally a game park in the traditional sense, and while it somewhat controlled the number of animals within its boundaries, they also bred those that were highly prized. It had been set up to entertain rich businessmen who paid a handsome sum to hunt the animals for trophies.

Trophy hunting had of course been around since discovery, but these luxury game parks were in their heyday about seventy years ago and are still immensely popular now under the banner of conservation. It wasn't called Saanastia back then, it was part of Hoogevelt which had been in the Veldsmaan family for generations.

The Veldsmaan's ran into trouble on a bad mining investment and needed money to get out of it, so this piece of land was grudgingly sold off to do that.

The Staadman's had a vision to change the tourism demographic from shooting animals with guns to doing so with cameras and promote experiences focusing on the beauty of the surroundings and not on the blood sport.

Then poaching started to impact the wild herds of animals, with bush meat fetching a high price. But it was the ivory and rhino horn that was most highly prized. The fallout from that were the many orphaned youngsters, if they hadn't already died as a consequence. So the Staadman's started hand rearing what orphans came their way.

The project took four years to get to operating status, and it was then named Saanastia.

Lloyds aunt and uncle had a baby at around the same time and were ecstatic because they had trouble conceiving and everything seemed to go from strength to strength for them in the few years to follow.

But it was short lived, the pair had no more children after that, which devastated them and was the start of a very dark time for the family and for the property.

Lloyd's uncle was found dead one day, just after the child's sixth birthday. The coroner's report concluded that he was trampled to death by a herd of elephants. The kid disappeared without a trace, likely taken by predators.

Then Lloyd's parents were tragically killed in a fiery car accident near Pretoria about two weeks later.

To add insult to injury, Lloyds aunt couldn't cope and committed suicide a short while later.

"Wow, that's so unbelievably tragic," Carley said sadly.

"Sure is," I agreed, having heard some of snippets of the story during my stay.

"So, with none of the family alive anymore, who looked after Saanastia?" Carley asked.

"The family had good people helping them, who worked on the business as much as in it. Martha and many of the keepers are some of the original staff. The Staadman's were old money and well funded. It ran in its original capacity for another five or six years until Lloyd came back from war and took it on."

"Back from war?" I asked in surprise, just as Alan slowed the car on approach to Saanastia.

"Yes, but that's a whole other story that is Lloyd's to tell," Alan said tactfully.

I had so many questions but likely wouldn't get any answers from Alan since none of it was my business and he struck me as very professional, but that didn't stop me from wanting to know why there was a cloud over Saanastia and what Lloyd's story was.

Alan's rendition also reminded me of that know-it-all lady, the tourist who suggested Pragtig was a killer and I wondered if perhaps she was one of the elephants that was involved in the stampede that trampled Lloyd's uncle to death.

# Chapter 25

With the wet season firmly developing, everything at Saanastia slowed down and most of the work was focused away from tourism and more on the maintenance of the property.

My days started early, and because of that, I joined the early breakfast crew with Lloyd and the keepers every morning. This gave us a chance to discuss any plans that weren't already on the schedule with everybody there.

I was kept busy as tracks started to become impassable and now that RED was based at Saanastia, the chopper did more work than she had ever done previously when Fred was in the right hand seat.

Martha had done a great job to utilise the asset to its best ability and we were put to work on supply runs, general border checks and would even ferry our anti-poaching friends to save them from the struggle of long detours thanks to flood plains and fast moving rivers that couldn't be crossed conventionally.

This became particularly important when trackers were needed. Evidence would likely be washed away with the regular thunderstorms that rolled through almost every afternoon. It also helped to fund the helicopter thanks to an agreement that was made between the organisations. If RED was hired to work outside of Saanastia's borders, which was surprisingly often because one of its boundaries bordered onto Kruger National Park – a prime poaching target - then all costs would be covered. It all worked amicably, and every little bit helped to keep the resource viable.

Then came the day of an important milestone. Jerry was booked in to check on Pragtig and give her the all clear before we would finally let her attempt to re-join her herd.

Kabri and I hadn't been waiting long before he joined us in her yard with my big grey girl cosying up to me.

Pragtig's health check was a brief one. Heart, respiration, eyes, mouth, feet and her general condition score. Jerry was just labelling a blood test, when Lloyd also joined us.

"Hey Jerry, how is she shaping up?" He asked before briefly glancing at me.

"You guys have done a remarkable job. She could do with a few more kilos, but apart from that I think she's good to go," Jerry said.

The result sounded like music to our ears and I could feel the collective relief flow between us.

"Yay," I chortled, celebrating with some light clapping while Kabri's earlier concerned look had transformed into one of his toothy grins.

"Well that's the news we needed," Lloyd said at the same time, "now all we need to do is cross our fingers that she picks up from where she left off with the herd dynamic."

"Well, there's no time like the present," Jerry said.

Kabri and I worked at opening the yard gate and leading Pragtig into the home paddock enclosure where the other elephants had been kept while she recuperated.

After encouraging the giant elephant on her way, we watched her amble quietly toward the group before we retreated back to the safety of the yard, just in case they had an elephant herd moment with the reintroduction.

Watching on through the heavy steel rails, we anxiously waited to see what would unfold.

Pragtig approached a large bale of hay that had been refreshed that morning, the herd parted for her to access the feed and that was it.

"Well, that was a non-event," Lloyd announced after a few more minutes of observation.

"Best result we could have hoped for," Jerry said, before Lloyd shifted uneasily and cleared his throat. After an awkward moment Jerry finally spoke again, "Well, as much as I would love to stick around, I have stuff to do," he said, backing off the fence. "Anna, see you soon yeah?"

"Sure," I nodded, taking a peek at Lloyd who was keeping his eyes on the elephants.

"Kabri, Lloyd," Jerry said, acknowledging the men with a cursory nod.

"Anna," Jerry said lastly, his gaze lingering until I responded with his name in kind.

"I gotta go," Lloyd said abruptly and left without another word.

We ignored Lloyd's surliness and stuck around a little longer.

"You know them all so well Kabri, leaving her near them all this time seems to have worked, just like you thought it would." I said, commending him.

"You must keep them as close to nature as you can to keep them happy Miss Anna, and you are here to stay now, she knows that too." He spoke softly.

"We'll see Kabri, we'll see." I said, knowing that I had made Pragtig a promise, all I had to do was wait for the trial to conclude before I could come good on it.

"Ah," he stated with a glint in his eye, "Yes, we will see, but I can already see that Saanastia is close to your heart and it will hurt you more if you leave than if you stay. That is something that you have in common with Mr. Lloyd."

"Psht," I huffed, "Well I think that'd be the only thing we have in common Kabri," I said, chuckling lightly in disbelief.

"I think you have more in common than you think Miss Anna," he said softly, keeping his focus on the herd.

Kabri's words hung in the air. I really didn't have anything to say to that, because the very thought of it was absurd and I really needed to not think about it.

"C'mon Kabri, let's get this yard cleaned up," I suggested, to divert the conversation.

We chatted about what we could do to help Pragtig further without my twice daily visits. We had already surmised that she needed to know that I was around even though I might not be what could sometimes potentially be days. We also knew that she was very scent driven and had been okay for quite a while in the past without actually laying eyes on me. Kabri, thought it might be an idea to simply make a conscious decision to rub and touch as many of the spaces that Pragtig spent time in.

With the regular rain, it would mean I'd have to do this consistently, but as long as my job included daily access to those areas, it shouldn't present a problem.

We had a laugh when Kabri suggested it was Pragtig's way of insuring that I couldn't leave the country.

"First you, and now Pragtig are conspiring to keep me here, what are you two up to?" I asked, only half joking.

Kabri winked at me and laughed, "That is because you fit in well here, Miss Anna," he said as we finished up.

The boys always ate lunch at the elephant barn if they were working near the resort and I normally joined them, but sometimes I ate at the homestead with Martha.

Today was one of those days.

I found her sitting at the kitchen island no doubt still working, since she had her tablet propped up in front of her.

"Hey Martha," I said in greeting.

"Anna sweetheart," she said brightly, looking up from the screen. "What wonderful news about Pragtig earlier today."

"It is good isn't it?" I agreed, grinning at the thought, "I might even be able to get an hour extra sleep in the morning," I said as a joke.

Martha chuckled. "Imagine what you could do with all the extra time."

Lunch continued to be pleasant and uneventful until my two-way crackled, catching my attention.

"Anna, you got your ears on? Over," Lloyd asked, the stress evident in his voice.

A lick of adrenalin jolted through me, "It's Anna. Go ahead Lloyd. Over."

"Anna, get the helo ready, we need to be out of here ASAP, we have a rescue to pick up beyond our border. I'll send you coordinates now. Over." Lloyd said, my heart dropping with the instruction.

"Onto it. Out," I said, looking up at Martha, who returned my troubled expression.

"I guess I'll see you later?" I called over my shoulder to Martha.

Martha gave me a weak wave, before I went to my room to grab what I needed, and then headed to the helipad to get the chopper ready.

The location came through and I logged the flight. Half an hour later Lloyd and Jerry arrived.

Lloyd addressed me with his usual brief eye contact and then went to check we had everything we needed in the back of the chopper.

"Hey," Jerry greeted, his smile not reaching his eyes.

"Hey," I said, parroting him automatically, "what are we picking up and what does it weigh?" I asked no one in particular and at the ready to work out my load figures.

"He's a two-month old elephant and about a hundred and fifty kilos." Lloyd answered.

I nodded and I asked for Jerry's numbers, knowing he was leaner than Lloyd, adding up the amounts to the fuel and the other gear. I still had fifty-three kilos up my sleeve, thanks to the excess seats and the doors I'd already removed from the Jet Ranger. We would also burn fuel on the way, so we'd be well within RED's lifting capacity.

Finally when all checks and balances were made, Lloyd asked, "are you going to be able to handle the scene when we get there? It's not always pretty. If we're lucky, the calf might have wondered off, but that rarely happens."

"Yeah, I'll be fine," I assured him, before we lifted off.

Due to the doors being removed, we couldn't travel as fast as RED's normal cruising speed. It was the compromise we had to make versus the weight and accessibility. It also meant we burnt more fuel because the air wasn't able to slide over the smooth shape the doors gave. But we only had about a hundred kilometres to fly, so none of that was really a problem.

What was a problem, was the scene that we were met with when we got there.

As we closed in on our location south of Saanastia, I watched for any circling birds that waited for an opportunity to scavenge.

Fortunately, for them at least, they were going to feast. I counted nine dead adult elephants strewn over a few hundred metres as well as a couple of younger elephants. I kept my focus on where the trackers stood and landed where Lloyd suggested.

Jerry asked me to bring his vet case when I was ready, he left the chopper with his tranq gun and dart case. Lloyd had the net and a small toolbox. I finished shutting RED down and followed the two men to where the trackers were busy explaining the turn of events.

Looking around I noted that the nearest elephant to where we stood had a gaping hole in the front of its head where the trunk and tusks used to be and it was laying in a large black pool of dried blood. The tusks were gone and the trunk was left discarded not far away. Its body was riddled with bullet holes, each one caked in the dark stain of the blood that had once freely flowed until the elephant could stand no more.

It was a devastating scene and one that would never leave me. Tearing my eyes away from the gruesome sight, I needed the distraction that came from lots of chatter, pointing and gesturing from the people on the ground. After some planning, and with everyone in agreement, we were led though the scrub to where all were asked to get down and stay quiet. I was prompted to hang back with three rangers while the tracker, Lloyd and Jerry continued on.

From our vantage and not too far from us, we could see another large female. Her face also mutilated as she lay there wasted, the flies gathered in a thick crust on the wounds and were hanging in clouds over the carcase.

And for what? Some pretty trinkets?

My blood boiled at the devastation. I took a deep breath of stale, still air, the smell of death not strongly apparent yet and I tried to calm my emotions.

A hand softly touched my shoulder before squeezing, and I turned to glance behind me. Dark eyes met mine, the flawless face of the fierce and proud female ranger sharing her strength with the gesture. She too was angered, but she had seen it all before and was much less animated and well-trained than I to keep calm and carry on.

Patting her hand in solidarity, we watched on. On the other side of the large grey mound, the calf was sadly feeling between his mother's front legs for her udder.

Who knew how long it had been since his last drink?

Who knew how long he'd last out here in this harsh wilderness on his own before the predators picked him off as he continued to weaken?

Who knew that once we interfered, if he'd survive the stress thereafter?

But we had to try.

Once the little elephant was darted and out for the count, everyone sprang into action. Jerry took vitals and covered the animal's head with a damp towel before taping it down.

Lloyd and I spread out the net and on three, the little guy was lifted onto it.

This made it much easier to carry him to the chopper and within minutes, I had laid out the long line and we made sure that every part of my precious load was properly positioned before I double checked that all the fasteners and fittings were safely secured.

I went through my start sequence and waited for the rotors to make speed and for the boys to jump in.

With a wave to our rangers, I engaged the collective and lifted off. By using the helicopter's floor windows and physically hanging my head out of the door, I monitored the tension on the sling and felt the new weight of the load. I eased us further off the ground and in a seamless motion, I pushed the cyclic forward before slowly and carefully making it to cruise speed.

The flight back was sombre and fairly silent, except for my radio calls and any necessary communication between the three of us. I knew that later, when I had time to process the gruesome scenes that I had seen today, I wouldn't be quite so stoic as I appeared right at this moment.

I thought of those brave women, the rangers and how focused they were. I wondered why they used women?

"They make better rangers." Lloyd's voice carried over the intercom.

"Pardon?" I asked.

"You asked why they used woman." Lloyd informed.

"Oh, did I say that out loud?" I asked in surprise.

He didn't answer me.

I squirmed a little. "So, why do they make better rangers? It's clearly a tough job and looks like hell."

"Anna, it's because they come from hell that they're so good at the job. What you saw there," he said thrusting a thumb over his shoulder from the scene we had left behind, "is a cakewalk by comparison. Dan, the CEO of the foundation that trains them, has given them an education, training, a way to support their children, escape abuse and keep a roof over their heads. It is tough, but those women? They're tougher. Tougher than most men." He said proudly.

He left me to process his words, until we finally started our decent into the Saanastia compound.

# Chapter 26

"Anna, wait up," Lloyd called out on the way back to the homestead after wrapping up another long day.

The young elephant had made it to the end of the day and was hanging in there... just.

"I wanted to say great job out there today." He said, catching up to me.

Wait what?

"Uh, thanks?" I questioned him, taken aback.

My expression must have shown my utter surprise at his compliment.

"Seriously, it was pretty rough out there and honestly, I..."

"...You didn't think I had it in me?" I asked.

"No! Not at all! I was going to say, I was pretty impressed. By the same token, I wouldn't have blamed you if you didn't have it in you, especially going in cold like that."

He looked decidedly uncomfortable, which was equal parts odd and amusing.

"Huh, really?" I asked, lost for anything else better to say.

Lloyd nodded, rubbing the back of his neck. "Yeah. And thanks." He said, continuing with his discomfort.

"Gees Lloyd, don't give yourself an aneurysm or anything," I said, no longer able to suppress the grin that had been threatening to bubble over.

"Ha!" He gave me a lopsided smile, "I guess I deserved that," he said, knowing as well as I did, that he wasn't one to give attagirl's out willynilly.

"Yeah well, I appreciate it, even coming from you." I said joking with him.

With the smirk staying on his handsome face, he narrowed an eye at me and said, "Just don't get too used to it."

"Right." I said with a nod.

"Say, are you coming to the barbeque tonight?" He asked, taking his cap off and running a hand nervously through his hair.

"Barbecue? What barbecue?"

Lloyd shrugged, "Just something me and the guys are putting on, it's no big deal. It'll be up on the deck. Fred and Martha will be there," he said, sounding like he wasn't actually asking under any duress and wanted me to come.

"And Jerry?" I asked, hoping he would be, even though I'd have liked to go either way.

Lloyd tensed his jaw for a moment, a gesture so subtle, that it could easily have been missed. "Yep. Jerry will be there," he said in a clipped tone.

"Ok then, count me in," I said with a smile.

Then Lloyd nodded and turned on his heel, before leaving me abruptly in his wake.

Was it something I said?

Later, at the homestead, I could hear Lloyd's agitated voice when I returned to my quarters to get ready for the barbie.

He was clearly on his phone, because I couldn't hear who he was talking to, but there was a tone of incredulity to his exchange.

It wasn't my business, so I drowned it out by taking a shower.

All cleaned up in plenty of time, I decided to make a quick salad while waiting for Martha to surface.

The restaurant wasn't open, so we had the deck to ourselves and the boys had already shuffled things around and had the grills sizzling before we even got there.

Dress code was smart casual, so I just popped on a patterned boho style maxi dress that I'd picked up at a town market while on one of Martha's shopping trips and I added a pair of strappy sandals. I loosely braided my hair and forwent any make up as I didn't see the point in dolling up too much. I saw these people every day, I had my "town clothes" on and that should have been enough.

Looking around, I recognised most of the faces, including many of the keepers, who weren't on duty, grounds staff and their families. Martha and I were joined by Fred and Jerry, who arrived together and only minutes after we did. After a warm greeting with a few cheek kisses, the boys were gentleman enough to get some drinks for us, before the energy changed and Lloyd made his grand entrance.

And he wasn't alone.

I could almost feel our whole gathering collectively look on in trepidation while the ever ostentatious Gloria hung off Lloyd like a leach. Dressed like she was going to a night club with everything either plunging or... not.

"Not leaving much to the imagination that one," Martha said under her breath with contempt.

Lloyd often looked some level of.... surly and more so this evening than I'd seen him in a while.

The attractive couple walked past us and towards the bar with Gloria radiating "mine" in her strange parade.

I turned to Martha. "Who invited that lovely ray of sunshine?" I asked her.

"Hmph," Martha grunted, "no invite needed apparently." She said in a hushed tone.

"I did hear him arguing with someone earlier while I was getting ready, couldn't understand a word though. Maybe it was with her and Lloyd made the invitation."

"Perhaps," Martha murmured quietly.

"Now, now, ladies. Let's not spoil the night, let's just eat well and enjoy ourselves," Fred said showing himself to be the voice of reason.

It didn't mean that Martha wouldn't throw a dagger Gloria's way every now and then.

I just needed to make sure to keep my back to them so I wouldn't be tempted to do the same.

After piling up our plates with the delicious food that everyone had brought with them, we found ourselves sitting well away from where the notorious couple were engaging themselves, and spent a comfortable hour enjoying each other's company before Jerry was called away early to check on the elephant calf. He apologised, excused himself and promised that he'd be back if he could.

Watching Jerry leave, I had a weak moment and glanced in the direction that I really shouldn't have.

Gloria and Lloyd were standing on the deck in deep conversation. Gloria caught me staring and sneered at me with narrowed eyes just as Lloyd was answering his phone. I was sure that if he didn't have her company tonight, that he would have mingled or even sat with us, but Gloria seemed to have monopolised him for the evening. She clearly influenced him, and not for the better, which was interesting, because from what I had witnessed, he was certainly a man who worked hard, he didn't flounce and wasn't interested in grandstanding.

Their complicated 'relationship' baffled me because Gloria seemed to have nothing in common with his lifestyle.

Perhaps the volatile conversation that I had witnessed between he and Gloria after the Gala had been negotiated. Perhaps their relationship was like his mood.

A constant state of flux.

How far would Lloyd go to get what he wanted? Not that it was any of my business.

My business or not, it didn't stop me from surreptitiously watching the couple from the corner of my eye as they appeared to be in a deep discussion. It also didn't stop my stomach from rolling when the couple left early. Gloria eyeballed me, looking extremely smug while walking past our table with Lloyd's arm possessively caught in her death grip.

It didn't take much for me to assume where they were probably heading off to, and from the way that Martha shook her head in disappointment, it looked as though she might have come to a similar conclusion.

The mood soured and it wasn't long before our little group also decided to call it a night.

The next morning, I wasn't feeling all that bright eyed and bushy tailed. I didn't sleep very well with all the thoughts that were rattling around in my head no matter how hard I tried not to think them.

Seeing Martha at breakfast led me to believe that I wasn't the only one who was short on sleep.

Lloyd didn't join us for breakfast, but that in itself wasn't all that unusual, because he often started early or had things to do off the property. But, more than that, Martha mentioned that he apparently didn't come home at all last night, which only served to confirm the things I was obsessing over.

Maybe his absence answered the question about how far he'd go to get what he wanted.

Aghh! Why, oh why was I letting this get to me like it did? Lloyd was a grown arse man who could spend time with anyone he wanted in any way he wanted. Jealousy was not a good fit on me, and I had no business wearing it in the first place.

So, with renewed vigour, I vowed to just work hard and not have these silly girly dreams, when it just wasn't worth wasting time entertaining the idea that I chase them.

I was an employee here and it would be best if I remembered that.

So from that day, I planned to buckle down and focus on work. Being too heavily invested in people's personal lives was only going to end in a world of hurt.

Of course, like with most things, the first day is always the hardest.

Kabri was quiet at the barn when we were doing our morning chores and informed me that Lloyd and Jerry had been up all night trying to save the little elephant. Unfortunately, he didn't make it and had passed away from complications on the operating table.

Guilt stabbed at me. Here I was assuming the worst in Lloyd when he was busy fighting for the calf's life.

It just served to cement my commitment even further. My assumptions were really messing with my head.

I did at one point, offer Lloyd my condolences, but he merely nodded and went about his work.

And that's how it continued. Apart from what had to be said, not much was said at all.

Eventually my days found a rhythm and thankfully nothing too 'exciting' happened and before I knew it, Christmas was almost upon us.

The build up to Christmas was surprisingly low key, because everybody thankfully had their own family commitments. So, we stayed in and I helped Martha with an Aussie style Christmas dinner to beat the heat. Prawns, salads, cold cuts, and I made a pavlova.

Lloyd remained subdued but not grumpy, thanked me for the pav and went to bed early.

Christmas morning was also a quiet affair.

We all made an effort to enjoy a hearty breakfast and then partake in the gifting of presents.

I received a lovely perfume from Martha, she gifted Lloyd his favourite aftershave which could easily become mine too. I wasn't that creative and stuck with gift vouchers. Martha had one to her favourite spa and Lloyd was happy with his from a hardware store, because what self-respecting man (or woman for that matter) didn't appreciate that?

And then Lloyd blew me away with his contributions.

I gasped as I took the wrapping off a framed picture of me and Pragtig sharing a beautiful moment.

"That was taken one day when you were leading her for a walk, and she was looking for those damn mints. She'd just placed her trunk over your shoulders to check your chest pocket and I happened to snap it at the right time." Lloyd said reminding me of the moment.

"I remember that day!" I giggled, "a second later, I moved her trunk aside because she felt me up, thank god you didn't catch that!" I said laughing, my eyes not leaving the endearing snapshot in time.

I even heard Lloyd chuckle.

"I didn't know that you took photos though, this is really beautiful!" I said, glancing at him. "Thank you so much," I said, desperately wanting to give him a hug, but forcing myself to refrain.

"There's a lot you don't know about me Anna," he said.

My eyes shot to his over his provocative words, his intense gaze meeting mine for a long moment before he broke off and handed Martha her present.

Another beautiful candid photo, but of her and Fred dancing together at the Gala.

I wondered when he had time to do that? How did he manage to notice these tiny details when he himself was so occupied with all the goings on, especially since Martha had not seemed quite herself that night.

It was clearly evident that Fred was as good for her as she was for him, because the pair appeared totally besotted with one another in that picture.

After Martha and Lloyd shared a warm hug, I had to agree that yes, there certainly was a lot more to Lloyd than he commonly shared with people.

With no rest for the wicked, I excused myself, left the table, washed up and headed towards my quarters to finish getting ready and to issue a flight plan for when I left the northern border of Saanastia later that day.

My photo got pride of place on my bedside table, where it would be the first and the last thing that I would see every day.

I picked up my overnight bag and supplies before meeting up with Lloyd and heading out to the helipad.

On this day, I'd be taking Lloyd to The Elephant Out Post for some routine maintenance. The camp was closed at this time of the year and with so much water lying about, the easiest access was of course by helicopter. There was a caretaker there for the off season, to look after things and do basic maintenance, but there were a few issues that required more than one person to address. We didn't know how long the projects were going to take, so we expected to glamp the night.

I was a little nervous at the thought, but it really wasn't any different to our arrangement here, only that Martha wouldn't be 'under the same roof'.

That's what I would tell myself anyway.

One of the ranger camps were also due for supplies. Luckily, the Out Post was almost on the way there, so after replacing RED's doors, we loaded as many supplies as weight restrictions would allow and that would kill two birds with one stone.

We set off mid-morning and were at the Out Post well before noon. There was water lying over the river flats and the muddy brown river itself was so fast flowing, that there were rapids and brown foam churning in a few places.

I set RED down in the gravel car park, the highest point near the Out Post that had enough rotor clearance and was hard enough not to sink into. A man stood next to a four by four to greet us. He looked a little rough around the edges, but I guess it didn't matter for he had no one to impress out here.

His sandy hair and scraggly reddish beard hadn't seen a trim in a while, and he wasn't dressed in a Saanastia uniform either, settling instead for a wife-beater, shorts and bare feet. It brought me back to growing up on the station where I'd often look the same for weeks at a time during the wet season. Minus the scraggly reddish beard of course.

This part of Saanastia was like a rain forest and so much more tropical than near the Resort, so I understood that having shoes on that were permanently wet wasn't comfortable or ideal to wear all the time.

"Well howdy Lloyd. Fred sure got a lot prettier since the last time I saw him." Were the first words that came out of the man's mouth in a heavy American accent.

"Randal." Lloyd said tightly, before he shook the scruffy man's hand. "Nice to see you dressed up for us. This is Anna," he said, before placing his hand at the small of my back causing a traitorous thrill to ripple up my spine, "and she's our gun pilot."

"If I'd known you were going to bring this lovely lady, I'd have made an effort." Randal said in his southern drawl. "Ma'am" he looked me up and down "I'm Randal, but my friends," he shot an impish look at Lloyd, "call me Randy," he said grinning wickedly although not in a creepy way.

He received a glare from Lloyd that didn't deter him in the least. "I'm very pleased to meet your acquaintance," he said further stirring the other man before holding out his hand for me to shake.

"Nice to meet you Randal," I said, giving his hand a firm squeeze.

"Oh, you're an Ossie, from the land down under," he said, causing me to suppress a laugh at his description, "that's even more lovely, may I take your bag, Anna?" He asked laying on the southern charm, that was clearly more for Lloyd's benefit than my own.

"I'll do it." Lloyd said in a rush, "you just see that you put some steel caps on," he said while Randal continued to grin mischievously.

I tried hard to hold in a giggle and shook my head at what I could see was the start of a pissing contest.

"That's fine gents, I can manage my own bag, thanks," I said, confounding them both.

"I'll show you to your room." Lloyd said eying the lanky man with a warning glare. Lloyd stuck to me like glue while escorting me down the board-walks to our quarters.

"You'll have to forgive Randal, he doesn't people very often," Lloyd said thinking he needed to excuse his friend's behaviour. "He's a naturalist and stays for nothing in return for the work he does around here and then spends the rest of the time in Indonesia's rainforests." Lloyd said, rambling more than I'd ever heard him do before.

"I thought he was charming," I said in response.

"Charming?" Lloyd asked in surprise.

I nodded.

With a shake of his head, Lloyd gave me a lopsided smile. "Damn Yankee," he said, mumbling under his breath.

Smiling, I asked, "How did you find him?" Knowing it had to have been an interesting story.

"In Afghanistan," Lloyd said simply, the conversation shedding its light hilarity.

Clearing his throat, he continued. "Here's your room, I'll be right next door and I'll radio the rangers and let them know you'll be leaving shortly."

Stepping into the familiarly of the high-end tent, I freshened up and had a drink of water before heading back out and knocking on Lloyd's door.

Answering it a moment later, he still appeared stoic.

"I'm good to go, boss," I said.

He nodded, and we both stood there awkwardly for a moment.

"Ok," I said letting out a breath, "I'll see you guys later this arvo," and I turned to go.

"Fly safe," he said.

I tamped down my rush of blood and continued to walk away, giving a single wave as a salute. "Always do" I said in acknowledgment.

Minutes later, I was skittering not too high from the treetops. My heading was north west, towards those brave female rangers, who risked their lives every day tracking poachers and often being shot at.

Sometimes they maimed or even killed those they tracked if there was an altercation. The job took them away from their kids and loved ones for long periods at a time, all to protect the animals and never forgetting that it was a vastly better life than the one they came from. The life where they were threatened, mutilated, beaten, raped and that's if they were lucky.

As the tall timber of the lush rainforest canopy thinned to scrub, I realised that I had certainly lived a very privileged life, and for all the hard times that I may have had, it all paled in comparison to these amazing and strong women. Crossing the road that separated Saanastia from neighbouring land, I radioed as soon as I flew into restricted airspace and I didn't have too far to go before I'd reach Camp November.

Once on the ground and while we were unloading RED, the women came across as very shy, very respectful and as always, very grateful for what they received for the fundamental basics that should be a right. Their english was actually quite good, and they said they admired the fact I was a pilot. Which was a bit funny coming from a woman clad in camo gear with a semi-automatic strapped to her back. We laughed girlish giggles when we admitted that we thought that both our bosses were handsome, and they thought I was lucky that at least my boss wasn't married and asked why I hadn't done something about that yet.

What could I possibly say to that?

Lord give me strength!

# Chapter 27

It was funny how girls were the same all over the world and like a dog with a bone when it came to hunky guys and gossip.

I don't think my ranger friends were at all convinced nor did I have the time to repeat my denials regarding any designs they thought I should have had on Lloyd, so I just let them continue to think what they wanted and we said our good byes.

I radioed Lloyd to let him know I was on the way and then a short time later, RED and I were soaring again, over the scrub-land at a good clip and heading back towards the Saanastia border.

Five minutes after passing the road, I spotted something on the ground, and turned back to see if it was anything of note. I circled the area and there under a thicket of acacia was a rhino laying on its side.

It looked dead.

"Shit," I mumbled to myself, before I radioed Lloyd on the ground channel.

"Lima one, Bravo one, do you copy?"

A few moments passed before the radio crackled, "Bravo 1, Lima 1 what's up Anna?"

"Lloyd, I've found a rhino, it looks recently dead, did you want me to take a closer look?"

"Yeah, go low as you can and assess."

I did as he asked and got low enough to be able to see things in more detail, gasping, I had to fight to keep RED steady as tears sprang to my eyes. I took her higher so I was safer because I could never unsee what I had just witnessed.

"Lloyd!" Procedures and formality went out the window, "it's still alive! It's still alive!" I said desperately. "Its horns are gone and I saw it move!"

I had been well versed on the despicable methods used to harvest the prizes that only the animals needed. I had already seen the aftermath of unloading hundreds of AK47 rounds into a herd of elephants, but this was different. This animal had been tranquillised. Poachers found this the easiest way to get what they wanted from a lone animal. They didn't need a good aim, they just had to hit the animal once and follow it until it dropped to the ground. They weren't interested if it was conscious or not, so long as the body was paralysed, that's all they cared about.

"Anna, listen to me," I heard Lloyd's steady voice cut through my musings when he asked me to dial up a closed channel so we could speak freely.

"Do you have enough fuel to come and collect me and still get back to the resort?" Lloyd's voice crackled over the airwaves,

Doing the quick calculation in my head helped me to focus. "No, even after reserves, we'll be short."

"Shit." He said.

The radio stayed silent for what seemed like forever.

"I'll do it." I said quietly, knowing that I couldn't live with myself if I continued to let the animal suffer a moment longer than it needed to.

"Anna you don't have to ok?"

"Yes, I do! Lloyd, I can't just leave it there!" I said, taking RED on a quick circuit to check if there were any predators about.

"If you're going to go through with this Anna, make sure you have enough rounds, it may take a few to do the job because you're not carrying a large enough weapon to guarantee a single kill shot," he said in a cool and calming voice. "And could you punch in the coordinates into the GPS for me? For our records..."

I complied, confirming with him and when I deemed it as safe as it was ever going to be, I set the chopper down, not far from the site and let her wind down to an idle.

We discussed where the ideal kill shot was, while I unbuckled from my harness and then unclipped the 308 from its cradle behind the front seats.

"They're pea brained Anna, your line needs to be accurate, and don't get too close, you'd be surprised how quickly they can get up no matter how injured they are."

"Ok." I said, noting his advice, my nerves on edge before I started to visualise my movements.

"Be careful, be aware of what's around you, you might have attracted predators by landing there, and remember I'll be right here for you." If he was anxious, I didn't hear it in his voice, but his support calmed me more than I could hope for.

"I know, Lloyd, I know."

Hanging up my headset, I opened the door and then proceeded to check the ammunition, counting four in the magazine. I gingerly climbed out of the helicopter and once I was clear from under the rotors, I looked around me, taking a deep and shaky breath before heading towards the prone rhino.

Carefully, I stepped into the thicket and to where the rhino lay. Its body came into view and when it heard me approach, It's ear twitched.

"Ah, you poor thing," I whispered to it and also to myself. Another few steps closer and I saw it struggle to lift its head, and the noise it made, I would never forget it.

A helpless squeak-like scream resounded, a huge animal like that, terrified of what was about to happen because it was barely living with what had already happened, its head was blackened and oozing and there was a pool of drying blood soaked into the earth beneath. The closer I got, the harder it struggled to lift its head, the continued squeaks of panic ripped my heart to shreds as it hammered in my ears. It was the second most awful thing I'd ever witnessed and the single most awful thing I'd ever had to do in my relatively short life.

Once there was only a few feet between us, I waited a few moments to position myself until I found my stable base.

Taking another deep breath, I finally locked the bolt, raised my arms and aimed. Feeling a distracting trickle of sweat run down my back, my hands and arms shook, so I delayed and regained my focus, licking my salty lips.

Again, I aimed, "Sorry, so sorry," I whispered to the pathetic creature before I fired.

It took all four shots.

Four! The last one echoed around me before all that was left was the sound of the idling chopper in the background.

I lowered the rifle and looked over this once beautiful animal before approaching it to check its eyelid reflex.

"Rest easy big fella," I said to him before I turned to walk back to the chopper. I suddenly felt so exhausted and my feet felt heavy as I trudged through the tall, green grass.

I needed to get away from here and all I wanted to do was get back to the Out Post and to Lloyd.

RED was waiting and ready to go, so I stowed the gun, buckled in and radioed.

"Lloyd are you there?" I asked in a flat tone. Talking was difficult and it was taking everything I had not to break there and then.

"I'm here," he said without delay, giving me a sense of relief.

"It's done, I'm on my way, ETA approx.," I looked at my watch, "fifteen thirty."

"Copy, I'll be waiting for you, are you ok?" He asked, so gently and with concern.

"I've got to go, I'll be there soon."

I changed the radio back to the open channel.

The thirty minute flight felt like forever and all I could feel was my tight throat whilst forcing myself to hold it together. I touched down and powered off before throwing my headset to the passenger seat, unbuckling and slumping forward over the cyclic, my arms leaning on the dash and my head resting on my arms. The images scrolled through my mind, not just the ones that I'd seen, but also those that I hadn't registered straight away and those that I started to imagine that led up to the rhino being left like that.

We could be so unbelievably cruel.

The cabin door opened, and a strong hand touched my back. "How ya holding up Bravo?"

"They just left him to wake up, they didn't even kill him first before chain sawing his face off," I whispered, "what kind of human does t...?" My voice cracked, and I could feel my features contorting in an ugly cry without my permission.

Lloyd gathered me to him where I sobbed into his chest, his arms were strong, holding me together, rubbing my back soothingly until the onslaught subsided. His voice murmuring in understanding as he tried to calm me.

I don't know how long we sat like that. But eventually I calmed down and Lloyd tilted my head back to check on me, smoothing the wisps of hair back from my teary and snotty face. As the moment lingered, my heart fluttered, and I reminded myself that nothing more could happen between us. I took a breath and it shuddered from my crying session, "I'm sorry about your shirt." I glanced at the damp khaki fabric.

He looked at me quizzically and held the sides of my neck, so I was facing him, we looked into each other's eyes and after a long moment Lloyd's brows knitted and a confused expression crossed his features before he smiled.

"You're kidding right?" He asked incredulously, stroking his thumbs over my cheeks, "you've just done one of the most difficult things that any of us could ever be asked to do, doing it on your own with, no real preparation or support..."

"You where there," I said, reminding him quickly.

"I really wish I was, I wish I was there to, to... well, anyway the point is you were the one that went through that and yet here you are, feeling all sorry for leaving my shirt with face juice on it?" He asked, staring at me with a questioning smirk.

"Face juice?" I asked, our intimate moment ending.

I pulled away and reached for the tissues stored in the door pocket.

"Help me put RED to bed?" I asked, slipping on my shades and lowering myself out of the chopper, causing him to step back a little before I blew my nose.

"Sure, just this once," he quipped, before lending a hand.

We both stayed silent after that. I was grateful that he didn't press the issue, I still had a lot to process without being prodded and staying busy was the best way for me to hold it together to stay focused, especially since I was our only means of getting out of here in any sort of good time.

Randal had also thoughtfully kept chit chat to a minimum and had prepared a light meal for us that was ready and waiting as Lloyd and I arrived at the fire pit where I'd eaten the last time I was here. The southerner was a pescatarian and his food was wonderfully prepared and flavoured with mostly food that he grew or foraged with only the basics supplied by Saanastia. We had fish curry with flat bread on the side and an amazing sweet yam dessert.

I looked like we were going to be staying longer than anticipated the following day due to the delay caused by the rhino drama.

I was just so tired, so I excused myself and retired early. I needed to scrub today off my body and have some quiet time to myself.

I struggled to get to sleep, first with a thunderstorm, then the inability to shake the visions in my head and then I also had a restless leg which annoyed me to no end so hours later, I finally had enough and got up to take a walk outside.

My bare feet padding the boards, I moved almost silently on the decking before I was attracted by the glow that shone from the flickering flames of the fire pit.

A swag with a mozzie net tented over the top was set up next to the fire. Sitting on one of a number of shaped boulders that were strategically placed to be benches, was Randal repairing a canvas awning by hand.

He looked up as soon as he caught my movement and gave a friendly wave.

"Hey girl," he said, before I propped myself up on a rock bench to sit across from him. Drawing up my legs, I wrapped my arms around them and rested my chin on my knees.

Randal didn't push for conversation and we sat there quietly for some time with only the night sounds and the crackling fire breaking the silence.

"No glamping when you have the opportunity?" I finally asked of his simple camp set up.

"This is glamping, for a man like me, Anna," he said in his drawling accent, pushing the thick sewing awl through the layers of canvas with his work hardened hands.

"Couldn't sleep?" He asked, looking up for a moment. I shook my head and another film role of graphic pictures flashed through my mind.

He sighed, "Mother nature can be a cruel mistress," he paused for a moment as he threaded the waxed twine to lock another stitch, "but humans are by far, so much crueller than mother nature could ever be. That's why I can only stomach them in small doses."

"That's why you're reclusive?" I asked and quickly adding, "for want of a better word."

"Suits me just fine," He said pushing the heavy gauge needle through the canvas again.

"Hmm, I kind of get that," I said, looking into the licking flames.

"I gather Lloyd told you we met while we were serving?" He asked.

I nodded again as he peaked up from his work.

He stopped what he was doing, "What else did he tell you?"

"Nothing really, he's my boss" I shrugged. "He's not in the habit of giving out free information and why would he? I hardly know him or anything about him, so ..."

"Just your boss huh?" He raised a brow in question.

"Yes," I reaffirmed, "why do you ask?"

He shook his head in disbelief, "Anna, my brother man there," he said tipping his head in the direction of our rooms, "gave off some pretty strong 'hands off' vibes after you flew off for the day."

"Oh, do I want to know why he felt the need to do that?" I asked.

"Let's just say that my lifestyle has allowed my gentlemanly manners to slip a little, and I may have said something that almost caused him to put them back by way of my rear."

"I see," I said, wondering what that may have been, but if I asked, he may actually tell me, and if he told me, I might wish he hadn't.

So, I didn't.

I continued to stare at the flickering flames of the fire pit. No good could come from this for Saanastia and therefore, for Martha and Lloyd either if I were to poke the bear.

Or as Carley would say, the bear were to poke me. Because she was crass like that.

"There's nothing going on and he's seeing someone so..." I shrugged and my eyelids started to feel heavy, "anyway, I really need to get some shut eye, I'll see you in the morning." I said, standing to leave.

"Anna?"

He halted me mid turn.

"Y'all hang in there, kay? He's a good guy and if there's one thing I know about him, it's that he has more integrity than just about any one I know."

I forced the sides of my mouth up, gave a weak nod, "I'm sure he does," I said before asking him something I'd been wondering about.

"Out of interest, what did you do in Afghanistan?"

He didn't answer straight away, so I turned to go.

He cleared his throat, which caused me to pause and look back.

"I was a medic." He said.

Well, I didn't expect that.

I nodded, not saying another word and walked back to my room.

If it wasn't enough for my mind to continue to go over the scenes I witnessed today, I was also kept awake thinking about the increasingly complicated thing between Lloyd and myself. I really had to get a handle on it and find some way to distance myself from him. Especially since it appeared as though almost everyone was apparently picking up what we were putting down. No matter how unintentional it was.

I sighed heavily and not just once.

Of course, I drifted off with not much time left before I had to get up again, and out here, I was reminded that with these thin canvas walls, nature woke very, very early.

Suffice to say I felt like crap.

Dark circles hung under my eyes and despite that, I was eager to get started so I could get home ASAP and so, I forced myself to get a wriggle on.

Lloyd also looked under the weather and didn't even bother to shave this morning. Not that it was an awful a thing to see by the way.

The sun hadn't risen over the surrounding range yet, and thankfully the soft light made it less irritating to my tired eyes because there was no way that they would accept contacts in that condition, so I settled for my sunnies and being annoyed with the too dark lenses instead.

Both Lloyd and I silently walked towards the fire pit. Clearly most of the tent like buildings where mothballed completely, including the mess hall. Randal had already packed up his camp and had the billy on, whistling to himself as we plopped ourselves down unceremoniously.

"Well, well," Randal took a second glance at our sorry looking arses, before he poured some hot water into tin mugs, "look at what the cat dragged in, if I didn't know any better, I'd say you two have either raided the mini-bars or had a... busy night."

Lloyd picked up his mug of black coffee and brought it near his lips, glaring over the rim at his friend. "Just as well you know better then." He said, blowing some heat from his mug.

"Yes Sir," Randal agreed in a jovial tone and was completely unperturbed.

He clearly enjoyed getting a rise from his friend. I continued to dunk my tea bag, letting the men banter. I was just too buggered to bother going all Le Femme on the conversation.

After breakfast, the three of us worked efficiently and by 1200, we were finally ready to fly out.

"I gotta say," Randal drawled, "it's been an absolute pleasure to meet you and there's nothing more attractive than a woman who can handle her tools."

"Is that your way of saying you like me Randal?" I questioned in jest, before I took the covers off RED.

"Don't mind him," Lloyd, cut in, "the isolation makes him the biggest tool in the camp," he said throwing his pack in the back of the chopper.

I let out a short sharp laugh, the light nature of the conversation finally cutting through the solemn mood, even if only for a short time.

The flight back to the resort was quiet and uneventful, Lloyd seemed to know that I didn't want to talk about it, and we kept to our fairly usual stilted exchanges and only speaking when it was necessary.

When we returned, he left me to look after RED and later, when we caught up again at the homestead, neither he nor Martha, said anything. In fact, I didn't think Martha even knew about what happened, going by her concern for my quieter than usual self.

"I think I might be coming down with something," I lied when she asked what was up.

And for the next few days, I laid low, my 'illness' giving me a little peace.

I just hoped that I could stay off the roller coaster and start the new year with a little less drama.

# Chapter 28

"Happy New Year Anna!" Pete's voice shouted through the phone as he battled the noise of the fireworks bringing it in over the town of Mackay.

"Happy New Year Pete," I replied flatly, while feeding up at the barn in the late afternoon.

"Not so happy Stedman? What's up darl," Pete asked, his jovial mood sobering.

I groaned, "rough week," I said, swallowing hard.

"Care to share?" He asked.

I sighed, "Not really," I said, shaking my head and trying to stop the horrible anguished feeling from creeping up on me again. All week I had been either low or lower and had broken down in private more than once.

As suspected, Martha and the rest of the guys and girls hadn't been told about the incident and the last thing I wanted was for everyone and their dog to ask, am I okay, am I alright?

Lloyd had continued to let me be, I think he understood that I needed space, he likely wasn't much different, hiding behind his often cold, brooding demeanour was a testament to that.

"Anna," Pete said, interrupting my internal monologue.

Shit.

"Anna," he repeated after another minute, his tone earnest now. "Don't shut down on me."

Double shit. I'd been there before. Shut down. For Pete to throw that card down was serious. I couldn't go there again and needed to snap out of it.

I could feel tears prickle behind my eyes and bit my lip to ward them off.

"Oh Pete," I looked around and headed outside to a secluded spot in the corner, under a low-lying tree next to where the elephant herd were busily munching on their latest bale of hay. "I think I get why Simmo topped himself during the last drought."

"Shit..."

"No, no it's ok, don't worry," I reassured him, "I'm fine... well not fine, fine, but not that bad, sorry, that didn't come out right." I sniffed hearing a crescendo of explosions through the speaker, before the crowd erupted in cheer. A stark contrast to my current position.

"Sorry to ruin your night, not a great way to start the year," I said, apologising.

"Anna, you're not ruining anything, c'mon what's wrong, talk to me, you could always talk to me. You'll always be a little sister to me, I miss ya, don't shut me out 'kay?"

"I'm sorry." I apologised again. I hadn't called Pete in ages and that was on me too.

"You're right, I've been so busy that every time I think to call, it's too late or early or whatever," I said offering a poor excuse with a shrug, knowing he couldn't see it.

"Anna, it's never too early or late if you're having a bad day, it's not like you'd ever call me over a busted fingernail now is it?"

I had to smile at that in spite of my mood, "No!" I sighed again, while Pete waited patiently, "it's just," I paused, "it can be so... devastatingly hard here," tears prickled behind my eyes again as I thought about the rhino, the elephants and my big girl Pragtig, who incidentally had the most amazing timing and had managed to sneak over to the fence to console me, feeling the tears on my face with her trunk.

I grabbed the big nose gently and let her play with my hand.

"You know how it is, people like Simmo, like Uncle Kyle and Aunt Rose, they raise cattle and face hurdles all the time, they're at the mercy of the weather, the market and bad press when they're tarred by a brush.

"They're forever making sure that their livestock get the best lives in order to produce a good product and almost nothing is wasted. Sometimes the wheels fall off even when all due care is taken and then all that pressure makes even the strongest people wonder why they bother."

I thought of Simmo again, and his family, who are now without a husband and without a father. Forced to the wall, he had to shoot his remaining, starving cattle after the worst drought in his lifetime, he then turned the rifle on himself and blew his brains out.

"Yeah," Pete agreed solemnly, "the black dog can get the best of us and sadly he's not the only one."

"No, he's not," I shook my head, "but I get it, I get why they lose hope. It's the same here, except with wild animals." I swallowed, "And I get that in the wild," I expressed with more inflection, "the animals are free to do whatever they like, yes, drought is natural, flood is natural, and yes, animals perish because of that, but the difference here is that being a 'wild animal' isn't really working for them anymore.

"If it's not natural causes that end them, the odds are being stacked against them by these bloody poachers, and unlike cattle and other livestock, there's not enough breeding programs to keep the numbers up.

"Pete, the animals here aren't even offered a humane death and it's only for the parts that get turned into trinkets and mystical phallic powder. They leave the rest of the animal to rot, it's just so heartbreaking.

"There is no such thing as a sanctuary Pete, I'm supposed to be living in one," I said, before telling him my accounts of the herd of elephants and the rhino all apparently within 'protected' borders even if not within Saanastia. "What hope do these animals have?" I rambled, "I just don't know how he does it…"

"Hang on a sec," Pete interrupted, "are we still talking about you here or someone else hmm?"

"What do you mean?" I asked.

"You said you don't know how he does it, who's he, is it that Lloyd fella?"

"I guess," I admitted feeling stupid at my slip, "I guess all of us really" I shrugged trying to cover myself and realised that I'd stopped crying.

"I see," Pete said thoughtfully. "Maybe you need to talk to these people Anna. Maybe learn from what they do to cope with seeing that sort of thing over and over. A bit like emergency service personnel, y'know? They can't cope on their own as well as they do as a team and no one expects them to."

"I- I just don't want to be a pain. A-and I think talking to you has helped…" I said honestly. I did feel a lot better now, getting all this off my chest.

"Knock it off, you're not a pain, the last thing I want is for you to suffer by yourself and come back here being a head-case or something," he said.

Pete always was the voice of reason.

"Gees Pete, don't you think that's a little melodramatic."

"Is it? Think about it Anna, it sounds like a war zone out there."

"Hm," I hummed, reluctantly agreeing.

"Look, I have to go, trying to leave the car park after these events is like a mass exodus," he said.

I could hear the garbled murmuring of the crowd in the background.

"Ok, thanks Pete."

"Look after yourself, chicken." Pete said endearingly.

"Sure, send my love to Rach. Happy New Year."

"Right back at ya. Night."

I hung up staring at the phone and let out a long and shuddering breath. Pragtig hadn't quit patting me the entire time, so I gave her back some love and kissed her trunk for good measure feeling better for the pep talk that both her and Pete had given.

I wondered who could be that someone that I trusted enough to talk to about these things.

Martha seemed the logical choice, but since she wasn't hands on out there in the bush, I wasn't sure she'd actually be the best one to bounce off.

And I was reluctant to talk to Lloyd because I didn't want to leave myself exposed to him like I had the other day. Besides, being a man who always held his cards pretty close to his chest, I couldn't imagine him being a very open conversationalist anyway.

But I did think I owed it to myself to at least consider Pete's advice and find someone to confide in.

"Labda nitakuongea tu, mpenzi wangu," I said to Pragtig, deciding that may actually not be a bad idea at all.

Giving Pragtig another cuddle, I got up out of my hiding spot and made my way back to the homestead. Almost everyone was going out tonight as far as I knew. Jerry had gone on a break throughout Christmas and was with his family in Cape Town and Carley had been thoughtful enough to invite me out to celebrate with her and Alan, but I really didn't feel like being a third wheel.

Most of the others also had commitments and there was only the bare minimum of staff, including myself, to hold the fort. I was actually sort of looking forward to having the house to myself for a change and it would likely be an early night for me.

Martha was rushing about getting a few last-minute things together for herself. "There are still some leftovers in the fridge lovey." She whizzed by, clipping her bracelet on.

"No worries, I'll have a poke around," I answered as I passed her, "Have a great night." I smiled, despite my sombre mood.

"I will, see you tomorrow, late morning," she added happily, reminding me she was staying with Fred that night.

"Will do," I called behind me, as I continued up the hall to my quarters.

A door across the hall opened, Lloyd stepped out catching my attention as I reached for the handle on my own. We both stopped in our tracks, me undoubtedly looking like a deer in headlights and he... looked amazing, like always in a casual button up shirt and jeans.

Well, this is awkward I thought to myself.

"Uh...Don't do anything I wouldn't do..." I said, kicking myself as soon as it came from my mouth.

He gave me a strange look. "Ha!" He huffed out mirthlessly, turning his back on me to leave. Without looking back he said not unkindly, "you have no idea Anna, no idea."

I was left looking down an empty hallway and then entered my room, locking the door behind me. Leaning back on it, I let out a long breath. "Good one," I admonished quietly and wondered what had him so jaded about this new year's eve.

Later, after some more self deprecation and a shower, I headed back to the kitchen and fossicked through the fridge. Deciding, rather than wallow in my own pity party, I'd go and make a 'healthy' lasagne of sorts with no pasta and my cauliflower cheese sauce, followed by an apple and rhubarb crumble with a macadamia and oat crust for dessert.

Four hours later, after a tidy up of the kitchen and a bit of telly, the large trays were cool enough to put in the fridge. There would be enough for the three of us for a few days, so my kitchen duty was done and dusted for the moment and I went to bed.

Sleep of course didn't come easily, with my brain refusing to shut off, even after trying to count backwards from a thousand.

As luck would have it, I was just about to nod off and I heard a loud giggle-snort echo through the hallway, followed by a "shhh," then a series of bangs, more giggle snorts and a "Jesus Gloria," whisper yelled by Lloyd.

Wide awake, it was like I'd been ripped from one nightmare, only to be confronted with another.

More banging, moaning, giggling, hushed murmurings, doors opening and closing and then silence - except for the occasional muffled moan and a garbled, "Lloydy," from Gloria.

Oh. My. God.

This was real wasn't it? I sat there in realisation, completely at a loss. And across the bloody hall from me too! I was mortified.

Stupid, stupid, stupid! I crumpled back into the mattress and used a pillow to cover my head, silently resigning myself to the reality that I was a little girl dabbling in an adult world that I just couldn't justify playing in at any level. I was not for this sort of drama, but for some reason I just managed to plonk myself right in the middle of it time after time.

It only served to strengthen my resolve to just work here and try to enjoy the unique experience while it lasted. The animals and Saanastia needed what I could bring to the table and that far outweighed my own personal issues.

I had never bawled as much in my entire life as I had in the last week and eventually, I even managed to pathetically cry myself to sleep. But the next morning... Oh boy, my eyes were that irritated, that I couldn't even get my contacts in, so I had to wear my Aviators instead.

I looked as though I'd had a hard night on the turps, and I may as well have I guess, because I certainly felt as though I'd been through the ringer. Only without the fun people were always bragging about, leading up to it.

Stepping out of my room, I was surprised with the scene playing out in the hall.

There, teetering on one leg, leaning up against Lloyd's door while struggling to get her other stiletto on, was Gloria in another little number. In red this time, with her hair a mess and panda eyes.

I sighed and creeping up my throat, was that dreadful feeling of nausea, combined with what was likely jealousy, anger, sadness and perhaps loss.

"Morning," I said in spite of myself.

"Shhh," she put her index finger to her lips, "Lloyd's still asleep, we were up all night and the poor darling needs his rest," she whispered dramatically, with a goading smirk and a condescending tone.

"I'm sure you were and I'm sure he does," I continued flatly, leaving her to sort herself out.

I had no desire to enter any sort of conversation with her, nor hang around long enough in case she might feel the need to get chatty, so I decided to skip breakfast and grabbed a banana out of the fruit basket, pulled my frozen bottle of water from the freezer and didn't pause until I got all the way to the yards.

There, I let out a breath that I didn't know I was holding.

The angered rush subsided the moment I spotted Pragtig. She wandered over and asked for my banana skin before I gave her a cuddle and an earful while I got stuck into my chores.

Head down and tail up was the motto.

I decided to concentrate on my work, because we all knew that there was never a shortage of it around here and it was probably the best way to avoid any distractions that may come my way.

As the days rolled on, flying every few days, working around the resort and of course doing the farm work, I ended up spending more time with my elephant too. I talked to her a lot, told her all about my concerns, she gave me the peace I craved and took the drama far away.

Sleeping came easier and I hadn't had a dream that I could remember or a nightmare that ripped me from my slumber.

But you know what they say. When things seem too good to be true, they usually are.

*-Sitting from my lofty height upon the broad neck of my best friend, the rhythmic flapping of huge ears at the side of my little legs, she took me across the river to our special place. A place we weren't really allowed to be, but if they never caught us, did we really ever go there?*

*I was surprised when I found the three older boys there this time. Trying to sneak away was a bit hard to do when you were atop a huge elephant.*

*"Go home!" Said one.*

*"You know you're not allowed out alone!" Said another.*

*"Chill out guys, she's just a kid..."-*

Sitting bolt upright again from another one of my odd dreams, I sat there catching my breath and waited for my heart to slow. One day that thing was going to fly right out of my chest or stop mid beat with the amount of crazy it had to deal with.

I checked the time. 0430, "Great," I said, murmuring under my breath and fell back onto the mattress with a huff.

Only a couple of hours later, I was working with Kabri in the yards and watching the men with their elephants while we pottered about.

Pragtig was hanging around like she usually did and casually wandered over to me, touching me with her trunk. "Hey baby," I said, acknowledging her.

Then she did something that I hadn't seen her do before. She bowed her head low. "Kabri, what's she doing?" I asked.

After the initial wide-eyed shock, he schooled his features before a warm grin spread over it, "Why Miss Anna, I do believe that she wants you to climb on."

I looked at him dumbfounded, "What? But I thought that she couldn't be ridden, that she just refuses to move?"

"She does not want to be ridden Miss Anna. Not by us anyway," he pointed out kindly. "She hasn't offered a ride like that in many, many years," he added, his eyes bright with excitement.

"She wants me to ride her?" I asked in disbelief.

"Perhaps, Miss."

"Can I?" I asked optimistically, my excitement growing by the minute.

"Nooo Miss," he said with a shake of his head. My heart sunk with his answer. "Not today," he added quietly, so no one could hear, he winked, and a mischievous grin crossed his gentle features.

"No, of course not," I said, my own smile forming without my permission, while I was secretly bouncing on the inside and maybe even a little on the outside.

So, there we were, chatting for a few hours and eventually I was brave enough to talk about a few of my concerns and Kabri proved to be exactly the wonderful listener that I needed to help me with my pains.

We also formulated a devious plan to sneak back to the yards, late at night, when everyone was asleep and only a few nights a month and when the moon was bright enough to light the area sufficiently so we wouldn't draw too much attention to ourselves by needing torches and other lighting. Kabri made sure to roster himself on for those nights, so that his wife or other staff wouldn't become too suspicious either.

Who knew Kabri had it in him?

We were acting like naughty little children and it was a joy to see Kabri's wise eyes brighten with an elfin glint.

It was all very exciting and the first time that we met late at night by the light of the moon.

With Kabri's detailed instructions, it was time to place my bare foot on the thicker part of Pragtig's powerful trunk when she offered me pride of place with a bow of her head. Feeling a long-lost surge of all that was happiness flow through my veins, she lifted me up high and I clambered carefully over her head and settled myself behind her massive ears like I'd done it for years.

I'll never forget that feeling and it was overwhelming. Collapsing in joyful emotion, I hugged that huge head, crying happy tears this time.

"Tembo yangu nzuri" I said rubbing her lovingly. Her trunk came up and I held it like a hand, like I always did when she reached for me.

And then I gave her a mint, like I always did.

Best. Therapy. Ever.

My clandestine meetings over the next couple of months with my elephant and my faithful partner in crime, balanced out the tension I felt when I was around Lloyd and to some extent Martha as well. I just didn't want to get into anything too personal anymore.

On the whole, things seemed to settle into a nice new kind of normal and thankfully, I didn't have any more major dramas or catastrophes to contend with.

I also went out with Carley and sometimes Alan tagged along too. We'd see a movie or go out to eat, but it didn't happen nearly enough because they lived a couple of hours away and it was hard to schedule something on a whim.

I did spend a couple of days at Carley's place in Pretoria in the last week of March. We were at a large shopping mall and had just wrapped up for the day.

"What do you want to do for your birthday A?" Carley asked, heading back to the car, "and don't say nothing, we haven't done anything since boarding school, so no more excuses," she said while we crossed the car park.

"No, and you know why, too many memories, I'd rather not go there." I said with a clipped tone.

"Anna, you can't keep going there, every time to the detriment of just about everything else, why not start some new memories, in this new country, with the new people in your life, well except me," she amended, "but I'm before that other stuff, so I don't count."

"I'd rather no..."

"Don't worry Anna, I got this," she said cutting me off and not taking no for an answer.

I was so screwed.

"What am I letting myself in for?" I grumbled under my breath.

"That's the spirit Anna," she said sarcastically and she started the car.

About fifteen minutes later, I was dropped off at the airport, just in time for me to catch the shuttle bus back to Saanastia.

As time went by, Pragtig and I were working as one. She wasn't as quick to react as Blue was, for example, but neither was a truck when compared to a car. And just like a truck she was also very utilitarian, that trunk and her tusks were very handy pieces of equipment. We had come to the end of our training because the rest would have to be done out in the open and for now that wasn't an option.

Blue was never far from my mind, I called Leonie, who was looking after him for me, on a regular basis. I missed that horse so much and felt horrible that I wasn't there for him. Leonie assured me that my boy was fine and he and his best friend, a Shetland called Nevil made a comical pair. I had the photos to prove it and I had to laugh when I was sent a video of Nevil and Blue playfighting and little Nev bit the big guy on the back of the legs, causing the tough black stallion to buckle at the knees and cut him down to size only to continue play fighting eye to eye.

Blue was even more so in my thoughts the closer that I got to the end of my trial at Saanastia. It had weighed heavily on my mind as to which way I would choose to go.

My Visa was extended for another three months, and we would take it as it came.

There was also a general increase in tension, Lloyd in particular was more broody than usual if that was possible. That's if he was around at all because he and Martha spent more time away from Saanastia these days. When they both came back, they looked more and more wrung out and everybody gave Lloyd a wide birth unless he approached them first.

I asked Kabri if he could shed some light.

"Ah Miss Anna, it is not for all of us to know and those that do know, cannot tell," he said wisely.

Lloyd hadn't accompanied me on a flight for ages either, which wasn't altogether an issue, because I often took one of the other guys.

On occasion, I went alone when I needed to cram in freight or when I had a dead leg after either picking up or dropping off passengers.

Getting into the air and away from the stress at Saanastia on my own was often just as cathartic as getting on Blue or that elephant.

Heading back to base one afternoon, after dropping off supplies at my last stop, I was running a line down the border between Saanastia and Hoogevelt, as it was sort of on the way back to base. I was at five hundred feet and about twenty minutes out, when I got the shock of my life and a white R44 settled beside me, only twenty odd feet to my right. Naturally I pulled away from it to give me a bit more room and collect myself. The registration was unreadable, which scared me a bit because that meant I couldn't really identify it. The chopper stuck with me, so I turned to take a better look. The pilot was unrecognisable but made the 'I'm watching you' action with his fingers before peeling off and heading towards Hoogevelt.

Shaken to the core, I willed myself to stay calm and not show my fear through my voice when I radioed my intent to base and casually asked who'd be in this evening because it was my turn to cook again. Thankfully it was a full house, so at least I didn't have to sit on the incident for too long.

I needed the time packing up after landing to get my wits about me before I reported the event. Once RED was put to bed, I radioed Lloyd on my way to the resort building.

"What's up, Anna?" He asked gruffly.

"Meet me in the office, something's happened and you need to know." I said, my tone serious and to the point.

"Ok, I'll be right there."

I relived the incident as I walked, feeling shaky again and once at the resort reception, I asked if Martha was in. She was and a moment later I knocked on her office door.

"Are you ok dear?" Martha asked the moment I closed the door behind me, "you look as skittish as a cat in a room full of rocking chairs."

"Lloyd'll be here in a second," I said, taking a drink from my water bottle, my hand now definitely shaking and my eyes glazing over even though I wasn't actually crying.

Right on cue, the door flew open and Lloyd rushed in without knocking.

"What's going on?" He asked calmly, even though his expression was far from it.

"Know anyone who owns a white unmarked chopper?" I asked, cutting straight to the chase.

They both indicated no.

"Well I was just intercepted by one about twenty minutes out near the Hoogevelt border, it snuck up unannounced and scared the crap out of me. The pilot had a bit of fun with this," I mimicked the 'I'm watching you action'"and no, I didn't recognise him, he had a helmet headset on, but he was white if that helps." I was visibly shaking now.

"Son of a bitch!" Lloyd swore and knelt in front of me, his hands hesitating before placing them on the arms of the chair I was sitting in. "I need to go, will you be ok?" I nodded dumbly.

He smiled weakly, "Ok" he said touching my hand momentarily before getting up quickly, "can you look after Anna please? I think she might be going into shock," he directed at Martha.

"Yes, of course, but Lloyd..."

"I'll take care of it."

And he was out the door as quickly as he entered it.

"I'm sorry," I apologised, my mind was a bit frazzled now and I was starting to get cold.

"Come on honey, I'll take you home, you need to lie down and relax a bit. Give yourself a little quiet time."

"Ok," I nodded, surrendering to Martha, I was just so tired. I seemed to be perpetually so, so tired, and all I wanted was the darkness that sleep provided.


Translation:

Labda nitakuongea tu, mpenzi wangu, - *Maybe I'll just talk to you, my darling*

Tembo yangu nzuri - *My beautiful elephant*

# Chapter 29

I stirred in my sleep and let myself wake slowly, eventually glancing at my bedside clock and I had to look twice.

That couldn't be right could it?

I checked my phone just in case.

Bloody hell!. It was already 1000 the next day!

Groaning, I rubbed my eyes and came to the realisation that I had slept straight for about sixteen hours and I still felt trashed.

Thankfully, the shakes seemed to be gone and with it, the cold, clammy, sick feeling. Sitting up, the world whizzed for a moment and I noticed a glass of water and a couple of tablets sitting on top of a note next to the clock.

Anna,

Take these if you wake up with a headache.

Call me anytime if you need me.

Martha.

I didn't take the pills and I didn't call Martha.

But I did start to feel a bit better as I shed the heaviness of my sleep haze and I did drink the water.

Unfortunately the uneasy feeling remained, which I simply put down to yesterday's events because I certainly wouldn't expect to get over something like that in a hurry.

I stood up to check my windows and door. They were both locked.

Telling myself off for my paranoia, I was secretly grateful that Martha had the forethought to secure the room on her way out.

After a shower, I was just tying my hair up into a messy bun when I heard a muffled crash from somewhere within the house.

Sticking my head out into the hall I listened intently.

Silence.

I then padded quietly out into the house, my senses heightened in the stillness, the large clock in the kitchen ticking rhythmically was the only sound apart from the fridge and what filtered in from outside. The place looked deserted as expected and I let out the breath I'd been holding and quietly gave myself another pep talk about my wariness.

With a gasp, I whirled around to the sound of another noise coming from the original wing of the homestead. It sounded like there was someone rummaging around in there.

For some reason, despite yesterday's episode, here I was, unable to help myself as my feet took me toward the door that had been forbidden to walk through the whole time I'd been here.

The homestead did have a heap of African handmade artefacts that were tastefully displayed throughout the main living area and since there weren't any cricket or baseball bats at hand, I picked up some sort of tribal club. Holding it up, it felt quite a bit heavier than it looked and would make an intimidating weapon.

Ever so carefully, I tried the handle to the door between the two residences and to my surprise I found it to be unlocked.

Easing it open quietly, I stayed clear of the doorway and pushed it open gently to swing wider on its own. Squinting into the darkened area and flattening my back against the door jam, I peeked into the long hallway which seemed to be the bedroom area of the original dwelling.

Carefully, I made my way down the hall and to the door at the other end that was already cracked open. Looking through the gap, I saw some shadowy movement on the other side and without thought I burst through "Hey!" I yelled holding the club up threateningly, startling the intruder so much that they tripped over some low furniture and fell on their backside with a loud crash.

With broken glass scattering across the slate floors, it was almost comical the way the thief had to scramble to get to his feet and in the brief moment he took to look my way, I couldn't say that I recognised him.

"Get out!" I roared at the top of my lungs and then lunged after him like a mad woman.

He managed to escape through one of the large French doors and with only the heavy drapes left waving in his wake, the room fell eerily silent.

With my bare feet picking their way around the large furniture covered in drop sheets, I called Martha and followed the man's path out through the doors. Scanning around the garden, I saw no sign of him.

"Anna dear, how are you fee...?"

"We've had an intruder," I said, not letting her finish her question. "There was a man in the house, I don't know if they took anything because I surprised them, but there's a bit of a mess. I didn't want to call 112," I rushed out in one breath as I picked my way back around the furniture.

"No, that's fine, I'll get onto Lloyd and we'll decide what to do, see you in a moment."

Left in the silence I noticed that the glass came from a picture frame that had been smashed on the ground and was facing down. They always say not to touch anything, so I left it there, but the other framed pictures placed on top of the sideboard, and displayed on the wall, showed the identity of the family that once lived here. A man with light brown hair, greying at the temples and a full beard, a beautiful blonde woman perched next to him, and there was a little girl of about four with almost white hair braided into thick plaits, who sat on the pretty lady's knee and was wrapped in her loving arms.

The perfect family photo set in the gardens in front of the resort entrance.

Then, in another picture, there was a teenage boy of about sixteen maybe, he had sandy hair and sat astride a young elephant. Perched in front of him was a toddler, who I assumed was the same little girl judging by that thick halo of golden mane. She was firmly secured by the young man's skinny, sinewy arms and had a delighted expression on her face.

The happy scene made me smile.

"What are you doing in here?" Lloyd's voice carried down the hallway, "I thought I asked you not to…" He stopped, realising that the break in was not in the other section of the homestead and I wasn't snooping.

Much.

"Oh." He said, looking around at the damage.

"The guy was going through the drawers, I scared him and he fell over the side table and then ran out that door," I said pointing to the open door with the broken hardware and gently moving curtains.

"Hm, they clearly thought no one was home, but c'mon, I need you out of here, I'll sort it out," he said looking a little spooked as he gazed around the room again.

I picked up the club and he started to escort me out of the room, "Do you want a hand?" I asked slowing my pace.

"Nope," he sighed placing a hand at the small of my back to guide me up the hall and I'd be lying if said that I didn't enjoy his touch.

Martha was fixing a cuppa for us as we emerged, and I heard the door click shut behind us.

Placing the artefact back where I found it, I felt both pairs of eyes on me. "What?" I asked.

"Are you ok dear?" Martha asked, concerned.

"Yeah, I'm fine," I answered, surprising even myself with my calm demeanour.

Martha and Lloyd gave one another a questioning look, which in turn gave me a pang of anxiety.

"It's certainly been an interesting couple of days, but I slept like a log last night and I feel so much better today." I said, while getting comfortable at the breakfast bar and looking up at them again.

My chatter stopped when I noticed their worry.

Lloyd in particular, looked as wrecked as I felt yesterday, just worn down and hollow.

He fidgeted under my scrutiny.

"Look, I gotta go, I'll be back later to clean up the mess and I'll get one of the boys to fix the door." He said as he strode from the room leaving Martha and I with three hot mugs sitting on the island bench.

"Is he ok Martha?" I asked turning my head in the direction that he took off in.

There was a long pause. "He's as well as can be expected, sweetheart," she sighed.

Then, I thought I'd be bold and ask the hard question that could shut me down, but I really did think she needed to at least give me a hint to what I wanted to know.

"Is it just me, or does it look as though this stuff that's happening might have something to do with Mr Veldsmaan?"

"Anna, I can't say anything ok?" Martha said in frustration.

I scrutinised her with narrowed eyes, I felt she owed me more than that now I'd had a threat made against me.

She sighed deeply. "Let's say that it's not just you."

I nodded but didn't push my luck. Her answer spoke volumes and we drank from our mugs in near silence with Martha only mentioning that she had some things to wrap up in Pretoria and then she would be staying with Fred again overnight and would be back in the morning.

I joined the land of the living that afternoon and went to work.

Someone had been stationed at the house with more than a club as a weapon to ward off any would-be intruders.

That evening I was back to being wide awake until the wee hours.

Lloyd was noticeably absent at dinner and of course that worried me. I couldn't help it now, I was too invested in all the goings on. I tried so hard to stay out of it, but the recent events had dropped me right in the middle of it.

Again.

I managed to doze a little from time to time and finally heard Lloyd come home at about one in the morning.

Not long after, I fell asleep.

*-He was laying on the ground bruised with blood clogging the whiskers that always tickled when he kissed my cheek. Screaming for him over and over, the tears streaming down my face, she grabbed me around the waist and lifted me to safety, a dark and looming figure standing over the scene, I reached out for the fallen man one last time. "Daddy!"-*

A blood curdling cry sent me jumping upright yet again, only I didn't know if it was from my nightmare, from myself, or something else entirely that had managed to morph into the broken images in my mind. Catching my breath, I seemed to be living on adrenalin filled interruptions lately that I couldn't even get away from it in my sleep. I took a few more deep breaths and strained my ears for any further sounds.

Those breaths were the only sounds in my darkened room, my hand had involuntarily found its way over my still frantically beating heart. I looked over at the bedside clock giving an eerie glow to the pale walls and it was just after three.

"Gees," I said under my breath, shaking my head at myself before I fell back onto the pillows to stare at the ceiling.

"Fuck!" I heard Lloyd's muffled voice through the walls, followed by a barrage of the same and other similar expletives in a grief stricken and angry tone.

I heard the water start running through the pipes in the walls, the knocking and then the hissing sound, that indicated he must've been having a shower.

I imagined the rivulets of water cascading down his body and then I pulled myself up abruptly.

Good lord! I scolded myself for the impropriety of my thoughts.

I shouldn't have been thinking that way about him, he wasn't mine to think about. But that didn't stop me reflecting otherwise, no matter the circumstances, I couldn't just turn that sort of thing off, regardless of how much I tried to convince myself.

I was promptly brought out of my reverie by a loud thump, followed shortly thereafter by another and some more expletives.

I sat up and strained to better hear.

First a sob followed by another thump, another sob and a heave of breath. I realised then, that Lloyd no doubt, was overly distraught and I was witnessing his breakdown.

I let him be for a while, the sobs subsided, but when after twenty minutes the water was still flowing, I thought better of it. The water had to be running cold by now.

We were alone and I was the only one here for him at this point. I took a deep breath to steel myself before throwing the covers off my bed and making my way to my bedroom door.

Closing it softly behind me, I tip toed across the hall.

It was dark in the hallway, with only a soft light coming from the great room at the end and also from a dull sliver that came from beneath Lloyd's own door.

Taking a step closer to Lloyd's room, I could still hear the shower running and before I could talk myself out of it, I opened his door and let myself in.

The softly lit room was the mirror of mine, taupe walls and white ceiling, the black bedclothes didn't surprise me, but the fact that the sheets were satin certainly did.

Lloyd was nowhere to be seen which probably meant one thing and that in itself was both alarming and exhilarating at the same time.

Without continuing to over think it, I followed the sounds to the bathroom. The door was ajar and as I approached, and I took a deep breath to brace myself.

But there was nothing in my imagination that could have prepared me for what I found. Lloyd's body, slumped in the shower, his broad back to me beautiful, muscled and glistening from the water, but that wasn't the most prominent feature. Not by a long shot.

Marring his skin were fresh bruises near his kidneys. He'd been in a scuffle, that much was plain to see, but even more noticeable were the injuries this man had been subjected to in his past. Old scars, long, wide and roughened and on the same side as those on his handsome face.

It was contrast to his perfection and a clone of what I knew of his personality.

He was covered in goose flesh and shivering from the cold, I snapped out of my creepy ogling and looked around the room for something to cover him, grabbing a fluffy bathrobe from the hook on the back of the door.

Quietly approaching him and trying to just stay focused on the skin above his waist, I needed to turn the water off and to do that, I had to reach past him. I swallowed thickly and tentatively stopped the flow of water and in a swift movement, I draped the robe over his shoulders.

He flinched at the contact, as if it was the first time that he'd registered my presence, but he didn't move away. I let out a breath and then started to help him into the robe. Much to my surprise, he submitted easily to my assistance, first one arm and then the other before I turned him to face me. My eyes never straying too far down or up to his face.

His scars were as prominent on his chest as they were on his back and met under his left arm. There was evidence of muscle injury everywhere and it amazed me that he even had use of his left arm at all. I quickly covered his chest and tied off the robe.

We stood silently for a moment, I needed to get him out of the bathroom and I couldn't get a read on him because I was too chicken shit to look him in the eye for fear of a rebuke.

Looking down, my nerves were getting the best of me, his feet were ... large, like the rest of him, his calves muscular, like the rest of him, the dark, coarse hair slicked to his skin, still damp, still cold and he continued to shiver.

I needed to get him warm, my hand had a mind of its own and found his while the other took a random towel off the rail. I found no resistance as he allowed me to lead him to the bedroom and guide him to his bed.

We stopped and I turned to face him, helping Lloyd to sit on the bed before he lay down and I dried him anywhere that wasn't under the robe and then covered him with the quilt. He hadn't let go of my hand, which made it awkward, and when I'd finally bundled him up, I straightened and looked down at where we touched.

I hadn't noticed that our fingers had entwined, the gesture was intimate, and I didn't know what to make of it, but I noted that his knuckles were pretty busted up.

"Stay?" He mumbled through his still chattering teeth.

After a moment, he squeezed my hand which caused me to finally snap my eyes to his face with what must have been a surprised expression, only my eyes grew even wider at the sight of him.

One of his eyes was swollen shut, he had a cut over the bridge of his nose and a split lip.

"Oh Lloyd" I said, my heart breaking for him, before I leaned forward to take a closer look. I tenderly wiped the damp hair from his forehead. "What did they do to you?" I asked in a whisper and I lowered myself to sit next to him on the bed.

"You should have seen the other guy," he mumbled, with a hint of humour. He shifted his position, hissing as his painful bruises gave him grief.

"Have you got a first aid kit?" I asked.

"Yeah, in the bathroom cabinet," he said hoarsely. I made a move to get it, but he still didn't let go of my hand.

"Um, Lloyd?" I dropped my gaze to our joined hands, squeezing his and he loosened his hold.

"Sorry," he said sheepishly.

Collecting the first aid kit, I sat back beside him and started tending to his wounds.

His easy compliance was quite disarming. "So, will you?" He asked.

"Will I what?" I said dabbing at the split lip with an antiseptic wipe.

He hissed again. "Stay," he repeated from earlier, "here," he said.

I sat back, worried about how that would be perceived, which he noticed.

"Please?" He asked, his eyes showed something other than the rigid steely gaze he normally held on his resting face. Instead there was a desperate pleading look, vulnerable even. "Please," he begged again, in a whisper this time.

I frowned at his words.

"Why?" My voice was hoarse.

He touched my hand again, forcing my eyes to seek his.

"You're a distraction," he said.

"A distraction?" I asked.

He nodded.

"You've got to be kidding," I scoffed, "you've been making an art form out of avoiding me and…" I thought of the morning Gloria did the walk of shame.

"I didn't, I don't want to avoid you," he said.

"Then why? I don't understand. Besides, you're with Gloria." I said, calling him out.

He shook his head, no.

"I couldn't… afford to have distractions Anna," he closed his eyes, "I need to keep my head in the game," he rubbed his thumb over the back of my hand.

"This is a game to you?" I asked. The revelations coming thick and fast.

"No," he said, "but it's a game to those that want what my family and what I have worked so hard for. A game to the poachers. A sick, sick game that I'm forced to play.

"And I'm not with Gloria." He said incidentally.

"What do you mean, forced to play? And she sure sounded like she was with you on New Year's Eve." I said, raising my eyebrow and countering him.

"Gloria." He said before he paused to think, "is part of the game."

I gave him a please explain look.

"Anna," he said sitting up, wincing again and made hard work of scooting back to the headboard, his robe fell open and my traitorous eyes glanced to his chest before I forced them back to his face.

He gave me a quick smile, "I might have taken advantage of her, but not in the way you think. She's desperate to be seen to be with me, it's actually an advantage for both of us both socially and personally. More so for me technically speaking." He said, shrugging with his postscript.

"I was just lucky that I had an opportunity to help get Gloria so wasted on New Year's Eve, that she couldn't even stand, so I carried her drunken derrière to bed to sleep it off." He said, "in the next room," he added, observing me intently.

I thought back to the scenes that I'd conjured up from what I'd heard that fateful evening and those that I'd seen in the morning and compared them to Lloyd's account.

I had to admit, it sounded plausible.

"Oh," I said, "Gloria sure made an effort to look freshly ravaged the morning after."

Lloyd shook his head. "Totally for your benefit no doubt and I'm sorry about that, she's a piece of work. New Year's Eve was a rouse, I have to walk a tightrope with her so that I can use her to delay the inevitable. In short, she's batshit crazy and the stakes are high."

"What stakes?"

My brow furrowed as I leant forward.

"All of this," he lifted his hands palms up, "Saanastia is under threat by more than the poachers Anna, and I don't know how long I can keep the wolf from the door.

"You need money?" I asked, "I thought that with the elephant tours and the helicopter in service, that most of that was sorted."

"Well, those things are enough to cover the running costs for the sanctuary, but not enough to buy fifty one percent by the 16th. Then this place goes on the open market," he said ominously. "That, or I marry Gloria," he said and if he intended to shock me with that news, he succeeded.

"What?" I asked in alarm, standing up abruptly.

"Yeah, Gloria has a grand plan," he said, with contempt. "I marry her and daddy's wedding gift is to buy Saanastia for us and it continues to run without any interference from him. "On one condition. Of course."

My mouth hung open in disbelief. " ...But that's blackmail!" I said angrily, pacing around to the other side of the bed.

"Yeah, you could say that." He said watching me. "I'm stuck between a rock and a hard place, everything's tied up in the sanctuary and both options I have at this stage, will force me to become just like them." His eyes lost focus and looked past me into some distant place.

"You've lost me," I said in confusion, sitting down again to listen.

He smiled without mirth, "What if I told you that the breeding program has inadvertently made Saanastia the biggest producer of rhino horn in the world?"

"Pardon?" I asked, completely perplexed.

He shook his head. "Some of the orphans are fifteen years old now, we have thirty three animals producing four kilograms of horn every nine months, being worth almost as much as gold, you do the math." He ran a hand through his hair. "And that's not including the horns we collect from the wild population."

"Are you saying you could buy Saanastia with rhino horn you have in storage?"

"Anna, I could just about buy South Africa with the amount of horn we have stored." He said explaining the magnitude of his dilemma.

"So, will you do it? Sell the horn?" I asked him, hoping he wasn't going to sell out.

"What?" He sat up, aghast and winced in pain. "No! Never! I'd burn every last gram myself before I'd lower myself that far, I'd even shoot every one of the breeding herd if I had to."

I gasped, "Surely not?"

"Anna, if Cyrus gets hold of this place," he gritted his teeth in disgust, "it all would have been for nothing," his voice cracked, "I'm screwed if I do and screwed if I don't." He slumped back defeated and shook his head, the anguish was rolling off him in waves.

His eyes were glassy. "It's so bad now that I dream about it," he said, his face contorted and a tear rolled down his cheek, "And on top of that number 246 showed up."

I gave him another questioning look.

"Number 246, was the rhino that you put out of its misery that day. We've since had the carcase scanned and it's number came up."

I sat there confused, "I still don't understand."

"The same number 246 that we dehorned that day that Fred had his heart attack."

My eyes grew wide and welled up before I even realised.

"Poachers have taken to revenge killing left, right and centre, they're killing the dehorned population out of spite now," he spat, "the bastards are taking whatever horn is still there. It might have only been a kilo and it had dye in it."

He threw an arm over his eyes to hide his grief, wincing as he made contact with the injuries on his face.

Now, I finally understood it all.

The pressure Lloyd was under, was as if he was carrying the world on his shoulders, his world, the safe haven, the utopia he and his family before him had created at Saanastia for the wildlife. It was all going to be taken from him. Who then would protect the animals? Who would protect the land? No wonder he was volatile so much of the time, I'm sure I'd feel the same in his place.

As I sat, I felt my own anger rise by the moment, helpless in this desperate situation. "Isn't there any legal recourse?" I asked him doubtfully.

He sniffed loudly before swallowing and shaking his head, "No, there's a clause in my aunts Will, she was the majority share-holder before she died, her daughter was her heir but the girl disappeared without a trace soon after my uncle died, she could have wandered off and been eaten by a lion for all we know," he shrugged, "I was in the States at the time, so I don't really know what happened here but you know how kids are?" He shrugged.

"No not really," I said truthfully, I'd never really been around them, "but I can imagine that you need eyes in the back of your head, especially around here."

"Yeah," he said with a chuckle, but there was no humour evident. His eyes were so tired, and I had unwittingly moved up the bed during his story and was now reclining beside him.

We stayed in quiet company, until exhaustion took over and eventually, I fell asleep beside him.

# Chapter 30

A comfortable warmth surrounded me as I woke, a slow breath fanned over my neck and a strong arm was wrapped around my waist, holding me close.

Wait... what?

I caught up with the memories from earlier on and could not believe that I, that we had ended up in this compromising position.

While it felt wonderful to be in Lloyd's arms, Lloyd might not think the same way, so I thought that I should make some effort to try to figure out how I could extricate myself without waking him.

Then he stirred and I froze.

Lloyd took his first deep breath upon rousing and groaned.

I waited for him to retract. "Good morning," he said in a husky voice.

Well, that went better than I thought it would.

I took it upon myself to turn in his arms and face him.

His good eye was cracked open and I flinched at the sight of his injuries and I imagined he was fairly uncomfortable. Being so close to him, for the second time his fresh war wounds weren't what piqued my interest.

The silvery lines that receded into his hairline on the left side of his face, drew me in. Tentatively I reached up and traced one of the jagged, raised scars that trailed over his temple and to my surprise, he let me.

His eye closed at my touch and his beautiful long, dark lashes feathered over those high cheek bones. He was devastatingly attractive even though he'd been thoroughly beaten. He flinched as I traced near his ear and I wondered if the nerves had been affected and if my touch felt different there.

Thankfully he let me continue and he relaxed after a few more gentle touches. I wondered how close he'd become to not making it, or at the very least not been mentally altered with the head injuries he'd sustained. Smoothing his hair behind his ear, "From the frying pan into the fire," I inferred, not meaning to speak aloud and I wasn't sure he'd even heard.

But he had and he simply nodded.

"Why, Lloyd, why war?" I asked him.

He rolled onto his back and opened his eye again. Clearing his throat he admitted with a sigh, "I was young and dumb."

"Will you tell me what happened?" I asked him in a tentative whisper.

He sighed again and for a moment, I thought the only thing he was going to tell me was that I should mind my own business.

"It was my last call of duty in Afghanistan," he said to my surprise. "I was leading a platoon of men back to base when we hit an IED," he shook his head, "a roadside bomb."

"I know what an Improvised Explosive Device is Lloyd." I said, only mildly offended. Did he not know I wasn't your average girly girl by now?

He attempted to suppress a grin, which clearly hurt him, so his fingers grazed down my arm and slid to my hand, "Of course you do," he said before he gave it a squeeze.

"And you were hurt?" I prompted.

"Yeah, you could say that" he whispered. "I should have died though," he said through clenched teeth.

With his eyes closed, he took a deep breath through his nose and I watched as he relived the moment in his mind. His head pressed deep into the pillows and his brow furrowed, but he didn't let go of my hand.

"But you didn't." I squeezed him back.

"I wanted to leave long before our mission was completed," he said with a shake of his head. "I had no idea what we were even fighting for anymore." His voice rose an octave, "and ..." he swallowed thickly, "and sometimes I just wish I'd have died along with my men."

He sounded resigned and drew another shuddering breath through his nostrils.

"Don't say that." I sat up and faced him cross-legged.

He huffed, shaking his head, my eyes found his. Glassy with unshed tears. "Why not? Do you know what it's like, to be the only one left? Do you know what it's like to have your body ripped open to the point where you can see your insides through the holes in your skin?" He asked, shutting me out by closing his eyes again.

I earnestly shook his shoulder. "Hey!" I said, getting his attention back.

"Maybe not, but I know loss Lloyd and I know what it's like to feel your insides ripped out figuratively speaking. I know what it's like to be the one left behind, but I don't feel it so much anymore, not since I've been here, which makes me feel good here." I said, my hand leaving his shoulder to splay over my heart.

"And despite all the chaos, I know it's the same for you," I said, placing my other hand over his heart in turn.

"You're fighting this battle because this war isn't over, and this war is one that's worth fighting for, or you wouldn't still be here!" I said sincerely, pausing for a moment. "I wouldn't be here."

We stared at each other and he covered the hand I held to his chest with his.

Patting it, he asked "How did you get so wise Bravo?"

His nickname for me endeared me to him even further and I had assumed that he didn't really believe my words, but I smiled at the effort that he made with his. Our eyes met and I felt the rush of butterflies with the intense way he observed me.

His brow furrowed. "Can I ask you a question?" He asked.

"You just did," I whispered, feeling like I was falling.

"Why haven't I noticed that you have two different coloured eyes before?"

And the spell was broken. How could I make such a grave mistake? I reeled back, broke my connection with him and I was off the bed in a flash.

"Um, contacts, I-I don't ... Um," I stuttered and fidgeted. Walking backwards, towards the door, I threw my thumb over my shoulder. "I have to get to work," I said and I left the room with Lloyd sitting on the bed, looking completely bewildered.

The timing of my exit turned out to be perfect because by the time I changed out of my PJ's, grabbed my things and started getting breakfast sorted, Martha had walked into the house.

"Morning dear," she greeted.

"Hey," I said, partially relieved that she was back, "can I get you a coffee?"

"That would be wonderful dear," she smiled though it didn't reach her eyes and it looked as though she might have had a hard time of it too.

Lloyd wandered into the room only minutes later.

With a gasp, Martha went straight to him, "What in the world did you do?" She asked in concern reaching for his face but hesitating the moment Lloyd flinched away.

"This is what you get when you cross a line," Lloyd said cryptically.

"Oh, Lloyd," Martha scolded in frustration, "now is not the time to go off like a bull at a gate, son."

I took it upon myself to fix Lloyd his cuppa too.

"I know, I know," Lloyd replied, sitting at the breakfast bar on the island bench, "but it did prove that I was right and they're up to something."

"Lloyd!" Martha warned, eyeing me cautiously.

"Don't worry, Anna knows the crux of it," he informed, "I think considering the circumstances and now she's caught up in it, she needed to know why it's been so crazy around here. So, how'd you go?" He asked Martha.

Once again there were three mugs on the bench, Martha picked up hers and took a sip. "Well, I managed to pin down a date finally. It was like pulling teeth, seems that because there's no record of Stasia's original birth certificate, that they just needed to agree on a date that was close to the date that everybody thinks it is and since no one's open over the weekend, the new date is now the Monday following the 16th."

Lloyd blew out a long, frustrated breath. "Ok, but I still don't like it Martha." He said with a shake of his head, shifting his gaze uncomfortably between Martha and I in turn.

"It's a last resort dear," Martha assured.

Lloyd shook his head, "Psht, I never thought I'd end up kowtowing to a bunch of suits," he said to no one in particular.

One could only assume that by suits, Lloyd meant either investors, lawyers, bankers, or all of the above. And I could also assume that Lloyd wasn't too happy about having to give away any sort of control to people who likely didn't have much idea on how Saanastia was run, because it usually came down to the figures, not the function.

Then I felt Lloyd's focus shift towards me.

"Which brings me to something else you need to know Anna," Lloyd said.

After an awkward silence, he took a gulp of his coffee.

The pause made me kind of nervous.

"Fred will be in tomorrow to pack up the workshop here, so if you can give him a hand with that and then fly RED back to Fred's hangar. Martha will be waiting for you. Helicopter operations will be suspended until further notice." He said with authority.

"What? Why?" I asked in surprise, putting my mug down.

"Because for now, with the threat made to you and the break in," he shifted and grimaced from his injuries. "I just can't afford for you or that bird to be interfered with."

"Ok, I guess that makes sense," I said, having to admit that he was probably right.

"For now, it's just too volatile out there," he said but he seemed uneasy and looked away from me.

Martha didn't look much better and I just knew that whatever they weren't saying was not going to be pretty.

"What's going on guys?" I asked.

"Please don't take this the wrong way dear." Martha said, a tear sliding down her cheek.

"Now you're really making me nervous," I said, scrutinising the two each in turn as the feeling of dread started washing over me.

Lloyd cleared his throat, "We need you to pack your stuff and take it with you tomorrow. Martha will take you to Pretoria and you will go back to Australia."

"What?" I asked in disbelief, tears springing to my eyes. "Your letting me go? What about Pragtig?"

"Just until this all blows over Anna," Martha said, her eyes also welling up.

I looked to Lloyd. "Will it? Will it blow over?" I asked hopefully, even though I knew in reality, that their backs were up against the wall. "What about Pragtig?" I asked again.

Lloyd's expression mirrored mine of utter despair. Shaking his head, he finally said "I'm sorry Anna, I just don't know, but I couldn't live with myself if something happened to you."

I couldn't believe what I was hearing.

After a long silence, I resigned myself. "So, I guess that's it then," I said not making any eye contact.

I stood and methodically rinsed my mug before walking past the two silent figures and heading out the door to do the equivalent of crying into Blue's mane. Off to my elephant, where I would both apologise to her for breaking my promise and be consoled by her.

Pragtig wasn't there that morning, which wasn't that unusual. She had taken the herd out onto the range, but I'd be lying if I said I was fine with it at that moment, so I had no choice but to save it up until that evening.

Most of the staff were also aware that major changes were looming and the day was understandably sombre for everyone, but we got on with our work and with the healthy camaraderie, we even had a few laughs along the way.

That afternoon, I was looking out for Pragtig to come back with the herd for the night, but they were later than usual. Kabri joined me sitting on the top rail of the highest fence at the yards to look out for them.

Another half an hour passed and still nothing. Kabri raised the alarm and the general consensus was that we needed to hash out a plan to find them.

This was not something that we needed right now and all thoughts of leaving Saanastia were put on the back burner.

So, over the next few hours we worked out the logistics and got every spare vehicle ready for a search party.

The elephants didn't stray more than twenty or so kilometres away from the homestead in almost any direction because Pragtig always made sure to come back every night.

Dan had been informed and after a bit of sorting, we were assigned with four rangers that were expert trackers and it would be my job to collect them first thing.

We just hoped the herd would be back before morning.

After yet another crappy night's sleep, I raced out to the yards first thing in the morning.

No elephants had made it home overnight and I was bummed.

We all were.

Before long, there was a flurry of activity as everyone was getting preparations underway for the long day.

I few out at first light as planned with Kabri acting as my guard and chaperone and was back with the trackers before 08:00.

Plumes of red dust rose from the ground as four vehicles sped out from the resort and then split off to follow the well-worn elephant tracks. The boys had enough experience to know where all the usual hangouts were and check on those while I stayed back to refuel. I'd head out again if they found something to go on and do a search by air, before taking Lloyd back to base to beat last light. He clearly couldn't help his protective nature and didn't want to leave Martha and I alone at the homestead overnight.

The rest of the crew could camp overnight, they were all experienced bush men and could look after themselves.

There was a breakthrough early that afternoon. Fresh tracks had been found, belonging to a herd of elephants that matched the number and size of the one we were searching for. Fresh dung had also been dropped confirming the fact because it contained the rhodes grass hay that we fed them.

This meant that the other three crews could then get themselves back to base and I could fly out earlier than expected.

It should have been a straight-forward trip.

And it was for the most part, until Lloyd radioed me with the worrying news that the herd hadn't simply been ambling along as they would normally. The footfalls revealed that the elephants were running and heading away from the resort.

When asked what that might mean, Lloyd informed me that he didn't know and that it might be nothing at all but said he couldn't ignore the possibility that it may have been induced due to a fright even though there was no evidence of any other movement on the ground.

Then my blood ran cold at the thought, knowing what I had previously done for a living. "Or they could have been chased from the air." I said, making the suggestion, because that would account for the lack of other animal, human or vehicle tracks on the ground.

"Shit," I heard Lloyd say. "You could be right. Listen, do me a favour and step on it, will ya? I'd feel better if I can make sure that you're safe."

I smiled at his concern and signed off.

Pushing RED across the landscape to maximum cruise speed and at about 500 feet, something rocked us like I'd flown through a downdraught. I righted her, keeping a firm hold, and scanned around me through the cabin windows, I spotted that white R44 turning to my left. Slowing RED down, while keeping an eye over my left shoulder, the white chopper had turned to face up and began a second charge.

"What the hell?" I wondered out loud when it repeated the manoeuvre from my left.

He was dive-bombing me!

And I wasn't having it, I was an aggressive pilot when I needed to be thanks to my mustering experience. This was where I shone and was more confident than most. There was no way I was going to let this guy bully me in my territory, so I went off after him, I knew RED well enough now to know how far I could push her.

Staying in the other chopper pilot's blind spot as best I could, I tailed him until he dropped out from under me. I continued heading up instead and made a hammerhead stall, settling back at the end of the manoeuvre to face the R44.

"Nice move young lady," the man's voice burbled in my headset.

He came closer and we were hovering near each other, circling like two dogs ready to fight.

It was then that it was apparent that the other chopper also had a passenger on board. He rotated the white machine, which had no doors so that he was facing me at ninety degrees.

"Shit."

I noticed the passenger take aim with a rifle and I wasn't about to stick around to find out what type. I peeled off and attempted to put a lot more distance between us.

"Hey pretty girl, where do you think you're going?" He mocked but I wasn't going to rise to his bait.

I needed to concentrate.

The only thing I could do was use my chopper and my skill to keep the gunman from being able to get a decent aim on me, he could only hang out of the door and shoot from that space, so it was my prerogative to stay on the pilot's side and out fly him.

And I did my best to fly the paint off RED, the other pilot was good and as time went by, I decided to go low. This was the only way I thought that I was going to be able to gain any extra advantage.

So that's where I went and he followed.

I ducked and weaved among the landscape and started to get the upper hand, I was flying rings around him and he kept trying to get me to fly high, but I continued to force the dogfight near the ground.

Taking cover at low level, I found a pattern in his flying. It may have been piloting skills or it may have been the limitations of that particular chopper, so I kept the pressure on, but he was lazy with his rearward pitch. My plan was to try to entice him to face up and allow the gunman to take aim while they were close to the ground.

"Now I have you my pretty," the pilot said menacingly, letting down his guard.

"I don't think so mate," I said and flew straight at him.

As expected he started to tip the chopper back, forgetting how low he actually was. The gunman desperate to stop me, started to shoot through the 44's windscreen at me, but was too late for them, and the tail rotor clipped a tree.

Like any unfolding disaster everything seemed to slow down. I pushed RED forward hard to get out of the way, her acute forward pitch allowing me to see both men through the windscreen as I bowled over the top of them. Their faces were filled with horror as they braced for what was to come and I left them to slam into the ground.

Spinning sideways to keep my eye on them, I continued to climb, watching as the R44's main rotors churned the dust and broke apart, the pieces flying off at all angles. The fuselage then bucked and spun from the force until finally all movement ceased, leaving only a large cloud of dust around the crash site.

I felt like I'd just run a marathon! Catching my breath, I eased RED closer to better assess the carnage, and hovered at a safe distance, noting that the other chopper had caught alight. If the crew survived the crash, they likely wouldn't survive the fire, and I wasn't going to hang around for another minute to find out.

Pressing down on the right foot pedal, I turned to leave, and registered a searing pain in my right thigh, looking down I spotted the blood ooze through the fabric of my shorts.

I had actually been shot!

"Oh crap," I said to myself, trying to tamp down my panic.

The pain became more acute now that all my senses had caught up with the injury and I found it increasingly difficult to put positive pressure on the right pedal.

Helicopters weren't like fixed wing aircraft, they flew like a brick if you let go of the controls, so I'd have to land before I lost the useful function of my injured leg.

I also needed to put pressure on the wound. I had a good look around me and found a nice clear area to put RED down, which was well away from the crash site, and landed. I figured that once I'd bandaged the wound, I'd be able to complete the flight and have the leg properly tended to.

Once I had safely touched down, I breathed a sigh of relief and looked down at my thigh.

It wasn't bleeding excessively, but that didn't mean that it wasn't serious, the bullet needed to stay in as it was likely stopping me from leaking all over the place. The first aid kit was strapped to the bulkhead behind me and even though it was a painful exercise, it didn't take too long to deal with my wound.

I decided to ditch my contacts, because having my eyes out on stalks for so long really irritated them. I was actually pretty lucky I didn't run into anything with the limited peripheral view the coloured lenses offered.

I was just about to initiate my start up sequence, and I radioed Lloyd.

"Lima one. This is Bravo one do you copy?"

Then there was a rap on the window.

I could feel the icy dread slowly creeping though my body, before slowly turning and finding two dark skinned men both pointing their AK47's at me.

I knew then that I was in a whole new world of trouble.

My radio crackled, I had no choice but to hang my headset, hearing Lloyd's garbled voice before powering down the chopper. Unclipping my harness, I took a breath and put my hands up. The men opened the cabin door for me and helped me out non too gently.

I winced every time the bullet pinched like an oversized splinter and with the guns to my back, I was forced to walk for quite some time before we came to an old Land Rover. The blood had now seeped through my bandage and my leg was really starting to throb.

"What do you want with me?" I asked after we climbed into the car.

"Be quiet," said the guy pushing his gun at me for emphasis.

They were the only words said for the whole trip.

We stopped at a shack made from corrugated iron and I was manhandled into the small, flimsy building and unceremoniously dumped on an old chair before being tied up.

The old shed looked like it could be a camera hide judging by the long, narrow rectangular hatches that ran along the walls.

The two men went outside and closed the door behind them. They didn't stray far, and I could hear them talking. I strained to hear what they were saying, but they were speaking Afrikaans and I only picked up a few words here and there. They sounded like they were talking to a third party over a radio.

The shed was dark, with the only light coming in through the narrow gaps around the hatches and from the old screw holes that were left in the reused iron. Multiple small beams of light dropped through the fine dusty air that circulated around me.

I was hot and I was thirsty, and I had all sorts of things running through my mind.

I wondered just how long I was going to be kept here, wondered how long it would be until it was discovered that I wasn't in the air. And I wondered why I had been targeted or whether I'd be rescued or let go. I even wondered if I would end up dying here.

One thing I knew for sure, was that I wasn't going to go any place fast and the ropes holding me were fairly tight. After spending some time trying to wriggle out of the bindings, I thought I'd conserve my energy, because even if I managed to get free, I wasn't in the position to escape anyway and could quite probably land me with another bullet lodged somewhere that could end me.

My leg was continuing to throb, and I was beginning to feel decidedly woozy. I lost track of time, nodding off occasionally and by the time the noise of another vehicle caught my attention, it could have been hours later going by the direction the meagre light was coming from.

I closed my eyes again, my last thoughts hoping that this was all just a bad dream.

I heard footsteps outside, and the door rattled, my eyes cracked open to reveal the blurry world around me. I was so thirsty, so tired. The rickety door creaked open and a tall, solid figure stood in the opening making an ominous silhouette. With the light that flooded in from behind, it was impossible to see who it was. Squinting against the sudden brightness, I moved my head to shield my eyes the best I could.

The large figure strode in and once inside, the door was closed, and then I recognised the man.

Cyrus Veldsmaan.

He continued his advancement until he crouched beside me. I tried to move away, but my bindings and my weakened state prevented it. He reached out and I flinched before he took a firm hold of my chin, tipping my face up to his and looked into my eyes. Smirking, he said, "so beautiful, just like your mother."

# Chapter 31

Drifting in and out of consciousness, I was disturbed at some point by a huge ruckus.

I remembered the feeling of being jostled. I remembered hearing the sound of people yelling, of gunfire and the mighty trumpet of an elephant. I remembered the smell of dust, of dung and of shot.

Then I remembered hearing Lloyd's voice close to my ear. "I've got you Bravo, I've got you." He said, but no matter how hard I tried, I didn't have the strength to open my eyes before I surrendered to the comfort of the darkness once more and the memories of a little girl flooding back in an array of mixed up dreams.

*-"I love you this much, Mumma," I was a little girl of four hugging my mother's neck as hard as I could to show her.*

*"I love you too poppet, now run along and have fun with daddy today," my mother said, kissing me before I ran into my father's waiting arms...*

*"Can I come sit up with you Cuzzy?" I asked my older cousin, who was sitting on my favourite elephant who was just the same age as me now that I had turned three that day.*

*"Sure kid, hop up..."*

*"Stasia! You can't stay up there on your elephant all day...," Nanny said, trying to reason with me at five years old.*

*"Yes I can Essy!" I said, evading my bath time for a little longer...*

*"You can't keep her away from me forever Richard!" The big scary man said, yelling at my father. I tucked my head into my father's neck, clinging onto him like my life depended on it...*

*"Take her far away, I don't ever want to see her again! I'll make it look like an accident..." I heard when I had finally been found with my elephant at the bush cubby in the trees...*

*"So lovely, just like your mother, child..." the man said when he visited my mother unannounced one day when I was four. I hid behind her skirt because I was so scared of him...*

*"I gave her that happiness Richard, when you couldn't," the giant man said as he watched his men use their bats on my father...*

*"If I can't have her, no one can..."*

*"Stop it! Stop it! Nooo! Daddy! Daddy! Daddy!..."-*

I struggled to get away from the images that invaded my mind and had trouble opening my eyes.

"Shhhh dear," Martha's voice cut through the chaos, her hand stroking my hair and settling me once more.

Finally, my eyes cracked open, letting in the bright light of my surroundings. I squinted as I took a moment to register where I was, with the beeping of the machines and murmurs of a busy workplace beyond the walls, I closed my heavy lids again.

Licking my dry lips, I tried to talk, but my throat was just too dry.

"Let me get some water for you, Anna," Martha offered kindly and I nodded my consent.

Braving the light, I opened my eyes again. Martha held a glass with a straw for me and I took a sip.

"How are you feeling dear?"

After drinking some more and clearing my throat I tried out my voice. "A bit like I went nine rounds with Danny Green. What day is it?" I asked, my voice croaky.

"It's Monday the 19th my dear, happy birthday," she said with a smile that didn't reach her eyes.

I couldn't help the tear that escaped and tracked down my cheek, "I'm so sorry to be so much trouble, there was this helicopter, and then I was captured and..."

"Shhhh Anna, it's ok, it's fine," she said, trying to placate me.

"What about Saanastia?" I asked as the door opened and a nurse strode in to check on me.

I was momentarily distracted then by poking and prodding and a few questions regarding the state of my health. "Doctor Benson should be here soon, ok?" The nurse assured.

I nodded and returned my focus to what was on my mind. "Martha?" I asked, prompting her.

"Yes dear?" Martha was clearly evading the conversation.

"Saanastia?" I repeated.

Martha looked towards the door nervously, "Now Anna, let's get the doctor to have a look at you before we get into that, hm?"

"What's - going on?" I asked following her gaze to the door.

"Well dear -" she hesitated, before being conveniently interrupted by the hallowed doctor and I didn't fail to notice her immense relief.

"Ah there she is," he grinned, "good to see that you're with us Ms Stedman. I'm Doctor Benson, you have been through quite an ordeal," he said as he read over the notes on the clipboard at the end of the bed.

Checking my latest Ob's, he asked me what the day was. I was honest and told him that Martha had informed me, and then he wrote a few things down before he put the clipboard away and looked at me with a warm smile. "Well, everything seems to be normal again. I'll schedule you for a scan this afternoon only because you were in and out of consciousness, just to give you a once over." He spoke with the perfect bedside manner. "I'll just have a look at your wound and see how that's going if I could?"

I nodded and he gently and thoroughly cleaned the wound and tested if I had sensation in my foot.

"That feel normal?"

I nodded.

"Good." He smiled with relief and then proceeded to explain that the bullet hadn't nicked anything major, but there was a little clothing contamination in there and we'd just have to watch for infection even though the wound had been thoroughly cleaned. It all looked great right now, there was a neat scar, with four outer stitches and about half a dozen internal ones and a drain. The drip had antibiotics added and I'd get an oral prescription when I left.

"If it all looks good tomorrow, you'll be able to go home late afternoon," he said rubbing some cream into my rope burns. "Now, Ms Stedman," his jovial demeanour became serious, "are you up to meeting a couple of visitors?" He asked.

"Um? Depends who they are I guess." I said warily, eyeing Martha suspiciously.

The doctor also looked to her, signalling her to continue.

"W-well dear," Martha started nervously, not helping me at all with the anxiety that was building, "with everything that happened, the police..."

"Police?" I asked in concern, wriggling to a more upright position.

"Yes dear, the police just want to ask you your version of events to help with their investigation," she continued, wringing her hands.

"Am I in trouble?" I asked looking between Martha and the good doctor.

"Of course not Anna!" Martha said aghast, "You've done nothing wrong, it's just that you're the only eyewitness that can fill a gap in the time line, that's all."

I let out a shaky breath, my head was admittedly spinning with the shock, but this wasn't going to go away, and I was never one to put off till tomorrow what could be done today.

"Ok, let them in I guess."

"You're sure?" The doctor asked.

"May as well rip off the band aid," I said with a shrug.

In a silent conversation, Martha gave the doctor a tight lipped smile before he nodded his assent and left the room to call the officers in.

A moment later two officers entered the room, a caucasian man and a dark skinned woman, their uniforms were a shade darker than I remember from those worn back in Mackay. Martha was asked to leave the room and wait outside but was allowed to come in if I needed her.

After the introductions and an explanation of the process, I was asked if I'd received any information regarding the case.

I shook my head, saying "No," and then they proceeded to explain why they wanted to interview me as soon as possible and not having any preconceived notions that could influence my side of the story was a priority, which made perfect sense to me.

... "Ms Stedman, can you please give us your version of events from the moment that you knew that the elephants were missing?" The female officer asked politely.

I had my session recorded and they paid particular attention to my interactions with the other helicopter, because there were of course a couple of men who weren't able to tell their version of events.

I could only recollect with any clarity, the memories of the dog fight, the crash, me discovering that I'd been hit with the bullet and the abduction.

Things started to get hazy after that; I did mention a tin shed and a large dark figure silhouetted in the backlit doorway, but nothing more afterwards for absolute certainty. I had so many images that had crossed through my head lately that I didn't want to inadvertently mix up what came from my mind and what was reality.

"Thank you for your cooperation Ms Stedman, we'll be in touch should we need anything else and if you remember more, please let us know ok?" The male officer concluded, while handing over a card with their details.

They left the room and Martha came in a few minutes later.

"How did you go lovey?" Martha asked before sitting in the chair beside my bed.

"Ok I guess," I answered, a little worn out by it all. "So, where were we, before we were so rudely interrupted?" I asked, sarcastically. "Oh yes! That's right, Saanastia, how's that all going?"

Martha appeared only mildly disappointed that I hadn't forgotten our track of conversation. "Well, after... what happened," she chose her words carefully, "It seems we have bought some time until some things get sorted out."

"That's a good thing... isn't it?" I asked, suddenly getting my second wind. "And what things?"

"Now don't you worry, sweetheart," Martha evaded nervously.

"Don't worry? Martha tell me!" I insisted. "Where's Lloyd, is he OK?" I said sitting up a little too suddenly. My head spun and I wobbled unsteadily.

"Anna dear, listen," Martha rose and took hold of my shoulders to stabilise me, "Lloyd is fine, everything has been put on hold for the moment because..."

Martha pressed her lips together and scratched her temple for a moment in thought, "uh, Cyrus was found dead with horrific injuries."

"What?" I raised my voice in disbelief, shimmying back on the bed. My leg gave protest and I winced. Martha fussed to arrange the pillows, and I settled propped up in relative comfort. "He's dead?" I asked.

"Indeed," Martha sighed, "anyway, let's not trouble ourselves with that right now, we need to concentrate on you getting better."

"No Martha!" I said with more authority than I intended. "How did Cyrus die?"

Martha cringed a little, "Well," she said with a thoughtful look on her face, "they think Pragtig might have killed him."

"That's not funny Martha," I frowned at her, thinking of the rumour that already surrounded Pragtig all these years.

"I wasn't joking Anna, but by all accounts, she was provoked and saved your life in the process."

"What provoked her?" I asked.

"Cyrus had you with a gun to your head, while using you as a human shield when Lloyd and the boys found you both." She fidgeted and if I didn't know better there was more to it.

"Oh, I don't remember." I closed my eyes tight, trying to recall it, but there was nothing that would stick.

"No of course not, you were apparently in a bad way and quite catatonic. We're only now starting to piece together all the details," Martha said pausing thoughtfully, before continuing to tell me about the turn of events.

The trackers had followed the prints that Pragtig and the herd made well into the Hoogevelt property, before something set them off back towards their home border. It was hours later before they caught up with them and just before they arrived at the hut.

Then all hell broke loose.

After a short scuffle and gunfire Lloyd and the boys had managed to secure the two men who were outside the hut, and then discovered that Cyrus was with me, he threatened to blow my brains out if they came inside. The elephants were agitated and a few of the boys tried to calm them. Cyrus finally appeared holding my limp body and created an impasse as he shuffled us towards his car to make his escape. Kabri was with Pragtig and wasn't able to keep her focus, so it didn't take long before she went nuts and charged.

Having Lloyd aim a gun at him quickly became the lesser of two evils for Cyrus, when the angry, six tonne elephant bore down on him. The standoff was over in an instant and Cyrus let me go, leaving me to fall in a heap to the ground, trying only to save himself. He fired a few shots at Pragtig and then high tailed it out of there with Pragtig in hot pursuit after him.

Martha told the story with perhaps a little too much enthusiasm, considering the circumstances, but she did eventually sober. "Anyway, you were whisked out of there and now here we are. You're safe and on the mend," she smiled warmly. "There's still a lot we don't know, but that will all come to light with the investigation."

"Is Pragtig ok?" I asked.

Martha distracted herself and went to pick up the pitcher of water without answering. She fastidiously poured two glasses and placed the pitcher back in its spot.

"Martha?" I asked, pressing her for the answer when she came back to my bed and placed a glass within my reach.

"Yes dear?" She asked vaguely.

"Is Pragtig ok? You said that Cyrus shot at her?"

My fears increased with Martha's silence as her face fell.

"Martha?" I repeated, my voice rising an octave.

She sat heavily in the chair with a sigh. "We don't know Anna," she whispered, "with all the ruckus. You needing to get to hospital, Cyrus being found dead and all the other furore, that when someone finally got around to account for her, she'd disappeared," she said sadly.

"But we can find her, right? I mean there were trackers and there was a team and..."

"Anna, they're looking for her, but she's proving very hard to track, she's crossed the river and they can't find any exiting prints. They don't even know which direction she went in," she said hopelessly.

I was relieved that they were looking for her. But I was also troubled with what this might mean for her if they did eventually find her. The realist in me knew that Pragtig had to take last priority over all the other carnage that had unfolded over that day. There were three men that had died under unusual circumstances, a kidnapping and the commotion regarding Sanaastia's future, which all far out-weighed the importance of a potentially injured killer elephant, who would likely be put down if she hadn't already perished when they discovered her because, she already had a chequered history and once a dog bites, that's what happens, right?

Martha let me know that the same team was looking for her in two directions and on both sides of the river. Lloyd had ordered them to keep going at least until we knew what was happening with Saanastia.

"So, when will that be?" I asked.

"Just as soon as the coroner's findings are published, it should be any day now."

"Ok," I nodded starting to get drowsy again. There was so much to process, but I could no longer keep my eyes open. I drifted off until I was woken for the scan. Martha stayed until I was done with that and announced that she needed to get back and would visit again the next day. I nodded and zonked out again until a nurse woke me to run my Ob's and give me some more medication before dinner was served.

The next day, Martha let me know that she'd been detained for the morning but would pick me up in the afternoon.

I felt anxious and bored at the same time while sitting by myself. I divided my time by dozing, watching T.V. and keeping an eye on the time while the seconds on the old style wall clock ticked slowly by.

Hours later, Martha finally arrived, making it well in time to hear the final scan results and ending my stint alone. She appeared a little uptight again, not making much eye contact and fussing around the room as she went about getting my things together for me. Pragtig still hadn't showed up and Fred, who had since been cleared to fly privately, had taken RED back to base with only the single bullet hole in the floor window on the pilot's side to tell her tale.

Martha explained that today, Fred had dropped her off and that he had a few errands to get out of the way. He would let her know when he was done, and he'd be waiting out the front for us once I was discharged.

I sat up in the bed, wincing a little as my leg twinged. "Well, you've certainly thought this through, haven't you?" I jested sceptically. "Seems like an awfully well orchestrated getaway."

Martha raised her eyebrows, "Maybe," she said simply.

I continued to watch her closely while she fussed a bit more before finally sitting beside my bed. She took a deep breath, "We might have a bit of a media presence to contend with," she said reluctantly, before she informed that we'd have to refrain from commenting on anything.

I fell back onto my pillows. "Oh great," I sighed, "I should have known that it was too much to hope this could all fly under the radar."

Martha smiled knowingly but not without her worry remaining etched on her features.

"Well, you do seem to have a knack for creating newsworthy stories, my dear."

I chuckled grimly just as the doctor announced his entry. "Ahhh Ms Stedman, how are we feeling today?" He asked warmly.

I always wondered why people addressed others like that as we.

"Well, Doctor, I don't know about you, but I'm ready to leave here ASAP," I answered giving him a little cheek.

He gave a small chuckle and shook his head at me. "Well hopefully we can help you with that," he said optimistically, while he gathered my charts and made a few notes.

"I won't draw this out," he said a moment later, "I have the results of your scans and the good news is that it came up all clear. You were in shock and dehydrated. That contributed to you coming in and out of consciousness, so that means you're all good to go."

Martha was on the phone in an instant calling Fred, while the doctor went on to show me my normal scans on an I-pad and then proceeded to check on my leg, redress it with a water-proof bandage and tell me how to look after it when I got home. He wrote my prescription and let me know that everything would be ready on my way out. He stated that the nurse would be along in a while to help me into a wheelchair and gave me permission to have a much needed shower after I asked, so long as I was careful with my dressing. Martha had the answer for that and whipped out a plastic bag and of all things, a roll of duct tape from her handbag.

"Fred had some in his car," she admitted as the question was raised.

Of course he did. I thought humorously.

"WD40 and duct tape fixes everything," I said. It had been a staple in almost every vehicle in my circle since I could remember. That and some high speed alloy tape in every aircraft toolbox ever.

"I knew you'd be crawling the walls to get clean. Sponge baths just don't cut it do they dear?" She asked.

"Martha. I'm sure the doc doesn't want to hear about my sponge baths," I said, under my breath and feeling a little embarrassed.

With that, Doctor Benson wished me luck and left the room with another friendly smile.

As soon as the door shut, Martha grinned and winked at me, "I'm sure he doesn't mind, not one bit."

"Lord give me strength," I said in mild frustration and with that, she helped me remove the pressure socks and taped my leg up.

I had been up only a couple of times to go to the toilet since I'd woken up and with the nurse's assistance, so I was glad that I had Martha with me in this instance. She prepared my clothes and then after the initial pins and needles feeling left my feet, she assisted me to the bathroom before leaving me to it. The feeling of the hot water streaming down my body was delicious and I actually had red sludge draining down the plughole while I washed my hair.

Martha had chosen a nice top and a long wraparound maxi skirt that would be easy to manage. With my leg wound on my thigh, it would be a while before I'd be in any sort of shorts, at least until the stitches came out in any case.

Martha received a call that clearly wasn't Fred and after all her 'uhuh's, I see's, and ok's,' she hung up with a big sigh as she rubbed her temples, leaving me none the wiser and also a little worried.

"That doesn't sound good," I prompted.

"Well, it's not awful," she breathed, "just the timing is a bit much, it seems we need to leave as soon as we can. That was Lloyd. Kabri has requested a meeting with us, he says it's important."

"Has he found Pragtig?" I asked.

Martha shook her head. "Lloyd didn't say, but for Kabri to make any sort of fuss means it is a big deal, so let's get our skates on," she said.

Her phone rang again.

Fred was on his way and he wouldn't be long, so after they ended the call, Martha organised one of the nurses to bring a wheelchair into the room and had a last minute look around for anything we may have missed.

Wheeling past the nurse's station, I thanked everyone who'd looked after me for the duration of my stay and then all that was left to be done was to pick up my prescription before we'd be out of there.

Martha was on the phone to Fred again, who was just about to swing past and it seemed like everything had worked like a well-oiled machine.

There were quite a few people milling near the entrance of the building, those coming and going, smoking etc.

We watched Fred's car pull up, so I put my sunglasses on, and we headed out into the open.

We didn't notice any media vultures circling and thought we'd might just have gotten off scot free.

But there was no such luck.

As soon as the doors slid closed behind us, we were pounced on by a handful of journos who had homed in on us seemingly from nowhere. Hearing a bevy of cameras clicking away, I put my head down and a number of eager reporters began flinging all sorts of questions at me.

"Ms Stedman, how are you feeling?"

"Ms Stedman, is it true that an elephant killed Mr Veldsmaan?"

"Ms Stedman, how did you manage to survive your ordeal?"

"Ms Stedman..."

"Ms Stedman..."

Agggh!

As carefully as possible, I was bundled into the back of the sedan and the rear passenger door was closed behind me.

Once Martha seated herself up next to Fred and she shut her door, the noise was finally muffled before we peeled out of the pickup area.

Fred was loathed to negotiate the hospital grounds at the notified speed, rapping the steering wheel in his impatience with every cross walk he had to wait at until we were finally on our way and on the open road.

"Good to see you again Fred," I said warmly.

I hadn't seen him for quite some time and had missed him and the like-minded aviation banter that inevitably happened when pilots would get together.

"Anna, it's wonderful to see you again too, who'd have thought that you and RED would go all Airwolf on us like that?" He praised.

Cue the aviation banter that warmed my heart instantly.

"Psht," I huffed, "Airwolf? Really? If she were that bird, both RED and I would not have had our matchy, matchy bullet holes." I joked.

Sobering, my thoughts went to my last flight. "Although I could do without knowing that I inadvertently killed two blokes, even if I was flying for my life." I said, regretting what I had been forced to do.

"Better them than you Anna dear," Martha said, weighing it up.

"I guess," I said, reluctantly agreeing and feeling very tired again all of a sudden. This sort of subject matter was stressful to deal with and not at all near anything I'd ever envisioned for myself, but it happened, and I couldn't undo it.

I sighed and put my legs up, sitting across the entire back seat and I soon dozed off again.

The sound of opening and shutting car doors roused me to a drowsy state. "I'll take her," I heard Lloyd's insistent voice in the background.

I was bundled up and I relaxed into him, savouring his scent as I wrapped my arms around him and buried my nose into his neck.

"I got you," he said, the words he used were so recently familiar to me.

"I know," I said groggily, snuggling into him. "I know."

Minutes later, I became more aware of my surroundings and found that Lloyd was carrying me through the lobby of the resort and towards Martha's office. Lloyd set me down gently on a seat.

Crouching down, Lloyd locked eyes with me. There was something different in them, his eyes were just as intense as always, only softer and less intimidating. Lost in his gaze, Lloyd reached to cup my face tenderly with his hand and asked. "Are you ok?"

Unable to stop myself from leaning into his palm, I nodded and his thumb gave my cheek a gentle stroke and the spell was broken when the door opened and Martha entered the office with Kabri, followed by his wife who was introduced to me as Essnass.

Lloyd stood to his full height before we greeted the new arrivals and sat on the seat next to me.

Kabri and Essnass sat on my other side and Martha explained that they would wait for refreshments before getting started.

Poor Kabri looked as though he was going to be sick, he was busily scrunching his terry towel hat in his hands and wouldn't make eye contact with me. Essnass kept glancing at me only to smile excitedly and when she wasn't, she was calming down her husband.

"Well, shall we get down to business then?" Martha started, after the tea, coffee and nibbles were delivered.

"Kabri darling, why don't you tell us what's worrying you so much."

"Yes, Ms Martha," Kabri said nervously.

Clearing his throat, he fumbled with his hat some more and looked to his wife for support, who nodded for him to continue.

Turning to me earnestly, Kabri looked apologetic. "M.. Miss Anna?"

"Yeah?" I asked, curiously. I wasn't the only one, Lloyd and Martha were also intrigued as to why he was addressing me.

"Anna is for Anastasia." He said, not making any sense.

"What is this all about Kabri?" I asked, glancing nervously at the others. I had always gone by Anna, my real name was Annabelle, but I dropped that at the same time that I went to school, preferring instead Anna and it simply stuck.

"Your name is Anastasia Staadman."

## Epilogue

We were left in the now silent office, staring at the closed door. Lloyd had slammed it so hard that it rattled in its frame after he swore and tore out of the room like a bat out of hell.

I was secretly devastated with the news that Lloyd and I were related, but also somewhat relieved that I'd been let off the hook before I ended up making a complete fool of myself and acted on my attraction towards him.

Kabri recalled as much as he could, so that we could fill in some of the blanks from my past.

He said when I disappeared, that I was found at an old photography hide with Pragtig and her herd watching over me.

Cyrus had eyes and ears everywhere and when he caught up with Kabri not long after the Mahout had discovered me, he suggested that the man should keep quiet about the little girl if he knew what was good for him.

Kabri had no doubt that Cyrus would make good on that threat. There had been many people in the surrounding communities that mysteriously disappeared or turned up dead and he had no choice but to surrender the girl and speak nothing of it.

Kabri never knew what became of Stasi and he never asked.

But he did know from the moment Pragtig first met me, that I was that little girl all grown up and it was quite the dilemma when I turned up the second time.

Kabri chose to simply stay quiet and hope that no one else would figure it out and that ultimately, this day would come.

And now here we were, the world turned upside down and wondering what the heck to do with it.

Kabri and Essnass were dismissed with great thanks from Martha and myself. They couldn't leave without a hug and Essnass was beside herself that her little Stasi was finally home and couldn't wait to catch up again soon.

With the office quiet again, Martha and I would make a start and try to figure things out.

Martha asked herself why she hadn't seen it earlier but apparently, she had barely set eyes on me as a child.

My mother kept me to herself most of the time. When I wasn't with her, I was with Essnass, who was my nanny throughout my childhood. Both her and Kabri were originally from Nairobi and they were incredibly loyal to the family. Almost to a fault according to Martha.

It was under their care that I picked up the second language that until recently I had no recollection of.

When my father Richard died, his wife, Isabella automatically became the majority share-holder and ultimately, so would Anastasia one day.

After all, the property's name Saanastia was an anagram made in honour of his little girl.

But Isabella wasn't ever going to be cut out to run the place, especially while grieving for a husband and her precious daughter.

Martha was instrumental in not only taking charge of the business, but also of all the legal process with the law firm that Alan's father owned.

When Isabella was found dead only days after the funerals, the paperwork came through that would lay the path for the future of Saanastia.

Richard had put in a clause that his fortune and his legacy was to remain in trust until Anastasia's twenty first birthday, that if left unclaimed, the trust could be bought out by Lloyd's side of the family, other shareholders could be found or Saanastia could be put on the market outright.

Of course, there was a lot more fine print to that, but that was the crux of it.

Who'd have thought that I would be the one to take it right down to the wire?

Then it was my turn to fill in the blanks from my side leading up to this auspicious day.

"I don't know what to tell you." I said thinking back to my childhood. "I don't have any memory of my life before the age of six, although I think I might have been dreaming and getting weird flashbacks since coming back here. They kind of make sense now, but they were pretty scary, random and fuzzy so I just didn't put it together."

"I see," Martha said with a thoughtful look on her face. "We won't force it, now is not the time. I think we first need to see where we're at legally and then we can piece things together. I expect you'll need to call your folks and involve them. They're bound to have some insight through their adoption information."

Nodding, I internally cringed at the thought of having to contact them again, but considering the circumstances, it was something that I probably couldn't avoid.

Martha called Alan, who was as shocked by the news as we were and said that he'd look into it and get back to us with an appointment time ASAP.

"Where's Lloyd?" Alan asked us two days later, when he arrived at Saanastia to go through the paperwork.

"Well," Martha started to say before a pause, "he seems to have gone missing."

"Missing?" Alan asked in surprise.

"Yeah, he upped and left as soon as we all got the news," I said, still perplexed by it all.

"Why is that?" Alan asked.

"We have absolutely no idea Alan," Martha said, shaking her head.

Before anything could be finalised, Alan said that we would need to find Lloyd and also get copies of my birth certificate and adoption papers to verify who I was, because he could find no record of them and that any of my current identification had likely been falsified.

In the meantime Alan said he could get the ball rolling on his side, while we did our bit.

I swallowed nervously as I looked at my phone, the station number displayed ominously on the screen. I decided to call them late that afternoon, the time difference meaning that I might catch them both at breakfast. Any later and they'd likely be too hard to pin down together during the day.

Pressing the connect button, I took a deep breath and let it out slowly.

"Hidden Valley Station," Rose's voice sang over the line after a short delay.

"Hi, it's Anna." I said tentatively.

Silence.

"Rose?" I asked, testing the line again.

"Hello, Anna, how are you?" She asked cautiously with an unsteady waiver to her voice.

"Is Uncle Kyle there? I was hoping to catch you both. There's something important that's cropped up," I said, managing to get it all out in one go. I thought the direct approach would help with any evasiveness.

There was a bit of mumbling in the background and I heard Kyle weighing into Rose's other ear before he took the phone from her.

"Look Anna, whatever has happened, we can't help you ok?" Kyle said abruptly.

"Wait! Please don't hang up!" I begged "I know who I am!" I said in a rush before he had a chance to end the call.

Silence again.

But the line was still open.

"Anna. We can't protect you anymore and you need to stay away from us now, it's all too late," he said dismissively.

"Too late? What do you know about my safety? Or is this more about yours? All I need is my birth certificate and my adoption papers and I'll be out of your hair forever." I said finding my courage.

"You're opening up a can of worms my girl." He warned.

"Yeah, they've already spilled all over the floor, and I'm not your girl." I said, getting more suspicious by the minute "What's your connection in all this, I'm sure you're not some needy random couple who adopted a six year old girl out of the goodness of their heart are you? You might as well tell me."

Then I had an epiphany. "Are you working for Cyrus?" I asked boldly.

Hearing an intake of breath, I took his silence as a resounding yes.

"Well I guess you haven't heard yet," I said, knowing I had rattled his cage.

"Heard what? What are you talking about, Anna?" Kyle asked and for the first time I registered his interest in the conversation.

"Your boss is dead."

"He's dead? Cyrus is dead? Rose!" Kyle called out to his wife with amazement. "Anna are you sure?"

"Of course I am, what's?..."

"Rose he's dead! He's finally out of our lives!" Kyle said in utter relief.

It was all very surreal and what I found out next, blew my mind.

Kyle and Rose had been forced to take the six year old Anastasia under the threat of death, not only for themselves but also their son Lloyd.

Another piece of the puzzle slotted into place.

Lloyd's parents were alive!

That of course meant that there were no adoption papers which we likely didn't need now anyway. As for my birth certificate? Well that was probably in the homestead somewhere.

Now we had three things to find.

Pragtig, Lloyd and my birth certificate.

Kyle and Rose would be on the first available plane to South Africa and hopefully able to make things right with their son.

Jerry rang early Sunday, only a few days later, he had found out where Lloyd was. One of Lloyd's childhood 'friends' decided to call Jerry to let him know that he, Lloyd and another chap had been on a weekend bender and that someone needed to... and I quote 'drag out his sorry arse', so that he could clean up the place so that his wife would be non-the-wiser when she came back from a girls weekend away.

Lloyd was apparently pretty paralytic, and Jerry would let me know when he was fit enough to show his face again.

"Some friends they are," I said, a little mad that a bunch of grown men would act that way, "what are they? Seventeen?" I asked.

"Don't be too hard on him Anna," Jerry said, always seeing the good in everyone. "They were really good friends as kids, but over the years they have lost touch with life getting in the way. From what I gather, Lloyd went to a bar and bumped into them. I guess he just wanted to get away for a bit, it's been..." he paused for a moment, "a bit tough on him lately."

"Yeah, it's been tough on everyone Jerry," I said, making a point. "Anyway, when he's finished being a moody teenager, get him to call us. He hasn't taken our calls and there's been a development I'd rather not text him about."

"I'll do my best," Jerry said, taking on what he knew would likely be a challenge.

Everything seemed to be happening at once and it was exhausting! Uncle Kyle and Aunt Rose arrived and stayed in the resort and it struck me as strange now that I had always addressed them as aunt and uncle, not mum and dad. Maybe deep down I always knew it and I would have, if only my memories hadn't failed me.

Opting to stay away from the homestead, My aunt and uncle felt it would be one step too far to stay there and that it would give everyone a bit of space and time to organise an amicable meeting, if it was at all possible.

They were aware that they were walking into a proverbial minefield but considering what the reasons were that kept them so far away, I was pretty sure that every mile would be worth it for them to come back.

The question was raised, if it wasn't Lloyd's parents that died in that car crash all those years ago, then who did?

Bringing up the reports, nothing seemed untoward. Clearly evidence had been tampered with, so that would be something that Alan and his firm would have to look into.

Worn out, my mind was frazzled by the turn of events but even so, fatigue took over and I had fallen into that dozy state somewhere between wakefulness and sleep, when some familiar images rolled through my mind causing me to jerk awake.

I winced. My leg pinched with the sudden movement while I tried to hold onto the image in my head so it wouldn't disappear before I had a chance to call Kabri about it.

The poor man had been so remorseful with what he had kept quiet for so long.

But he did want to make it up to me and extended his availability. "If you need anything Miss Anna," he said, "I will be there, day or night." – not that he wouldn't drop everything if one of his friends needed him anyway, but he did make a strong point to tell me like I was one of them. He, his wife Essnass and his family were safe now and that over-bearing pressure was now gone. It was comforting to know.

"Miss Anna, so soon you call me? What is the matter?" He asked in concern.

"I'm not sure Kabri, but I think I remember something," I said to him. He stayed quiet, prompting me to continue, "Was there ever a time that I snuck out with Pragtig and came back really late from somewhere when you were babysitting me?"

"Not just once, Miss Anna," Kabri chuckled knowingly.

I smiled at that, who knew I was such a hell raiser as a small child and that Pragtig was my partner in crime?

"Do you know where we went?" I asked.

"No Miss Anna." He replied.

"Oh," my heart sunk, I hoped that by describing it, Kabri might know where I was talking about.

"Was there ever a tin shack that was small, like the one I was held captive in but built high, like in the trees or raised up on poles. I remember young boys, not sure who's kids they were, used to camp out there," or something, I thought, if they were anything like the station lads with a day off here and there, they could have been up to anything. "It overlooked the river I think."

"Ah! Yes Miss Anna, they were the hides that Mr Richard built for photographers, I know the one, it was where we found you after Pragtig took you there for safety when your father..." Kabri said, stopping in mid-sentence.

I felt the hair stand up on the back of my neck, but I had to know where this place was.

"Has anyone looked there Kabri?" I asked.

"No, I do not think so, because that hide was washed away in a flood many years ago, but I will look into it in the morning, good work Miss Anna!"

The next morning, as promised Kabri sent a search party to the old location and Pragtig was found! She was a little worse for wear but not in bad shape. Apparently, she had been shot twice in the right shoulder and through her ear but she didn't appear lame at all, just agitated with her intruders.

Being found and bringing her home were two totally different things and it was with some argument how we were going to do things, especially since Lloyd chose to use that time to reappear.

Everyone said I needed to rest while I argued that she could die of infection or depression while I did that.

Lloyd thought I was being 'melodramatic', but I maintained that since she clearly wouldn't respond to any coaxing even with feed from the others, there could be a chance that she was in the same state she was in last time, and who was the one that brought her out of that?

I suggested that Fred could take me there in RED at first light, that in itself would save a half day in travel time and then I would come back with the others in the Landcruiser. In all likelihood, Pragtig would follow. It would be a slow trip, but it shouldn't take more than a day if we took the same route back as that of the elephant back tours.

"Yeah, except for one detail," Lloyd pointed out, "we can't get the ATV's across the river, it's too deep."

"Well, could someone drive one to the other side via the main road as we do with the tours? I could ride Pragtig across," I said.

"Absolutely not!" Lloyd scoffed, "no way, no how, are you going to ride that elephant, she's not safe!" He said angrily.

"She's fine Lloyd, I've been riding her for a while," I said, accidentally letting the cat out of the bag.

"You what!?" He bellowed at me.

"I know, I know," I said sheepishly, cringing a little, but I figured since I had every intention to ride her again at some point, we'd likely have this discussion anyway. "But Lloyd, she's not put a foot wrong and she asked me to get on, I'm perfectly safe up there," I said, giving him a weak explanation, even to my own ears.

He folded his arms across his chest as he thought it through and there was no mistaking he was pissed off.

He glared at Kabri asking, "You knew about this?"

"Yes boss." Kabri said looking guilty.

He wiped his hands over his face in frustration. "Figures," he said. "And she's been ok?" Lloyd asked, raising an eyebrow at him, which in turn raised my hopes.

"Yes boss, better than I have ever seen her," Kabri said confidently.

Kabri definitely had my back. And Pragtig's too!

Lloyd stayed quiet in contemplation, glaring at us in turn, before finally settling his gaze on me.

I felt pretty smug and I knew it was likely the best idea that we'd come up with, no matter how cautious we might be.

Groaning loudly, he said "Alright then," throwing his arms up in surrender. I grinned victoriously.

"But," he leaned forward pointing at me, "you're going with him," he said, turning the finger to Kabri, "so, that way, if you come unstuck, you both go down together, got it?"

"Yay!" I clapped and turned to Kabri. I raised my hand to him, and he hi-fived me with a big grin on his face, "I recon this is going to be the start of a beautiful friendship Kabri."

Lloyd just shook his head and grumbled some more. "I'm glad this amuses you both," he said sarcastically, and I could tell he was trying very hard not to turn any part of his frown upside down.

Thankfully the plan worked beautifully, Pragtig was clearly overjoyed to see me and wouldn't stop touching me and crying like an elephant did. Before we left her sacred place, we made sure she had a huge drink and she ate almost everything offered to her.

The two bullet wounds had already started to close over, but we sprayed some antiseptic on them and gave her a shot of antibiotics anyway. Jerry said the bullets likely wouldn't cause her any problems if they hadn't already, so it would be fine for her to make the trip. They likely also wouldn't need removing when she got back home unless the wounds got an infection, which of course we would watch for closely.

As we led her back, she had her trunk in the window the whole trip and it didn't matter to any of us that it would take hours.

Once we got to the river, it proved to be a real challenge to get up on her with my leg injury, it was made easier with the boys helping me up onto the roof of the Troopy first, and Pragtig was oh so patient as she manoeuvred willingly into the right position for me to gingerly climb up.

Pragtig picked her way carefully across the river with both Kabri and I atop her four-metre high and dry shoulders.

By the time we got back, I assumed that Lloyd had finally discovered that his parents were still alive. Martha said as much and apparently he took it hard, so we were all asked not to fuss over him and leave him be so he could process it all.

In the meantime, Martha and I started turning the house upside down looking for my birth certificate.

It had been hours and we were fast running out of places to look.

"Hey, remember when we had that intruder?" I asked her peeking behind another picture on the wall.

"How could I forget dear," Martha said digging through yet another drawer for the second time.

"He was searching for something in the living room, around that big old sideboard."

"We've already worked through it with a fine-toothed comb," Martha said with a sigh as she put everything back in a drawer of a bedside table.

"But we haven't looked behind it," I said, making a point.

"What makes you think there's something behind it?" Martha asked looking up from her task.

"As you sometimes say Martha, I have a hunch," I said giving her a knowing smile.

Minutes later, we had removed all the loose items from the top of the sideboard and slid the heavy piece of furniture away from the wall.

I was a little disappointed that there wasn't a hidden safe or something built into the wall, but I continued to check out the back of the sideboard and did discover a small hidden pigeon-hole with something in it.

I pulled out one of those old-fashioned diaries, complete with a lock on it.

"I got something," I said, showing Martha.

She took a close look. "Does it have a key?" She asked.

"No, But I'm sure we can just cut the strap." I said.

We walked back through to the other wing of the homestead and I ended up using a pair of kitchen shears to snip through the leather closure.

Fanning the pages full of script, that could have been all of my mother's secrets and confessions, I found a folded piece of paper tucked next to the back cover.

I opened it with trepidation with Martha looking on expectantly and it proved to be the document we were looking for, with all the shocking proof we needed.

"Oh my God," I said, looking up at Martha in utter shock. She too had a similar look of surprise.

"How...?" I started to ask before we heard raised voices from outside in the garden that got louder as their owners approached the house.

It was clearly Lloyd and his parent's, and it didn't sound good.

"...No! I haven't told her! What good would it do? Was it not enough that I'd been to hell and back, only to find the one thing that might have made it bearable was taken away from me at the eleventh hour?"

"Son, why do you say that?" Uncle Kyle asked in a bewildered tone.

"What? I can't believe this. How can you not find that disturbing? She's my cousin for crying out loud!" Lloyd's voice pitched in frustration.

Aunt Rose chuckled, "Oh Lloyd, you aren't aware?"

"Aware of what? And I can't believe you would think this is remotely funny," Lloyd said, sounding highly offended.

"Oh honey, Anna's not Richard's daughter." Rose explained, the humour still evident in her tone while trying to calm him.

"What?" He asked, completely surprised.

"She's Cyrus."

Lloyd must have been too stunned for words because he didn't say anything. Martha encouraged me to move, my feet carried me out to the garden where the family stood facing one another.

The three of them turned to look at me as I stepped out into the open space from the doorway. My mind went to the previous varying images, none of them complete, none of them pointing to anything in particular, but together they certainly painted a picture that might point to the same conclusion, if you willed it hard enough.

"It's true" I said holding up the slip of paper. My birth certificate revealing the proof that what Aunt Rose is saying was true.

I was in fact Cyrus Veldsmaan's daughter!

It turned out that Cyrus and I both had heterochromia iridis, a rare genetic mutation, where we had two completely different coloured eyes and while it was hereditary, it was more rarely seen in successive generations. With my mother taking such great pains to keep me from meeting many people, it was now clear that she knew.

Perhaps because I was Cyrus' daughter, I avoided meeting the same demise as Richard, who everybody thought was my father.

With Uncle Kyle and Aunt Rose forced to take me somewhere, anywhere, so long as it was out of the country.

We ended up in Australia.

They were paid hush money for their trouble not that they needed it. As if a death threat wasn't enough to stay compliant.

In his weird and twisted way of thinking it was the 'least' that Cyrus could do for his bastard child.

It paid for anything I might have needed and my education.

The trust fund that had so generously been handed to me was to set me up for my future. It was no wonder that my aunt and uncle were so unenthused about handing it over. It was blood money.

Who knew that the fund that was designed to keep me away from Saanastia, was the very catalyst that ended up bringing me back?

Later in the conversation and after a long, extended silence, my aunt and uncle decided to, 'leave Lloyd and I to talk some more.'

Lloyd and I made our way into the house and sat on the over-stuffed couch in the great room to tell his side of the story.

Lloyd kicked himself that he hadn't seen it earlier. Twenty, twenty hindsight is a wonderful thing.

Lloyd spent most of his childhood in the USA and only visited South Africa a handful of times as a kid throughout the holidays. He was a typical rowdy teenager and spent more time getting up to mischief with the local boys than he did with his whole family let alone his little cousin who he knew had a crush on him.

So while he was apparently never unkind to me, he never encouraged a close relationship either and simply didn't pay a lot of attention to me. That just wasn't cool as a teen.

Not that he was given much opportunity to anyway, my mother saw to that. Most of the interactions he'd had with me were when Richard insisted on family gatherings.

He also discovered girls and he met his first girlfriend at fifteen.

He saw Gloria during two summers until all the tragedy unfolded. From there, Lloyd went off the rails and his appointed guardians put him into boot-camp.

Lloyd thrived with the discipline which led him to enlist, where he had his life altering moment and almost died a few years later.

Then of course, he came back to South Africa to run Saanastia, Gloria swooped in and thought she'd try her luck and start where they'd left off.

They became the local 'it couple' and Cyrus loved to show them both off, making sure they were at every social event and sparking the rumour that they were to marry.

Of course, it all came to a screeching halt when Lloyd found out that they were playing for cattle stations (as they say in Australia) or in this case conservation parks, when Gloria let slip in one of her drunken episodes.

The Veldsmaan's had hoped to be able to turn Lloyd with the promise of wealth by selling the rhino horn to Cyrus' wealthy Asian clients and therefore keeping the man's virtue intact by using farmed horn.

That was more than enough for Lloyd to end it with Gloria and that's when shit got real.

Rhino horn was an illegal product. Black market was black market, and it would likely never become a regulated industry, because the prestige and therefore also the value of it would diminish.

To have powdered rhino horn in possession was a status symbol in these countries, just like having a private jet or car collection was for example.

Unfortunately, the Veldsmaan's still wanted what they wanted and if they couldn't get it through the front door, 'they'd play dirty'- Cyrus' words, not Lloyd's - which would have been laughable if it weren't so appalling, and they were willing to get it at almost any cost.

It was only fortunate that Gloria was so obsessed with Lloyd. Because she was the only thing that was standing in the way of having him killed off all along, and it was only by the grace of God that Cyrus indulged his daughter the way he did.

Who knew what would become of her, my dear half-sister?

It was out of our hands now. Gloria had been arrested and all family assets seized pending an investigation with multiple charges laid on her and a number of others involved in the scam.

I swear, you couldn't make this stuff up!

"The rest as they say is history," Lloyd said in conclusion.

Then the mood changed in the room.

Lloyd took a deep breath glancing at my lips. "And then I bumped into you," he said softly, leaning in a little more.

He had shuffled closer during our talk and his arm had already found its way to the back of the couch and had been gently playing with my hair for some time.

"And then you bumped into me," I replied, repeating his words dreamily.

Hesitantly, he approached me like I was a skittish foal and little by little, the gap between us disappeared until our lips touched ever so tenderly.

The world fell away and all I could feel was just the two of us.

I was finally home.

## Two months later.

It was a beautiful afternoon and we had managed to take the time out together for a date, completely organised by Lloyd.

Who'd have thought that he had such a romantic side? A picnic in the bush near an old well, a small oasis in an otherwise almost barren landscape. No hippos, no crocs... maybe a lion or two, but not on that day and we had a gun with us and a watch elephant as a lookout for our protection.

The day was ending and the ever-present fine dust gave a golden glow to everything around us in the late afternoon sun. Sitting astride my elephant's broad neck, with Lloyd shadowing me, his strong arms wrapped around my waist was my idea of pure bliss.

To our left were the vast plains of Saanastia and to the right and not more than a couple of kilometres away, was our homestead.

"I have a surprise waiting for you," Lloyd murmured as his five o'clock shadow scratched my neck gently.

"You know I don't like surprises," I said.

"I'm sure you'll like this one," he said confidently, before kissing me under the ear, sending shivers down my spine, despite the warmth still lingering in the air.

We had moved into the original part of the house together, Martha had moved out with Fred, and Kyle and Rose were looking for a place of their own. They had handed in their resignation as managers at Hidden Valley Station and decided to return to their homeland permanently after having finished things up properly in Oz.

As we lumbered through the two great gates towards the yards and stables, I spotted a black and white form moving around in one of the larger grassed yards.

"No way," I said in disbelief, grabbing Lloyd's leg to ground me.

"Surprise babe," he hugged me from behind and kissed my cheek, I turned so I could kiss his lips, before I turned back and whistled to Blue.

He answered with a long and excited neigh. He remembered!

I watched him gallop toward the closest fence, screaming and snorting at us as we came closer on the huge elephant. His eyes were on stalks, but he'd get used to these big grey animals in no time, I was sure.

We dismounted and left Pragtig with the other elephants to munch hay and then I wasted no time to be with my horse. Hugging his thick neck felt just so good and I took a long whiff of him. I'd missed that beautiful horse smell and couldn't wait to ride him again once he'd settled in.

Ecstatic couldn't even begin to describe how I was feeling, it was at that point the happiest time in my life, so elated and carefree that I didn't even notice the other people including Kabri, Essnass, all the other guys and their girls, Alan and Carley, Jerry and his new girlfriend, Vanessa and surprisingly also Pete and Rach, who were all in on it and had gathered to watch on. I thanked Lloyd over and over, kissing him as the sun turned everything around us from radiant golden light to burned orange while it set to the west.

For now, everything was as it should be, and I just wanted to bask in the glory of it for as long as I could.

When the time of bliss came to an end - and I knew it would - I was going to be more than ready for the new challenges I'd – we'd face.

Together.

## The End.

# About The Author

Professional Horsewoman, Ardent aviation enthusiast, and Fiction author.

L N O'Rourke spent her formative years growing up all over the world, joining her father, who was a sought-after Aircraft Maintenance Engineer, and all the while, she wished for a pony.

Although she loves all animals, horses are incredibly close to her heart. She eventually got that horse, and one horse became many horses. However, aviation also stuck with her.

She expanded her interest in anything mechanical, which she draws off to create realism in her genres of science fiction, adventure, drama, and intrigue, all inter-woven with a touch of romance that appears in her stories.